THE HANGING OF HETTIE GALE

TESS BURNETT

BLOODHOUND
BOOKS

Copyright © 2024 Tess Burnett

The right of Tess Burnett to be identified as the Author of the Work has been asserted by them in accordance with the Copyright, Designs and Patents Act 1988.

First published in 2024 by Bloodhound Books.

Apart from any use permitted under UK copyright law, this publication may only be reproduced, stored, or transmitted, in any form, or by any means, with prior permission in writing of the publisher or, in the case of reprographic production, in accordance with the terms of licences issued by the Copyright Licensing Agency.
All characters in this publication are fictitious and any resemblance to real persons, living or dead, is purely coincidental.

www.bloodhoundbooks.com

Print ISBN: 978-1-917214-70-4

*To Mum and Dad for your unconditional love.
Long gone, but with me forever.*

CHAPTER ONE

JUNE 1772

Whether 'tis truth or n'e'r but a lie, who sees?
With his bright button eyes, and focus so keen,
Spies the crow.

Picture this: a young girl lies atop a blanket of grass, grass so green and soft it seems as though it must be made of the finest silk. Above her is a sky of bluest blue, dotted with little clouds what look like wool from the sheep that sit lazily around, chewing and fussing. The air is scented with honeysuckle and meadowsweet, filled with the gentle singing of birds as they swoop for insects and call for their loves. She is alone, yet she is not lonely, and her head is full of dreams. Oh, 'tis a sweet scene.

But 'tis not real.

The girl is real enough, for she is me. But I am not lying on soft grass, rather the bed that I share with my sister and my brother. The ropes beneath the thin straw mattress dig into my flesh, and I feel I must be bruised all over. Above me are the beams what hold up the roof, draped in webs spun by busy spiders, beyond them dark, dusty shadows. The air is thick with sweat and greed, and disgust.

And I am not alone.

But 'tis not Greta and Daniel who lie with me. 'Tis my da. My da what's laying atop of me, squeezing the life out of me and into me, both at the same time. 'Tis not the right way, but 'tis what is happening. His eyes are closed and he's sobbing. I can taste the salt of his tears as they fall on my face, mingling with my own.

'Stop, Da, it hurts.'

His breath smells foul with the ale, and his face is red with the effort, but he don't stop. Seems he can't stop. My ma is through the door. I know she can hear his groans and my pleadings, but she chooses not to listen. My little sister runs in.

'Why's Da fighting with Hettie? Has she been naughty?'

'Hush, child. Come away. Go back to your brother, go.'

Have I been naughty? I have not, and that's a fact. I'm Hettie Gale, I've seen fourteen summers, and my da is doing what he oughtn't. I shut my eyes and try to think about the day that just passed, but 'tis a blur of haymaking and goat herding, fetching and carrying.

'Please stop, Da!'

Da finally shudders and climbs off me, unsteady with the ale and the grind, his eyes still shut tight, denying my existence, oblivious to the sin he has just committed. He shambles off, tightening the belt that holds up his breeches, shouts cruel words at Ma and I hear a slap, and then the cottage door slams shut.

I lay still for a moment, feeling the wetness atween my legs, wondering whether I've been broken. I feel like I might be sick. Ma comes in, her face pinched and bitter.

'Get up, child, the linens are ruined.'

I can tell she is angry with me and with Da, but she holds

pride in her bosom and will not be put upon, despite the mark reddening across her cheek. I sit up, pain searing at my insides, and see that my dress and the linens beneath me are spotted red with blood. My blood? I must suppose so, though there is less than when I have my monthly bleeds and my stomach bloats with the cramps, and I must fetch sheep's wool from the fields so my linens stay clean. I know a little of the way of things and a woman's obligation to a man.

Ma hands me a rag and tells me to clean myself and dress in fresh clothes, while she takes the soiled linens from the bed. She says nothing more, her face set in a mask of sufferance. I walk, pain stabbing like an accusation, into the other room. My sister, playing with our little brother, looks at me askance.

'Did Da cut you, Hettie? Have you been naughty?'

'I've not been naughty, Greta, and Da didn't cut me. Look, see how Daniel tries to walk.'

I scrub myself down there, put on a clean frock, and try to forget. I want to burn my bloodied dress, but Ma rubs and scours the fabric until it almost falls apart, forcing me to bear the pink stains of shame as the months pass, until the fabric is stretched beyond its own bounds.

I cannot forget. None of us can.

CHAPTER TWO

FRIDAY 24 MAY

Alice was sitting at her desk, tentatively nibbling the edge of a ring donut, when the call came. She usually politely declined the Friday freebies when they were brought round, but there was something about today that made her feel reckless.

She put the donut down, licking the sugar from her fingers, and stared at her phone. No one ever called her. It was a withheld number, so she nearly didn't answer, but her instincts took over; maybe this was important.

'Miss McKenna?'

'Speaking.'

'Alice McKenna?'

'Yes, that's me. How can I help?'

The voice on the other end was calm and professional. Her curiosity rose.

'My name is Sergeant Cooper – Keith Cooper – stationed at Monkstown. On the Moor; you're aware of the Moor?'

Alice's eyebrows shot up. 'Yes, of course. I holidayed there as a child; my aunt and uncle owned a cottage at Nether Dennyfold.'

'That would be Crag Cottage?'

'Yes, that's the one. I haven't been there for years. What's this about, Sergeant Cooper?'

'You have a cousin, Fleur Hennessy-Blair?'

'Yes, Fleur's my cousin. Her parents were killed a few months back – my aunt and uncle. Is everything okay?' A shiver of concern trickled down Alice's spine. She didn't much like her cousin, but she wouldn't wish her any harm.

'The thing is, Miss McKenna – may I call you Alice? – the thing is, Fleur has been staying at Crag Cottage recently, with a view, I believe, to placing it on the market.'

A stab of anger, mixed with dismay, caught Alice unawares. The thought of Crag Cottage – the place of her dreams, her favourite childhood memories – being sold to some stranger was dreadful, but it didn't surprise her. Fleur had always hated it there.

'I see. I didn't know that.' She tried hard to stop her voice shaking.

'The thing is, Alice, she's gone missing.'

'Missing? Since when?'

Sergeant Cooper gave a little cough. 'We're not sure exactly, but we think it must be at least six days ago.'

Alice frowned as she considered this information. 'She has homes all over the place, now her parents are dead. I expect she's gone to one of those. How did she get to the cottage? Did she drive? Is her car still there?'

'Well, that's the thing, see. It appears she got a train from London, and then took a taxi to Nether Dennyfold. We've checked that out. But her personal belongings are still at the cottage, and the last person we think she spoke to said that he saw her walking in the direction of Crow Pond. That would've been on Saturday.'

Crow Pond. A fresh twist of alarm clawed at Alice's stomach. It was the most beautiful, idyllic spot, but to reach it you had to navigate Pedlar's Quag, a treacherous quagmire riddled with deep pools. She'd been taken there just a handful of times in all the years her family holidayed at Crag Cottage. The myths and legends about evil fairy folk who lived in the bogs, scaly monsters that lurked in the pools – which were, of course, bottomless – and the large number of people who'd gone missing in the area over the years, had both delighted and terrified her. Even now, the only images that would come to mind were of sinister ripples in still, black ponds, twisted figures sprinting through the reeds not-quite-seen, and the thick mists that would rise out of nowhere and then disappear as quickly.

'Oh, I see. That's a bit of a worry. So, this person who spoke to her last: are they a suspect? Has a search taken place?'

'No, not a suspect, he's been eliminated from our enquiries. The search and rescue lads have been mobilised; they're due to finish today. Nothing found yet, I'm afraid.'

'But that's good, surely? If they haven't found a... a body, then Fleur must be somewhere else. I can't imagine her walking across the Quag, to be honest; it's not really her thing.'

'Well, let's hope so. But the thing is, you seem to be Fleur's only living relative.'

Fleur was an only child, doted on by her wealthy parents. Uncle Graham was also an only child, so there were no more cousins, something that Alice had always been very grateful for; Fleur had been quite enough of a handful.

'Yes, that's right, no other cousins... except I have a brother, Luke. He lives in Australia; we're not really in touch. Why?' She was beginning to worry about where this might be going.

'Well, we thought it might be an idea for you to come down to the Moor; you might be able to tell us a bit more about your cousin, and it's easier face to face, like.'

'I'm owed some holiday, but I'll have to check with my supervisor. I'm sure he'll understand, especially if I tell him the police have asked me to come down. I might even be able to make it down tomorrow, if that would work?'

Sergeant Cooper said that would work very well, and they agreed that Alice would let him know when she arrived. She wrote down his number on a page of her notebook, said goodbye, then doodled flowers all around the numbers as her head filled with a mixture of alarm and anticipation.

Life had been so empty for the last few months since Mum finally lost her grip on life. Alice had repeated an endless, empty round of work, home, work, home, unable to fill the void of loneliness.

She picked up the donut and resumed her nibbling, a tentative smile curling her mouth. First a donut, now a trip to the Moor – whatever next?

It was the boxes of old photographs that Alice had found hardest to confront. The endless knick-knacks and pointless, dusty ornaments had been easy to deal with; she'd taken a grim delight in wrapping each item in newspaper and consigning them to a dozen cardboard boxes, hauling each one to the charity shop on a dozen melancholy bus journeys.

Even sorting the clothes had been relatively stress-free. She'd resisted the urge to breathe in the scents that were still faintly discernible on her mother's floral dresses and bobbled cardigans: the rose-based eau de toilette she'd favoured, mingled with the aromas of teabags and long, drawn-out death.

Her father's suits and shirts had hung dormant in the fusty mahogany wardrobe that occupied the spare bedroom for fifteen years, gathering a patina of mildew and sorrow; her mother had refused to throw them out, unable to accept the loss of the man she'd loved so dearly. Alice had the benefit of a healing cushion of time and had shoved it all into black refuse bags, and put an extra bag out on each rubbish collection day, disposing of another little bit of her misery along with the clothes.

But the photographs had been a step too far, and it had taken the unexpected invitation to return to Crag Cottage to push her to finally look at them.

There were folders full of faded sepia photos of people she didn't recognise, and now she'd never know who they were. She'd get rid of those one day, but for now she was searching for one special box.

Holiday Box. She picked it up – it wasn't very heavy, as the McKenna family holidays could be counted on the fingers of two hands – and took it downstairs to the kitchen, placing it carefully on the table. She wanted to take some time with this, so she made herself a mug of tea, and then gently peeled off the tape.

The first item was a long cardboard folder; the photos inside were much more recent than the ones she'd been sorting through earlier. One photo caught her eye, and a smile twitched at the corners of her mouth, transforming her pale, pensive face. It was her father Philip, her brother Luke and herself, sitting outside a stone cottage in bright sunshine. She looked about seven years old, with the same delicate features and mousy, straight brown hair she had now. Luke would have been four or five. Her dad was smiling, but he had an air of sadness about him. She hadn't known then, of course, when she was only seven, that he was wracked by the guilt of only being able to afford to take his little family on holiday to his brother-in-law's holiday home. The adorable Crag Cottage was nestled in a tiny hamlet on the edge of the Moor in the West Country; the holidays her family had spent there provided some of her most cherished memories, despite her father's melancholy.

She slowed down, and peered carefully at each photo, reliving those balmy summer days, revelling in the warmth of family life. There was her mum, looking slim and pretty, though dressed in a shocking floral high-necked number. And Luke; such a sweet-looking child, it was a shame the way he'd turned out. She hadn't seen him for years, though he'd come back from Australia for their mother's funeral; it turned out he was coming over for something entirely unconnected anyway. Being Luke, he'd basked in the praise that had been showered on him: such a good son, to come all that way; his mother would have been so proud.

Another photo shook away any thoughts of Luke: Pigswhistle Clump, her favourite place of all. An ancient woodland comprising mainly oaks, but also chestnut trees and beeches, silver birch and sycamores: to Alice, it was her own private wonderland. When she was little Mum and Dad would take her there, and they'd walk the stony paths and marvel at the variety of toadstools and leaves they'd find. As she grew more independent, Alice took off to the woods whenever she could for some blissful time alone, usually making her way to her special rock. She was happy in her own company, spending hours at a time exploring the secret paths that had been made by a fox or a badger, or simply sitting on the rock, dreaming.

As the memories came flooding back, Alice wondered what Crag Cottage looked like now. The last holiday they'd had was the year before her father had died so unexpectedly. Her mother couldn't face it without him; she couldn't face life without him. Places could change a lot in sixteen years; maybe it wouldn't seem quite so magical to a jaded thirty-two-year-old.

The last folder she picked up had more holiday photos, this time with her Aunt Mari and Uncle Graham, and her cousin, the dreaded Fleur. It was the only time they'd ever holidayed at the cottage together, when Alice had been twelve and Fleur a sophisticated fourteen. Crag Cottage might have belonged to Uncle Graham, but his family hardly ever stayed there. Once he'd become so successful, so rich, they could jet off to anywhere they wanted.

There were more folders, but Alice had found what she was looking for, and set aside a small pile of photos. Closing the box, a flash of colour caught her eye and she remembered the book. Smiling, she carefully pulled it out, placing it with reverence on the table. It was a cheap scrapbook with multi-coloured sugar paper pages, the front decorated with photos cut from magazines: sunny beaches and blue skies, green fields full of cows, and across the middle, carefully crayoned and cut out letters forming the words, *My Holiday Diary*.

Alice had started this diary the year she was nine, and she'd since forgotten all about it. She'd written something every year they'd stayed at Crag Cottage. She slowly turned the pages, amused by the pictures she'd drawn to go alongside her entries, which in the first few pages were very simple.

> *25th July 1996*
> *I love being back here!!! Here are some things I saw in*
> *Pigswistel Clump this afternon.*

She laughed at the terrible spelling, and the childish drawing of a red-and-white spotted toadstool. There was a dried oak leaf and a piece of fern, partly disintegrated and stuck down with yellowing tape. She read on.

> *It was funny, it felt ~~breazie~~ windy under the big tree. I*

thought Luke was strocking my hair but he was up the tree, so I think it must of been a fairy.

Alice remembered with a start how she'd really thought someone was stroking her hair, almost as though trying to get her attention. She used to love drawing fairies when she was little, but this one looked more like a malevolent imp, with crossed eyes and huge hands.

> *The fairy lived inside the tree,*
> *Her friends a fox, a ~~bird~~ crow and a bumblebee.*

Grimacing at her childish attempt at poetry, she read on.

> *We had fish and chips from the village for tea!*

An empty miniature vinegar packet had been taped to the page, a sour tang still evident after all these years. Fish and chips had been a real treat for Alice and Luke; Dad had never been one for spending frivolously, and Mum had always turned her nose up at eating out of paper. But on holiday, it seemed, she allowed her standards to drop.

Leafing through the diary, she came to a section where the writing was neater and there were fewer drawings. 1999: the year her aunt, uncle and cousin had stayed at Crag Cottage with them.

> *1st August 1999*
>
> *I don't like Fleur being here. She doesn't like doing the things I like doing, but Mummy says I should be friends with her.*
>
> *Mummy made a big shepherd's pie for tea, it was delicious, but I heard Aunt Mari whisper that it was like canteen food. I*

think she's a bit of a snob. Fleur hardly ate anything. She says she's on a diet. But she's already too thin!

Alice sighed; she and Fleur were so different, it was no wonder they'd never been close, even though there were only two years between them. It was a shame, really. Fleur was an only child, and Alice was as *good* as an only child, now that Luke was so far away. But they were like chalk and cheese; she'd always been unconcerned about her appearance, and being on a diet was something that had never crossed her mind, even though she felt a bit squishy at the edges.

3rd August 1999
Luke's being stupid, he follows Fleur like a puppy. She wears make-up!! And a bra!!!!

Alice giggled at her ridiculously childish drawing of what she must have supposed was a bra. She hadn't needed to wear one herself until she was nearly sixteen, and then only did so because the other girls at school had teased her; it had clearly been something of a marvel to her twelve-year-old, flat-chested self.

I went to Pigswhistle Clump, and it was nice and quiet. I like being on my own, so I can think about things. I thought someone was there, but it was just a shadow on the ground. I wasn't scared for long.

A fleeting memory of being terrified by something unseen and unheard crossed Alice's mind, and a shiver ran up her spine. But she'd been young and impressionable then, with an overactive imagination.

Shutting the diary and shoving it back into the box with the folder of photos, she shook away thoughts of Fleur and the Moor, and spooky shadows. Her cousin had probably simply left the Moor without telling anyone; she wasn't too worried. But she'd had enough for one day; the other photos could wait. It had taken her a year to look at them – they wouldn't be going anywhere. And anyway, she had a suitcase to pack.

CHAPTER THREE

SATURDAY 25 MAY

Watching the last of the drab high-rises and commercial units disappear, Alice felt a surge of excitement. Her suitcase was packed with very little: a pair of flat walking sandals, a couple of T-shirts and a warm jumper; all grey or navy, not a spot of colour amongst them.

Weather on the Moor was always a bit more, well – *weathery* – than in the city, so she knew she should be prepared for anything. She'd also packed her favourite navy-blue raincoat and a pair of grey welly boots, which took up most of the space; the ground around Nether Dennyfold was boggy, and if she was to help look for Fleur, she needed to be appropriately shod. Freshly laundered, utilitarian underwear and her woefully meagre toiletry bag completed the packing, and it was all currently stowed above her head, as the train sped towards the West Country.

John had been surprisingly relaxed about her taking some time off at such short notice, but he'd recently started dating that girl from comms he'd been going on about, and he was sweetly relaxed about everything.

She'd never really been one for dating, herself. She liked

men, and she'd had a few crushes over the years, even been on a few dates, but relationships had never lasted long. It didn't help that she was so painfully shy. She probably didn't give off encouraging vibes, which was why she was ignored. Or perhaps she simply wasn't noticed. She was average looking, certainly not a head-turner. Not like Fleur.

Delving into her backpack, she grabbed a bag of wine gums, her holiday diary and an envelope of photographs. Last night, after looking through all the images, she'd cried tears of concern for her cousin, though she was still convinced Fleur had simply taken off for one of her other homes. She wouldn't stay any longer at Crag Cottage than she needed to – not when she had homes in London, Paris and New York. Alice assumed *those* hadn't been sold off yet.

Crag Cottage would be the first to go; Fleur had always hated the place, lacking the luxury she'd become used to. She'd even referred to it as *creepy,* once. But its bare stone walls and floors, its wood burner and big old Aga, the breezes that found their way through the rickety windows, the overgrown garden with its little stream, and the way it was tucked into a tiny hamlet as though it had been there forever, had always enchanted Alice. She wondered if she'd still feel the same about it.

Slowly chewing a wine gum, she leafed through the photos. They all had Fleur centre-stage, which was where Fleur liked to be. Her lovely face shone out in each one, overshadowing anything – or anyone – else. Fleur in front of the cottage; Fleur in her bedroom in the London house, surrounded by hundreds of dolls and teddy bears; Fleur with her parents, the Eiffel Tower a blurry smudge in the background. There were even some of Fleur and Alice together, taken on that single holiday the two families had shared. Alice looked small, shapeless and very young in her home-made, badly fitting cotton shorts and matching top. Fleur was only two years older at fourteen, but she'd already morphed into the beginnings of the smartly dressed woman she'd later become, proudly thrusting her well-developed chest at the camera.

Relaxing into the rhythm of the train as it whirred along, Alice let her mind wander back twenty years to that summer at the cottage.

That particular year, the Hennessy-Blairs' plans for three weeks cruising around the Caribbean had been ruined by an outbreak of illness on the cruise liner. With no time to make other arrangements, they'd decided to join Alice's family on the Moor. It hadn't been a success, and had never been repeated. There was too much of a gulf between the two families. Mum had insisted on Aunt Mari helping her with the washing up after every meal, and Dad had organised a rota for the children to do little chores – sweep the floors, tidy the beds, shell the peas. He'd tried to encourage Uncle Graham to help him collect firewood and plan long walks across the Moor, but the Hennessy-Blairs were used to luxury and having people do things for them, and it had all got a bit awkward.

Luke had spent the whole holiday gazing at his cousin with puppy dog eyes. Fleur had flirted madly with him, despite him being only nine. She'd flirted with everyone; it was her way.

Alice had still been very much a child, and loved nothing more than getting up early and taking her fishing net to the little brook that edged the far end of the cottage's wild and wonderful garden. She'd catch tiddlers in an old jam jar, and watch them as they darted here and there. Fleur preferred to have a lie-in, then spend her mornings experimenting with the expensive make-up her mother had presented her with on her thirteenth birthday. Alice remembered wondering whether Mum would give her make-up as a present when she reached thirteen. Of course she hadn't; her parents had given her a big, glossy encyclopaedia of trees, plants and wildlife, which had been much more satisfying.

One morning during that holiday though, she'd bounced down the stairs to find her cousin sitting morosely at the scrubbed pine kitchen table, leafing listlessly through a magazine.

'What's the matter?'

Fleur hadn't answered, just thrust out her lower lip and hunched further down. Alice had got herself a bowl of cornflakes, and sat munching in silence. There was one surefire way she'd known of that would cheer Fleur up, and that was to suggest a walk to the big house.

The Manor House, as it was properly called, was a gorgeous, crumbling Georgian pile, rebuilt in 1726 on the site of an earlier house that had been destroyed by Cromwell, or so it was said. The Denny family had owned it since those early days, but it was Sir Rufus Denny-Hurst who'd lived there when Alice was small. Fleur had been impressed to hear about another family with a double-barrelled name, and they had two sons: Jenson, who was eighteen, and Finbar, a very good-looking sixteen-year-old. It had usually been easy to persuade her to go for a walk, just in case the boys were at home.

Fleur's face had lit up. She'd flicked her long blonde hair into a chic bun, and they'd pulled on their trainers. Alice had never really known what caused Fleur to be so open when she'd started talking on the short walk to the big house. Perhaps it had been the sun, which warmed their skin and cast golden light over the pretty hamlet, with its golden stone cottages and over-abundant gardens... or perhaps it was just that Fleur had needed to talk to someone, and Alice had been there at the right time. She'd listened quietly as Fleur had poured out her troubles and her innermost feelings, though she hadn't really understood, and had buried the memory until now.

Soft rain was falling when Alice finally stepped from the train onto the platform at Monkstown. It was coating everything with a mist of nostalgia. She'd been planning to take a taxi as far as Dennybridge, stop for a bite to eat then walk the mile to Nether Dennyfold, but the drizzle was faintly depressing and even though her suitcase was small and had wheels, she couldn't face the long trudge along muddy lanes. So she asked the lone taxi driver parked on the station approach to take her to Crag Cottage. He peered at her curiously, eyes dark behind thick glasses, brow furrowed under the brim of his battered tweed cap, as he deposited her suitcase on the back seat.

'You'll be the cousin then, I s'pose?'

'I beg your pardon?'

'Cousin of that woman what's gone missing? Hop in the front. My name's Harry. Harry Deegin. I s'pect you'll be using my cab a lot.'

With that, he leapt back into the taxi, revved the engine and patted the passenger seat. Alice was slightly taken aback, but had no choice but to clamber in as gracefully as she could, and hope that he wasn't expecting to have a conversation. Small talk didn't come naturally to her, but unfortunately Harry seemed to be the chatty type.

He started humming as the cab made its way through the streets of Monkstown, and Alice distracted herself by gazing out of the window. She was delighted to see that some of the shops and buildings looked exactly as she remembered them. She was thrilled to see that Hamble & Addie still looked much the same, its golden stone facades adorned with hanging baskets, its windows as hideous as ever they were, filled with outdated mannequins wearing ridiculously frumpy clothes. The old-fashioned department store had been a place of wonder to Alice, who'd never been taken to the enormous stores in London as a child. Her mother had always said they were for the rich, *'not for the likes of us'*. She visited them now, of course; Liberty's was her favourite, with its wooden staircases and nooks and crannies, and she always remembered Hamble & Addie as a smaller, madder, mustier version.

'So, how long since you visited here, Miss...?'

'Alice. McKenna. It's been sixteen years, but some places don't seem to have changed much.'

Harry snorted. 'Monkstown don't never change. Same old shops, same old people. Bleedin' tree's still there, look, looming like some great evil judge.'

They were passing the town gardens, walled in golden stone, the wall pierced by metal gates. She could see young mothers rushing through the rain with buggies, small children running around, and a dog cocking its leg on a lamppost. Taking centre stage was an enormous tree, an ancient oak known as the Hanging Tree, due to its grisly role in the past. The last hanging to take place in Monkstown was in eighteen-something, but its history clung to it like an executioner's shame, and it was now something of a tourist attraction in a town that lacked much else.

'I was always fascinated by it when I was little,' Alice ventured. 'I loved all the gruesome stories, but now I'm older...' She shivered as she thought about how it must have been, to be hanged in public from such a beautiful tree.

'There's a few want it cut down, but the council won't have it. Say it should be kept, outta respect for the dead. Though they wouldn't have been hanged if they wasn't guilty of something bad, so what's to respect? That's what I want to know.'

Harry grumbled on about the council, and taxes, and pretty much everything to do with Monkstown, so Alice just kept quiet as they passed through the rest of the town. Some new housing estates had sprung up on the southern edge, the grey brick and huge windows jarring with the feel of the town itself. They were ugly, and Alice wondered how on earth they found enough people to live in such places; what did they all do for jobs? She supposed they must work from home, or travel to the nearest city; there certainly wasn't enough on the Moor to sustain hordes of workers.

The cab took the road towards Dennybridge, passing the ruins of Greyfriars Priory, the only other significant site in Monkstown. It looked gloomy in the drizzle, but Alice had loved playing there when the sun was bright, casting a maze of shadows formed by its columns and empty windows that had made for an exciting game: she and Luke pretended that the shadows were solid ground and the sunny bits fiery pits. She missed the good times with Luke; they hadn't lasted for long.

They were soon passing through the village of Dennybridge, with its grey stone buildings. Turnpike Bridge took them over the River Denny, its little octagonal toll house now a gift shop. It was very picturesque. A few shops clustered along the banks of the river. A supermarket occupied what had once been a butcher and a baker, but the ironmongers was still there: an Aladdin's cave of boxes and shelves, and trays of this and that, where Alice's dad had spent many a happy hour, and where she and Luke had bought their fishing nets. The last shop in the village was still there, too: Turnkey Books. She frowned as the cab sped past; it looked gloomy, and she'd never have known it was open if there hadn't been a small, handwritten sign saying *Open* on the door.

Browsing through the second-hand books had been one of her favourite things. The smell of paper and bindings, ink and mildew had thrilled her, and she longed to go in now and run her hands over the spines, take volumes carefully from the shelves and open them, dust flying out in little puffs as she thumbed through forgotten pages. But then she remembered old Mr Turnkey, a dour man with a scowl and ever-present cough. She'd been terrified of him, always trying to evade his prowling presence; the cough had been helpful in that respect. He clearly hadn't been fond of small children rummaging through his precious stock.

Harry must have read her thoughts. 'He's not there now, old Mr Turnkey. He's been packed off to a nursing home, due to his going a bit potty. Shop's not what it was without him.'

'Oh! That's a shame.' Alice was secretly delighted, and vowed to visit the shop as soon as she could. 'Who runs it now?'

'His son, James. Nice enough chap, but he don't have a clue about how to run a bookshop.'

'I don't remember him having a son.' Alice's brow wrinkled as she tried to recall. Mr Turnkey had lived in a flat above the shop, but she couldn't remember him having any family. 'You like reading, then, Harry?' She was warming to the cabbie; anyone who liked books must be okay.

'Well, I don't mind a good thriller, some of them Scandinavian ones is good.' He blushed, and darted a quick look at her, as though weighing up how much he should say. 'It's not something I'd like bandied about, but I'm trying to write one myself.'

Alice's mouth dropped open. 'Seriously? I like writing, too. Poems mostly. It's hard, isn't it?'

Harry chuckled. 'I'm thinking about going to a writer's retreat that's being held soon t'other side of the Moor. If I'm brave enough.' He pulled a face, then brightened. 'Well, here we are.'

Alice hadn't noticed that the cab had turned up the narrow lane that ran for a mile from the main road to Nether Dennyfold, and she couldn't help but smile as she recognised the cottages of the tiny hamlet. Honeysuckle Cottage, picture-perfect with its picket fence, but the honeysuckle that had been draped abundantly over the porch was no longer there; was it just a little neater than she remembered? And Pedlar's Cottage, still empty by the look of it; ancient and gloomy, partially hidden behind a bank of hedges that had grown taller over the years, its strange ornate chimney disappearing under cords of ivy. She and Luke had always believed it was haunted.

Then, as they turned the corner, she had her first glimpse of Crag Cottage, and her heart did a little leap. It still looked the same as she remembered: a solid house built of the local golden stone, with a wide wooden door in the middle, the windows sporting freshly painted white frames. A single-storey addition to the left side was a coal shed, a place of terror when she was small, with its thick, greasy cobwebs and mysterious objects covered with coal-dusty sheets. The strip of garden in front of the cottage looked neglected and overgrown; when Alice's family had holidayed there it had always been overflowing with roses. At least, that's how she remembered it.

She realised the cab had stopped, and Harry was expecting a reply to something he'd said.

'I'm so sorry, it's just...'

Harry chuckled, shaking his head. 'Don't fret, Alice. Memories are powerful things. You'll need some time to explore, rekindle some of what you loved, as I don't s'pose it's all the same as it was when you was last here.'

Cash was handed over, with a generous tip, and Harry pushed a small card into her hand. 'My number, next time you need a ride.'

He pulled the case from the car and placed it by the gate, then held out his hand, gripping Alice's with strong, warm fingers. 'Don't forget, not a word about the writing thing.' He grinned, leapt back into the cab, and was gone before she had time to react.

Strangely nervous, she hesitated. The lane, puddled and grey in the subdued light, the hedge she'd once hidden in dark and riddled with brambles, looked both familiar and alien. Harry was right: this place wouldn't match up to her childhood memories. She grabbed the suitcase and unlatched the gate, gathering her courage.

Sergeant Cooper had told her the key would be left underneath a flowerpot, and there it was. She smiled. No one would ever do such a thing where she lived; it was far too obvious, and houses were burgled regularly, with or without the nicety of leaving out a means of access. Opening the door with a shiver of anticipation, she walked into Crag Cottage.

CHAPTER FOUR

NOVEMBER 1772

Whether 'tis truth or ne'er but a lie, who dreams?
With her head full of visions of beauty and hope
Dreams the crow.

I love to roam, but the crow knows 'tis getting harder now, and I don't go so far. I've not been to Pedlar's Quag in a goodly while, though most'd say that was a good thing. More folk than I can count've been lost in that treachersome quagmire. They say those men must've been bad 'uns, as the bog holes are bottomless and surely the doors to hell. But I don't see as that's true. I found bones in the Quag as wasn't from no sheep nor hound, not a bird nor any beast, but was surely the leg bones of a man. And if his bones was still on this earth, then the bogs are no more bottomless than my slop bucket, and his soul wasn't gone to hell.

'Twas the woods I loved most when I was little. I still love 'em now. Pigswhistle Clump, they're known as, though why, I have no notion. There's no pigs there, and that's a fact. I love the way the sun makes shadows through the branches, and the ground is all soft with fallen leaves and ferns. I sit on the big rock in the clearing and let the sun warm my bones. I look for mushrooms what grow under the trees, some blood-red, others white as dumplings. I like the little cracking noises as the wind blows through and nuts drop to the ground. I used to pick 'em up and put 'em in my bonnet and take 'em home to Ma for roasting on the fire.

But not no more. Ma sent me away from the cottage on account of my belly, what's growing bigger than seems possible. My old linens don't fit, so Ma gave me a new set what she said'll clothe an el'phant, whatever that might be. But she don't want me in the cottage, and she don't want me near my da.

My new home is the old bakehouse on the path to Pedlar's Quag, what's not been used for many a year. 'Tis cold and gloomy, but it has a roof, and a door what almost shuts, and I made a bed of straw what's comfy enough. 'Tis lonely and the night noises scare me, and the wind blows harsh through the window, but what choice do I have? Who'd take in a girl who has nothing but a growing belly? I keep to the big room what was the bakehouse; there's another, behind the chimney what was used for brewing, but I don't go in there, only if a storm makes the door blow in and turns everything wet with rain. 'Tis darker than the blackest night in there, and it fair frightens me.

I don't have much to call my own, but those few rags for to clothe me, and my most precious thing, my box with shells stuck all over. I keep it safe in the space what was used for baking. I never did see the sea, though Ma told me tales of big ships and pirates and suchlike, when I was a child. I look at the shells and can almost smell the salt in the air and hear the crashing of the waves. I got a good 'magination, and that's a fact!

In the daytime I go to the woods, and I pretend I'm a princess with long golden hair, and a soft bag of silver coins, and a platter of meat, dripping with juices. 'Tis a fine dream, but in the end I always must return to my little barn, light a fire to keep away the cold and the night beasts, and eat whatever has been left for me. My ma does have a heart, see, though she don't often show it, and the crow knows she won't let me starve. Tonight it's a big hunk of bread, hard on my teeth, but 'tis smothered in dripping, and I like a bit of dripping, so I'm happy enough. I fetch a pail of water from the well just beyond the bakehouse, gather some turf what my da's cut and left out, and I'm as blessed as any princess.

Sometimes I walk the lane to Ma's, see if I can spy my sis. I miss Greta, and little Danny. Soon as I see the chimney what my da built atop the roof, my heart sings a little. 'Tis a strange affair, with its twisted bricks and jaggedy top, and he's fair proud of it. I wish he had pride in his Hettie, but I reckon he don't ever even think about me.

'Course, I know why my belly's swelling. I might not know my letters, but I know a bit about life, and I seen my ma's belly grow more'n once. My da planted a seed in my ma, and that's what growed me. And now he's planted a seed in me too, what he shouldn't have done, and my belly's growed, and one day out will pop a child. I don't rightly know how, or when, so's I must bide my time until it happens. Ma won't help; she won't hardly ever come near me, like I got the pox, but she talked to Miss Patience in the big house, who's going to send me her woman when my time's near.

I don't like Miss Patience. When she was given her name they can't have known what sort of woman she'd grow into. She scares me. Her da, ol' Sir Michael Denny, is a kind man, though I've not seen him in a goodly while, and I fear he's near his end. Miss Patience is married to Mr Wickens, so I s'pose I should call her Mrs Wickens, but it don't sit right. Anyway, she'll send me the woman what helped her birth young Charles, and that makes me feel safer. I seen the lady with the boy, and though she looks diff'rent to most of us, I can tell how she's gentle and kind with that poor lad.

My belly has stretched so big, I'm afeared I'm going to burst open like the plums on the trees in the orchard what get too ripe. I like to run my hands over the skin, tight like a drum, and feel the strange bumps underneath, what I must s'pose is the child. Sometimes the bumps move, and I feel the oddest feeling, like my insides is full of wriggling fishes, but I'm not scared. Ma let me feel her belly when sis and little Daniel were inside her, so I knows 'tis not a thing to be afeared of, but a thing of wonder.

What sort of ma will I be to my child? And will it be a boy or a girl? I s'pose I must be patient. I will know soon enough.

CHAPTER FIVE

SATURDAY 25 MAY

Milky light puddled on the flagstones in the kitchen, lay in pools on the long, scrubbed pine table, and highlighted the ancient Aga, its red paint flaking after years of neglect. The beamed ceiling was embroidered with a multitude of cobwebs, a huge stone fireplace at the far end similarly festooned, an old wood burner lurking in its shadows, cold and blank.

Alice gazed around the room, so familiar and yet so different. This place had always been full of laughter and activity, the table laden with food, the wood burner blazing, whatever the temperature outside. Mum would be bustling around baking, sweeping, nagging. Dad was always happy as a lark, chopping wood, lighting fires, dodging the nagging as much as he could. Alice and Luke would explore the house and play hide-and-seek, squashing into shadowy corners, squeezing into empty cupboards, and climbing the narrow stairs that led to the attic, home to the worst sorts of monsters that both thrilled and terrified them.

She'd never been happier than on those holidays, when even the rain seemed sweeter, the breezes sharper, and the air more luminous than in the suburbs of London. When she was younger, she'd felt as though she was her real self at the Moor, and just a shadow everywhere else.

There was a musty smell in the air now, a mix of rotten wood and damp stone, but then another scent hit her: a sophisticated blend of jasmine and sandalwood. Fleur loved her perfumes, even as a young girl, never leaving the cottage without a cloud of rose or vanilla wafting around her. It had always made Alice cough and splutter, and she'd never worn anything more than a dab of her mother's eau de toilette.

Fleur. Alice remembered why she was here, with a pang of guilt. She studied the various items on the table. A wooden bowl that had been there since forever, that Mum used to fill with the not-quite-ripe apples and pears that Alice and Luke collected from the orchards. Now full of dust and dead insects, it had been pushed to one end of the table. At the other end was a pile of leaflets and papers, marketing stuff for estate agents and solicitors, by the look of it. Fleur's handbag, baby blue leather by a seriously expensive designer, lay on its side, contents spilling out.

Sergeant Cooper had already explained that the police had taken Fleur's phone and purse, including her credit cards, but there were lipsticks, a tiny mirror, and several other personal items lying on the table in disarray. A little bottle of anti-bacterial hand gel made Alice smile; that was Fleur all over. While Alice had never been happier than when knee-deep in the stream building a dam, fingers clawing at mud and slimy pebbles, Fleur had been the one to wail about germs and getting dirt under her beautifully manicured nails. Alice carefully put everything back into the bag and placed it on a side table.

A Chanel jacket was slung over the back of a chair, as though Fleur had been in a hurry. Normally it would have been hung up neatly on one of the padded silk hangers she favoured. Alice felt a shiver of concern, followed by a shudder of fatigue. What she needed was a cup of tea. There were a few teabags in the battered Tetley's tin she remembered from her childhood, but they smelled stale. They might have been there for years. Two new boxes had been opened, though: Earl Grey and some organic fennel mix in little organza bags. Typical Fleur. What was wrong with good old-fashioned tea?

There was a half-empty bottle of skimmed milk in the fridge, which smelled okay, so Alice set about filling the kettle and finding her favourite mug. The *decent* mugs, as Aunt Mari had called them, were at the front of the cupboard, floral bone china in shades of lilac. Alice moved them aside so she could reach to the back, where her beloved sheep mug lurked in all its brown-stained glory. A quick rinse in cold water sufficed, and the mug was soon filled with a steaming brew.

It had been a present from old Mrs Furbelow, the housekeeper at the big house, the very first time Alice had stayed at the cottage. She'd been picking wildflowers in the lane, and Mrs Furbelow had hobbled past. On a whim, she'd thrust the wilting bunch at the old lady, who'd been so charmed she'd immediately called back to the cottage with the mug. Alice had treasured it ever since. She might even take it back home with her; Fleur certainly wouldn't miss it.

Sipping at the tea, she sent Sergeant Cooper a text, as she'd promised to, and then she was ready to check out the rest of the cottage, make sure the immersion was turned on so she could have a shower later, and make up a bed. The kitchen led back into the small entrance hallway, a door into the sitting room on the opposite side. She glanced around the room, which was stale and dusty with a distinct air of neglect. It had never been used much, except when the two families stayed that one time, and Aunt Mari had insisted that the grown-ups sit in there after supper. Mum and Dad would much rather have been in the kitchen, everyone together, sitting around the table playing board games.

At the back of the cottage, behind the kitchen, was an empty room known as the scullery, which housed an ancient range and the boiler. It had once been the original kitchen and had a door leading to the storeroom and coal shed, which was dark and cobwebby, and scared Alice so much she'd always refused to go near it. She chose not to go there now, and instead made her way up the stairs.

There were three bedrooms and a bathroom on this floor, with two further rooms tucked up in the attic, reached by a set of narrow stairs hidden behind a door. That had been where Alice and Luke had played on rainy days, though they only slept up there on that one joint holiday – Luke on an old-fashioned camp bed in the larger room, Alice next door on a narrow bed with the lumpiest mattress in the world. They'd tried to scare each other with stories about the monsters that lived up there, but she'd adored the attic's sense of solitude and secrecy.

She remembered with a pang what else was up there, but first looked around the bedrooms. Fleur had clearly chosen to sleep in the largest of the three, her suitcases stacked neatly in one corner, and the sheets were crumpled, a heap of decorative cushions lying on the floor. Why hadn't Fleur bothered making the bed when she'd last got up? It was very unlike her to be so messy.

She opened the old oak wardrobe, and found several garments on their padded hangers, lined up neatly according to type and colour. Jackets, trousers, crisp shirts, floaty skirts, smart dresses – nothing suitable for wearing in a place like this. Alice suppressed a scornful giggle, then remembered again that Fleur was missing. She'd have a good sort through later, see if she could find anything that might give a clue as to where her cousin had gone.

Choosing one of the remaining bedrooms, Alice spent a happy half-hour finding bedding, making up the bed and tidying away her own meagre selection of clothing. Sergeant Cooper would be there soon, so she decided to leave exploring the attic till later. There'd be plenty of time to find the book and the poem – *her* book, and *her* poem – later.

Sergeant Cooper had brought a box of proper teabags and a bottle of milk with him, together with a packet of chocolate digestives, a loaf of bread and some cheese. 'I thought you'd not've had time to do any shopping.'

He'd also brought with him a young man, good looking in a scruffy way, though with a scowl that rendered him unattractive. They were sitting at the table, mugs of tea in hand while Sergeant Cooper prattled on about the weather and the state of the local police force, as though he was desperately trying to avoid his reason for being there. He was a cheery looking man, perhaps in his fifties, and Alice had taken to him immediately.

'Alice – I can call you Alice? – It's so nice to meet you in person. As I said, this is James Turnkey. I've asked him to come along, as we think he was the last person to see Fleur. I should reiterate that he's not a suspect, but I thought it would be best for you to speak to him directly, as he might be able to offer some clues as to Fleur's disappearance.'

Alice looked solemnly at James and offered her hand, which he ignored. She wondered whether he was anything to do with her favourite bookshop. It was starting to feel awkward as they all sipped at their drinks, Sergeant Cooper gossiping while James gazed into his mug and Alice tried, but failed, to think of something to say.

'I suppose we should get down to business.' Sergeant Cooper

had a little cough and produced a notepad from his bag. 'Well now, James, you say you saw Fleur... when was it, exactly – a week ago? I know you've already given me a statement, but perhaps you could tell Alice what you told me, so she understands a bit more.'

James frowned, dark eyebrows drawn together over grey, secretive eyes. Alice guessed he was a similar age to herself, perhaps a little older... mid-to-late thirties, maybe. She also thought he could do with taking a bit more care over his appearance; his beard was untrimmed, his clothes shabby. His voice was quiet but rich, with an attractive local lilt.

'I'd come here to see Fleur. We... We had a bit of a row, nothing major, and she stormed off. I started to follow, expecting her to have gone down the lane, or up to the big house, but she wasn't there. I scouted around, looked in the orchard, walked along the stream. I wondered if she'd gone to the woods, but then I saw a flash of the pink dress she was wearing, on the path to Hettie's Hovel. I followed, but by the time I'd reached the ruin, she'd disappeared. There's nowhere else she could have gone but Pedlar's Quag.'

A silence descended on the room as Alice digested this information. Something wasn't right. 'So, you didn't actually see Fleur walking on the Quag? But you didn't follow to make sure she was safe?'

James cast his eyes down, sweat pricking his forehead. He looked extremely sheepish, Alice thought, and so he should if he'd just let her cousin walk over the treacherous ground that made Pedlar's Quag so infamous. He looked at her then, a gaze so direct and penetrating it made her stomach lurch.

'I didn't see her on the Quag, no. And I'm not proud of myself, but it was difficult. I was angry. Fleur isn't an easy person to be with. She'd been acting weirdly. And it's not an area I know well. It was getting misty, there are stories...'

His eyes dropped again to the mug he was cradling, and Alice noted that his hands were shaking slightly. From anger? Shame? Guilt?

Sergeant Cooper coughed again, perhaps picking up on the tension that had slowly been building. 'James, could you tell Alice why you were visiting that day?'

James looked sheepish again, his eyes roaming around the kitchen, as though looking for something. He looked anywhere but at Alice. 'I came to give her a present. I was hoping to impress her.'

Alice noted the blush creeping up beneath James's beard. She frowned. 'Were you dating?' She didn't mean to sound so surprised, but this scruffy, angry man wasn't at all like the slick city suits Fleur favoured.

'Is that so surprising?' James snapped, his fists balling.

Sergeant Cooper gave another little cough, and intervened. 'James gave Fleur a present, didn't you, lad? A carved box. He's a terrific carpenter, is James. Thing is, we haven't been able to find it. We wondered if perhaps you could keep an eye out for it, Alice?'

'Why? Is it important?' Alice realised she sounded dismissive, but she was still struggling with the idea of Fleur being with this man. It unsettled her. 'I'll look for it, of course.' Something else James had said bothered her. 'You said she was acting weirdly?'

'She seemed distracted. As though she wasn't really listening to me, as though there was something else she was more interested in, something not quite tangible. I know that sounds odd, but I can't put it into words.'

A silence descended on the room, broken only by the ticking of the old grandfather clock that stood guard by the door. James shifted in his chair, while Sergeant Cooper munched slowly on a biscuit. Alice desperately cast around for something to say. Her eye caught the pile of leaflets she'd hurriedly pushed to one side.

'Is Fleur trying to sell this house? Is it on the market?'

James looked at her. 'Yes, she's selling it. She hates it.' He gazed around the kitchen. 'I think it's lovely.' His gaze dropped, the emotion that had briefly softened his face gone, and he resumed his angry examination of the table. Well, that was one thing they had in common, Alice and James. They both loved Crag Cottage.

Sergeant Cooper shut his notebook, brushing off biscuit crumbs, and packed it away in his bag. James and Alice sat for a moment longer, each stuck in their own thoughts, but the scraping of Sergeant Cooper's chair on the flagstones brought them both back to the present moment, and James hurriedly rose.

'Well, Alice, it's been lovely meeting you. James here has agreed that he'll let me know if he can think of anything else that might be relevant. Perhaps you could contact him if you have any questions? Would that be all right, James?'

A flicker of annoyance darkened James's eyes, but he mumbled, 'Yes, I guess so.'

'You can find him at Turnkey Books, in Dennybridge. You know it?'

Alice took a deep breath. She'd been looking forward to visiting her old haunt, but perhaps it wouldn't be such a pleasure, not with James being there.

'I know it.'

The grumbling tension that Alice had felt during the meeting drifted away as she climbed the narrow stairs into the attic. She and Luke had played up here, in the good times. Sometimes they'd pretended they were in a castle, besieged, hiding from the enemy (their parents, of course); or they'd been prisoners trying to escape from the bad men (their parents, again); often, they'd just revelled in being high above everyone else, alone in their own little world. After the first couple of years, Luke had become difficult and refused to play with her, so she'd often had the whole attic to herself.

It had seemed huge to two small children, but now, as she stepped into the space with its sloping ceiling and tiny windows, it felt quite claustrophobic. There were two rooms: a large one taking up most of the area, with a tiny bedroom created by a thin wall between the beams, sectioning off the far end. Old rugs were scattered across the floor, dusty and threadbare, a couple of old camp beds, and a few broken chairs and bits of small furniture.

A bench ran around two of the walls of the main room, under which were stored boxes of things that Aunt Mari had decided she didn't want in the main house. Alice remembered a happy morning spent with her mother, who'd rarely ventured up here, when they'd sifted through all the boxes, laughing at some things, astonished by others.

'Such a waste, when there's someone somewhere who could do with this,' Mum had muttered about this item or that. 'Money to fritter!'

Mum's taste had always been geared towards the traditional; she'd never been a very adventurous woman, whereas Aunt Mari had liked everything to be shiny and new, and had followed trends meticulously. That's why so many things were stored up here – where once they'd been in vogue, they'd become old-fashioned almost overnight. A lot of it would now be considered retro, and fashionable once more.

The windows were grimy from being unwashed for years, motes of dust dancing in the rays of fragile light that managed to filter through. Alice walked towards the door that led into the smaller room, excited anticipation quickening her pulse. The door opened with a loud creak, her footsteps on the bare floorboards deafening in the silence. There was a tiny window, no rug, furniture or boxes – just a small iron bedstead, its mattress gone, springs broken, poking up like so many jagged teeth – and one small bookcase in the corner. She switched on the light.

Alice had slept in here the year Fleur had stayed. Luke had wanted to but for once, she'd got her own way. It was the books that drew them, albeit for very different reasons. One shelf held nothing but paperbacks: *Lady Chatterley's Lover, The Country Girls, Lolita, Tropic of Cancer.* To small Alice they'd looked boring, but Luke had constantly leafed through, searching for *'the dirty bits',* as he'd so charmingly put it.

The other shelves held a collection of old books with beautiful covers. Some were about the landscape of the Moor, one had exquisite illustrations hand-painted by a lady botanist from centuries gone by, and there were a few dull ones detailing the geology of the area. But the books Alice had loved most were those that told the Moor's history, and the myths and legends that made it such an intriguing place. She'd spent many blissful hours holed up here on rainy days with a mug of tea, wrapped in one of her mother's hand-crocheted shawls. She'd read everything she could, and it had set her imagination on fire.

But there was one book that she loved more than any other, and she sought it out now. There it was, on the bottom shelf, covered in cobwebs but otherwise looking the same as it always had. She pulled it from the shelf, dusted off the thick layer of time that had settled on its shabby cover, and sat herself down on the floor, her back against the wall. She took a deep breath, and opened the book, the pages falling open at the place they always did – the page with the poem. There was no reason why that should happen, no crease in the page or other defect that might cause it to stick, and it had always intrigued her. When she was little she'd thought it must be because the book wanted her to read the poem, but of course that was childish fantasy. But the poem had become very special to her, nonetheless. She read it out loud slowly, relishing the words that were so familiar.

The Hanging of Hettie Gale

'Twas a fearsome dark night when the soldiers arrived
In Monkstown, men battered and brave,
With a girl in their care all tattered and torn,
A wench they had battled to save

From herself, as she struggled and wailed with the
    crows
On the Moor, by the light of the moon.
At Crow Pond she did drown her golden-haired child,
A precious young life gone too soon.

Nine souls there were, nine men to judge
The witch who had murdered her boy.
Hettie Gale was her name, a murderous whore
Though she acted so meek and so coy.

The clergyman, called for his nearness to God;
The constable for upholding the law;
The physician to vouch for the girl's state of mind;
The blacksmith to speak for the poor.

An artist, a soul with the vision of gods;
A man from the purest of castes;
A writer of words to make sense of the charge;

And an Earl of the Realm at the last.

*The soldiers, distraught as their stories were told
To the judge, cried tears that they fought.
But young Hettie Gale showed no sign of remorse
As her fate was pronounced to the court.*

*Crowds jostled and jeered as they gathered that morn,
For the spectacle they had travelled to see.
Hettie Gale was strung up and met her due end
At Monkstown's Hanging Tree.*

*It is said that her soul cannot rest for her sin,
That she searches alone for her child
In the mists that enshroud Pedlar's Quag, damned and
 doomed
And her name forever reviled.*

Alice felt herself transported back to the eighteenth century, wondering as she always had, about Hettie Gale, and whether the story was true or just another Moors myth. She'd tried asking her mother once, when she'd first found the book, but Mum had been horrified that her daughter was reading such morbid things and took the book away. It hadn't taken long for Alice to find it, hidden at the back of a cupboard. She'd quietly retrieved it and put it back in the attic, and it hadn't been mentioned again. But she'd never forgotten Hettie, and every year she'd looked forward to the moment she could sit down, the book would fall open on that page, and she could immerse herself again.

The book that contained the poem was called *Myths and Legends of the Moor,* an unimaginative name, but it was full of the most weird and wonderful stories about this place that she loved so much. Apart from *The Hanging of Hettie Gale*, she particularly loved stories relating to Pedlar's Quag, and there were lots of them. *Betty's Frock*, *The Laughing Squire*, and *Yellow Eyes* were her favourites. Oh, and *The Lonely Child*, that was a sad one: a young boy, abandoned on Pedlar's Quag, roamed the paths and pools crying never-ending tears, raising a mist around him as he wandered for all eternity.

No longer scared of her mum finding her with the book, Alice decided to take it down to the kitchen so she could pore over it in comfort, warmed by the fire she'd set in the wood burner, and with the added pleasure of another mug of tea. There was something a little creepy about this attic. No, not creepy, but there was something about it that sent a shiver through her bones. As a child she'd been scared by the silly stories of monsters she and Luke would tell each other, but now there was something else she couldn't quite put a finger on. It was almost as though she wasn't alone.

CHAPTER SIX

SUNDAY 26 MAY

Sergeant Cooper had arranged for one of his constables to guide Alice across Pedlar's Quag the following day, so that she could see the area for herself. PC Berry was very young, very tiny, and the least likely police officer that Alice could imagine. She'd arrived on Sunday morning, a few minutes later than they'd arranged, explaining that she'd stopped to help a calf that had got its head stuck in a fence. Alice had liked her immediately.

Briony (such a lovely name, Briony Berry – perfect for someone born and raised on the Moor) was already dressed for a trudge across the quagmire, wearing a heavy-duty raincoat and wellies, so Alice pulled her boots on and stuffed her raincoat into her backpack. It was warm outside, but you could never tell if the clouds would roll together and unleash their loads, so it was best to be prepared. They set off down the path that ran behind the hedge that formed the western boundary of the cottage's land.

'How did you sleep, Alice?'

'Very well, thank you. I was tired from the train journey, and there's something about the fresh air here that makes it easier to sleep.'

She'd slept extremely well, despite the mustiness of the sheets she'd chosen for the bed, and had woken feeling ready for anything.

'Do you know this area well, Briony? I know lots of people are supposed to have disappeared here over the years.'

'Pretty well, really. I helped the other day in the search for your cousin, so I know the way, and how to avoid the most dangerous bits. Don't worry, we'll be fine!'

'My dad took me to Crow Pond once or twice, but he was never very confident, and we always went with an old man who worked at the big house. I can't remember his name, but he loved telling me about the monsters that lurked in the pools. I don't think Mum was very happy about it.'

'Well, whoever that was must be long gone. I don't suppose you've met the current lord of the manor?'

There was a sarcastic tinge to Briony's words, which surprised Alice. Sir Rufus was a charming man, a real gentleman, who'd taken great pains to talk to everyone.

'Sir Rufus?'

'Goodness no, he passed away ten years ago. Heart attack.'

That was sad; he couldn't have been that old, although he'd always seemed ancient to her ten-year-old self.

'So, it must be Jenson?'

'Sadly not. Jenson was a lovely man, according to my parents: generous, kind, looked after the manor very well.'

'Was?'

Briony stopped to poke at a bit of plastic that had become embedded in the grass. 'It was such a shame, really. He died five years ago, of bowel cancer. The place has gone to wrack and ruin since then.'

Satisfied that the plastic was nothing of interest, Briony walked on.

'So, it's Finbar?'

'Yup, that's him. Handsome, loaded, useless–' She stopped abruptly. 'I'm sorry, do you know him well?'

Alice shook her head. 'I don't know him at all, really. Fleur used to fancy him like crazy when we were younger, the year we all stayed at Crag Cottage together. She'd have been fourteen, I think. She made me walk up to the big house every day, just in case Finbar was around.'

'Well, she won't have found him there this time. He lives in London, just comes down once or twice a year to show off the family seat to his wealthy friends. The parties are quite something; we always know he's back when the calls start coming in, complaining about the noise and the traffic.'

'But what about Finbar's mother? I can't remember her name; I never met her. Is she still alive?'

'Lady Emilia: she was a lot younger than Sir Rufus. Bit of a party animal by all accounts, took an accidental overdose. Quite a sad family, really.'

Alice felt dejected; there were too many changes, but then she should have expected that after all this time.

They'd reached Hettie's Hovel, the last building before the Quag began to puncture the ground with its pools and ponds, though there was little left of the solid barn it must've been back in the day. Three walls still stood intact, but the tin roof had caved in at one end and the rest had crumbled into piles of stone. The story went that Hettie Gale lived here with her little son, disgraced because she'd had the child out of wedlock.

'Do you think Hettie was a real person, Briony?'

'Oh yes. There are supposed to be court records from when she was tried, in the council offices somewhere, and I think there might be some relevant stuff in the museum. And she was definitely hanged in Monkstown.'

'The Hanging Tree,' Alice mused. 'Hanged for drowning her own son. How could any mother do such a thing?'

'Well, don't forget it was nearly 250 years ago; things were different then, I suppose. Perhaps she was struggling. I think I'd go mad, living here all on my own.'

'But that's so sad. Not having any support just because you made a mistake. I mean, there wasn't any birth control back then.'

Briony gave a hearty laugh. 'Only birth control was to not let the bastards get you!'

Alice walked around the outside of the hovel, peering through the holes that had once been windows, though there was no indication they'd ever been glazed. The Council had erected a sign by one wall, that she was sure hadn't been here when she was child.

HETTIE'S HOVEL
The last known home of Hettie Gale, who was hanged in Monkstown for drowning her young son in 1776.

It wasn't much of an inscription, but then, Hettie was a murderess; perhaps she didn't deserve any more than that.

'Can I just have a look?'

Ignoring the shiny red *"Danger: Do Not Enter"* sign that hung above the opening, Alice walked through, the door hanging on by one rusty hinge. Once her eyes had adjusted to the gloom, she could see the old beams that held up what was left of the roof, the original thatch hanging down in great greasy clumps, the rusting metal visible beyond. It didn't look at all safe. There was no flooring, just compacted earth, and the remains of what looked like a feeding trough took up much of the space. A vast chimney separated this room from the one beyond, but the blackness through there was so complete, she didn't venture in. Alice tried to imagine how it would be to live here with a baby. Perhaps Hettie had a breakdown; she could see how that might happen. Life must have been hard here, in the cold, all alone. And she guessed postnatal depression wasn't something people knew about back then.

As she turned to rejoin Briony, Alice felt the faintest whisper of a breeze ruffle her hair, and goosebumps prickled her arms. She realised the weather must be turning, and she was glad she'd brought her raincoat, but when she stepped out it was into brilliant sunshine – not even the suggestion of any wind. Something tugged at her thoughts, but she couldn't quite grasp what it was, so she quickly dismissed it as Briony urged her on.

'Come on, we'd best get moving. I don't expect this weather will last for long.'

They made their way to the end of the path, where there was a small wooden gate and an old weather-beaten, hand-painted sign saying *"Keep Out. Danger"*. Alice remembered the sign, which had been put up many years ago to keep people from wandering into the Quag; it clearly hadn't stopped anyone, as so many had gone missing here. *It hadn't stopped Fleur.*

Briony opened the gate and they both went through, following a clear path for a few metres before it petered out and the ground became slightly softer underfoot. Dark clouds were beginning to gather, blocking the sun and casting everything into bone-chilling shade.

'No mist today, so that's a bonus. It's scary, the way it just suddenly appears; no wonder people have got lost.'

Alice thought of Fleur, crossing the unstable and unfamiliar ground, perhaps enveloped in a sudden swirl of fog that would've blinded her. She made sure to follow Briony's exact footsteps as she made her way across the quagmire, zigzagging between clumps of coarse grass and small puddles of black water. Sometimes the ground felt hard beneath her feet, sometimes it shook and wobbled, which was alarming, but Briony seemed very confident.

From their current viewpoint, she could see the trees of Cleator Forest, way in the distance, forming a dark slash across the horizon. As they progressed, the puddles became small pools, then ponds some several metres across, the areas of solid ground between them growing narrower.

The water looked cold and faintly disturbing, and Alice's thoughts turned to the myths and legends of Pedlar's Quag. She'd taken a perverse delight in the stories of monsters that lived in the pools and grabbed small children for their supper when she was little. Now she thought of them as silly and childish. It was the other, darker tales that hinted of evil fairy folk and death, which fascinated her now. Yellow eyes that blinked under the water, luring you in; hairy arms reaching out to grab your ankles and pull you under the surface; strange, hypnotic voices that rose with the mists and caused delirium.

It was certainly true that quite a few people had gone missing here. If you didn't know which way was the safe way, it would be so easy to fall into a pool, but she was pretty sure they weren't bottomless, and she couldn't really understand why a person wouldn't be able to get out of the water and save themselves. Unless the tales were true, of course...

'Here we are, Crow Pond.' Briony had stopped, and was pointing towards a range of low granite hills, reminding Alice of the curve of a croissant, which held the western edge of the Quag in its rocky embrace. Alice had been so wrapped up in watching where her feet went, she hadn't noticed the ground looming up ahead. At the foot of the hills was a large, sparkling pond, the grass around its rim green and velvety, punctuated with clumps of reeds and blueberry bushes. There were so many berries, still green at this time of year, but another few weeks and they'd be ripe and delicious.

One side of the pond was enclosed by a large rocky outcrop, with a single tree jutting almost horizontally from the rock.

Some branches plunged beneath the surface, others lay just above, casting deep shadows on the water. Its roots formed a giant, gnarled claw clinging on to the stone for dear life, though the trunk itself was long dead. But a shoot must have grown from the trunk, as a second tree soared heavenwards, its pale green leaves and clusters of small cones proving its health and fortitude.

'Do you know the story of the tree, Alice – why it's growing like that?'

Alice frowned, trying to remember what she'd read in her book. 'Was it hit by lightning?'

'Yep, that's it. In seventeen-something. There's a lovely drawing in the museum in Monkstown, of how it used to look before it fell. It must've been so beautiful here then. Looks a bit rubbish now.'

Alice didn't think it looked rubbish at all. There was a sadness to the scene, a melancholy that lay like a shroud over the whole area, but also a tender charm that she hadn't appreciated as a child. The atmosphere was heightened by the brooding presence of several crows, some circling overhead, others sitting on the tree or the rocks. The occasional squabble broke out, piercing the silence that otherwise filled the air. Crow Pond was well named.

She turned to Briony. 'So, the theory is that Fleur came walking through the Quag, and may have got into trouble somewhere between the gate and here? Mightn't she just have walked on, towards the forest?'

'Well, it's a possibility, but it's quite a walk to the forest. We think she was wearing inappropriate footwear, so it would have been very difficult for her. Plus, the search teams didn't find anything.'

'Inappropriate footwear? What, like high heels?' Alice could just imagine Fleur walking off in a huff wearing a pair of shiny Louboutins.

'Our witness said he was expecting to take her out to dinner, so she was quite dressed up, I think.'

'Your witness, as in, James Turnkey?'

Briony frowned. 'Mm, that's him. Although...'

'Although what?'

'Well, this is me saying this as me, not as PC Berry, okay? I just can't see someone like James romancing someone like Fleur. It doesn't sit right.'

Alice laughed. 'No, I didn't really think he was her type when I met him. Too scruffy, and so grumpy.'

'He's not really grumpy. He's had a hard time of it, with his dad and everything. He hates running the bookshop, but feels he has no choice while his dad's still alive.'

'You seem to know him very well?'

'Not really. He dated my sister for a bit, but it was never going to work; they're too different. But he's very sweet, honestly; I think he's just lonely.'

Alice wasn't convinced. She hadn't taken to him, but he was probably the last person to see Fleur, so he was important.

'Sergeant Cooper told me James had given Fleur a present, a carved box, that isn't anywhere in the house. Do you think she could have taken it with her and dropped it somewhere? Was nothing found at all when you did the search?'

'Nope, we poked around in every single pool and pond; a diver searched this one, but there was nothing apart from some animal bones, sheep probably, strayed from a farm. Perhaps you could have another look around? I don't think the search of the cottage was that extensive.'

Alice thought it a bit sad that Fleur would be so callous as to throw away a present she'd only just been given, but she agreed to have another look.

'Well, you've seen Crow Pond, and the way here, and now you can feel satisfied, I hope, that there's no trace of your cousin. She must be somewhere else, though why she left all her stuff in the cottage is a bit of a mystery. We'll be widening our enquiries now, I expect, contacting our counterparts in the places she has other homes, see if she's upped and left for some reason. One of my colleagues is already checking with airlines and ferries.' Briony turned and started making her way back across the Quag. 'Come on, looks like rain.'

Alice stayed for a moment, her eyes searching Crow Pond for any tiny hint that Fleur might have been here. Briony was right; clouds were gathering above in an angry knot, and rain was certain to follow soon. But something held her there, an unease that twisted her stomach and made her skin prickle. The air was still and thick, yet she experienced that same whisper through her hair she'd felt in Hettie's Hovel.

Unsettled, she tore herself away and followed Briony, her fear of going the wrong way overshadowing her other anxiety, but an image had formed in her mind that she couldn't shake away: a young girl, a cruel noose around her neck, hanging from a large oak tree.

CHAPTER SEVEN

MARCH 1773

Whether 'tis truth or ne'er but a lie, who gives?
With love to spare and a generous heart
Gifts the crow.

I never felt this much pain, I surely never did. Is it right? Is this what my ma felt, birthing me? 'Tis a hard thing, being a woman, then, harder than ever I thought. I feel as though my insides are on fire, and then 'tis all just embers, but again and again the flames flare up high.

Rose has told me how the babby will come out, but I don't rightly believe her. 'Tis not a big enough hole, unless the babby will be like a tiny mouse. Rose is sitting with me now, placing a cold linen to my cheeks and my brow. I look at her face, round and glistening with sweat from the fire she's set to keep us warm. Her eyes are large and darkest brown, searching deep into my soul, it feels like. When she smiles, which she does often, her teeth are white as snow 'gainst her skin, her mouth full and wide and filled with gentle words to calm me.

I never saw a woman like her, with her skin as black as coal, and she says how folks think she's the devil come to carry away their children; yet to me she's the kindest person I ever did meet. But her stories! She tells me how she came to be in this little place, how she travelled on a huge ship full of people like her to get here, across a big, angry sea, and tales about the place she come from. A land where the sun shines all day long, and it hardly never rains, and the ground is dust. I find it hard to 'magine such a wondrous place, when here it rains most of the time, and 'tis a reason to cheer when the sun does show her face.

Arggh! Another pain what seems to rip me in two, but Rose gently wipes my eyes as the tears stream out. I can't stop it. I don't know what's happening to me. She parts my thighs to peer at my pipkin, and even though 'tis nothing I 'sperienced afore, somehow it don't seem awkward.

'Babby soon be here, my darlin'. Good girl, you doin' just fine.'

Rose's voice is deep and soft, and sometimes she bursts into song, though no songs I know. Another pain rips my insides, but Rose just hums and sings, and carries on with her boiling and swabbing. Seems to me like we're two people outcast from the others. Rose is diff'rent 'cause of her skin, and I'm diff'rent 'cause of my belly. P'raps that's why we like each other so much.

'You need to push now, my darlin'. Push out your babby, an' Rose'll be here to catch it.'

Push it out? I don't understand. Arggh! My insides are on fire, again and again. I want it to stop. I hate my da for making me hurt so much. I hated him then, and I hates him even more now.

'Push, little lady, push!'

I don't know how, but Rose understands, and tells me to 'magine I'm pushing out a big 'un on my bucket, if you gets my meaning. So I does just that, and oh my, I feel as though my pipkin'll tear apart.

But then – then I manage one huge push, and I feel like a ball is caught atween my legs, and then a slither and there it is, safe in Rose's arms: a tiny, bloody thing, looking like one of the gargoyles on St Brigid's porch. Rose wraps it up in a cloth she brought special, and it bawls, the noise tearing at the cold morning air. Then I scream as I sees a fat, purple snake what comes from the babby.

''Tis a demon!' I cry, but Rose laughs and wipes my forehead again as she hands the grumbling bundle to me.

'No, my darlin', it's just the cord that feeds babby while he's in your tummy.'

Rose busies herself doing something to that horrid snake, and I finally look at my babby. 'Tis bigger than a mouse, so I fears for my pipkin; but one look at that little, wrinkled face and I fall in love and forget everything else. I unwrap the bundle, and see two perfect little pink hands, two perfect little pink feet. And 'tis a boy, I can tell that by his winkle, what looks too big for such a little scrap. But Rose gazes with me and tells me he's perfect, and I believe her.

I never did feel this much love for a person, I truly never did. And that's a fact.

CHAPTER EIGHT

MONDAY 27 MAY

Alice sat bolt upright in the middle of the night, woken by a dream that had disturbed her, but which she couldn't quite remember, and she felt so out of sorts that she got up and made herself a mug of tea. Then she decided to send her brother a message, asking if he'd heard from Fleur recently. At this hour of night in England, it was probably daylight in Australia. There'd been a stage, when he'd first moved away, that Alice would've known precisely what time it was on the other side of the world, but not anymore.

The reply from Luke was prompt, short and emotionless:

'No. Heard nothing.'

She wasn't at all surprised at the brevity of the response, but was pleased he'd answered at all. She'd given up trying to keep in contact ages ago. What was his life like? What job did he do? Did he have a girlfriend? Alice had no idea, and it saddened her.

Luke had packed up and left as soon as he'd turned eighteen. There'd been constant, bitter arguments with their father, but he'd reacted badly when Dad had died so suddenly.

At fourteen, Luke lost his figurehead, and he became angry. He'd always hated school and left with precious few qualifications; he'd gone on to do odd labouring jobs, and caused Mum to cry far more tears than she should have. It had been something of a relief for Alice when he'd gone, but Mum had never really got over it, and when she was ailing it was her one hope that she'd see Luke again.

He had returned, but too late, and it was just a coincidence that he'd happened to be in London at the same time as her funeral. He'd looked very healthy: tanned, lean, and well dressed, but had barely said a word to Alice, just given her a dutiful hug. He was a stranger to her. No wonder she felt so alone; her whole family had disappeared, in one way or another.

So, Fleur hadn't contacted Luke. Where on earth was she? Sergeant Cooper had messaged yesterday evening to say he'd call by later today with an update; perhaps he'd found evidence she'd flown to America, or something. Alice had managed to get a week off work, but no more, so time was precious; she had to make herself useful while she was here. But not in the middle of the night – she needed sleep more than anything.

After restlessly dozing, she finally got up at 8am. Refreshed by a shower followed by a mug of tea, she felt ready for action and decided to look for the box James had given Fleur. The bins that were kept just outside the coal shed door seemed a good place to start. It would be just like Fleur to throw away something that had been given to her, simply because it didn't live up to her refined taste. A home-made wooden box was probably not up her street at all.

Walking gingerly into the coal shed, Alice was transported back to her childhood holidays again. She'd always hated the smell of dirt, rusting metal and coal dust that stretched into every corner, the darkness that sat like a shroud and the spiders that scuttled across the stone walls. Now, her stomach clenched as the smell hit her, and fear rose in her throat. But she was thirty-two, for goodness' sake; this was just a coal shed, there were no monsters in here, just the spiders, and they were a lot smaller than her.

The outside door pushed open with a reluctant screech of wood on stone, letting sunlight flood in to banish the shadows. There were two bins set against the wall: a black one for general rubbish, green for recyclables. She poked about in both, holding her breath at the stench, but there wasn't much in either bin: a few plastic containers and a couple of wine bottles in the recycling bin, a black plastic sack tied at the top and some discarded wrapping paper in the other. She gingerly picked up the bin bag and felt its contents, hoping for something hard and square, but it was all squishy. The box wasn't in the bins.

Walking back into the shed and picking up the old torch that had always sat on a shelf, Alice was amazed to find that it still worked; she'd thought the batteries would have given up long ago. A quick glance around in the beam of yellowing light was all she needed to satisfy herself that there was nothing else to see in the coal shed, and she made her way back to the kitchen.

The worst was over, and a search of the rest of the house was easy in comparison, but equally unfruitful. After opening every drawer, every cupboard, looking under beds and behind wardrobes, Alice found nothing. Perhaps the box was in the garden somewhere, or Fleur had thrown it behind a wall down the lane. Maybe she still had it with her. It could be anywhere, but the important thing was, it wasn't here. Alice could tell Sergeant Cooper she'd found nothing, and he could tick that off his list.

Making herself another mug of tea, and craving the intimate space of the attic, Alice picked up the book of myths and a cushion off the sofa, and made her way up to the top of the house, settling herself down on the floor by the bookcase. If this was her house, she thought, she'd have a comfy chair up here, a colourful rug, and fill the space with books. She'd probably never tear herself away.

The book opened on Hettie's page, as always, but Alice browsed through to find some tales she hadn't read for a while. She briefly scanned the story called *A Message From The Heavens*, about how the tree at Crow Pond had been hit by lightning, causing it to fall and killing all the crows that lived in it; all but one, who lived there still, unable to escape this world.

She flipped through the pages, stopping at *The Lonely Child*. It was a heartbreaking story about the ghost of a toddler that roamed Pedlar's Quag. There had been many recorded sightings of the tiny, bedraggled figure that flitted about from pool to pool, with its mop of blonde hair and distressing cries, raising a thick mist wherever it went; a child who, the story went, had been abandoned by its cruel parents. Alice hadn't liked the story when she was younger; her own parents had hearts of gold and would never have knowingly caused her distress, and she'd found it hard to believe that there were such awful people in the world.

Now, she knew different. This story dated from the late eighteenth century, when life in rural England must have been hard. Perhaps the story had a kernel of truth in it, but like all these myths and legends, they'd been elaborated and embroidered over time.

Alice shut the book and put it carefully back on its shelf. Somehow it didn't belong in the kitchen, but here it was safe; she was safe. She was beginning to feel a deepening concern for her cousin; Fleur may not have been very likeable, but she was family, and she was missing. She decided to visit Turnkey Books after lunch, and see if she could draw any more out of the reticent James. She wouldn't feel comfortable talking to him, but then this whole experience was way out of her comfort zone. And she was coping, wasn't she?

A soft drizzle glazed everything a uniform grey as Alice made her way the mile from Nether Dennyfold to Dennybridge, but the air was warm, birds were singing in the hedgerows and she felt a freedom, a happiness that had eluded her for a long time.

Fleur hated the stillness of the Moor, preferring frenetic activity and noise. She was prettier, more talented and far more confident than Alice, who had tried, and failed, to hide her jealousy. But where Alice had a mundane, unexciting life, she had at least had the love of her family. Fleur had a hidden side to her, a sadness and fragility that she kept buried away. A secret. Alice would never have known, had Fleur not told her that day on the Moor when they were still children, and the knowledge was beginning to haunt her now that Fleur had disappeared.

Lost in her thoughts, Alice was suddenly jolted back to reality by the sound of cars whizzing along the main road, and she realised she'd reached the end of the lane. Approaching the grey stone building that housed Turnkey Books, her stomach twisted with anxiety. The shopfront looked shabby, its sign faded, the little paint that was left peeling sadly away; the windows were slightly grimy, and the path unswept. Old Mr Turnkey had kept it all gleaming, which was one good thing she could say about him; he'd be horrified to see it like this. She crossed the road and peered through the glass, feeling a little leap inside as she saw the familiar jumble of books piled haphazardly in the window. There was no welcoming light, but the sign said *Open,* so she went in.

Shutting the door quietly behind her, Alice closed her eyes and breathed deeply. That smell! It took her right back to her childhood, and she couldn't stop a big grin from creeping across her face.

'Can I help you?'

Alice snapped her eyes open and felt her cheeks burning as she realised how daft she must've looked. James Turnkey was standing by the counter, a chisel in one hand, his grey jumper covered in flecks of sawdust, dark hair unwashed and straggly, his beard overlong.

'Oh, hello. James, isn't it? We met on Saturday.' Alice struggled for something to say, her summoned confidence gone.

'We did.'

An awkward silence stretched between them, as she fought to find some words, any words. James clearly wasn't one for casual chat.

'Can I have a look around? I used to love this shop when I was little.'

James simply nodded and waved his arm around, as though it was too much trouble to speak. 'I'll be in the back room.'

Choosing to ignore the frosty welcome, Alice wandered around the shop, checking out the shelves of novels, paperbacks and hardbacks, haphazardly plonked down with no apparent care. She was sure it had been set out in alphabetical order before, but there was little order to it now. Two long benches took up much of the middle of the shop, laden with coffee table books: huge volumes on a variety of subjects, full of flashy photos, but with precious little text.

It had always been the back corner, where a pair of shelves jutted out to create a little nook, that Alice had loved the most. She made her way there now, fingers running along spines as she went. She was pleased that the sign was still hanging from the ceiling on its little chains: *Local Interest*. The books here covered the whole region, but were mostly focused on the Moor. There were history books; books on geology, vegetation and local wildlife; locally written poetry, and books about famous local people and places; books on art, artefacts, and of course, myths and legends. Some volumes were almost new, others were worn with age, but every single one was a source of pleasure for Alice.

She was sure a lot of these had been here when she was little, and wondered whether James ever sold anything. He certainly didn't seem very enthusiastic. A spine with the words *Murders on The Moor – A History of the Hanging Tree* caught her eye, and she pulled the large volume out. It clearly hadn't seen the light of day for years, as a cloud of dust puffed into her face from its ornately tooled cover. There was nowhere to sit, unlike her favourite bookshops in London, which had coffee shops and crèches, and comfy sofas dotted around. So she sat herself down on the floor, cross-legged in her usual fashion, and opened the book in her lap.

Gruesome tales of beheadings and shootings, stabbings and poisonings going right back to medieval times were accompanied by illustrations, paintings and photographs. Alice was sure she'd never seen this book before, and was immediately gripped by the stories of cheating wives, violent highwaymen and cruel landlords. Then she came to a page that was titled "The Murderess Who Drowned Her Child". It was the story of Hettie Gale, and a version she'd never read before. She was so absorbed, she failed to hear the footsteps approach.

'Cup of tea? No sugar, if I remember correctly.' James held a steaming mug towards her. Startled, she scrambled to her feet so she could take the offering.

'Thank you. That's kind.'

'I can get you a chair, if you like. I imagine it's none too clean down there.'

'That would be lovely, although a bit of dust never did me any harm.'

A smile twitched at his mouth, little lines radiating from the corners of his eyes, and Alice caught a glimpse of sweetness beneath the sour exterior. She waited, clasping the mug in hands that were chilled despite the sun warming the world outside, until James dragged a small, shabbily upholstered chair from the back room. He placed it by one of the long benches, so Alice could put both mug and book down.

'Thank you.'

James turned to leave, and Alice knew she had to grab the moment.

'Do you still live in the flat above? I don't remember ever seeing you when I used to come here years ago.'

'I do, yes. We weren't allowed in the shop, and I can't say I was ever really interested in books.'

He turned to leave, his expression dismissive. Alice tried again. 'James... Do you know Fleur well?'

He turned, wearily, his gaze directed towards the floor. 'Not very well, no.'

'Please, tell me everything you can. I'm worried about her, and it would be useful to know what happened before she left.'

James turned and walked into the back room, and Alice began to think she'd overstepped the mark, but he swiftly returned with another chair, an old-fashioned bentwood one covered in sawdust. He placed it on the other side of the bench, and sat down, one hand wiping sweat from his forehead. Did James know more about Fleur's disappearance than he was letting on? She kept her mouth shut and her expression neutral, waiting for him to speak.

'Fleur only arrived here a couple of weeks ago, on the fourteenth, I think it was.' He hesitated, looking anywhere but at Alice. 'She caused a bit of a stir in the village.'

'Why? I mean, how?'

James looked at his lap. 'She's quite... glamorous. Sophisticated. Not like most women here.'

Alice was unsurprised. Fleur exuded star quality, and the few times she'd been with her cousin as adults, heads had turned as Fleur walked by. Always immaculately, expensively dressed, hair shining, make-up perfect, Fleur had an enviable figure and walked with an assurance and grace that Alice could only ever dream of.

'So, how did you meet her?'

James hesitated, passing his hand over his brow. 'It was in the pub, the Monks Arms. You know it?'

Alice nodded; the pub was further down the road, close to Turnpike Bridge. It had always looked inviting, with its baskets of flowers hanging outside, and painted benches filled with customers, but she'd never been inside. Her parents hadn't been ones for going out, and rarely drank alcohol, so they'd never even thought of taking the children there.

'I don't often go there, but I'd had a bad day with Da– well, I needed a drink. I have a friend Cory who's an estate agent. He was there with Fleur; she was talking to him about selling the cottage, I think. Cory introduced us, and... well, she was lovely. She looked amazing.'

James had flushed pink, and was clearly flustered, so Alice decided to help him out. 'I expect she made you feel like you were the only person in the room. Made you feel special, as though you were the only one she needed at that moment.'

James nodded, miserably.

'She was always good at doing that.' Alice didn't mean to sound bitter but couldn't help it. That's how Fleur had been with her; she'd made Alice feel like she was the most important and interesting person in the whole world one moment, callously dumped the next. It was Fleur's way with everyone. 'You asked her out?'

'I couldn't help myself.' James finally looked at Alice, his eyes shining with the memory. 'I don't know where I found the courage, to be honest.'

'Did you see a lot of her?' Alice realised with a shock that what she really wanted to know was whether they'd slept together, and she felt her own face burning.

'We met up a few times.'

James was clearly not going to give away anything more personal, so Alice swiftly changed the subject, partly to ease the tension that had grown between them again.

'I don't remember ever seeing this book before.' She indicated the book that lay open in front of her. 'Have you had it long?'

James shrugged. 'I don't recall it, either. But then, I can't pretend to have much interest in this old rubbish.'

Alice wasn't surprised at James's attitude; the whole shop screamed for someone to love it. She wondered how he made any sort of living. A chime as the door opened, together with a simultaneous buzz from James's phone, brought them both out of their reveries, and he leapt up.

'Please, stay as long as you like,' he muttered, distractedly checking his phone, as he grabbed the bentwood chair and disappeared into the back room.

The newcomers were a pair of exuberant American tourists who blustered around the shop, commenting loudly as they went. 'Don't ya have any new books?'

Alice realised the question was aimed at her. 'Erm, well... I don't actually...'

'Honey, there's real English antique books here, come look.'

The woman had found the local corner, and there was soon much exclaiming and gasping. James reappeared, and self-consciously approached the pair, enquiring whether they needed any help. Alice watched as he tried to deal with their bombardment of questions; he really wasn't very good at this.

'But d'ya have any about the gory stuff that happened hereabouts?' the man was asking. 'We love a good murder, don't we, Belle?'

His partner whooped, 'Oh yeah, honey, we do. We saw that Hanging Tree just now; what a place! D'ya have any books about that?'

James glanced towards Alice, and started to tell the Americans about the book she was cradling.

'No, I'm sorry, I'm buying this one,' she interrupted, as they advanced on her. She had no idea why she said it; the book was probably expensive, and she'd just done James out of a lucrative sale, but she couldn't part with it. The Americans left the shop, empty-handed, disappointment clear in the glares they sent Alice's way.

'Thanks.' The sarcasm in James's voice cut Alice deeply.

'No really, I do want to buy it. How much?'

James sighed. 'Just take it. I need to close the shop early.'

'Is everything okay?' Alice noted the strained look on James's face, and wondered if the phone call had anything to do with it.

'Please, just take it and go.'

Jabbering her thanks as she tried, and failed, to stuff the book into her backpack, then hearing the door being locked behind her as she left, Alice was bewildered by James's manner, and vowed to give him a wide berth.

CHAPTER NINE

MONDAY 27 MAY

The Hanging Tree was a huge oak, its massive branches spreading high and wide, the girth of the trunk proclaiming its great old age. Alice stood just inside the park gates, taking it all in. She'd been to this park when she was younger so the sight was familiar, and she'd always been aware of the tree's grisly past, but now she could somehow *sense* the melancholy that surrounded it, too.

As soon as she'd left James and the shop, the book safe beneath her arm, she'd known it was here she'd wanted to come, so she'd found the card Harry had given her, and luckily he'd been between jobs.

'You been talking to young James, then?'

Alice had grimaced; it was true what they said about village life: everyone knew everyone else's business. But Harry seemed harmless, so she'd relaxed as the cab slowly made its way towards Monkstown.

'I have. He's quite... Well, he doesn't really say a lot. He seems a bit angry?'

Harry had nodded, his eyes firmly on the road. 'He's a nice

enough lad, really. Lost his mum at an early age; would've been about twenty years ago now. Tragic, that was. Tragic.'

'What happened?' Alice had been curious to know more about James, find something that might explain his grouchiness.

'Poor Kath, hit by a car, she were, while she was cycling along this road. Sixteen's a difficult age for a boy to lose his mum.'

'Does he have any sisters or brothers?'

'Jenn, lovely girl, she is. Married to a fine chap called Kenneth, expecting their first child. They live in Monkstown. Then there's Billy. He's a wild lad, lives in the city, only comes back when he wants money.' Harry had bitten his lip, as though he knew he'd said too much.

'What about old Mr Turnkey? You said he was in a nursing home?'

'Poor old sod, got dementia. He was never right after Kath died. It's hard on James. Feels he has to keep the shop running while his dad's alive, though he'd rather be making his boxes. Have you seen them, his boxes?'

Alice had said no, she'd not seen the boxes, but she'd been trying to remember whether she'd heard anything about a tragedy in the village; she'd have been twelve when James's mother was killed – the year that Fleur was here. But nothing came to mind. It explained why old Mr Turnkey had been so grumpy back then, though. Poor man, losing his wife and then losing his mind. No wonder James was grumpy, too. She resolved to try and bear that in mind next time she saw him. Then her face had flushed as she realised she wanted to see James again, despite how she'd felt earlier.

'Here we go; the park.'

And so here she was, walking towards the Hanging Tree, the scent of freshly mown grass infusing the warm air, the drizzle gone, replaced by warm, hazy sunshine. The park was quiet, just a few mums with toddlers or babies in buggies, a group of schoolgirls sitting on their raincoats on the damp grass, sketchpads on their laps, and an elderly couple sitting hand-in-hand on a bench. Mum and Dad had never held hands, and it was lovely to see.

It was cooler in the shade beneath the branches and Alice shivered, goosebumps prickling her skin. A large plaque had been fixed to the trunk: *"The Hanging Tree, over 700 years old".* There was an information board too, by the path.

```
THE HANGING TREE
The site of 36 public executions between 1647
and 1863. Amongst the more infamous cases are
those of Billy Podmore, aka Billy the Brains,
who murdered three friends over a debt in
1712, Hettie Gale, who drowned her son in
1776, and the Ninth Earl of Collymore, who
shot his parents in 1851.
```

Alice felt a deep sadness as she returned to the tree itself, circling the trunk, reaching to touch the rough bark, wondering how something could live for so long. She didn't go quite so far as to hug it, but she wanted to; she wanted to feel a connection with Hettie.

The thought slapped her in the face, and she retreated to the path, uneasiness shivering up her spine. Why had she become so interested in someone who'd drowned their own child over 200 years ago? She studied the tree, identifying the branch where she thought the rope would have been tied, the rope that had ended so many lives, including Hettie's. A swell of emotion came from nowhere. Her stomach clenched, her throat closed, and the peculiar-yet-familiar breeze rippled through her hair.

Alice hurried towards the park gates, disturbed by how she

felt, and in need of a strong coffee. The nearest café was a tiny place called Bean, which boasted *"Monkstown's Only Trained Barista!"* and *"Home-made Scones!"* on handwritten signs on the pavement outside. She'd skipped breakfast that morning, and realised she was hungry. Stepping into the brightly lit interior, with its furniture made from wooden pallets, and hessian coffee sacks adorning the walls, she ordered her coffee and scone, and sat at a table near the window, her spirits lifting.

She placed the book on the table in front of her. She opened it, but it didn't open on Hettie's story, rather on one about a mummified hand, and she breathed a small sigh of relief. It would have been too much if this book had *also* automatically opened at the same place every time. As she was flipping through the pages, a girl brought over her coffee and a plate with a scone, and two small china pots, one with butter, the other jam.

'Did you want cream with your scone?'

'No thanks; I'm not keen on cream, really.'

'I have to ask; sometimes the tourists get a bit narky if they don't get their cream tea, even if it's breakfast time.' She placed the items carefully on the table, peering over Alice's shoulder to see what book she was reading.

'You must be a visitor; don't think I've seen you before. Interested in all the old stories, then?'

Alice liked the girl's directness. 'Yes, I'm just visiting, but I've been here before, a long time ago. I love all the myths and legends; they give the place such atmosphere.'

'I expect you've already seen the Hanging Tree? Gruesome, that is, if you ask me.'

Alice let her gaze wander through the window towards the park. She could see the highest branches of the tree from here. 'I think it's rather lovely. And very sad. All those people, even young girls, dying in such a brutal way. Different times, I suppose.'

The girl snorted. 'There's still some in this town would deserve being strung up, different time or not.' She must have noticed Alice's shocked expression, as she quickly changed the subject.

'If you're interested in those old stories, you should visit the museum. There's a whole section on stuff like that: murderers, deaths, that sort of thing. My grandad works there; he'll show you around if you tell him I sent you.'

Alice beamed at the girl, delighted with her suggestion. 'Thank you, that would be lovely…?'

'Maddie. Just ask for Joe. He looks like Father Christmas; you can't mistake him. He'll tell you all sorts.' Maddie's face had lit up; she was clearly very fond of her grandfather.

'Thank you. I'll do that.'

Something about Maddie's manner made Alice feel bolder.

'Did you ever see a woman in here called Fleur? Tall, blonde, very glamorous?'

Maddie frowned. 'Woman from London? The one that's gone missing?'

Alice nodded.

'Hmm, I did serve her a few times. Snooty so-and-so she was, very snotty about our coffee, kept telling us how much better it is in the city. Never left a tip, never smiled much either, just moaned about the coffee and turned the men's heads. Nice clothes, though.'

Alice grimaced. That sounded like Fleur.

'D'you know her, then?'

'She's my cousin.'

Maddie turned bright red. 'Oh God, I'm so sorry. I shouldn't have said anything.'

'Please, don't worry. Fleur can be difficult to like. She's used to having the best of everything.'

'The police were in here last week, asking questions. I think they visited all the shops in case anyone had noticed anything.' Maddie began to back away, still pink with embarrassment. 'I hope she turns up. I'm so sorry.'

Alice gazed out of the window, wondering where on earth Fleur had gone. If only she knew the worry she was causing. But then, Fleur didn't care about other people, didn't trust anyone. Not surprising, really, after everything she'd been through – the death of her parents, and the other thing.

A growling from her stomach turned her attention to the scone, which she split, buttered, dolloped with jam and demolished before she so much as sipped the strong, black coffee. She'd go to the museum next, another old haunt to revisit.

Alice thought Joe looked more like a heavy metal guitarist than Father Christmas; perhaps that was just the age difference between her and Maddie showing. His white beard almost reached his chest, and his eyes were crinkled from the smile that seemed to be permanently etched onto his weather-beaten face. Long hair was tied back with a leather thong, and he was wearing jeans and a T-shirt that proudly pronounced him to be a *"Staff Member - Here to Help You."*

Alice had paid the modest admission fee, then spotted him straight away. She'd introduced herself and told him Maddie had sent her, and he'd clearly been expecting her. He'd immediately taken her arm and steered her through several rooms that were stuffed with glass cases of artefacts, paintings on every wall, and various random items poised atop tall marble plinths. One room seemed to be full of agricultural items, another had clothes and domestic stuff. Memories came flooding back of happy times spent here on wet days, Alice and Luke wandering around the museum looking for specific items as illustrated on a sort of quiz sheet one of them would have attached to a clipboard. The sense of freedom had been delicious, as their parents were content to let them roam, with only the basement out of bounds.

Joe stopped just as they reached a set of steps disappearing into the dark below.

'Did you ever come down here, when you were a child?'

Joe was indicating the steps, and a sign above, which said: *"Enter at your peril! Dungeon of Death. (Over 12s only, to be accompanied by an adult)."*

Alice shook her head. 'No, my parents never let me or my brother go down there. I never really wanted to, but Luke did. He had a massive row with my dad about it, and we never came back here after that.'

Joe started descending the steps. 'Well, it might be scary to a kid, but I think you'll cope.' He chuckled as he went, Alice following. Although it had looked dark from the top, it was well lit with wall lights designed to resemble oil lamps, but there was a definite chill in the air, and Alice felt her skin prickle as they arrived in the Dungeon of Death.

She'd been a great fan of the Chamber of Horrors at Madame Tussauds in London, revelling in the gruesome stories, the death masks and instruments of torture. This exhibition had a similar feel to it, though much smaller, and without the terrifyingly real wax models.

'So... What is it you specially wanted to see?'

'Anything about the Hanging Tree. And Pedlar's Quag, too... missing people, that sort of thing.'

'There's plenty about both those things; the crow knows they're the popular ones!'

Alice smiled at Joe's use of the term. It was commonplace

around the older generation here, a tradition begun centuries ago due to the high numbers of the black birds that bred on the Moor. She'd heard it uttered by lots of people already, and found it quite charming. He led her past several tableaux where mannequins had been dressed up to represent various notorious characters. The poor things had seen better days, with noses missing here, hands there, and the effect was anything but scary.

Joe stopped at a large glass case set back against the wall, a sign pinned to the top saying *"The Hanging Tree, Monkstown".* Inside the case were dozens of photos and drawings of various characters, mostly men of questionable appearance, dating from the 1500s onwards – together with reproduced newspaper articles, printed stories and several items of clothing. The remains of a hat belonging to one John Burbidge, a farmer who'd murdered his wife in 1622; a pair of spectacles, which had been taken from the corpse of Sergeant Penney, who had gone mad and shot two of his companions *"as they did drunkenly dance a jig"* in the Monk's Arms.

But it was the section dedicated to Hettie Gale that immediately drew Alice's attention. Several articles of the day detailed her crime, and there was a court report, naming the judge and jury. There were a couple of badly worn illustrations, and most exciting of all a small, tatty wooden box, stuck here and there with shells, though it was clear most had fallen off leaving dark, greasy marks. The label beneath the box stated:

> This shell box is believed to have belonged to Hettie Gale, given to her as a child by her mother. It was discovered in 1922 in the bread oven in an outbuilding at Nether Dennyfold, now known as Hettie's Hovel, where Miss Gale

lived with her son. Kindly donated to this museum by Sir Matthew Denny.

Alice gazed at the sad little box and could almost feel the delight of the girl as she'd held it in her small hands. She wondered if Hettie had ever seen the sea; probably not, people didn't travel so much in those days. It was incredible that it had survived so long.

She turned her attention to the illustrations, one of which was a faded ink drawing of a young girl, long hair twisted into braids framing a small face. Alice recognised the image from the book James had let her take. Such a sweet face; it was impossible to think that such a person could have harmed her own son. The second image was of the Hanging Tree itself, a small body dangling from its branches, a crowd of people gathered around: men, women and children.

Alice could barely look at the drawing, it caused her so much distress. She tried not to think about how Hettie would have felt, how the crowd would have bayed and hollered, the terrifying feeling of a rope around her neck, knowing her life was about to end. She pulled away from the cabinet, tears pricking her eyes, and felt a ruffle of breeze catch at her hair. She shivered and pulled her jacket tighter around her. It was chilly down here; perhaps they didn't have any heating on, on purpose, to enhance the sensation of fear.

'If you're interested in Pedlar's Quag you'd best look over here,' Joe called from the far end of the room.

Alice gladly left the Hanging Tree exhibit and hurried over to Joe, who was standing beside a large, glass-topped display case. It was labelled *"The Quagmire of Doom".* A little bit dramatic, Alice thought, although the number of people shown to have gone missing at Pedlar's Quag was quite surprising.

'I'll leave you here, shall I?' Joe asked. 'Unless there's anything else I can help you with?'

'No, you go, Joe. I'm quite happy looking at all of this. I'll come and find you if I've got any questions.'

Joe nodded, grinned and made his way back towards the stairs. Alice liked him; he made her feel comfortable, and she knew he'd be a great source of information if she needed it. She returned to the case and scanned the names of those who'd gone missing. The only one she recognised was Peevish Pat, real name Patrick O'Dwyer, an Irishman who'd farmed at Nether Dennybridge in the late 1890s. He was a notorious drunkard, and had failed to come home one night, after telling his wife he was off to check the sheep. Remains thought to be his had been found some months later, snagged in weeds in one of the larger black pools. When she and Luke were little, Mum had told them that Peevish Pat would jump out of the water and drag them down if they ever went near the Quag on their own. The story had scared them both sufficiently to stop them wandering; Alice had been easily taken in then, and the thought of ghosts had terrified her. It was funny to see the same name and story here, in black and white. It wasn't terrifying at all.

But Peevish Pat was the only one whose remains had been discovered; there were quite a few others who'd never been found, and that she'd never heard of. One name caught her attention, though she couldn't quite place it: Jeremiah Nisbet, who'd gone missing in the early 1780s. Try as she might, she couldn't remember where she'd seen the name before; perhaps it was in one of the books she'd been reading.

There was too much information to take in, so glancing around to make sure she was on her own, and ignoring the signs dotted around saying, *"No Photography Permitted,"* she took out her phone and snapped several images, which between them captured most of the information. Then she returned to the

Hanging Tree exhibit and did the same. Finding a bench, Alice sat down and took the notepad out of her rucksack. She jotted down a few things that she'd found particularly interesting – names that stood out, that sort of thing – it felt good to write, even just a few notes. There'd be time to go through it all at her leisure when she got home.

Alice arrived home to find Sergeant Cooper sitting in his car outside Crag Cottage. She felt a surge of hope, invited him in, and made them both a cup of tea.

'I'm so sorry to keep you waiting. I got a bit sidetracked in town.'

He brushed her apology away. 'I see you've been busy.' He indicated the notepad, and the *Myths and Legends* and *The Murders on The Moor* books, which Alice had spread out on the table.

'I've had a very busy day. I've been to see Mr Turnkey; he gave me this book.' She pointed to it. 'Then I went to Monkstown to see the Hanging Tree, and then the museum. I've had a lovely time.'

Feeling suddenly self-conscious, and knowing she'd been inappropriately chirpy, Alice frowned, bit her lip, and became serious. 'Do you have any news, Sergeant Cooper? About Fleur?'

'I'm afraid not, Alice. We've had another team out searching the woodland at Cleator, and all the farmland that surrounds the Quag: outbuildings, sheds, that sort of thing. No trace of her anywhere. We've contacted every airline, train and ferry, but there've been no bookings in her name in the last few weeks. And we've managed to talk to most of the names in the contact list in her phone, but no one's seen or heard from her.'

'She must have gone somewhere! Was the argument she had

with James very serious? Perhaps she was so mad, she just upped and left. She'd have access to money somehow, even without her purse and cards. Wouldn't she?' Alice knew she was clutching at straws, but the thought of Fleur being lost somewhere was too much.

'Don't know about that. But we did wonder if you could help with something we found in her handbag. You know we took her phone and purse for evidence purposes; we also found these.' He produced a small plastic bag from a pocket; inside was a packet of tablets. He pushed the sealed bag towards Alice. 'We've had them checked out; they're anti-depressants.'

Alice picked up the bag to examine the box and label, but didn't recognise the name of the tablets. Prescribed by a doctor, according to the label.

'Did you know your cousin was suffering from depression?'

Alice shook her head, feeling bad, as though this was something she should have known about. 'I'm not really surprised though, to be honest. Her parents both died last September; you'd expect her to be depressed.'

'But that's the thing, see; we managed to get access to her medical records, and it seems she's been taking anti-depressants for years.'

'I had no idea. But then, we hardly ever saw each other. We weren't close. Although...'

Sergeant Cooper tilted his head, encouraging her with a smile. 'Although what?'

Alice felt silly; she thought of the time Fleur had poured her heart out all those years ago. But that was all teenage angst, surely?

'Well, it's probably nothing, but the time we stayed here on holiday, and Fleur and my aunt and uncle stayed here with us, Fleur did tell me something. But we were just children.'

'Go on.' Sergeant Cooper sipped at his tea, and nibbled a biscuit from the packet Alice had put near his mug.

'Like I said, we were young. I was twelve, Fleur must've been fourteen. I was still a kid, she was much more... sophisticated, I suppose. She was always into clothes and make-up, lounging around and listening to pop music. I just wanted to muck about outside.'

He nodded, a serious expression on his ruddy face. 'What did she tell you, Alice?'

'I came down one morning to find her looking miserable; she may even have been crying, I can't quite remember. Anyway, it was a lovely sunny day, so I suggested we go for a walk up to the big house. That usually cheered her up; she had a crush on Finbar Denny-Hurst.'

A snort from Sergeant Cooper quickly turned into a cough. Alice was getting the impression that Finbar really wasn't much liked by anyone.

'As we walked, Fleur poured out her heart to me. How she was lonely, being an only child; how she never felt she was good enough for her parents, or beautiful enough, or slim enough; that she wasn't very clever and had no idea what she wanted to do when she grew up, and...'

Alice hesitated, unsure whether she should tell this man sitting in front of her what Fleur had really been trying to say, even though he was a police officer.

'And?'

'She told me something that she said she'd never told anyone else. I didn't really understand what she meant then, but I understand now.'

Alice felt a growing sadness for her cousin, mixed with a huge sense of guilt that she'd never said anything, even though Fleur had made her promise not to.

'She told me she'd... Oh, this is so hard to say...'

'Take your time, Alice. Fleur told you something had happened? She'd done something bad?'

Alice felt tears building in her eyes, and blinked rapidly to stop them falling. 'She told me she'd been... abused. By her father.' There, it was said, and now Alice let the tears run down her face.

'Abused? Physically, do you mean?'

Alice could tell by Sergeant Cooper's face that he didn't think she'd meant physical abuse. She continued in a very small, quiet voice. 'No, sexual abuse.'

A shocked silence filled the void between Alice and Sergeant Cooper, as they both considered what she'd just said.

'I didn't really know what she meant. I was clueless about sex, and that sort of thing. I just knew that Uncle Graham had hurt her, and she was really upset about it. We never spoke about it again. To be honest, I'd never really given it much thought, until now. Fleur could be very dramatic when she wanted to make people feel sorry for her.'

Alice could barely raise her eyes to look at Sergeant Cooper; the feeling of guilt and shame at not having taken Fleur seriously beginning to wrap itself around her, crushing her chest, making the tears flow out of nowhere.

'You were a child. No one could have expected you to do anything.'

'I could have told my mum. Why didn't I tell anyone?'

'Because Fleur asked you not to? Because you didn't want your uncle finding out? It was a long time ago, Alice, but it could explain why Fleur is on these.' He picked up the tablets. 'Something else for us to consider.'

Alice was openly sobbing now. He produced a tissue from his pocket and handed it to her.

'I'm sorry if I've opened old wounds, but we need to know everything we can if we're to have a chance of finding Fleur. And we will find her.' He stood up. 'I've taken enough of your time. Please don't be hard on yourself, Alice. Your cousin told you something you didn't really understand when you were a child. You're not to blame for any of this.'

As he let himself out, Alice sat, unable to move with the weight of a new understanding heavy on her shoulders. She'd let what Fleur told her be shoved to the back of her mind, choosing to forget it, even when she *was* old enough to understand the seriousness of the claim. She'd always found herself giving Uncle Graham a wide berth after that holiday, but never admitted to herself the reason why. She should have reached out to Fleur, offered a chance to talk about what had happened, instead of succumbing to the easier option of forgetting about it.

Alice felt wretched. Her lovely day had turned sour, and there was no one to blame but herself.

CHAPTER TEN

NOVEMBER 1773

Whether 'tis truth or ne'er but a lie, who loves?
With a passionate soul and a yearning to please
Loves the crow.

My ma han't seen him yet. My da han't neither, nor will he ever, and that's a fact. But my little sis comes down to my barn on a Sunday, and brings me bits and bobs: a threadbare blanket what Ma threw out, a bit of mouldy cheese, a sugary cake for my boy. She loves my boy, and pulls faces at him to make him laugh. And how he laughs!

He's getting heavy now, and I fears I won't be able to carry him around much longer, but his little legs are getting stronger, and I made him a pair of boots from some old leather scraps sis brought, so p'raps he'll get the hang of walking soon.

His hair is growing as golden as the sun, and his smile could light up the darkest sky. He's my best love and I'd die for him, swear I would. I never did feel this much love in my heart. Sometimes I feel I'm about to burst with happiness as I watch him shuffle around on his bum, though he don't have no toys but an old butter pat, what he chews on to make his little pearly teeth grow strong. I can't believe 'tis almost winter and he was born as the daffodils was just poking their heads through the grass. I must prepare for the cold, and the crow knows it will be cold.

Dear Rose, she brought me a pile of old blankets what Miss Patience was throwing out, and some of Master Charles's baby clothes what Miss Patience wouldn't miss. Rose is so kind to me, and we have a laugh when she comes to my barn. Though that's not very often, as she has to spend all her time with Master Charles, being the way he is and all.

I wonder why that boy is so diff'rent to my own sweet child. Mr Wickens runs a comfortable house, as far as I can tell. 'Course, I never been inside those grand walls, but when I was little, I confess I crept through the garden once or twice to peer through the windows. What sights I did see! And Miss Patience wears the finest silks and pretty bonnets with flowers an' all, though a bit more colour would brighten her hard face.

But though they have more money'n I could ever dream of, their boy is a shame to 'em. He's hidden away like a dirty secret. But he's just a bit diff'rent, like me and Rose. He walks a bit lopsided, and he makes funny moaning sounds, not proper words, but he smiles with such a big grin as makes me chuckle, and I can see the makings of joy in his sweet face. Rose is so patient with him, and with me, and I don't know why Miss Patience has no love for her own son.

She has another boy, William he's called, but I've not seen him for a goodly while. Ma said he and Mr Wickens have come a cropper, and William has run off to a place far 'cross the sea to fight in a battle, though he's not yet touched sixteen years. I don't think Miss Patience has much love to spare for him, neither. I do wonder whether she has love in her heart for anyone, even for herself. 'Tis a shame.

I don't have much what I can call my own, and that's a fact. But I have a roof of sorts over my head, I have a bed what's comfy enough, though the straw do get damp and the rats get too curious. 'Tis a good thing the crows like a plump rat for their dinner, else me and my boy would be sharing our little home with a 'normous family of 'em. But I have my health and I have my boy, and I can find joy in my heart and in the beauty of the world that we live in, and that's more'n some folk have.

I didn't know so much love existed in the world as I have for my own boy. But though my heart is filled to the brim, 'tisn't all sunshine in our world. 'Tis cold in my little barn, and when the storms come, and p'raps the snow, 'twill be tough keeping him warm and safe from the sweats or the pox. But I have my Rose and my sis to bring me things, so I'll survive. We'll survive. Me and my golden boy.

CHAPTER ELEVEN

TUESDAY 28 MAY

After a night spent alternately being wakeful and thinking about nothing else but Fleur and what she must have gone through with Uncle Graham, and dreams filled with angry, ugly images that she couldn't quite remember, Alice woke feeling surprisingly refreshed. A hot shower cleaned away the previous evening's turmoil, the sun was streaming through the kitchen window, painting everything in a warmer, friendlier light, and a mug of tea soothed away the last of her uneasiness.

Uncle Graham was dead; if he had done what Fleur suggested, then she hoped he'd felt remorse, and *he'd* deserved to have his life shortened. But Aunt Mari was dead too, and perhaps had never known what happened. Her own parents were dead, and she was certain they'd never had an inkling of anything wrong. So, it was only poor Fleur who still lived with her demons – if she was still alive.

To stop herself being drawn back into these dark thoughts, Alice turned to the books and notepad that were still laid out on the kitchen table. Remembering the photos she'd taken at the museum, she took out her phone and went through each picture, making notes of anything she found particularly interesting.

The first batch of images was of the Hanging Tree exhibit, but she soon found herself focusing on the Hettie Gale story instead. There was a copy of a newspaper report from the *Monkstown Mercury*, dating from November 1776. The copy wasn't very good quality, and some words were hard to decipher, so there was a typed version next to it, which read:

> Hettie Gale, eighteen years, of Nether Dennyfold in the Parish of Dennybridge, was brought before Court at Monkstown on the seventh day of October 1776. At a quarter before seven the prisoner was brought into Court, and placed before the judge, Jeremiah Nisbet. Being sworn in, the prisoner did fail to make a coherent statement, being unable to read or write.

Alice found it hard to imagine being charged with murder at such a young age. Poor Hettie had been found guilty, and hanged for her crime, but a niggling doubt had wormed its way into her thoughts. Hettie had pleaded her innocence, though not very eloquently by the sound of it, and the only witnesses were three soldiers, recently arrived in Plymouth following postings overseas, and supposedly on their way home. Were they entirely innocent? Why were they at Crow Pond at all? Something didn't add up.

Turning to the second batch of photos, which all related to people who'd gone missing at Pedlar's Quag, Alice stopped in surprise at the first case. Yesterday, she'd thought there was something familiar about the name Jeremiah Nisbet. Now she knew what it was: he was the judge who'd tried Hettie Gale;

who'd sentenced Hettie to be hanged. And it seemed he himself had gone missing ten years after Hettie's death. She read the article more closely.

> One of the Moor's most influential men of the late eighteenth century was Judge Jeremiah Nisbet, an imposing figure in his black silk gown and full-bottomed wig. Nisbet presided over many of the more notorious trials of the time, including those of Benjamin "Bennyboy" Cavendish, an over-privileged young man who strangled his parents and two sisters in 1769, in an attempt to secure his inheritance and pay off amassed gambling debts; Hettie Gale, a young woman who drowned her son in 1776; and "Inky John", a local printer who went mad and shot an entire herd of cattle, together with the farmer, in 1784 because "The cows were laughin' at me, yer honour."
>
> Judge Nisbet was a highly respected member of society until the mid-1770s, when he became something of a laughing stock due to his capacity for imbibing high volumes of alcohol, and his predilection for "ladies of the night". He resigned his position in 1785, and disappeared in mysterious circumstances from The Manor House, Nether Dennybridge, in 1786. No trace of him was ever found,

but it is thought he may have been the victim of a disgruntled employee.

Alice was fascinated. There was nothing in the article about why Judge Nisbet was visiting The Manor House at Nether Dennybridge, but she assumed it was a social visit. Nisbet was probably acquainted with whoever was lord of the manor at that time. She wondered how she could find out, and thought perhaps a visit to the library in Monkstown was worth a try. Then it occurred to her that the big house was just a couple of minutes' walk from where she was right now. Finbar obviously wasn't at home, but that might be a good thing, from what people had said. The housekeeper might be, though, if a live-in housekeeper was still employed, and Alice thought that was quite likely, given that the house was empty for most of the year.

It certainly wouldn't be sweet old Mrs Furbelow, who'd given Alice the sheep mug; she must be long gone. For some reason she was intrigued by the Hettie Gale case, and something was gnawing at her to find out more. She'd just have one more mug of tea, and then perhaps she'd walk up to the big house before lunch.

Nether Dennyfold was a typical English hamlet, consisting of the manor, a church, a handful of cottages, and a farmyard. The Manor House was as typical an English Georgian house as could be imagined. As Alice walked up the lane, she glimpsed the golden stone through the trees, and then she was at the walls that bounded the property, pierced with fancy double wrought-iron gates. The house itself was set back from the lane, a wide strip of well-tended garden lying between the gates and the front door. Alice stood and gazed for a moment, admiring the symmetry of the building: two large windows either side of the central door, a window above the door and another pair either side of that, with three dormer windows up in the roof. Big, but not too big; grand, but not too grand. And perfectly silent just now, with no sign of life anywhere.

She gingerly opened one of the gates, and stepped onto the gravel path that led to the door. The crunch of stone beneath her trainers sounded horribly intrusive in the silence, but she was at the door before she had a chance to turn back. A heavy knocker in the shape of a lion's head made such a loud, clanging noise when she rapped it against the back plate, that she leapt back in surprise.

Nothing happened for a moment, and Alice was on the point of retreating when the door opened just a crack, and a small, freckled face peered through.

'Can I help you?'

'Erm, my name's Alice. I'm staying in Crag Cottage, just down the lane.'

The door opened a little further, revealing a head of curly red hair framing the freckled face.

'Oh. Hello. Have you come about Fleur?'

The question knocked Alice's hard-fought composure, as she realised that her own cousin should be the first person on her mind, not some missing people from centuries ago. Perhaps all this was a way of dealing with her sense of helplessness amidst Fleur's disappearance.

'Well, yes. Did you meet her?' The door stayed half-closed, and suspicion lingered in the freckled face. 'I'm Fleur's cousin. I'm really worried about her.'

The door swung open, the guardian revealed as a small, middle-aged woman wearing jeans and a tie-dyed top, which was further decorated with spatters of paint.

'Come in, Alice, come in. I'm Genevieve, a friend of Finbar's. I'm house-sitting while he's away.'

Alice stepped through the door, and into a wide hall, a flight of stairs curving elegantly upwards in one corner. The flagstone floor was scattered with rugs of differing styles; an ornate coat stand stood to the side of the door, empty apart from a rain jacket and a pair of hiking boots, and a side table stood on the wall opposite the staircase, piled with unopened post and a half-dead plant in a stunning antique pot.

'Finbar's not been down here for a while, and isn't planning a visit until mid-summer. So he can party in the garden, I suppose.'

Genevieve's tone was hard to read, so Alice said nothing.

'D'you fancy a cuppa?'

'Yes, please, that would be lovely. If I'm not intruding.'

Alice was led to the back of the hall, where a door led into a curved anteroom with an elaborate tiled floor, and large windows looking onto the garden. This led into the kitchen, a huge room with appliances and cabinets that had seen better days.

'Did Fleur come here?'

'She did; we had a couple of chats.' Again, Genevieve's tone was obscure. 'Earl Grey or builder's?'

She bustled around making the tea, while Alice sat at the table, studying her surroundings. Fleur would've had a field day in here. She'd done some hideously expensive interior design course in Rome when she'd left school, but as she'd never had to earn a living, being the recipient of an enormous allowance from Uncle Graham from the age of eighteen, she just played at it. But she did have naturally good taste, and although Alice didn't share her love of the sleek, the expensive and the ultra-modern, she could tell from the few designs she'd seen, that

Fleur could have made the grade as a top stylist. She certainly had the right contacts.

Tea made, Genevieve sat at the table opposite Alice.

'Genevieve's a lovely name. I don't think I've ever met anyone called that before.'

'I was named after a car in a film my parents saw when my mother was pregnant with me.'

This time, Alice could see the mixture of indignation and humour in the redheaded woman's face, and she decided she liked her a lot.

'Tell me about when you met Fleur.'

Genevieve propped her dainty chin on her hand, and sighed. 'She knocked on the door out of the blue, just like you did. I was in the middle of a tricky bit of my painting, so I might have been a bit curt with her.'

An artist. That explained the spattered clothes.

'She was asking about Finbar, then she wanted to look round the house. I found her a trifle demanding, to be honest.'

Alice nodded. 'Yes, she could be very demanding.' She couldn't help a giggle. 'And she fancied Finbar like mad when we were younger.' Noticing Genevieve's puzzled expression, Alice told her about the holiday she and Fleur had spent in Crag Cottage, the differences between the two families that had made things so awkward, and the countless times she and Fleur had walked up to the big house, just in case her cousin caught a glimpse of her idol.

Genevieve laughed. 'You and Fleur are very different, Alice. Don't tell her, but I find you so much easier to get on with.' Realising what she'd said, Genevieve reddened. 'I'm so sorry... I didn't mean to... Is there any news yet?'

'No, there's been no trace of her. I still think she's gone to one of her other homes, though it's odd she left all her stuff.

Apparently she had a row with James Turnkey, just before she stomped off. Do you know him?'

Genevieve sighed. 'He's a nice chap. Quiet, introverted. Not surprising really, with his dad in such a bad way. I don't know him well, but I wouldn't have thought he'd be interested in someone like Fleur.' She gave a sly smile. '*You'd* be more his cup of tea, I should've thought.'

Alice felt her face flush. 'I don't think he likes me, actually. He couldn't wait to get rid of me when I went to the bookshop.'

'Now that's an interesting shop. It's a shame he doesn't have a passion for books; it could be so much nicer if he made an effort.'

A silence descended while the two women sipped at their tea. Then they both spoke at once.

'Do you know anything about the history of...?'

'You're into old books...?'

They both laughed, and Genevieve let Alice speak first.

'I seem to be getting a bit obsessed with Pedlar's Quag, and all the people that've gone missing. And with Hettie Gale; you know about her?'

Genevieve nodded. 'That was a sad case, by the sound of it. I sometimes walk to Hettie's Hovel; it has a melancholy feeling that I find inspires my work. The history here is incredible.' She paused, as though weighing something up. 'Would you like to see my work in progress?'

Alice thought it was probably an honour to be asked to see her new friend's work. 'Yes please.'

When they'd drained their mugs, Genevieve led Alice back through the anteroom and into the hallway, then up the staircase, which was lined with paintings; portraits of the old Denny family, Alice assumed, though she barely gave them a glance. Then along a corridor, and up another flight of stairs that were hidden behind a plain door. They were now at the top of the house, and Alice gasped as she looked around her. This vast space was lit by the three gable windows visible from the front of the house, matched with a further three at the back, seen through a fretwork of ancient wooden beams. Shafts of light radiated into the space, creating multicoloured prisms flecked with spirals of dust.

But it was the paintings that made Alice gasp. Several large canvases were propped against the walls, and a couple more mounted on easels in the centre of the room. They were stunning. Abstracts, mostly, but with landscape form: swirling skies, fields a patchwork of colour and texture, looming hills.

'I can't seem to get to grips with this one. What do you think?'

Genevieve stood by an easel that held a smaller canvas. The painting was mostly dark in tone, with energetic brush strokes in a range of greens and deep blues, suggesting a density of trees. A lighter patch to the bottom left had wistful daubs in muted greys.

'Oh, it's lovely! It reminds me of a place I know in Pigswhistle Clump.'

The smile that split Genevieve's face couldn't have been any broader. 'Seriously? That's exactly what it's supposed to be. The Whistling Rock. That's what it's called in the old stories; the place where the very first man to arrive on the Moor whistled for his pigs, and they all came from every corner of the land. It's such a beautiful story. And a beautiful place.'

Alice laughed. 'I've never heard that story, or that name. I always thought it was my secret place when I was little; I imagined no one else knew it existed.' She smiled shyly. 'But I'm glad you love it there too.'

She wandered slowly around, gazing at each of the paintings in turn. They all had the beautiful, sweeping brushstrokes that were clearly Genevieve's trademark style, but there was something else about them that Alice couldn't quite put her finger on, until she returned to the painting on the easel.

'The others, they've all got one pale brush mark, which gives some sort of focus, I suppose. I don't know anything about art, but this one with the Whistling Rock doesn't.'

Genevieve frowned and looked around at all the other paintings. 'You're right. Why haven't I noticed that before? I'm pretty sure I never meant to do that; consciously, I mean.'

Alice smiled. 'It looks like there's a little ghostly figure hovering in the background of each painting. Or an angel. That's it; they're your guardian angels!'

Genevieve laughed. 'You don't believe in all that nonsense, do you?'

'No, but who really knows what lurks just beyond the surface of this world?'

'Oh crikey, don't let's get all weird.' She studied the painting on the easel again. 'But it's true; there is something missing from this one. I'll have another go at it later.'

As they made their way back down to the ground floor, Alice spotted a door on the other side of the hall that stood partly open, revealing a wall lined with bookcases.

'Is that a library?'

Genevieve grimaced. 'Yes, it is. Horrible room, it makes my skin crawl. You can have a look, if you want. I'll make another brew.' She skittered off towards the kitchen.

Alice wondered at how such a tiny slip of a woman was able to create such vast, profound paintings. She turned towards the library and felt a thrill of excitement as she walked in.

Three of the walls were completely covered in shelving, from floor to ceiling, stuffed full of books. The fourth was pierced by a tall sash window, with an ornate fireplace angled to the side. Displayed above the fireplace were glass cases holding various stuffed creatures, all in poor condition. Pairs of antlers were dotted here and there, and even whole skulls, which added a sombre air to the room. There was a tang of decay tainting the air. No wonder Genevieve found it creepy. The walls were painted a deep, blood red, and everything was covered in a thick layer of dust, including the rugs on the floor, the heavy desk and the well-worn armchairs; as Alice stepped carefully across the floor towards the shelves, little puffs danced up around her feet.

But she forgot the gloomy surroundings as she gazed at the books, reading the titles on the spines with a mixture of delight and disbelief. All the classics were here, mostly very old editions. There was a large section of books written in French, and another dedicated entirely to vintage cars. Books from every decade of the last two centuries, some even older than that. Alice was alarmed that this treasure trove appeared to be entirely neglected; the whole library had clearly been untouched for years. Old books had to be kept in decent conditions if they were to withstand time; that much she knew.

As she wandered along each wall, wondering whether the wooden steps that stood in one corner were safe so she could see what was stacked towards the ceiling, Alice noticed a section of shelving that had been closed off with an ornately carved door. Curious, she bent down and tried to open the door, but it was locked, and no key in sight. It was probably nothing of interest, anyway, and she resolved not to be so nosy. As she stood, the back of her neck prickled, and a shiver ran through her. A clattering sound drew her attention to the desk, and she noticed that a little silver inkwell had tipped over. A chill was seeping through the room; a draught from one of the windows must have knocked the inkwell over, but Alice couldn't help feeling uneasy, as she walked to the desk and set it upright. The windows were closed.

A drawer in the desk was slightly open, so she pulled it out, and amidst a jumble of stuff was a bunch of keys. Would one of them open the cupboard? With a quick glance at the door, hearing sounds of activity in the kitchen and satisfied that Genevieve was still occupied, she took the keys and tried each one in the lock on the cupboard door, until one clicked, and the door opened. Squatting down, Alice peered into the dark interior, which was lined with shelves and yet more books. She giggled as she realised that she'd stumbled across a collection of erotica. How many Dennys had shut themselves away in this room, she wondered, studying this assemblage of antique filth?

The bottom shelf was arranged slightly differently, the books unique in appearance, and she carefully pulled one out. It was a slim volume bound in rich brown leather, with the word *"Journal"* inscribed in gold, and was entirely handwritten. The first page gave the date as 1786, and she flipped through, opening it at random. In amongst the dense, beautifully written passages was a name she recognised: *"Judge Jeremiah Nisbet"*. The words almost jumped out at her, and she was taken aback. This was clearly a diary, and although the entry was hard to decipher in its entirety, she managed to make out a few more words: *"has been missing"*, and *"Mr Wickens feels most guilty."*

'Ah, you've found the smutty cupboard, then?' Genevieve stood in the doorway, arms crossed, a big grin on her face. 'Tea's ready, if you can tear yourself away.'

Alice felt embarrassed, but Genevieve's giggles were infectious, and she found herself chuckling too. 'I was just curious; now I know why this cupboard was locked. But did you know *these* were in here? Do you know what they are?'

Genevieve scrutinised the journal Alice still held in her hands.

'They must be the old diaries. The Denny Diaries. Finbar told me once that the wives of each generation of Dennys had written personal journals, going right back to seventeen-something, even before that, perhaps... but the original manor house was burnt down, so I suppose anything earlier would've been lost. It was something of a family tradition, I think.'

She looked at the journal Alice was holding. 'That's such beautiful writing. Can you make any of it out?'

Alice shook her head. 'Not easily. I'd need to sit down in good light to try and decipher some of it.' An unexpected boldness took hold. 'I don't suppose…?'

Genevieve looked apprehensive. 'I don't know. They're so old, and probably precious, though Finbar didn't seem too impressed by the diaries themselves, more by the fact it was women who wrote them.' She sniggered. 'I imagine he's far more interested in the rest of that cupboard's contents.'

Closing the journal, Alice started to place it back with the others.

'Oh, I don't suppose it would hurt, if you promise to be careful. Finbar's not due back here for weeks; what he doesn't know won't kill him.'

'Thank you, Genevieve. I promise I'll be careful. Books to me are the most precious things, just like art is to you. Can I take a few? I'll bring them back in a couple of days.'

As she walked back down the lane, Alice's head was full of what she'd just found. She was carrying five of the journals wrapped in a bin liner, nestled safely in a supermarket carrier bag, and she felt a thrill of anticipation for her evening ahead. A mug of tea – several mugs of tea, probably – maybe with the wood burner lit to warm her bones, the angle-poise lamp plugged in, and her notepad and pencil at the ready.

When she'd seen the name of the judge, and the words *"has gone missing"*, she'd felt an inexplicable sense that she was about to unravel some part of history. She doubted it would have anything to do with Hettie Gale, and she was still mystified as to why Hettie should be so frequently on her mind, but she felt uplifted, and had a new spring in her step.

Turning the corner, she noticed a car parked outside Crag Cottage. At first, she thought it must be Sergeant Cooper with news, and her heart pounded... but then she realised it wasn't a police car; in fact, she didn't recognise it.

As she neared the cottage, the car door opened, and a figure climbed out. It was James Turnkey.

CHAPTER TWELVE

TUESDAY 28 MAY

'I'm sorry.'

The words were spoken quietly and, Alice thought, with sincerity. She was sitting at the kitchen table, James opposite her, the ever-present mugs of tea steaming on the table between them.

'What for?'

'For being rude yesterday. I really should have been more welcoming, considering...'

James was looking at his hands, which were clasped around his mug; fine, strong hands, but with bitten fingernails and dirt grained into the knuckles. Alice took the opportunity to study his face. His hair was on the long side, wavy, dark brown, unbrushed. His beard, which could do with a trim, had a few white hairs vying with the brown. But there was kindness radiating from him that she hadn't noticed before: gentleness, shyness, even. And he'd apologised.

'Don't worry about it. I suppose I should have let those Americans buy the book I was looking at. I'm sorry you lost a sale.' She got up and walked to the high-backed wooden chair by the wood burner, where she kept her backpack, and delved into it, bringing out her purse. 'How much is it?'

James gave a wry smile and shook his head. 'Don't be daft. I gave you the book. My pleasure.'

Now she could see that his grey eyes were flecked with brown and were rather attractive; the fleeting smile brought out a sparkle. His deep voice was soothing to listen to.

'Besides which, I very much doubt people like that would have read it. They'd have displayed it on their hideous gilded coffee table, along with the replica Hanging Tree and plastic bog sprite they'd bought from Monkstown, and they'd have declared to all their friends how English they felt.'

Alice couldn't help but giggle at this unexpected outburst of vitriol. She'd seen the ugly tourist tat that was on sale in several shops in the area, and she thought the Americans probably would've fallen for it, just like all tourists did the world over.

'Tell me about your dad, James.' She scrabbled for something to say. 'Someone told me he's in a care home?'

James's eyes narrowed, the sparkle gone, and he resumed the scrutiny of his hands. 'That's the trouble with villages: everyone knows everyone else's business.'

Alice felt awkward; perhaps she shouldn't have mentioned the subject, but she had, so she couldn't just leave it. 'I remember being a bit scared of him when I was little. I don't think he liked me touching his books.'

James sighed. 'He didn't really like kids at all, me and my brother and sister included. I've never understood how he and mum managed to have three of us.'

'I heard your mum was killed in a cycling accident?'

Shaking his head, James suddenly stood up, filling the kitchen with his tall, stocky presence. 'It was twenty years ago. I was sixteen, Jenn nineteen. Billy was only twelve. Jenn pretty much brought us up after that; Dad went to bits and couldn't cope. It was hard.'

James ran out of words, and Alice felt a surge of sympathy for this man she barely knew. He paced around the kitchen, restless, and then it all came out in a flood. He told Alice how his dad had started to say strange things, forget words, wander off and get lost in the village. It had been amusing at first, when he'd put the shopping in the oven instead of the cupboards or tried to open a tin of beans with a corkscrew, but then things began to get more serious. Over the years, he'd slowly become a danger to himself.

James had reluctantly taken over the shop when it became clear his father was no longer capable, despite having been accepted onto a woodcarving course somewhere in Scotland. Jenn was by then married and working as a teaching assistant, and Billy had moved to the city, conveniently away from the family home, so he'd felt like he had no choice.

'One day, Dad went out and didn't come home. He'd got lost and wandered off into a farm a mile or so beyond Dennybridge. They found him sitting on a hay bale, smoking a cigarette, oblivious to the danger.' James sat down again, resting his head in his hands. 'The whole lot could've gone up. I talked to Jenn, and we agreed he'd be better off in a home.'

Alice felt another surge of compassion. Her own parents were dead, but at least they'd been there to the end. It must be devastating to watch your parent become a stranger.

'Is he nearby? Do you visit him?'

James finally looked Alice in the eye. 'He's in Friarswood Manor in Monkstown. I try to visit most days, but sometimes it's hard. That call I had when you were in the shop... It was to say he'd had a fall. It was the one day I'd not visited at lunchtime. I felt like it was my fault.'

Walking to the kettle, James said, 'Let's have another cuppa, and you can tell me about yourself.'

Wednesday 29 May

Sunlight poured through the thin curtains, waking Alice with a warm caress. She'd slept very well again. As she lay snuggled under the duvet, unwilling to move even though such a lovely day beckoned her, she thought about yesterday afternoon, and the conversation she'd had with James. Perhaps he wasn't so bad after all. He'd seemed genuinely interested in her life in the suburbs, particularly wanting to know about transport and how she got about. He'd never been to London and had developed a fascination with the Tube. It was the map, he'd insisted; he loved the iconic map of the Tube system.

Alice remembered that, in her new enthusiasm for this man, she'd made some off-hand comment about him getting a train to London so she could give him a tour. She felt her face burning; hopefully he'd forgotten, better still never heard her say it. The subject of Fleur hadn't come up, but Fleur was the reason she was here, she mustn't forget that.

She forced herself out of bed, drew back the curtains to admire the golden fingers of sunlight that striped the hedgerows, the new leaves glistening on the trees, and tried to forget about James. She'd meant to spend yesterday evening reading the journals from the big house. But after James's visit, they'd completely slipped her mind, and she'd spent her evening curled up with a romantic novel she'd found stuffed at the back of her bedside cupboard. This morning, she'd sit down and read them. After that she'd have another search for some trace of her cousin, venture out for a walk, if the weather held.

Alice felt a tingle of excitement, as she filled the kettle and prepared her breakfast. The journals were lying in their bin bag on the kitchen table, and she was itching to get to them, but the chances of her spilling her cereal over them was too great, so she ate quickly, drained her mug, and was ready.

She laid them out side by side. These were the first five she'd randomly picked up, and were dated all over the place. The oldest was titled *"A Journal of Life at The Manor House, Nether Dennyfold"*, the author named as *"Mrs Patience Wickens (née Denny)"* and was dated 1776. The date leapt out at Alice as the year Hettie Gale was hanged, so she selected that volume and settled down to read, relishing the feel of the dark blue leather in her hands, and the musty smell of paper and old ink that wafted out as she turned the pages.

> *1st January 1776*
> *My mood on this first day of the year is low. Mr Wickens has begun as I fear he means to continue, by shouting at the girl who stoked his fire, at Mary who brought his morning meal, and at myself for simply being his wife. I fear that the year ahead bodes ill. I am disquieted, though why, I cannot say.*

Leafing through the pages, Alice was in awe of the writing – tiny words, crammed together, slanted slightly to the left with long down strokes – and impossibly neat, each carefully written letter as perfect as the one before. There were long, dull passages describing the running of the house, fabrics that had been purchased, visitors that had attended for tea, and several bits that she found hard to decipher, but then an entry caught her eye.

> *12th June 1776*
> *I do wish Mr Wickens would afford me a little more consideration. Though dear Rose is a boon to me, I find it wearisome entertaining poor Charles after his tea. The boy is so difficult to please, and his needs so far from those of others of his age. He would benefit from his father's command, yet Mr Wickens refuses to have anything to do with the child. I fear Charles will not make old bones. William has attained nineteen years of age this very day. Though he is my firstborn, I confess I have found little in him to please me. My prayers are most fervent, and I plead with the Lord to bring William home safely, but I do worry whether he will be much changed on his return. I sometimes wonder whether Mr Wickens lays the blame for our sorry family entirely at my door.*

Alice wondered what Charles's needs were, and thought how sad it must have been to have a husband who took no interest in his own child, but she supposed things were very different 250 years ago.

She carefully flipped a few more pages, her practised eyes scanning the paragraphs, searching for something of interest. The name *"Hettie"* suddenly leapt from the page, so she stopped to read that day's entry, her heart hammering in her chest.

> *19th November 1776*
>
> *The physician called this morning to tend to Charles, who has again suffered an unexplainable fit of the nerves. The boy becomes more of a burden to me, though I would not confide that treacherous thought to another soul. Yet not so much of a burden as his brother. I thank Our Lord for William's safe return in the month of August, though I despair of the boy's increasingly wayward behaviour, but I fear Mr Wickens's choice of punishment will only deepen William's resolve to agitate this family.*
>
> *This afternoon, I have been to see Mrs Gale at Pedlar's Cottage, whose eldest daughter was hanged in Monkstown this very morning. It is said that the wretched girl drowned her child, a boy of no more than three years, born out of wedlock. I have discovered nothing of the father of the poor boy, despite urging Mrs Gale for answers. That woman must have a heart of iron to match her stony face, for she shed not one tear over her daughter's loss. The cottage was disorderly, small children cluttering up the floor around Mrs Gale's feet, all of them filthy.*
>
> *I saw young Hettie with the child but a handful of times, and each time, she bestowed upon him such love and affection that even my dull sensibility was touched. I have decided I will attend her burial on the morrow, but I will not tell Mr Wickens, for he would disapprove most sternly.*

Tears prickled at Alice's eyes. She shut the journal, her heart racing. She was beginning to wonder if Hettie had been hanged for a crime she hadn't committed. That poor girl, and yet there seemed to be so little sympathy from those who were in positions of power.

She picked up the next book, which was a much more elaborate affair bound in emerald green leather, decorated with floral patterns in rich gold. It was dated 1821, the author's name "*Mrs Florence Denny-Hurst.*" The handwriting in this one was rounder, less controlled, as though the author was barely able to contain her enthusiasm.

> *1st January 1821*
>
> *And so a new year begins. Our petulant and odious monarch will be crowned in the summer, and I shall not cheer for him. Instead, I shall concentrate on my own dear family, although Mr Denny-Hurst's mood last evening was one of sombreness and sobriety. I shall make it my goal to induce laughter in that wretched man at least once in a day.*

The next entry Alice stopped to read fully was halfway through the journal.

> *24th July 1821*
>
> *I am in despair! My dearest friend Lady Fitzwarren has sent me an account of the coronation of our extravagant monarch, which she was honoured to attend just five days since. Oh me, that I had been there. The King wore a red velvet robe with a long train, held up by pageboys, as though he were a comely bride, and the sun beat most ferociously upon him, causing him to appear somewhat faint. It seems that a commotion was witnessed at the gates of the Abbey, where poor Princess Caroline tried to gain entrance. To my mind, she is well rid of that corpulent peacock.*
>
> *But it is the banquet that Lady Fitzwarren describes so eloquently that causes my despair. Venison and veal, lobster and goose, braised pork and cold ham, all of the very highest quality. My friend is of large dimensions, but even she was unable to taste but a tiny portion of the delicacies the banquet offered. My mouth salivates as I imagine such a feast. Ah me, I dare say we will dine*

again this evening on the stringiest lamb Mrs Jenkins can manage to conjure up.

Alice had always loved history lessons at school; along with English, it was the only time she'd found pleasure in learning. She was fascinated to read the thoughts of this woman who was a real person such a long time ago. She flipped through the pages. Florence was certainly more fun than Patience; she and her husband Edward seemed to host parties practically every week, and there were entries about the food that was served, problems with the staff, and accounts of some of the guests, which were very amusing. Alice decided she liked Florence. Then she came across a more thoughtful entry.

5th September 1821
Today, my boy reaches adulthood and becomes a man. Tobias is more handsome than his father, and more intelligent than his mother. He will be successful in life, of that I am certain. But I cannot quite believe how swiftly the years have flown by since I lay in the birthing bed so young, so ignorant of the pain I was about to endure. And three more times I was to suffer that pain, such is the miracle of a mother's love that obscures agony of the body in favour of the sweet tenderness and adoration of her new child. Edward, being a man, has no notion of such deep and devoted love. Only one of our darling daughters lived, yet I am blessed, and must never forget to greet each new day with joy and thankfulness.

Alice found herself wishing she could go back in time and reassure Florence, give her a hug. She sighed, and was just about to close the book, when a twitch in her hand caused her fingers to flip another page. How odd. She was overtired from all the reading, probably. Scanning the page, an entry caught her eye.

> *7th September 1821*
>
> *Oh me, what a day I have endured. Mr Denny-Hurst has been most perturbed, which has led to a lack of civility towards myself, though I am in no way accountable for the boy's disappearance. Yesterday, the farriers came from Dennybridge for the quarterly shoeing of Mr Denny-Hurst's mares. It is such a usual occurrence, I feel no need to detail it here in my journal; it is simply of little account. Dear Joe Biggin, with his moustaches as wild as ever they were, had with him a new boy, by name of Jack Malaface, a sweet child with flaxen hair and dimples, apprenticed to Joe for some two months, though he seemed so very young. The boy's hands were red raw from the newness of his profession, but he was eager to learn, and Mr Denny-Hurst was most satisfied with Jack's attention to the task in hand. But when it came time for the men to take their leave, Jack was nowhere to be found.*
>
> *A search took place, first of the stables and the grounds, but when one of the gardeners who had been working in the orchards reported that he had spied a young man walking the path towards the old bakehouse, a handful of men were dispatched to search Pedlar's Quag. Nothing was found, no trace nor sound of that poor child, and today his mother has been found quite dead from the shock. It is my belief that the boy has been taken by one of the bog spirits down to the doors of hell, though Mr Denny-Hurst tells me that my imagination is over-wrought, and the boy must have simply drowned in one of the pools. May his soul rest in peace. And may Mr Denny-Hurst reclaim his propriety on the morrow.*

A young man, missing on Pedlar's Quag. Alice wondered if he was one of the disappearances documented in the museum. She didn't recognise his name, but there were so many. She remembered the photos on her phone, and flicked through until she found the images of the Quagmire of Doom exhibit. Sure enough, there was a small reproduction of a cutting from a local newspaper, dated September 1821.

> UNACCOUNTABLE DISAPPEARANCE
>
> A young man in the employ of Master Blacksmith Mr Joe Biggin, of The Forge, Dennybridge, has vanished in unknown circumstances whilst carrying out his work as an apprentice farrier at The Manor House, Nether Dennyfold, home of Mr and Mrs Edward Denny-Hurst. It is believed that Jack Malaface, of Cherry Cottage, Dennybridge, was last seen heading for the treacherous Pedlar's Quag. A search party was despatched, each man carrying a blazing torch and shouting in the hope they would be heard. However, throughout the night of the sixth, not the slightest trace of him could be discovered. Mr Malaface's widowed mother Mrs Elsie Malaface was distraught to the point of death, her heart succumbing to grief just one day later.

Poor Jack. Alice wondered what had happened to him, then found herself picturing a similar piece about Fleur in the local press. Had there been any reports of her disappearance? It would be easy to find out by googling, but she didn't really want to see anything in stark black and white – that would make Fleur's disappearance too real.

She made some notes so she could check it out later, and decided she'd given herself enough of a headache for now; the rest of the journals could wait. What she needed was fresh air, and the sun streaming through the kitchen window made her mind up: this would be a perfect chance to take a long walk and see some of her old haunts, as well as looking for clues about Fleur.

Alice headed to Pigswhistle Clump first, her favourite place of all when she was young. The woods lay just to the east of the cottage and could only be reached by taking an almost hidden path that ran between Honeysuckle Cottage and Pedlar's Cottage. It was really overgrown now, with thick ropes of ivy and whips of bramble completely concealing the stone walls that she knew edged the path. Thorns snagged her clothes as she fought her way along.

She felt her insides clench as she passed the back of Pedlar's Cottage, just like they had done years ago. It was such a gloomy place, and still empty, by the look of the grimy windows and grass growing from the gutters. She and Luke had teased each other about the ghosts and monsters that flitted around inside the walls, and she'd usually ended up running full pelt up the path to get past quickly.

As the path angled away from the cottages, the brambles grew thicker and more aggressive, and Alice had to use her backpack as a shield as she pushed on through. But then it cleared as the walls ended, and the narrow track expanded into an open area, dense with young bracken, brilliant green at this time of year. Fields ran along one side, a herd of brown and white cows sitting together, lazily chewing the cud. She recalled that cows sitting down were a sign of impending bad weather, or was that just an old wives' tale?

The first trees heralding the edge of the woods were on the far side of the patch of ferns, and a spurt of energy took hold as Alice made her way towards the oaks and hawthorns, the hollies and rowans, her mood lifting with each step. When she'd first come here with her family, always in August, she'd been enchanted by the stillness beneath the canopy, the softness underfoot, and the thick, velvety silence. She'd almost expected to see fairies dancing in the mounds of fallen twigs, elves leaping from branch to branch, or a white unicorn appearing through a magical mist. She'd sat for hours on end, just watching, letting her imagination go wild.

Following the faint track through the trees, stepping over moss-cushioned roots and avoiding large clumps of fungi, she went deeper into the woods now, the unexpected scent of wild garlic and flashes of violet from the last of the bluebells delighting her senses, until she reached a place she recognised. A small clearing, the trees forming an incomplete circle, a large flat-topped rock sitting incongruously in the middle. To the young Alice it had been a theatre, the rock a stage, and she'd spent many happy hours pretending to be someone else – anyone else – as she told stories to the invisible crowd seated around her. Until the year Fleur came on holiday, and Alice had brought her here. Her excitement and pride at showing off this most special and secret of places had been met with a yawn, a shrug, and a speech about how it was just a silly bit of rock, and it was time Alice grew up.

But she still felt the old enchantment, still appreciated the peace and the feeling of solitude, despite being a grown woman. And thanks to Genevieve, she now knew it had a name: the Whistling Rock. She settled down on the smooth stone, happily sitting for a while, munching on sandwiches and reminiscing as the sun crept overhead, filling the clearing with warmth and light.

Her thoughts turned to her cousin. Where on earth had Fleur got to? Alice felt a shiver as the sun was obscured by a dark cloud that appeared out of nowhere. The treetops began to sway as a breeze picked up, and the bright theatre of the clearing suddenly felt more like a gloomy dungeon. A tingle ran through her shoulders and down her spine, her scalp prickled beneath her hair, and an unearthly vision forced its way into her mind: Fleur – or was it Hettie? – trapped somewhere, cold and scared, and alone.

As the unsettling vision evaporated, Alice felt a sting of guilt as she packed her lunch things away; she should be searching for her cousin, not sitting here having a picnic, happy and carefree. Fleur had to be somewhere, and Alice had travelled to the Moor with the sole purpose of helping to find her. The clouds above were gathering into a black bundle, and the temperature dropped; rain was on its way, but she had her jacket, so she'd be fine. She knew where she should be, and it wasn't here. She'd make her way back to the cottages, and then take the path that led to Pedlar's Quag. For some reason, she knew that was where she'd find answers, and a drop of rain wasn't going to put her off.

CHAPTER THIRTEEN

JUNE 1776

Whether 'tis truth, or ne'er but a lie, who dares?
With his puffed-up breast and feathers of steel
Dares the crow.

Oh, I never did feel so happy as I feel now. Two more winters have passed and my boy is becoming a proper little man. His plump baby legs have grown strong and straight, his blue eyes shine with laughter, and his hair grows more golden and full of curls than ever. 'Tis a struggle to hold him still while I pull an old comb through each morning, and that's a fact.

We're at our favourite place, but 'tis a secret place, what no one knows, and 'tis a dangerous place to find, unless you know the safe way 'cross Pedlar's Quag. My da showed me the way soon as I could walk, and I thank him for that, though for not much else. And now I've shown my boy, and he leaps and dances on the solid ground atween the treachersome bog holes, and never once has he slipped or fallen. Most times, the air is chilled and full of a thick mist what glimmers above the Quag, but today the sun is queen of the sky, with not a cloud to cover her face.

We're at Crow Pond. 'Tis called that on account of the birds what gather on the tree. Big birds, they are, with their black feathers and cruel beaks, but they make us laugh with their bickering and squabbling. The tree's a pretty thing, with branches dipping down; it grows on a little rock jutting out into the water, and its roots cling onto the rock like a giant's fingers. An alder, my da said, what likes a drink o' water more'n most other trees. Around the edge is the greenest grass, soft for us to sit on, like a posh lady's cloak. We pick the blueberries when they turn from green to purple, and they taste like happiness.

The water is the bluest blue I ever did see, with sparkles all over like tiny dancing fairies. I'm teaching my boy to swim, and he laughs as his head dips 'neath the surface and pops out again, his hair darkened and stuck all across his pale little face. He shakes, just like Ma's old dog Bess after she's been in the river. He laughs, and his laughing is so infectious I catch it, like I catch a cold only much, much nicer.

There's no one here; there's never anyone here, 'tis too remote, and that's just how we like it. There's a little hill what shelters the pond and keeps the world away. We have a secret, see, a secret hidden 'neath the rock with the tree, and I know we're the only ones ever to have seen it, me and my boy. And that makes me happier'n almost anything. The secret is a little cave, but 'tis tricky to get to. I did find it by happy chance, but now I knows its mysteries, and my child knows, too.

'Shall we go to our cave, my love?' I ask my boy, and he nods, a smile lighting up his sweet face. I strip off my dress and my shift, and I help my boy take off his frock and petticoat and watch as his lean little limbs stretch as he heads for the pond. Soon he'll be wearing breeches and looking like a proper boy, but for now he's my golden child. There's surely plenty of time for him to be a man.

I fold our clothes safe on the grass, and follow him into the water. It makes me gasp as the cold hits my warm skin, but I know 'tis best to duck under straight away, and we both bob and duck till we feel right. My boy swims like a fish already, he does, and he wastes no time in swimming for the cave. We must hold our breath and go right under, feeling for the right place, 'neath the rock. I can't rightly remember how I first found it, but there's a hole, black as the night sky, atween two big roots. We wriggle through the hole, and here 'tis. Our secret. Our own piece of heaven.

The cave is low and wide, and a little beach of stones rises up t'ward the back-most edge. Tree roots plunge through the rock above, making a curtain of sorts. There's room enough in here for a host of men, but 'tis just me and the boy, which is how we like it. 'Tis dark, as hardly no light reaches this far in, but we fill the darkness with our laughter and song, and 'tis a place filled with love.

'Tis nice to have somewhere I feel safe. My sis brought me talk of soldiers roaming the Moor, homeward bound after some battle over the sea in a place what's name I can't remember, and I have a fear of men of any shape. But soldiers are known for their drinking and fornicating, and I don't want that sort near my innocent child.

I does worry a bit 'bout what our future holds. Rose still comes by when she can, but Miss Patience is with child again, and Rose'll soon be needed elsewhere. I hope the new child'll have its wits, for all our sakes, for poor Master Charles gets more muddled and more helpless with every passing day. 'Least, that's what Rose says.

But here the world shrinks, just for me and my own sweet

child, and his smile lights up the gloom, and we're safe as can be. And that's all that matters when all's said and done, and that's a fact.

CHAPTER FOURTEEN

WEDNESDAY 29 MAY

Alice knew as soon as she stepped through the gate near Hettie's Hovel that she was being reckless – she was *never* reckless – but something drew her on, deeper into the Quag. The amiable summer day had turned hostile, the rain, at first a gentle patter, now throwing itself to the ground in fury. A fierce wind ripped at her jacket and threatened to blow her over, but she was determined to make her way to Crow Pond.

Trying to remember the way Briony had shown her, she half-ran between the pools and bogs, finding solid ground beneath her trainers. But the further she went, the darker her surroundings became, and the ground grew less stable. She should have stopped at Crag Cottage to change into her welly boots, but it was too late now; her trainers were black with mud, which had also splashed up her jeans so the fabric clung damply to her skin. Her feet felt heavy, her legs tired with the effort of pushing on through the downpour.

Alice quickly lost track of her surroundings; she'd reached a place where several faint paths forked off in different directions, and she had no idea which one to take. The rain slowed to a drizzle, but the air had thickened, and mist was beginning to rise from the ground, hampering her view. Her stomach clenched, a knot of fear clawing at her, urging her sensible self to turn back. But something drew her onwards. What was it? A suggestion? A compulsion? Was that a faint golden light dancing along one of the tracks? She chose that one, even though it went against her other instincts to continue. The glow disappeared so quickly, she began to doubt it'd ever been there in the first place. But the track was clear enough to follow, and even though the pools either side were growing in size and blackness, she felt an unexpected confidence taking hold as she hurried along.

So she wasn't at all surprised when the ground rose ahead, forming the hill that shielded this place, and through the mist the slender form of a strong, young tree that reached for the sky, growing from its parent, which slumped forward, its decayed branches plunging deep into the water. The tree was filled with small, dark shapes, silent until her arrival, which broke out into squawking and squabbling as she approached. She'd made it to Crow Pond, and elation replaced any fear.

As Alice made her way cautiously towards the rocks, which fringed one side of the pond, the clouds parted, allowing a tentacle of light to snake down and set the water afire with little flashes of brilliance. The mist began to drift away, and the rain finally stopped. She found a flat-topped rock and sat down; her jeans really couldn't get much wetter. Relief flooded through her veins. Never one to take a physical risk, allowing her imagination to run riot instead, Alice felt a sense of achievement at getting to Crow Pond on her own, but anxiety wasn't far away – she still had to find her way home.

Did Fleur make this journey? How could she possibly have got this far in high-heeled shoes? Perhaps she'd taken them off and gone barefoot, but in that case, what had she done with the shoes? Alice really couldn't imagine her cousin here, in such a remote place. And she still felt angry with James for not following Fleur after their argument. Perhaps if he had done, he'd have seen where she went. Or if he'd hung around, waited for a while, he'd have been there when she turned back, which she must have done, surely? Alice couldn't see any alternative. The thought of her cousin here, alone, shoeless, was too much to bear, so she forced herself to think of childhood memories instead.

After the doomed holiday with Fleur and her aunt and uncle, Alice's family had holidayed alone at Crag Cottage for four more years. They would probably have carried on, but Luke's behaviour had become unmanageable by then; he'd got into trouble with the police for shoplifting, vandalism and an array of other minor offences, and her parents couldn't cope anymore. Alice had been devastated; she'd felt as though she was being punished for her brother's crimes, and she'd probably not helped matters by withdrawing further into herself, becoming sulky and silent.

A year later, her father died suddenly, his heart simply giving up its constant battle. She'd loved her dad deeply, and still regretted never telling him that. They'd never been a hearts-and-flowers sort of family, but she should have told him how much he meant to her. Her mother had crumpled, so Alice had put all her energy into helping her keep some semblance of normality.

Luke had spiralled out of their lives, leaving school at fifteen and disappearing into the depths of London. They'd barely heard from him in three years until, out of the blue, he'd returned home one evening looking clean, well dressed, and reeking of dirty money. He'd hugged his mother, even hugged Alice, and told them he was off to Australia, where he'd apparently got a job in finance – something dodgy, presumably. And that was that, until he'd turned up at their mum's funeral last year.

Aunt Mari had been very sniffy about Luke, constantly holding Fleur up as an example of how young people *should* behave, but Uncle Graham made so much money it had been easy for his daughter to do whatever she wanted. Alice remembered the year Fleur had been given a pony for her birthday; even though she'd never been interested in riding herself, jealousy had balled up inside her, and she'd spent miserable hours imagining scenarios where Fleur fell off the pony, or it got stolen, or it kicked her and broke her leg.

Now, sitting here at Crow Pond with no clue where her cousin was, she felt an enormous sense of guilt and shame. She might be quiet, a low-achiever, and of little interest to anyone, but at least she was here, in the place she loved, even if only for a short time. Where was Fleur?

Fighting off the pall of gloom that had settled around her, Alice decided she should make her way back to the cottage while the weather held. The sun had reappeared, burning the last wisps of mist away. As she stood up, something caught her eye beneath the tangle of branches that thrust into the water. She made her way around the edge to take a closer look, but it must have been a shadow, as there was nothing to see but gently rippling water.

Laughing at her overactive imagination, Alice felt her mood lift, and she began to make her way back across Pedlar's Quag. She was certain now that Fleur must have doubled back after James had gone, and for some reason she'd left the Moor in a hurry, without her phone or purse. It didn't make sense, but the Quag had been thoroughly searched; Fleur hadn't drowned in a boggy pool, she was sure of that.

A loud rapping at the door brought Alice out of the bathroom, clouds of steam following her as she tiptoed down the stairs. She'd thrown on Fleur's dressing gown, and wrapped her hair in a towel; she really didn't feel like talking to anyone in this state, but what if it was important? What if it was Sergeant Cooper or Briony, with some news?

Another bout of knocking, more urgent this time, persuaded her to open the door just a crack so she could see who it was.

'Oh. Have I come at a bad time?'

It was James. Alice hesitated, feeling a rush of embarrassment at being caught at such an unguarded moment. His expression was almost unreadable, but did she detect a faint whiff of anger in his eyes?

'No, come in. I've just had a bath. Sorry about...' She gestured vaguely at her feet, which were bare, and had left wet prints across the flagstones. 'Cup of tea?'

James didn't answer but walked across the kitchen to the wood burner, which Alice had lit as soon as she'd returned from Crow Pond. Despite the warmth of the day, she'd felt shivery, and she needed to dry out her jeans, which were draped on a rack above the fire and her trainers, caked in mud and stuffed with newspaper.

'You've been to Pedlar's Quag.'

It wasn't a question; it was a statement, spoken with a noticeable veneer of displeasure.

'Well, yes, but...'

'I spoke to the old woman who lives in one of the cottages, she said she'd seen you go up the track.'

'Yes, I did, but...'

'Are you crazy?'

James turned to look at Alice, his eyes flaring with emotion. He'd trimmed his beard, and his hair looked as though he'd dragged a comb through it. He looked so much nicer, and a flush of heat raced up her neck and into her cheeks.

'Tea?'

Without waiting for an answer, Alice pottered about filling the kettle, washing the mugs and finding the teabags; composing herself. She could feel James's eyes burning into her back.

'It's not safe to be out on the Quag on your own; anything could've happened.'

Alice put the mugs on the table, unable to meet his gaze. 'Sit down, James. Please.'

He walked across the kitchen, with some reluctance it seemed, and sat opposite her.

'I just needed to be there on my own – Crow Pond, I mean. I don't know why; something drew me there. I suppose I wanted to make sure there's really no trace of Fleur on the Quag.'

James reddened, presumably at the mention of Fleur.

'I was fine. I remembered the route Briony took, and it only rained for a little while. Honestly, I'm perfectly okay.'

He looked at her then, and his eyes softened. At the same moment, a tendril of hair snaked free of its cover, a pearl of water dripping sinuously down her chest and disappearing under the dressing gown. She saw James's eyes stray downwards as he, too, noticed the drip, and she couldn't help a nervous giggle as he snapped his gaze to her face, clearly embarrassed.

'I'll go and get dressed. Won't be a minute. Enjoy your tea.'

She practically ran to the stairs and up to her bedroom, where she shut the door and stomped to the bed, annoyed with herself that she'd found James's reaction so endearing. He was the *enemy*, right? The one who'd abandoned her cousin.

Rubbing her skin dry, Alice realised she'd only brought the one pair of jeans with her. She donned fresh underwear and a clean top, but there was nothing else for it; she'd have to put her damp jeans back on, though they were hanging over the fire, and she'd have to walk half-naked across the kitchen to get them. Then the wardrobe caught her eye – the wardrobe that contained Fleur's clothes. They were a similar size, although with wildly different taste in clothes, but maybe Fleur had some jeans she could borrow. She rummaged through the hangers; so many clothes, but nothing appropriate for the Moor.

There were a couple of pairs of jeans, one black with diamanté decorations on the pockets; the others plain blue denim, clearly expensive and beautifully cut. She tried them on and they fitted, though only just. Admiring her reflection in the mirror attached to the back of the wardrobe door, Alice marvelled at the shape the jeans gave her, making her legs look long and slim, even though she had to turn up the cuffs a couple of times; Fleur was taller. But she had to admit she felt good; perhaps there *was* a point in investing in expensive clothes, after all.

Towelling her hair, she ran her fingers through to smooth any tangles, then, feeling slightly self-conscious, she returned to the kitchen. James had pulled out one of the journals and was leafing through the pages.

'Please be careful with those. They're from the big house. Genevieve shouldn't really have let me bring them here, but I bullied her into it.'

James raised an eyebrow. 'I work with precious old books every day. I know how to handle them.'

Alice ignored the barb. She felt good; she wasn't going to let James undermine her.

'Which one have you got?'

He showed her the cover: *A Journal of Life at The Manor House, Nether Dennyfold, 1910, by Iris Denny-Hurst*. Patterned in art deco style, white, green and crimson, it was a jolly looking book. Alice wondered at all these women who'd lived in the big house.

'I was just reading this bit, about some poor vicar who'd obviously had enough of female company.'

Alice stood behind James, peering over his shoulder at the looping handwriting that flowed haphazardly across the pages.

> 6th June 1910
>
> *Well I never! This afternoon's tea party for our new vicar was going swimmingly when all of a sudden, in the middle of sampling Mrs Dunlop's marvellous Battenberg cake, the Reverend suddenly took off. He'd become flustered not, I believe, due to the cake, which was quite delicious, rather he was compelled to leave for reasons unknown. I wonder whether a gripe of the stomach caught him, although the rest of our merry party was unafflicted. When he had failed to return some two hours later, I instructed the staff to conduct a thorough search, but no trace was found. The wretched man had simply upped and left. How very impolite! I shall ask Valentine to call on the vicarage tomorrow, and I fully intend to put on a display of frostiness at church on Sunday next.*

Alice laughed. 'Well, Iris sounds feisty. I suppose 1910 is quite recent, really, compared to the ones I've been reading.'

James closed the book and placed it carefully back with the others, and she felt a sense of relief. She'd been entrusted with the journals, and she was determined to keep them safe.

'More tea?'

'No. Thank you. I must visit my father before he has his supper.'

Alice waited for James to say something more about his reason for visiting her, but he seemed a bit reticent. For once, she felt the more dominant, the more confident; she quite liked the sensation.

'Why are you here, James?'

He blushed, and fiddled with the half-drunk mug of tea.

'Erm, well, I just wondered if you'd...' His words trailed off.

'Wondered if I'd what?'

'If you'd like to... have dinner with me?'

Alice was taken aback. She'd got a strong sense that this man didn't think much of her, and she wasn't quite sure what to make of him yet. And more to the point, he'd already been out with Fleur, who was the polar opposite of herself.

'Oh! Well... I'm not sure, really. Wouldn't Fleur be a bit peed off if she found out? I mean, you and she were a thing, right? *Are* a thing?'

James looked angry again, his eyes darkening as he stood hurriedly. 'Don't worry, I didn't really think you'd want to.' His face had taken on the sullen expression he'd had when she'd first met him.

He strode to the door, barely looking at her, and she felt a little silly. She was a bit lonely here, to be honest, and it might do her good to get out for an evening instead of burying her nose in those journals on her own.

'James! Wait, I'm sorry. I didn't mean I don't want to have dinner with you. I'd like that. Really.'

He turned, and his expression softened, his smile making delicious little crinkles around his eyes.

'Tomorrow? I'll call at about seven. There's a nice little place in Monkstown that does great tapas. You're not vegetarian or anything, are you?'

'No, I eat pretty much anything, really. Tapas sounds lovely.'

After James had left, Alice wondered whether she'd done the right thing in accepting his invitation. It would probably be one of those awkward evenings when neither of them had much to say to the other. Still, it would be nice to have a decent meal. So far, she'd been existing on cereal, toast and cheese sandwiches. Tomorrow, she'd go to the supermarket, buy some fruit, find something healthier to eat. She'd meant to go this afternoon, but the impromptu visit to Crow Pond had put paid to that.

She decided not to worry what she'd wear for now. The kitchen was super cosy with the wood burner still glowing brightly, she had just enough bread to make some toast, and of course there was tea.

Rather than look through the journals, Alice found the *Myths and Legends* book and settled down to a quiet evening of reading and dreaming. She'd read four of the stories when a rush of sleepiness flooded her. It had been a strange day, and she just wanted to get to her bed and switch off. Tomorrow, she'd do something normal; shop for some food and forget about Fleur and the Quag for a while.

And of course, she had dinner with James to look forward to.

CHAPTER FIFTEEN

THURSDAY 30 MAY

Alice woke early to the sun streaming through the curtains, a gentle breeze flapping them against the wall. Birds were in full song, but alongside that was the low hum of some sort of machine, and she could detect the scent of freshly cut grass. Full of energy, she showered, donned her now-dry jeans and trainers after brushing off as much mud as she could, drank a mug of tea and then walked into Dennybridge. Inhaling great lungfuls of fresh, clean air, enjoying the subtle scent of the cow parsley that threaded through the hedgerows edging the lane, she was in high spirits.

The village was quiet at this time, with just a few cars making their way to and from Monkstown. After negotiating the pathless section of road, she entered the village, crossing over after she'd skirted Turnkey Books, not wanting to be seen. She wandered around the supermarket, admiring the produce, much of which was local.

As she smiled at other shoppers and exchanged remarks about the lovely weather, Alice thought again how much more confident she felt here, in a small village, surrounded by nature. The air was purer, the colours brighter and the people friendlier than in the London suburbs. Or perhaps it was simply that here, she was Alice McKenna, not *"poor Angela's daughter"*. It was cheesy, perhaps, but she really was beginning to feel like a different person. There was a danger that she'd become known as *"the missing woman's cousin,"* but for now she was enjoying her comparative anonymity and freedom.

Laden with two bulging carrier bags, Alice didn't really fancy the walk back to Crag Cottage, so she decided to find the teashop and then call a taxi. Walking towards Turnpike Bridge, she picked up the aroma of freshly baked bread, and followed her nose until she came to Mrs Biddy's Tearooms. This place had been here forever, and Alice had fond memories of visiting as a child, when she'd happily devoured not one but two huge teacakes smothered in golden butter.

Today, the tearoom was almost empty. Selecting a table near the window, she gratefully set the heavy bags down on the floor and gazed around. The chintzy ruffled curtains had gone, along with the awful plastic tablecloths and clashing carpet, to be replaced with rustic wooden flooring and jugs of fresh flowers on the mismatched wooden tables. It was pretty, she thought, and still retained a certain charm, with painted milk churns and vintage bits and pieces adorning every spare inch.

'Good morning. What can I get you?'

An older woman, perhaps in her early seventies, appeared at the table, notepad in hand, a warm smile lighting up her crumpled face. She looked familiar, and Alice wondered whether it was the same lovely waitress who'd worked here twenty years ago. Surely not?

'Hello. Isn't it a lovely morning? Could I have a pot of tea, please, and...'

She quickly scanned the menu. She'd not had breakfast yet, and noticed that teacakes were still there, though right down at the bottom, under croissants and pain aux raisins.

'Could I have a teacake, please.'

As the waitress disappeared into the back, Alice settled down and watched people walking past the window. She admired the relaxed pace of life here, no rushing about looking at wrist watches, no manic shouting into phones. There were a few tourists, identifiable because they were taking photos of almost everything they passed, groups of teenagers looking either bored or mischievous, and others simply going about their normal daily business. So many smiling faces.

In the months following her mother's death, Alice had managed to keep herself occupied, at first by going through the process of grieving, which she'd tackled by offering to work extra hours every week, making the empty mornings and solitary evenings shorter and more manageable. But then John had told her to take time off. She'd spent a whole week in her PJs, eating whatever she could find in between prolonged bouts of crying, watching mindless daytime television, and sobbing miserably to herself about the injustice of everything.

After that chaotic and exhausting week, she'd resumed her normal life, got back to regular working hours and eating patterns, and kept her emotions firmly tucked away. But she'd felt desperately lonely, and still had no idea how to fix that. Even though her mum had been barely able to hold a conversation in her final few weeks, Alice had had a purpose, and plenty of things to do: cleaning; preparing tiny mushy meals; ironing bed sheets; reading bits from books she knew Mum had always loved. Afterwards, there seemed to be no purpose to her existence, and she'd become more and more robotic, less and less a part of the real world.

Coming here to the Moor had changed all of that, and Alice had never felt more alive, the world never so filled with possibility. Just gazing out of this window and seeing how life could be – should be – made her apprehensive about returning to her so-called real life. She just needed to keep in mind why she was there in the first place – to help find Fleur, or figure out where she might have gone.

'Here you are. I put an extra pot of jam on there for you.'

The waitress winked at Alice as she set the plates and pots down on the table.

'Lovely, thank you.' Alice felt her mouth begin to water as she gazed at the teacake, toasted to the perfect colour, and she could barely wait to spread it with so much butter that it would melt and drip onto her fingers as she ate.

'Erm... excuse me.'

The waitress was walking away, but turned back with a quizzical expression.

'Have you been here for a long time?'

A big smile stretched across the woman's face. 'Here in Biddy's, or here in Dennybridge?'

Alice felt suddenly shy. 'Well, both, I suppose. It's just... you look a little like the lady who worked here when I visited as a child.'

'And how long ago was that, my dear?'

'I was last here sixteen years ago, when I was nearly seventeen. But we mostly came here when I was younger, so maybe twenty, twenty-two years.' Alice was beginning to wish she'd kept her mouth shut, but the woman's smile grew even wider.

'Well now, I been working here for over thirty years, so's it's entirely possible it was me, though I 'spect I've changed a bit!' She chuckled as she patted her generous backside. 'We've had a lot of kiddies in here over the years, and I dare say you've changed a bit, too. So I'm sorry as I can't quite remember you.'

It was Alice's turn to laugh. 'Oh, I wouldn't expect you to. But I always loved coming here, and I'm so pleased you still do the teacakes.'

'What made you come back after all this time?'

Alice hesitated, but in a small village like Dennybridge she wouldn't be able to keep her purpose to herself for much longer... and anyway, she was beginning to sense that people here wanted to help rather than hurt her.

'I'm staying in Nether Dennyfold. My cousin's missing, and I've come to see if there's anything I can do to help find her.'

'Oh, my dear, I'm so sorry. That shiny blonde woman with the clothes?'

Alice grimaced at the description. 'Yes, that's her. Fleur. My name's Alice, by the way.'

'And I'm Mary, and if there's anything at all I can do, you just come and ask. Crow knows she'll turn up; folks like her don't just vanish, you'll see. Though there's been that many disappearances from hereabouts, it's no wonder our visiting friends from abroad get taken in by all the stories of snatchings and hauntings. Oh, I'd best go. You enjoy your teacake, Alice.'

She spread on a little jam and nibbled carefully, as she thought about what Mary had said. So far, she'd got the impression that Fleur hadn't been very well liked. It was a shame, really, because although Fleur had always craved attention, she just hadn't gone about it in the right way.

Feeling suddenly deflated, Alice wanted to get back to the cottage. She rummaged about in her backpack for the card Harry had given her and phoned him. He answered on the second ring, was available, and only a couple of minutes away. Leaving a generous tip for Mary, she picked up her things and waited outside the tearoom for the taxi to arrive.

'Climb in, Alice.'

Something about Harry seemed a bit different, Alice thought, though she couldn't say exactly what it was. The usual smile was stretched across his face, but didn't quite reach his eyes, and his voice was a little less full of cheer.

'How are you, Harry?'

'Oh, same old.' He sighed as the car pulled into the flow of traffic. 'Any luck with finding your cousin?'

It was Alice's turn to sigh. 'No, nothing. I don't know what to think. Sometimes I feel worried, other times I'm annoyed because she's probably just flounced off somewhere.'

'Must be hard for you.'

There was a long silence, each of them locked in their own thoughts.

'She isn't... you know?'

'Sorry?'

'Well... she doesn't suffer from... ever feel a bit... down?'

Harry was struggling to find the right words, but Alice understood. 'Do you mean, does she have depression? I think maybe she does, they found some tablets in her handbag, and I know–' She stopped suddenly. 'I shouldn't have said that; please don't tell anyone.' Alice looked beseechingly at Harry, but could tell by his expression that this was not something he'd be bandying about. In fact, was that a tear on his cheek?

'Don't worry, Alice, I'll say nothing. And in any case, there's no one to tell.'

'Thank you.'

The taxi was passing through the end of the village. Alice couldn't help glance at Turnkey Books in case she caught a glimpse of James, but there was no light in the shop, no sign of life.

Harry must have noticed. 'He's taking you out tonight, then?'

'How on earth did you know that?'

A snort was Harry's first response. 'Everyone knows everyone else's business. Or think they do.'

The taxi turned into the lane leading to Nether Dennyfold.

'How's your writing coming on?'

Harry snorted again, then gave a long sigh. 'Can't seem to get anywhere.'

'Well, don't give up, Harry. You must keep going.'

'Keep going...' He said the words with such dejection, that Alice didn't feel she could say any more, and the rest of the journey was spent in melancholy silence.

The fridge was filled with ham and cheese, tomatoes and salad leaves, pasta sauce and eggs, but Alice had lost her appetite. She decided she might go for a walk that afternoon, try to clear her head, but first there'd be time for a rest and a cup of tea.

The journals were still sitting on the table, and she instinctively reached for the earliest one, which was Patience's diary, dated the year of Hettie Gale's hanging. She flipped through the pages towards the end of the year, looking for something that mentioned Hettie, and came across an entry that both intrigued and saddened her.

> *20th November 1776*
> *This morning brought with it a sky full of winter's first snow. I instructed Rose to dress Charles in his warmest coat and muffler, and we left the house on the pretence of taking a bracing walk. I do not like to deceive my husband so, but I bear an inexplicable obligation to the Gale family, which Mr Wickens would simply not tolerate.*
>
> *It was a sorry little gathering that bore witness to the poor girl's final journey. As a convicted murderess, she could not be laid to rest on the church's land, and Reverend Bacon declined to attend, which does not surprise me one whit. Mr Gale had dug the grave with his own hands, close to the old bakehouse where the girl had made her home. Mrs Gale tried hard to console the*

> *smaller children, a boy and a girl, but she was in a sorry state herself, poor woman, her stoicism of yesterday quite gone.*
>
> *I offered a few words, we said a prayer, and Rose sang a most melancholy song very beautifully. I believe it was a comfort to Mrs Gale. I returned quickly to the Manor with Charles and Rose, and we took cups of posset to ward off the chill. I said another prayer for young Hettie, but silently, for fear of displeasing Mr Wickens. I cannot shake the notion that I am somehow at fault, though I cannot say why.*

Alice frowned; she couldn't remember ever seeing a grave near Hettie's Hovel, or reading anything about Hettie's last resting place. She felt such tenderness towards this girl who'd lived so long ago, which she couldn't explain. And she was beginning to doubt whether Hettie really was guilty of drowning her son. Closing the journal, she picked up the *Myths and Legends* book again, and read the poem. She almost knew the words by heart, and was, as always, slightly cross about the way Hettie was portrayed. Something wasn't quite right; she was sure of it.

> *Nine souls there were, nine men to judge*
> *The witch who had murdered her boy.*

For a start, it sounded like Hettie hadn't been given a fair trial, was found guilty before she'd even had a chance to defend herself. But Alice supposed things must've been very different in 1776. And after all, this was just a poem, written by an unknown person at an unknown time. Hadn't Briony mentioned something about court records being held by the council? Perhaps she'd find out if they were available to the public; it might be worth a go. The last verse had always given Alice the shivers.

It is said that her soul cannot rest for her sin,
That she searches alone for her child
In the mists that enshroud Pedlar's Quag, damned and doomed
And her name forever reviled.

The black-and-white illustration accompanying the poem was of gloomy bog land, a ghostly apparition floating above the pool-riddled quagmire, a bunch of crows circling aloft. It had given Alice nightmares when she was little, and she didn't blame her mother for taking the book away. But it wasn't just a picture of a haunting; it was a picture that haunted Alice.

She closed the book, on the one hand determined to find out more about Hettie's trial, but on the other, nursing a growing concern that she was becoming obsessed with something that happened centuries ago, something she could do nothing about, when she should be actively doing something about Fleur.

To prevent herself from becoming further mired in history, Alice decided to get some fresh air. She grabbed her phone, but left her bag in the kitchen; she didn't intend to go far, just an amble around the hamlet.

As she stepped outside, the aroma of freshly cut grass drew her in the direction of the big house. It was one of those smells that reminded her of sunny summer holidays, and it was irresistible. She decided to walk up past the house and carry on along the track that led to the church, and eventually to the old farmhouse and yard, long abandoned… but as she neared the house, she could see a familiar figure in the small garden behind the front wall.

'Hi, Genevieve. What a lovely day!'

The artist turned and waved, putting down a pair of secateurs and the basket into which she'd been placing cut stems of roses and chrysanthemums, peonies and some other flowers.

'Hello, Alice. Any news?'

Alice shook her head. 'No, nothing. I don't know what to do with myself. I can't think of anything else I can do to help, really.'

'I'm about to stop for a break, and to sort this lot out. Want to join me?'

Alice grinned, happy to spend some time with her new friend. She opened the gate, following Genevieve around the side of the house, then through to the back garden, and found the source of the enticing smell of cut grass. A huge lawn, neatly striped in shades of green, stretched behind the house, bounded by a tall brick wall.

'This looks very smart.'

Genevieve pulled a face. 'His lordship's coming down for the weekend, and he likes everything just so. Bill's just finished the mowing.' She raised the basket. 'And hence the flowers.'

'Oh, I thought you said he wasn't coming until the summer?'

'It'll be the usual, I imagine: a party for his so-called friends, to show off his ancestral pile. Though he never normally comes until July or August, so I don't really know why now. He never tells me much; I'm just the house-sitter.'

Genevieve clearly wasn't too fond of Finbar, but Alice found herself wondering what he looked like now, and wishing Fleur was around so she could gawp at her childhood crush. They entered the rear of the house through a back porch, from where a maze of small utility and storerooms led them into the now-familiar kitchen. Genevieve put the basket of flowers on the table.

'Are you any good at arranging flowers?'

Alice laughed. 'No! I'm hopeless with anything like that.'

'Me too. Oh well, in magazines they always show flowers that are supposed to look like they've just been shoved in the vase. How difficult can it be?'

Half an hour later, hands green from the stems and clothes spotted with fallen petals, the women had several large vases overflowing with a mixture of blooms, and cheeks that were sore from laughing so much. Genevieve carried one into the sitting room, and Alice put another on the dining room table, which smelled strongly of beeswax.

As she stood back, admiring the scene, she noticed the paintings that covered the walls of this formal room. They were portraits, mostly: some of men in splendid uniforms, standing rigidly in heroic poses, others of elderly gentlemen with white whiskers and thoughtful expressions.

'Gruesome lot, aren't they?' Genevieve joined Alice in gazing at the paintings.

'Are they all Denny-Hursts?'

'Yup, and Dennys, of course, from before they went double-barrelled.'

'Was that a marriage thing, or just snobbishness, do you think?'

'It was a marriage thing. Back in the 1700s one of the Denny forebears had no sons, and his daughter married, but was widowed young. Patience, I think her name was. She remarried, but wanted to keep the Denny name going, wanted to stay in her family home. I think she lost two of her sons when they were young, too. One was disabled, the other succumbed to a mystery illness, or so the stories go. It must've been hard for women, back in those days.'

Alice nodded, thinking about Patience's journal entries. 'And there are no portraits of women here. Why's that?'

'Oh, but there are. You must have noticed them!'

Alice followed Genevieve into the hall and up the elegant staircase, where the walls were lined with more portraits, this time women. She had noticed the paintings on her previous visit, but hadn't really paid them much attention; now she looked closely, they were magnificent. The women were in varying styles of dress, some solemn, others cheerful. Here was one, an endearingly shy smile lighting up a pretty face, blonde hair studded with flowers, her salmon pink dress trimmed with copious amounts of coffee-coloured lace. Alice liked the look of her and peered at the tarnished brass label fixed to the opulent frame: *"Mrs Violet Denny-Hurst, 1883"*.

The next to catch her eye was a stern-faced woman of middling years, who had an air of grief about her not helped by the deep blue, almost black, dress she was wearing and the background of dark trees, a glimpse of river and mountains seen far off in the perspective-defying distance. The portrait was exquisitely painted, but Alice could see a deep sadness in this woman. Her label said *"Mrs Patience Denny-Hurst, 1795"*. Patience, again. Alice felt as if she almost knew this woman from reading her journals. How lovely to put a face to the name, even such a flinty face.

As she climbed the stairs, she started to feel a sense of solidarity with these women from long ago. The paintings didn't seem to be in any date order, and it was charming to see the different clothes and hats and hairstyles. Towards the top were two paintings very different in character. One, in a bright pop-art style, intense neon colours splashed across the canvas, depicted a middle-aged woman wearing a black-and-white dress with a Peter Pan collar, her face heavily made up with dark eyes and bright pink lips: *"Susan Denny-Hurst, 1961"*.

And the last painting, on its own, right at the top, was a dreamy portrait in gentle pastel colours, of a younger woman with long blonde hair wearing a floaty white lace dress: *"Lady Emilia Denny-Hurst, 1976"*. She looked like a bit of a hippy, Alice thought, and felt sad that this woman – the mother of Jenson and Finbar – had died from a drug overdose. Poor Finbar; no wonder he'd turned a bit wild. He was the only Denny-Hurst still alive.

'Space at the top for another, but personally, I can't see Finbar ever getting tied down. He's not the marrying type. Lady Emilia is probably the last of the Denny-Hurst women.'

Genevieve disappeared back down the stairs and into the kitchen, leaving Alice to wander slowly down, taking a picture of each of these formidable women with her phone, wishing that she could talk to them. At least now when she read the journals, she could put a face to the writer.

Back in the kitchen, Alice washed the mugs and put them on the drainer. 'Genevieve, is there any other stuff here about the Denny-Hursts? Any other books or information? Other than the journals, I mean.'

'Not that I'm aware of. Why, is there something specific you want to know?'

'Not really. I just get the feeling that there's something that links some of the disappearances on Pedlar's Quag with this family. I'm probably being silly.' She grimaced. 'I've got an overactive imagination, always have had.'

Genevieve laughed. 'Nothing wrong with a good imagination. Mine goes into overdrive when I'm staying here. I start to feel that there's some sort of... I don't know... presence. And I don't believe in ghosts, or any of that nonsense. It's strange, though...'

Genevieve stopped and frowned.

'What's strange?' Alice was intrigued.

'Well, I haven't felt anything like that for a few days, now. Not once.'

Alice laughed. 'Perhaps that's why you've been struggling with your painting?'

Genevieve frowned. 'I can't seem to get the Whistling Rock

picture right. I tried to add a few paler strokes, like you pointed out on the others, but it's just not doing it.'

'Your guardian angel must have deserted you!'

Genevieve grinned. 'Perhaps it's because you've arrived. He must have transferred his attentions to you. I expect you'll be getting visions and things now; you just wait.'

Alice pulled a face, and giggled along with Genevieve, but felt a grip of nervousness in the pit of her stomach at her memory of the vision at Whistling Rock the previous day.

'Anyway, you want to know more about this family. Why don't you have a look in the graveyard? I think most of them are buried there. And there may be some church records, or something. Though you won't find anyone in the church to ask; it's rarely used these days.

'I'm going to get on with my painting, see if I can get it right. Thanks for helping with the flowers. Perhaps pop in again before his lordship returns? It's nice to have some company, and as soon as Finbar's back I shall scurry off back to my tiny house in the city.'

'I will. It'll be a shame to see you go, but then I suppose I'll be off back to London soon, anyway.'

CHAPTER SIXTEEN

AUGUST 1776

Whether 'tis truth or ne'er but a lie, who kills?
With his fearsome black cloak and his talons of iron
Slays the crow.

'Tis the sort of day what makes me think I'm the luckiest girl there ever was. The sun is on her throne, high above in a sky as blue as the forget-me-nots in Ma's garden, and it warms our skin as we cross Pedlar's Quag. There's been no rain for a while, and the ground holds firm, and my boy skips atween the pools like his feet are lifted by the bog sprites.

Do you know 'bout the bog sprites? Folks round here are afeared of 'em, for there are tales of drownings, and stolen babbies taken into the depths, and coming out again reborn as evil spirits. I don't believe a word of it. I never saw nothing what afeared me, and I travel the Quag more'n most. 'Tis sometimes misty and that makes strange, dark shapes of the trees, and it goes so quiet, like God's muffling the world with his beard. Mind you, I don't rightly believe in no God, neither, and that's a fact.

Crow Pond lies still and calm. Mr Crow sits atop the tree

with his wife, and they're bickering and shouting and making me and my boy laugh. We race to see who can strip off our clothes first, and slide into the cool water. He wins, though in truth I goes a little slower than I could, and we're soon splashing and dipping under.

But there's summat not quite right. Clouds are blackening, and gathering into a big knot, and I feel like me and my boy's being watched, though there's no one to be seen. I gaze around, water flicking from my lashes, making me blink... but though I still sense summat, there's not a body anywhere. Me and my muddled head! 'Tis just a summer storm threatening the calm, what's making my skin tingle so.

We climb out of the water and lie down on the grass, water striping our limbs, shivering even though the sun warms us. I tell my boy a story as we gaze upwards, shading our eyes from the light. He loves stories! Specially the one 'bout the fat ol' hen and the gentleman goose. He laughs as I tell it, though he's heard it many a time afore.

But my skin starts to prickle as I get to the bit with the puddle, and I know my instincts is right. The sun disappears behind the clouds, casting us into shade, and I sit up and have a good look around. My boy begs me to go on with the story, but I can't. My heart leaps into my mouth, feels like, and I can't stop shivering.

I can see 'em. Three men, standing atop the little hill that shelters the pond, watching us. Soldiers, by their garb, and dirty brutes at that, their breeches smeared with mud, their beards and hair long and filthy. I don't like the way they sneer and stand with their hands on their hips, swaggering, like.

I pull my dress over my head and tell my boy to don his frock, but they're coming this way, and the air becomes chilled of a sudden. I try not to frighten my boy, but I heard what soldiers can do when they've been without a woman for a stretch, and my stomach lurches with fear. I never did feel so much fear, but mostly for my boy.

And now I see one of 'em, the biggest, ripping off his breeches as he runs, and just for a moment I think, p'raps they want a dip in the pond, to wash away their grubbiness. Just for a moment. But then I see the lust in the man's eyes, and the state of his cock, and I know just what he's after.

He's not having my boy! Whatever happens to me, my boy must be safe. I grab his hand and pull him into the pond afore he can ask what's happening, and we sink down 'neath the water. I can feel the waves pummel my skin as the man leaps into the pond, and I know my time is up, and I won't be able to hold him off.

We break the surface, and I hiss into my boy's ear, 'These men are bad men, you need to hide while I see to 'em. Dive under and find the cave and stay there till I come to get you. Quick now, for Ma.'

My golden boy looks scared, the first time I ever did see such a look on his sweet face, but he does as I tell him, and I dive under too, make sure he finds the hole in the rocks, and he's gone to our cave. Safe.

And then big hands grab at me, and though I try, oh how I try, I cannot get away. I'm dragged from the water onto the grass, and now I can feel spits of rain on my face, and the world has turned dark, as though night has come too early.

The man's face is close to mine, the stench of his breath filling my throat with bile. He's had more'n one ale, and that's a fact. His big, rough hands claw at my dress, and he rips the bodice, exposing me, and then he's on top of me, and it's happening all over again. I shout but get a slap for my pains, and he gets rougher, so I shut my mouth and my eyes and try and pretend it's not happening, though I cannot, for the pain is too great. All I can hear is the soldier's grunting and the others laughing and saying foul things. All I can see is my da, and all I can think of is my boy. I'm glad he can't see what's a-happening, but I fear for him, and all I want is for this to be over so I can hold him safe in my arms.

But it isn't over. Even when the soldier grunts his last and rolls off me, another jumps on. He stinks of ale and sweat, and he hurts me, his calloused hands grabbing and grasping. I feel the tears what are flowing down my face being washed away as the raindrops thicken and soak the grass beneath me. A flash of lightning brightens the sky, followed quickly by a rumble of thunder. My boy hates thunder, he must be so afeared without his ma to comfort him. I want this to be over more'n anything, but I must endure, for his sake.

The second soldier grunts and is spent, and he rolls off me, and I wait for the third. What else can I do 'gainst three big, strong men what don't care for anything but that I'm a woman? A woman to be used as they want. Just like my da. Are all men like this? I know they're not. Some are gentle and kind, though that's no good to me now.

But when I open my eyes, I see the last man, the youngest, looking at me with something like disgust in his eyes. His face is gaunt, with unshaved whiskers, mucky and unwashed, and I feel there's something familiar 'bout him, though that can't be true. The others urge him on, foul language and obscene words mingling with the rain, but he don't move on me. Instead he makes for the water, and starts shouting, 'Where's the child? The boy?' My heart almost stops, and I start to clamber up, but the grass is slippery 'neath me, and the rain heavy on my poor, bruised body.

The young soldier wades into the pond, thrashing around with his arms, while the others laugh at him. I feel a shiver of hope while I try to pull my tattered dress around me. He's not a bad man after all; he wants to save my boy. But I'm wrong. The others laugh and tell the young 'un he should be a real man like them, and take a woman for a change, not poke little boys.

I feel sick, and the vomit pours from me, covering what's left of my dress. The men turn and stare at me, disgust contorting their faces. Not a shred of compassion, nor care for anyone but their selves. The first comes at me again, telling the young soldier he'll show him what a real man does to a woman, and I wait for the pain to split me as the rain pelts down, but a yell echoes from the hill, and the pain never comes.

The men quickly stand to attention, the one in the pond splashing his way out of the water as quick as he went in, adjusting their clothes, wiping the lust from their faces, as a figure walks calmly t'wards us. I raise my aching body and again try to cover my nakedness as best I can. 'Tis an officer, I can tell by his garb, the cap he's wearing and his bearing. He's a handsome man, and I feel ashamed as he looks me up and down.

'What's this?' he demands.

I can feel the three soldiers bristling with fear. Another flash lights the sky, the whole world seeming to buckle 'neath the sound of thunder. My boy!

'She drowned him!' one of them shouts. 'The witch drowned a defenceless little child!'

They all start shouting then, telling the officer all sorts of lies. They found me drowning my child. They tried to stop me. That's why they're all so bedraggled.

I cry and I plead, I try to tell what they done to me, but the officer don't listen. I try to show my ripped dress, the bruises on my arms where I was grabbed so roughly, but he don't look. He don't even look at the pond to see if there's truly a drowned boy there.

'She's no more than a common whore. Cover her up and

we'll take her to Monkstown, where she'll be dealt with as she deserves.'

I'm pulled roughly to my feet. One of the soldiers takes off his jacket and shoves it round my shoulders, though it's so wet from the rain what's pouring down, it don't make my shivering stop. They can't take me away! My boy sits in the cave and waits for me. I try to tell 'em, but they won't listen.

'They defiled me!' I cry. 'My boy's alive, hiding in a cave 'neath the tree. I must go to him.'

They call me a murdering witch and much worse, and the officer laughs as he wonders why any decent soldier would want to take a filthy slut like me, covered in vomit and all. 'Course, the men don't want the officer to know the truth, but he has his own story already in his head, I can tell: return to Monkstown the hero, with a murderess in tow.

I use all my strength to get away from the soldier's grip, but he's too strong. I kick and scream and I try to bite, but I gets a bash on the head for my troubles, and it knocks the stuffing right out of me. I'm dragged away from the pond, my whole world as black as the sky above, and my heart bursts with fear for my boy.

I look back and see the pond in turmoil as the rain pelts down, a seething cauldron, overflowing the edges. A mighty crack deafens me, and I watch, helpless, as the tree overhanging the pond is hit by a flash of lightning, split in two, one half crashing to the ground, the other into the pond, causing the water to 'splode with a noise louder'n any thunder. My boy!

I beg, I plead, I tell the soldiers they can take me as many times as they want, if only they'll let me go and save my boy. But 'tis no good, they are deaf to my wails. They know me to be a murderer. And p'raps, in a way, I am.

CHAPTER SEVENTEEN

THURSDAY 30 MAY

The Church of St Brigid bore an air of neglect, but though small in stature it retained a sense of godliness. Not that Alice was much of a churchgoer. But she did like the buildings. Sometimes, for a change from the library, she'd visit the local church back home. It was a modern, modest affair, but she loved the coolness of the plain stone interior, and the echoes that bounced off the walls from the smallest sound.

St Brigid's was set back from the lane, a parking area in front, overgrown with weeds and brambles. The graveyard was to the side, surrounded by black iron railings, flaking and rusty, laced with thick ropes of ivy. The gate stood open, so Alice made her way through, carefully keeping to the gravelled path.

She'd been here once before, with Luke, the year after the disastrous joint holiday. They'd been playing what she'd thought to be a game of hide-and-seek, but Luke was just looking for opportunities to scare her. He'd hidden and jumped out from behind one of the larger gravestones, frightening her out of her wits.

Many of the gravestones were sloping at discordant angles, some had fallen over completely, and most were so badly worn it was hard to believe they'd once been carved with names and dates. The area towards the back, spreading behind the rear of the church itself, was a little neater. As Alice stooped to read the inscriptions, she realised this was where the Dennys and Denny-Hursts were buried. The gravestones were grander, with carved wreaths and marble inserts.

Here was Florence, next to Edward, and Octavia beside Tobias. Violet and Charles shared a stone, as did Iris and Valentine. Susan's stone was much newer, its glossy black marble standing out from the crowd, outshining its pair: Susan's husband Matthew, killed in action in World War Two – *"He Died That We Might Live"*. Then there was Lady Emilia's stone, white marble with a gilded lily curving above the inscription. Next to this was a pair of granite stones, with the names of Sir Rufus and Jenson carved in plain, sombre letters. Someone had placed flowers on all three of them some while ago, the blooms now brown and brittle.

But there was one stone she hadn't yet found – the one for Patience – and that was the one she most wanted to see, though goodness knows why. She wandered along the path, stopping every now and then to check the inscription on a stone, finding more Denny-Hursts than she'd realised existed. At the far end, just as the path turned a right-angle to skirt the other side of the building, stood a large rectangular tomb. It was a huge marble box surrounded by a low, wrought-iron fence, rusted and warped with age. This was where Luke had jumped out at her, she remembered now, with a pang of nostalgia.

A plaque was mounted on the tomb. Alice reached over the fence to pull aside a tangle of ivy and wipe away years of accumulated dirt and grime, and could just make out the inscription:

HERE LIE BURIED
Gerald Wickens
April 1726 - September 1778
Frederick Denny-Hurst
June 1762 - September 1783
William Wickens
May 1757 - March 1786
Charles Wickens
March 1729 - January 1789
Patience Denny-Hurst
July 1736 - December 1800
Edward Denny-Hurst
September 1776 - December 1843

REUNITED FOREVER IN GOD'S HOLY ARMS

Ah, Patience at last, with her two husbands and three sons – the start of the double-barrelled surname. It was satisfying, somehow, to see them all together, and Alice felt a warm glow as she reread the names. But as she was turning to leave, a cloud obscured the sun, throwing the graveyard into shade and causing a shiver to run down her spine. The iron railings with their ropes of ivy, and the thick clumps of brambles and cow parsley, took on a malign appearance as though seeking to throttle the graveyard and everything in it. Alice nearly jumped out of her skin as a black feather floated from the sky above, caressing her cheek. A second feather floated down, this time falling against the tomb, catching in the dirt and ivy and landing, gracefully, by Patience's engraved name.

Heart thumping in her chest, Alice felt just like she had all those years ago when Luke had scared her. She hurried quickly along the path that led to the front of the church. Glancing back as she turned the corner, she saw a large black crow sitting on top of the tomb, for all the world looking like it was laughing.

She couldn't close the gate quickly enough behind her, but now the cloud had passed, the sun once again warmed her skin, and she cursed her foolishness. Determined not to be cowed by her silly thoughts, she walked to the church door, and tried the handle. It was unlocked.

The interior was cool and dark, with a musty smell that reminded her of Dad's clothes in the wardrobe, untouched for so many years. Small and simple in layout, it was nothing out of the ordinary. She wandered down the aisle, gazing at the stained-glass windows that threw a kaleidoscope of multi-coloured slashes across the wooden pews and the stone floor. The windows depicted various religious characters: saints, perhaps, or apostles; she didn't know much about the Bible, but they were very beautiful.

The window behind the altar was in three parts and was exquisite; the centre panel depicted Mary, dressed in a glorious blue and holding the baby Jesus, with two kneeling figures in the panels on either side. Alice gazed at it for ages, thinking about the women that must have gazed at this window over the years. Did all the Denny-Hursts worship at church? She supposed so; it would have been the done thing. She thought Patience would certainly have knelt here, and Florence, and Iris, even though she was cross with the vicar. But what about Hettie and her family, and the other cottage dwellers? Would they have been allowed inside the church? She didn't know enough about how things worked over 200 years ago, but she rather hoped Hettie had knelt here, too.

Wandering back towards the door, a plaque caught her eye. A large, smooth piece of white marble, it was inscribed with a long list of names and dates. The first name read: *The Reverend*

Thomas Alnwick 1633 to 1639. Alice let her eyes travel down the list, until one caught her attention: *The Reverend Peter Bailey-Bew 1909 to 1910.* That must be the vicar who was mentioned in Iris's journal, the one who'd disappeared. Strangely, he wasn't in tenure for long, and finished the same year that Iris's journal was written. Alice made a mental note to read further, to see what had happened to Peter. But that could wait for now.

Feeling suddenly sleepy, she decided to return to Crag Cottage and have a nap. She'd need to find something of Fleur's to wear to dinner. Maybe even apply some of her make-up; Fleur's cosmetic bag was overflowing with expensively packaged stuff. Or was it unhygienic to share? She really had no idea, as she never usually used anything more than a blob of moisturiser. How funny: being here at the Moor was bringing out a bold streak she didn't know she had.

Alice was beginning to panic. She'd only meant to have a half-hour nap, but when she woke it was just gone six o'clock; she'd been asleep for nearly three hours. A super-quick shower was followed by a rummage through Fleur's clothes, but she didn't have a clue what she should wear, or whether James would expect her to dress up. She should have asked him, but it was too late now, he'd be there within the hour.

She'd already tried on and discarded the black jeans with the sparkly pockets – not her style at all, and the only top that went with them was very low-cut. On Alice, with her almost flat chest, it looked ridiculous.

The black trousers were smart, but paired with a linen shirt they made her feel as though she was off to a business meeting. The dress looked shapeless on her. There was one skirt that she liked, in a lovely rich burgundy. On Fleur it would have been midi length, but on Alice, who was a good six inches shorter, it came to just above her ankles. A simple burgundy silk top, splashed with spots of pearly grey, matched well. Alice swirled around in front of the mirror, admiring herself.

She found Fleur's jewellery case and selected a long pendant set with a russet stone, and a matching bracelet. Her hair would just have to stay as it was; she didn't have time to do anything other than run her fingers through it. She'd sometimes considered buying a bottle of hair colour – a bright auburn, perhaps – or visiting a hair salon and having blonde highlights through the mouse-brown, but she'd never plucked up the courage. She'd rather fade into the background than be noticed. But now, seeing how good she *could* look, she wasn't so sure.

She found a small black clutch bag – she couldn't possibly take her backpack – and then noticed her short, unshaped nails and wondered whether they'd benefit from some of Fleur's nail varnish. The idea was quickly dismissed; she'd probably get the stuff over everything, and her nails would still look short and unshaped. But she did choose one of Fleur's perfume bottles and dabbed a little scent behind her ears, and on her wrists. She started to rummage through the make-up and picked out a lipstick. Dare she?

A knock at the door startled her. A quick glance at her phone told her he was ten minutes early. She put the lipstick back, relieved she wouldn't have time to apply it, had another glance in the mirror to satisfy herself that she wasn't a complete disaster, and ran inelegantly down the stairs.

James looked amazing. Handsome, even. He was wearing jeans, but matched with a white linen collarless shirt and a tweed jacket in the loveliest heathery colour. His hair had been trimmed, as had his beard, but what topped it all off was the shy smile he wore on his face.

'I'm sorry I'm early. I'm always early.' The smile grew

broader. 'You look lovely.' He thrust a bunch of flowers at Alice, wrapped in brown paper. 'They're from my garden. Sorry about the paper.'

Alice took the flowers, a mixture of daisies, roses and peonies, and beamed at James. 'Thank you, they're lovely. Come in, I'll put them in a vase, then we can get going.'

There were a couple of ornate vases stuffed at the back of one of the cupboards, but Alice chose a simple white jug, filled it with water and unwrapped the blooms, which she stuck in as they were. She'd discovered with Genevieve that she was a rubbish flower arranger, but they looked lovely anyway.

'They're so pretty. Will I need a jacket?'

James laughed and shook his head. 'No, we won't have far to walk and it's a lovely warm evening. I'd recommend you wear some shoes, though.'

Alice looked in horror at her feet. She'd completely forgotten about shoes. She couldn't borrow any of Fleur's; Fleur was a size seven, Alice a four. She felt her face reddening. The only footwear she had were her trainers, her flat sandals and the wellies, all of which would look ridiculous with the lovely skirt.

'I haven't got anything... only my walking sandals.' Well, this was going as badly as she'd feared it would. She was stupid, a failure at everything, she couldn't even get dressed properly.

'The sandals will be fine. They'll give you a bohemian look.'

She was sure James was just being kind, but slipped her feet into the sandals. They hardly showed under the skirt, and there wasn't any other option. Locking the door behind them, Alice followed James to his battered old Volvo, and climbed into the passenger seat. Her heart began hammering in her chest, a sense of dread building. This was why she'd hardly ever dated; she couldn't cope with the stress. The evening ahead loomed over her like a black cloud; she wished she could retreat to the sanctuary of the cottage.

An hour later, Alice was totally relaxed and enjoying James's company. The tapas place Bravas was small and intimate, filled with the sounds of people chatting, glasses chinking and Spanish music in the background. They'd ordered several dishes, which they were sharing, dipping their forks into bowls of spicy potatoes, fat juicy olives, chewy calamari, oily chorizo, and Alice's favourite – gambas – the prawns swimming in a hot garlicky sauce.

Alice was slightly shocked; she hadn't expected James to be so entertaining and charming. They talked about their childhoods, Alice concentrating on the years she'd holidayed in Crag Cottage. She described her shock and sadness when her father had died so suddenly, and the feeling of abandonment when her mother had passed away last year.

James told her again how he'd lost his mother in the cycling accident twenty years ago when he was sixteen. His father had been stoic at the time, but James thought that had probably been the trigger for the depression that had enshrouded the suddenly elderly man, and perhaps even the creeping dementia that followed.

They studied each other's faces, comfortable in the knowledge that they both understood loss; they had a shared sense of displacement in this busy world, and a relief at being able to talk to someone else who understood. Alice asked James about the bookshop, which led on to her fascination with the myths and legends of the Moor, and especially her infatuation with Hettie Gale.

'I don't know what it is, but ever since I first came on holiday to Crag Cottage, I've had this feeling that Hettie and I have a connection. Does that sound daft?'

'I guess you just feel sorry for her. I mean, she lived in

Nether Dennyfold, so you'd have picked up on that when you were a child.'

Alice shook her head. 'No, it's more than that. I almost feel like she's trying to talk to me.'

She realised how ridiculous that sounded; it must have been the wine. James chortled, clearly unconvinced.

'I visited the museum on Monday. A man called Joe showed me around the Dungeon of Death. It was fascinating.'

'Joe Crabbe? Big fellow, long beard?'

'That's him; he was lovely. Knows a lot about the Moor, and some of the exhibits were fascinating. Have you been?'

'Not since I was at school. We went every year, had to fill in silly question sheets. I was always more interested in eating my packed lunch.'

Alice laughed. 'I loved filling those in. How funny, we might have been there at the same time, though you're a bit older I suppose.'

A comfortable silence followed, James sipping his wine, Alice gazing around at the cheerful faces crowding the bar.

'One of the things I found most interesting – well, sad, really – was a little box that belonged to Hettie Gale. Someone found it in her hovel, 150 years after she'd died, and gave it to the museum. A sad, battered little box, covered in shells. I don't expect she ever saw the sea, do you?'

James frowned, looking slightly distracted. 'Probably not.'

His face had darkened, so Alice changed the subject. 'I searched everywhere, but never found the box you gave Fleur. What was it like?'

A look of discomfort spread across James's face. 'It was small, square. Cherry wood. Lined in padded satin.'

'Was it decorated? What did you carve on it?'

A few tense beats passed, before James answered. 'Shells.'

'Oh!' Alice's eyes widened. 'That's quite a coincidence, isn't it?'

A prolonged silence squatted between the pair of them.

Eventually, Alice broke the silence. 'I'd love to see some of your work.'

James squirmed. 'It's sort of personal, really. I don't sell the boxes or show them off, or anything. I find it relaxing to carve. That's all.'

'But you gave one to Fleur. She must be very special to you.'

Another silence stretched between them, this time taut with emotion.

'I do like her. She's beautiful, intelligent, full of an energy that I've never seen before. But...'

He tailed off, and his face closed over. It was clear he didn't want to say anything more, but what he'd said was quite enough. "Beautiful, intelligent, full of energy": words that would never apply to Alice in a million years. What on earth was she doing here with this man, who would obviously have been much happier if Fleur had been sitting opposite him?

'But?'

He looked up, his grey eyes full of an emotion that Alice couldn't quite decipher.

'She was just playing with me. I was a distraction while she was sorting out the cottage. I'm pretty sure she was playing the same game with Cory.' He noticed the blank expression on Alice's face. 'My estate agent friend; the one who introduced us. Cory's married, but hey, who am I to judge?'

Bitterness had crept into James's voice, which wasn't at all attractive. Alice scrabbled to change the subject. 'So, tell me about your sister. Did you say she's expecting a baby?'

James slowly unwound, and their conversation stayed on the light side, chatting about his family, the music they preferred, films they'd enjoyed. The wine bottle was empty, the plates mopped clean, and the bar getting even more crowded, making it difficult to hear each other.

'Shall we get some fresh air? Then I can call Harry; it'll be easier outside.'

Was that a look of relief flashing across James's face? He was probably keen to get home and away from her. Not surprising really, she must be as entertaining as a bag of dust after Fleur's glitz and glamour. They fought their way through the crowd to the door, and then again through the group of smokers clustered on the pavement.

'That's better. I had to hold my breath to come through that lot.'

They stood a little way down the street, in front of a shoe shop. Alice sighed as she looked longingly at the pretty high-heeled shoes.

'I could have done with some of those tonight.' She kicked up one of her feet, encased in its flat, practical brown sandal, and grimaced.

'No, you look fine, honestly. I like the down-to-earth look. It suits you.'

Alice winced from this backhanded compliment. Her first impression had been right: he wasn't really her type, and she clearly wasn't his.

She pulled her phone from the borrowed bag and tapped Harry's number. There was no response. She tried again, letting it ring for longer this time. Still nothing. Perhaps he wasn't on duty this evening, but it was strange there wasn't a call-back message.

'Harry must be off this evening. I don't have any other numbers.'

'Not to worry. There's a taxi rank just down the road; it doesn't really matter who drives us. They all talk too much, and charge too much.'

They walked slowly along the pavement, neither of them speaking. Then James suddenly stopped just before they reached the taxi rank, turned towards her and took her chin gently in his fingers, tilting her head upwards so she had no option but to look at him. 'I know you think I'm besotted with Fleur. She's beautiful and wealthy, yes. It's a boost to my self-confidence and my image to be seen with such a sexy woman at my side. But she's not here. You are. And there's something about you... something sweet, and ordinary...' He tailed off as he realised his badly chosen words had misfired spectacularly.

Alice felt her face redden, not with embarrassment, but with anger. 'She's not here because you let her wander off on her own into dangerous quagmire, but I'm here now, so I'll do. Is that it?'

Alice stomped off to the taxi rank and stooped to talk to the cab driver waiting first in line.

'Alice, wait. I'm sorry. I didn't mean...'

She ignored him. 'Can you take me to Nether Dennyfold, please.' She glanced at James, who was looking quite distressed, clearly mortified at his clumsiness. She softened, just a tiny bit. 'And stop first at Dennybridge.'

They climbed into the back seat, keeping as much distance between them as possible. The driver set off, chattering about nothing, which was just as well as neither James nor Alice were listening, each wrapped in their own miserable thoughts.

As the cab left the bright lights of the town and sped along the road towards Dennybridge, sudden blackness swallowing them whole, James tentatively reached out his hand towards Alice's. 'I'm truly sorry, Alice. I've enjoyed this evening. I like your company. Really, I do.'

Alice had enjoyed herself too, until just now, but wasn't ready to admit it yet. She pulled her hand away, and spoke to the cab driver instead.

'I tried calling Harry Deegin. He gave me a lift this morning; doesn't he work Thursday evenings?'

The cab driver caught Alice's eye in the rear-view mirror. 'Haven't you heard?'

'Heard what? Is he ill or something?' Alice felt a shiver of anxiety run through her.

'He's gone missing. Not been seen or heard of since this morning. He should've been working all day, but after his last job before lunch he just upped and left, said something about feeling anxious, and disappeared. He's not at home and not answering his phone. Not like our Harry at all, most odd.'

CHAPTER EIGHTEEN

FRIDAY 31 MAY

Alice had a restless night, unable to sleep for the thoughts racing around unchecked inside her head. Some had been about James, and the confusion she felt; she'd enjoyed her evening with him, but then he'd spoiled it all at the end by blurting out his true feelings. He'd rather have been with Fleur. As usual, Alice was second best.

But mostly, she'd been worrying about Harry. He'd not been his usual cheery self when he'd driven her home yesterday morning, and now he'd gone missing. She hadn't been able to dispel the notion that somehow his disappearance was either her fault, or was linked with Fleur, and that had kept her awake most of the night.

So now she was on the phone to Sergeant Cooper, her voice breathless with anxiety and lack of sleep. 'I found out yesterday that Harry Deegin the taxi driver has gone missing. Do you know about that? Has he turned up yet, Sergeant Cooper? I'm really worried about him; he was a bit odd yesterday morning.'

'Not yet Alice, no. It's out of character, I would say, and there's a fair bit of concern amongst his colleagues. *How* was he odd, can I ask?'

'I don't know, really. Just a bit quiet. He seemed sad. Does he have a wife or family?'

'No, never been married as far as I'm aware. Lives on his own just up from the Priory. One of my officers went round there. The door was open, but no sign of Mr Deegin.' He hesitated then, and Alice could sense there was something else he was not saying. But he coughed instead, and carried on. 'But you know, it's been less than twenty-four hours since he was last seen, so I don't reckon we need to worry just yet. He's probably just gone off for a bit of peace and quiet. I'll be in touch if we need any more information from you, but don't worry yourself, Alice. I'm sure he'll pop up soon.'

But Alice *was* worried. She wafted around the cottage listlessly, going from room to room, up and down the stairs, with no purpose other than to keep her feet busy enough to stop the thoughts whirling around her head.

Eventually, she filled the kettle and sat at the kitchen table, pulling the journals from their bag and laying them out. She remembered the one James had been reading. Iris's diary; the woman's indignation at the vicar leaving the tea party had been funny, but then Alice had seen the plaque in the church, which had shown what a short tenure the vicar had held. She flipped through the pages, till she came to the right entry, then read some of what Iris had written following that day.

10th June 1910

My darling Valentine brought my breakfast tray to me this morning, with a pink rose he had plucked from our garden. I do declare he is the most attentive husband, and though we have been wed not quite seven weeks, I do believe he will remain as attentive until we reach a ripe old age. That is my most fervent wish.

There has still been no sight of Reverend Bailey-Bew. Poor

Mrs Bailey-Bew is beside herself, and lays the blame at her own feet as she failed to follow him from the tea party, electing to finish her Battenberg first. A deputation from the Abbey at Monkstown has been unsuccessful in their scrutiny of Pedlar's Quag, and the police have said they will conduct more searches and make closer investigations into the Reverend's circumstances. A curate from Monkstown will be dispatched to St Brigid's to preside over Sunday's services. We shall include prayers for Peter. Pray God he is found soon.

This was intriguing – another missing person. She read some more.

22nd June 1910
It is entirely too much! My poor heart can take no more of this anguish. Poor Fred Middleton has been helping in the search for the Reverend, and he, too, has now disappeared. Only four days ago, I wrote that Fred was in this very drawing room, where we gave the Sergeant and his three constables refreshments whilst on a break from another search of the area. He excused himself, and simply never returned. It is most unlike Fred; he is a man of such fortitude and level-headedness, with a loving wife and four children who are desperate for news of their father. I am beginning to wonder if this house is cursed.

A shiver ran through Alice, starting at the base of her spine and running up to the top of her scalp. *Cursed.* That was quite a word, but *something* was wrong, that was for sure. So many people disappearing, and many of them seemed to be connected to The Manor House in some way or other. She picked up Patience's diary, the one dated 1776, and searched for the entry about Hettie's burial. She read and reread it until the tears were flowing down her cheeks. Damn! Why did she feel so deeply about this girl who quite possibly murdered her own child? Alice knew she had to find Hettie's grave. She didn't know why, but she had to find it.

A soft mist pooled around Alice's feet as she trudged along the path that led to Hettie's Hovel. It was rising ever-so-slowly up her legs, clinging damply to her jeans and making her shiver, even though the sun shone brightly. She hummed a little tune to herself in an attempt to dispel the feeling of dread that was beginning to seep through her bones. She'd walked this path many times before; there was no reason to feel scared, but still she trembled.

Reaching the ruin, Alice stood for a moment, trying to picture Hettie and her son as they pottered about, living their simple lives. But why were they living in such a lonely, cold place? It was hard to imagine the hovel as someone's home, and more shivers ran up and down her spine.

Alice remembered her first visit here, with her parents and Luke. Mum hadn't told her anything about Hettie, but had focused on the building's original purpose, which was as a bakehouse and brewhouse, dating from medieval times; a place where ale was brewed, and the yeasty froth on top of the fermenting beer then used to make bread dough. Enough would have been made to feed everyone living in the hamlet. Mum had pointed out the remnants of the bread oven built into the side of the chimney breast, but other than that, the building was pretty much in ruins. Not surprising, really, given its age.

Walking through the entrance, Alice hesitated, allowing her eyes time to adjust to the dark. The window was curtained by braids of ivy and tall nettles that were growing unchecked, both inside and out. She almost tripped over the old iron animal feeder that stretched across the space, as she made her way to the second room behind the chimney breast. She'd never ventured in there before, but wanted to see it all today. She needed to, so she could imagine better how Hettie must have felt, living here all alone with her little boy.

Activating the torch on her phone, Alice got as far as the opening. The light didn't touch the shadows, and the blackness was too creepy to entice her any further. Would Hettie have slept in here? Or perhaps cowered in here during a storm? She'd never know, but there was nothing to convince her that it was worth exploring further. Not when she couldn't see what might be lurking in the shadows.

Shutting off the torch, Alice hurried back to the door and stepped into the sunshine, relishing the fresh air. The mist had vanished, leaving the grass covered in tiny drops of moisture that reflected the light, twinkling like a carpet of diamonds. Where *was* Hettie's grave? She'd never been aware of its existence, and couldn't remember any of the tourist information saying anything other than that Hettie had lived in this barn with her child. There'd been no mention of a grave; it would have been the sort of thing she and Luke would have searched for with childish, ghoulish enthusiasm.

Wishing she'd brought her wellies, she began to push through the damp undergrowth that surrounded the building. She found a stick propped against the wall and used it to thrash her way through the nettles and long grass, poking at any clumps she came across, hoping she'd find something that could be a burial mound. A full circuit of the building proved fruitless, so she decided to sit for a while, and take in the atmosphere of the place. A cluster of rocks lay just beyond the path, so she sat on one of those, lost in her thoughts.

She was wondering whether there was anyone who would know more about the site of the grave – someone in the council, perhaps, or maybe Joe at the museum – when a pair of crows appeared out of nowhere, cawing and wildly flapping their wings as they circled in a sort of dance. She was delighted with the display, thinking it must be some sort of courtship ritual. But then the pair swooped down to the ground by a large patch of brambles that had caught at her jeans earlier as she'd made her way around the corner of the ruins.

The crows bobbed their heads up and down a few times, nodding at each other, scratched at the earth with their clawed feet then flew off, disappearing as quickly as they'd appeared. Alice didn't know much about crow behaviour, but this seemed very peculiar. She was intrigued and wondered what they'd been scratching at so eagerly.

She inspected the ground where the crows had been, but there was just bare earth – no sign of insects, or anything else that might have caused them to become so agitated. Grabbing the stick that she'd left propped up by the wall, Alice poked around in the brambles, but they were dense and tangled, and the stick was useless.

She was about to give up when a breeze caught at her hair, tingling her scalp, and she noticed a feather caught between the brambles, right in the middle of the patch. A black feather, just like the one that had fallen onto Patience's tomb in the graveyard. But there were crows everywhere; it wasn't surprising their feathers fell out sometimes.

Alice felt vaguely unsettled. Perhaps she should go back to the cottage, change into her wellies and find some sort of tool to help her clear these brambles away. She couldn't shake the feeling that she had to find the grave, that someone was urging her to find it, although she knew that was ridiculous. And even if she did find it, how would that help anything? She had no intention of digging into a grave; she'd probably find bones, maybe a whole skeleton, with slugs and beetles and other things slithering through the eye sockets of a skull, lacing a ribcage with a ribbon of slime.

Shuddering, she tried to banish the images from her head, but nevertheless, as she walked back towards Crag Cottage, she found herself thinking about what tools might be in the coal shed that would help, whether there'd be some shears that would cut through the brambles easily, and a spade to dig.

But as she reached the cottage, her stomach lurched. A police car was parked on the road, and Sergeant Cooper was knocking on the front door.

'I'm showing you this as you're the last person we know to have seen Mr Deegin.'

Sergeant Cooper placed a notepad on the table in front of Alice, after urging her to sit down. The notepad was sealed inside a clear plastic bag. An evidence bag.

She'd read the words over and over, but was finding it hard to make sense of them. The handwriting was sloppy, as though the note had been scribbled in haste. As though the note had been written by someone who was rushing out of their home. Out of their life.

> *I can't go on like this anymore. My thoughts have turned against me. I must find solace in that other place. There is no comfort for me on this earth.*

A solitary tear ran down Alice's cheek. 'This is crazy. Harry was a bit sad yesterday, but he wasn't... you know...' Her words fizzled out.

Sergeant Cooper placed a hand on her arm, squeezing reassuringly. 'I know what it looks like. But whatever this means, there's nothing to blame yourself for. I just need to take a statement from you, if that's okay. So we have a clearer picture of Mr Deegin's state of mind. And could I ask you not to mention this to a soul?'

Alice answered his questions, and he wrote it all down. She didn't think there was anything much she could tell him, really. Harry had been a bit miserable, not his usual cheery self, but not... Well, not obviously suicidal. Granted, he'd asked after Fleur's well-being, but even now, in light of... everything... that didn't ring any alarm bells. She sniffed back the tears.

'Have you found anything more to do with Fleur, Sergeant Cooper? It's nearly two weeks since she went missing. If she's in trouble – if she's stuck somewhere on Pedlar's Quag – she'd be dead by now, wouldn't she?'

The look of anguish on Alice's face caused Sergeant Cooper to leap up from his chair and give her an awkward hug. 'People are very resilient, Alice. A human can exist for three weeks, even more, without food. As long as she's got access to water, she'll be fine. But she's not on the Quag. We've searched several times, in every pool and hollow; we even had a diver in Crow Pond. She's not there.'

But Alice wasn't comforted. If Fleur wasn't on the Quag, and wasn't in any of her other homes, where was she? And now Harry had gone missing, too. Something strange was going on, and she felt as though she was being drawn into some sort of hideous nightmare.

CHAPTER NINETEEN

OCTOBER 1776

Whether 'tis truth or ne'er but a lie, who fibs?
With her head full of tales and a cunning so keen
Cons the crow.

There's nine of 'em. Nine men, good and true, they say, though I doubts it. Nine men to save my life – or send me to the gallows, more like. I can feel nine pairs of eyes travelling all over me as I stand afore 'em, trembling so much I fear I must look like I'm dancing a jig.

And behind me, a braying crowd, amongst 'em my ma. But not my da. I s'pose he must be drunk somewhere. 'Tis a pleasure of sorts to see her face, though her mouth is set in a hard line, and her eyes full of bitterness.

I been held in Monkstown Gaol for days now, weeks p'raps, and though I've tried to tell about my child, no one will listen. He must be so hungry and scared, and I don't rightly know if he will get out from the cave, now the tree has fallen. I don't care if they hang me. I feel dead inside for what I've done to my golden boy.

I shut my eyes and try not to faint. The smell of herbs is strong: lavender, rosemary, sprinkled all around to hide the stench of sweat, and ale, and fear. And I *am* afeared, for I know what's a-coming.

The judge is a big man, name of Jeremiah Nisbet. He puffs out his chest to show he's important, but I think he looks daft in his wig. Sir Eustace Denny is here, brother to Sir Michael from the big house, but he don't look so kindly as ol' Sir Michael, and next to him is some earl what I never heard of. They whisper and gossip like a couple of washerwomen.

There's Reverend Bacon from St Brigid's, all pompous and holy; a young constable what I never saw afore, no more'n a boy, who looks as scared as I feel; a smartly-dressed man they call *"doctor"*, who looks most uncomfortable; a man what must be a blacksmith, his hands are so rough and dark, and two more, florid types dressed in garb unbecoming for their task, I'd offer, and who they are I can't rightly say. All men, here to judge me based on what them soldiers tell 'em. Lies, all of it. But who will they believe? 'Tis a young girl's word 'gainst three soldiers and their captain, and nine more, judge and jury. Men, all of 'em. I know who they'll believe.

I hardly hear what's being said, my heart's pounding so loudly, and then the first soldier struts in like the biggest cockerel in Ma's yard. He sneers at me, and I want to scream at him, *"Go and save my boy!"* but I know 'tis too late. I try and forget the feel of his hands all over me, the stinking breath, the pain, but 'tis burnt into my head and will never leave, and that's a fact.

The soldier tells how he came upon me drowning a child, and like a hero from a story he raced to save the child, but 'twas too late. I hear mumbling behind me, and I know folks is thinking me a witch, even without no soldier telling tales. The jury sit with faces like stone, each pair of eyes drilling into me like I'm everything that's evil.

The second soldier comes in and tells the same tale. Then the third, the one what wanted to poke my boy, the one what still seems familiar. He told the worst tale of all, said I was strangling and thrashing the child before I pushed him under. I can feel the tears wetting my face as I fight to remember how we was laughing and splashing afore those hogs arrived. Me and my golden boy, the best, purest love that ever could be, and they defiled it. Defiled me.

The same man as stood up at the start stands up then, a man with a face pocked with great pimples and slashed with scars, a real ugly brute. He talks in words I don't understand, and then the gaoler stood at my side pokes my ribs and tells me to listen to the judge. The ugly man reads summat from a paper, and then the judge asks me to tell my side. I got no one to speak for me, so I must speak for myself, though my words are simple and childish.

My voice seems to have forgot how to make itself heard, but I cough and does my best. I try to tell about my golden boy, about how we'd play in Crow Pond, and about the secret cave, but the judge snorts and as good as calls me a liar. I tell about how the soldiers stood and watched, then how they came towards us, and how I told my boy to go into the cave, but I can't say no more as I get to the bit where the first soldier grabs me. I can't stop trembling, and I hear the sniggers behind, the shouts of *"Witch!"* and *"Harlot!"*

My voice is no more'n a whisper as I tell how the first two soldiers attacked me. I feel the tears, hot on my face, but I can't wipe 'em away as my hands is shackled. How did it come to this? My life weren't easy, and that's a fact, but 'twas a good life. I'm a good girl, and my boy is an innocent, but I must've done summat to anger God. Though I don't rightly believe in no God. P'raps that's where I gone wrong?

My words've dried up; I can't say no more. The ugly man says a piece, then the judge speaks with the jurymen, but I don't listen. I'm in the cave with my boy, we're laughing and singing, and the sun outside makes the water twinkle like a million stars. I wish I could turn back time so none of this would've happened, but it has, and a slap of the judge's hand on the bench brings me back to now. His face is solemn, like he's 'bout to tell off a naughty child, but then... then he reaches for summat and puts it on his head. A piece of black stuff. I know what that means, and my insides can't stay inside no longer. I throw up what little was in my tummy, and the gaoler stood next to me leaps away, cursing loudly.

I can hear shouts and clapping behind me, cheers and whistles, but in amongst 'em I hear a low sobbing. My ma, I know it is. Why didn't she sob for me when it might've made a diff'rence? 'Tis no good now. She's lost me and my golden boy both, and 'tis too late for hollow sadness.

CHAPTER TWENTY

FRIDAY 31 MAY

Alice couldn't shake the feeling of dread that was knotting her stomach. She didn't fancy going back to Hettie's Hovel, not just yet anyway, so instead she decided to lose herself in some more reading. She'd read most of Patience's diary, so she picked up another that she hadn't yet opened, its royal blue leather binding worn at the corners. The author was Mrs Octavia Denny-Hurst, and it was dated 1870.

> *1st January 1870*
>
> *On this, the first day of the year of our Lord 1870, I shall resolve to spend my time less as Mr Denny-Hurst wishes, in other words embroidering, and arranging flowers, and keeping my "pretty little mouth" free of words or opinions, and rather I shall spend more time in London, away from his haranguing and surliness.*
>
> *Would that I had been allowed to attend dear Lady Hamling's soiree in Russell Square last evening, where at least I would have dined well, become silly on champagne, and been amused by her circle of outrageous friends. Instead, we dined with the Reverend and Mrs Bertram Pratt in Monkstown, a*

couple as dull and flabby as their name suggests. There was no wine and the meat, whatever it was, was tough, the potatoes undercooked and with no butter. We were home and in our beds by ten o'clock. Life must become less dreary and more vigorous, else I swear I shall be dead from boredom before this year ends.

Alice giggled. This Octavia sounded like quite a character. She wondered what she looked like, then remembered she'd taken photos of the paintings on the staircase at the big house. Scrolling through the photos, she found Octavia's portrait. The painting was dated 1838. Octavia looked very young; she had the sweetest face, her dark hair elaborately curled, caught up in some sort of silvery clasp. Strings of pearls adorned her elegant neck, and her dress, pale, water-coloured satin, accentuated her lily-white skin and her dark, mischievous eyes. It was an exquisite painting.

Leafing through the diary, Alice read about Octavia's days. She clearly wasn't happy being a meek and dutiful wife in this quiet little pocket of England.

27th August 1870

Mr Denny-Hurst is most grumpy this morning. He has been reading about a new Act of Parliament that allows that women may now be the owner of their inheritance, with the power to command their own destiny. Poor Tobias! He can no longer tell me what I should do with my pretty little house near Hanover Square. I believe I shall make ever more use of its proximity to my beloved Regent Street, where I shall be content to spend my own money, and not be beholden to any man!

Most of the entries gossiped about London life, and Octavia's various friends and acquaintances. Many were about her forays to Regent Street, and the purchases she made there. It was very entertaining, pulling Alice out of her melancholy. But then, towards autumn, Octavia had returned to the Moor, which must have been as much of a shock to her sensibilities as it was to Alice reading it. One name leapt out, and Alice's eyes widened in surprise as she read.

1st September 1870

Poor Cora is in a pickle. She becomes overwrought whenever we have guests, and even more so when the guest is Tobias's brother. Her kitchen is in a state of sheer panic! I warrant those poor girls are exhausted from all the washing and scrubbing and chopping, and Clifford is not arriving for another ten days. I am quite exhausted myself, just listening to the constant barking of orders. Cora is, I think, much in awe of General Sir Clifford Denny-Hurst, though I find him as overbearing and oafish as his brother.

I risked a short walk this afternoon, between the showers that have been so plaguing us. As I reached the old bakehouse, a most peculiar thing occurred. A mist rose quickly from the ground, as it is wont to do, but my skin began to prickle as I approached. I swear I witnessed two figures disappearing into the building. They were slight – no more than wisps of pale air – a young girl with long, fair hair holding the hand of a small child. I truly believe that what I saw was an apparition of the poor, wretched girl who was hanged nearly a hundred years ago, and the child that she drowned. Her name was Hettie Gale, and she was buried at the side of the bakehouse, which had been her home. Her burial mound is still to be seen, beneath a blanket of weeds, its paltry wooden cross rotted with age and half hidden beneath the brambles. I do not believe in ghosts, and I chide myself for turning into one of those silly, whimpering women I so despise. But I know what my own eyes saw, and I shall not walk that path again.

Alice reread the entry several times, before gently pushing the journal away. This was the first time she'd seen, in black-and-white, the idea that Hettie's ghost truly did haunt the Moor. And it had been Octavia, one of the Denny-Hurst women no less, who'd witnessed it. Something was beginning to form in Alice's consciousness, but she couldn't quite grasp what it was, and it was starting to frustrate her.

She walked to the fridge and took out the makings of lunch. She'd not eaten breakfast, and now she was hungry. Just as she began to slice the tomatoes, there was a knock at the door.

James stood there, sheepishly, his hands clasped behind his back. She was still cross with him, and she didn't feel like making this easy for him, so she said nothing.

'Can I come in? Please?'

He looked so crestfallen, Alice couldn't keep the act up. She pulled the door wide. 'Come on, then.'

She strode back to the counter, where she continued to prepare the salad, leaving James to shut the door. She turned to see him hovering by the table, one hand plucking at the buttons on his jacket, the other thrust deep into a pocket. Her anger dissolved, just a bit, and she found herself offering him lunch.

'I'm going to eat, so you might as well join me. It's only simple.'

He took off his jacket, and slung it over the back of the chair, sitting down with a gentle sigh.

'Thank you.'

Silence stretched between them, broken only by the click of Alice's knife on the board, and the clatter of plates she pulled from the cupboard and set on the table. She put the bowl of salad between them, a barrier of sorts, then laid out bread, butter and ham.

'Help yourself.'

'Thank you, Alice. This looks lovely.'

James hesitated.

'Go on, then. Or don't you like simple food?' Alice couldn't stop the bitterness from entering her voice.

James squirmed. 'No, really, it looks lovely. It's just that I was brought up to let the lady go first.' He squirmed even more. 'That's not really the done thing these days, is it?'

Alice found herself melting a little bit at the confusion in James's eyes. His beautiful, grey eyes. 'Don't be silly. I think it's lovely when a man is gracious to a woman... if he does it out of respect, not because he thinks he's superior. I know there are some women who don't like it, but I'm not one of them.'

She sat down and began to cut chunks off the loaf of rustic rye bread, then helped herself.

'I've been reading more of the journals. Women had it pretty hard in the 1800s; they really were treated like men's possessions in those days.'

James glanced at the journal lying open at the other end of the table, as he took some bread and buttered it thickly. 'Have you found any exciting stuff, or is it all about what they ate and wore?'

'That's my point, really. These Denny-Hurst women were strong and intelligent, not just silly clotheshorses. They wanted things to be different, better, more equal.'

James put his hands up in a sign of defeat. 'Sorry. I sometimes say things which aren't quite what I mean to say.' His face had reddened, and he concentrated on his food, eating carefully and slowly.

Alice picked at her plate, her appetite gone. 'There's still no sign of Harry Deegin.'

James looked blank.

'Harry, the taxi driver. He's such a sweet man. I don't understand why he'd write something like that...'

She stopped suddenly, realising that she shouldn't have mentioned the note Sergeant Cooper had shown her.

'Write what?'

'Oh, nothing, I shouldn't have said. It was just a note.'

James's eyes widened. 'A suicide note, you mean?'

'No, really, it was nothing. Please forget I said anything.' It was Alice's turn to squirm. They'd both finished eating, so she busied herself with clearing up.

'I won't tell anyone, Alice. I might be a bit of an idiot, but I'm a man of my word.'

'Thank you.' She stacked the dirty dishes in the sink, then wiped crumbs from the table. James had pulled the open journal towards him.

'So, what's this one like, then?'

'Octavia. 1870. She seems quite lively, and she doesn't seem to have much affection for her husband.'

He turned a couple of pages, reading quickly. 'This is interesting.'

Alice leant over to read the section he was pointing to.

3rd October 1870

I have wished so hard over the last few days that Clifford would leave. He is insufferable on his own, but when paired with my dear husband! It seems they are trying to outdo each other.

But it seems my wish has been granted. Clifford left the house after luncheon yesterday, and has not been seen since. His man swears that he was given no prompts that Clifford intended to leave early, and his belongings remain here. It is most odd. Tobias is beside himself, one moment outraged, the next in the depths of despair.

I have an inexplicable sense of dread, a sensation I have never before encountered. Since I witnessed the apparition near that girl's grave, I have been unable to eat more than that which is sufficient to keep my body hale... and though I chide myself for being oversensitive, I fear that Clifford has gone the way of others before him, and that perhaps there is some truth in the old tales about evil spirits that roam the Moor. I believe I shall return to Hanover Square as soon as is seemly.

'Oh!' Alice felt a shiver run through her as she reread Octavia's words. 'Not another missing person?'

'What's the apparition she mentions?'

Alice showed James the previous entry. He laughed, a bit too heartily.

'I thought you said they *weren't* silly women?'

'Don't you believe in ghosts, then?'

'Of course not. The Moor is steeped in myths and legends. *You* know that; you've read them. All stories, made up over the centuries to scare little children.'

Alice felt a wave of irritation. James would clearly think she was a "silly woman" too, if she believed in such things. 'Well, I'm not sure whether I believe in them or not, but I do think there's something strange going on here. Something I can't explain.' She hesitated, unsure exactly how much she should tell him. But something in his expression, a softening of the eyes and a look of genuine interest, encouraged her to go on. 'I visited Hettie's Hovel earlier. I was looking for her grave.'

'Hmm. I don't think there's anything to show where that is, is there? I can't remember reading about a grave in any of the stories. I imagine, if she was buried there, any evidence would have disappeared after all this time.'

'I couldn't find anything. But there was a big patch of brambles, and a crow's feather dropped from the sky, right in the middle. I thought it was a sign–'

She stopped again, realising that she *did* sound silly, after all.

James grinned. 'A lot of people believe the stories. I think it's just a sign of a fevered imagination. But then, my imagination has never been particularly vivid.'

Alice frowned. 'But you're creative, you make things. You need a good imagination for that, surely?'

James kept his eyes firmly on the table, and his face reddened. He seemed about to say something, but instead he worked his mouth as though chewing, his brows knitted together in thought. He suddenly delved one hand into the pocket of the jacket he'd slung over the chair, and brought out a small object wrapped in blue paper. He thrust it towards Alice.

'I made this for you.'

Hesitantly taking the object, Alice looked quizzical. 'Oh, thank you! What is it?'

'Best open it and see.'

She carefully peeled the sticking tape from the joins of the paper, unwrapping the present and folding the paper back neatly.

It was a small wooden box. The sides were carved with loops of ivy, and Alice gasped as she inspected the tiny, delicate leaves. The lid bore a crow, a feather tucked into its large, sharp beak, its eye so real Alice felt it was watching her.

'This is amazing, James! Beautiful. Did you really make it yourself? Thank you so much.' She turned the box over and over in her hands, then opened it to reveal a pair of silver earrings shaped like delicate feathers, nestled into the lining of burgundy satin. She gasped again. 'Oh, they're lovely! How did you know about the feathers?'

'The feather in the bramble patch? What's so important about that?'

Alice realised she hadn't mentioned the other feather that had fallen onto Patience's tomb, and she felt a bit daft. 'Oh, nothing. Feathers just seem to be a thing for me at the moment. This box is exquisite; did you really make it? You're so clever.

Why don't you make lots, and sell them in the shop? The tourists would go mad for them.'

James sighed. 'No time, really. What with running the shop, visiting Dad. And I'm not convinced they're good enough to sell.'

'Well, I think they are. You should have more faith in yourself.' Inwardly, Alice grimaced. She was a fine one to talk about faith and self-confidence. She placed the box carefully on the table. 'You said the box you gave Fleur was carved with shells. I didn't know she had a thing for seashells.'

'I don't expect she did. That box was one that I'd made a while ago.' James began to look uncomfortable.

'So you didn't make it specially for her?' Alice felt a pang of triumph, which quickly faded into shame.

'No. It was just lying around.' James looked embarrassed. 'I wanted to impress her.'

'Oh.' Alice fidgeted with the wrapping paper, a thought tugging at her that she couldn't quite decode. 'And did it? Impress her, I mean.'

James looked uncomfortable, sadness clouding his eyes. 'I doubt it. I don't think the box was to her taste, and I don't think I was, either. She probably dumped the box in a bin somewhere, and she'd have dumped me too, if she hadn't–'

Alice sprang up from her chair. The thought that had been niggling at her had suddenly found clarity. 'This paper. Did you wrap Fleur's box in the same stuff?'

'Yes, I think so. Why?'

Alice walked towards the door that led to the scullery, excitement coarsening her voice. 'Come and see.'

She heard the scrape of wood on flagstone as James rose from his chair, and paused so he could follow. Opening the door to the coal shed, feeling not the slightest flicker of fear of the dark or the spiders, she led James to the outside door, unlocked it and dragged it open, then showed him the bins. She triumphantly opened the black one, and pointed to its contents. James looked confused as he peered inside.

'The paper. See? Blue wrapping paper, the same as you used for my box. This must be the paper from the box you gave Fleur.'

James looked baffled. 'I guess it must be.'

'But don't you see? The box isn't here! Fleur didn't throw it away, just the paper. And it's not anywhere in the cottage; I've checked every nook and cranny. Fleur must have taken the box when she left. It meant enough to her, to take it with her.'

James's face brightened, and Alice felt a tinge of jealousy, but she was right, she knew it.

'If we can find the box, we'll find Fleur.'

But something else was bothering Alice, another thought she couldn't quite grasp.

Back at the kitchen table, mugs of tea steaming between them, Alice and James sat and stared at their hands, neither knowing what to say next. It was James who eventually broke the silence. 'I really am sorry, Alice. I'm not very good at being sociable. Not very experienced with how to talk to women. I say stupid things that I don't mean.'

Alice waved her hands generally in his direction. 'Don't worry. I'll try and remember that in future.'

She reddened as she realised she expected there to be a future with James. She'd be leaving the Moor on Sunday, though she hadn't yet bought a train ticket. She'd only asked for a week off work; she had to go back on Monday. The week had flown by so quickly, she'd lost all track of time.

'I have to leave on Sunday.'

'Oh.'

Did James look a little crestfallen, or was it just her imagination running riot?

'There's nothing else I can do in the search for Fleur. Sergeant Cooper's got people making enquiries with all the contacts on her phone, the Quag's been thoroughly searched. I don't really think I've been any help at all, actually; I'm not sure it was worth me coming here.'

'Don't say that. Fleur would appreciate you being here. If she knew...' He tailed off, looking uncomfortable again.

'I just don't get it. She would have taken her handbag, her phone and purse, if she'd been planning to travel somewhere else. Her credit cards haven't been used since she disappeared, so how could she have travelled anyway? It doesn't make sense.'

James just sat, fiddling with his fingers, his expression unreadable.

'What did you two argue about, James?'

He looked even more uncomfortable, squirming in his chair. 'It was nothing. She's very temperamental, just took something I said the wrong way.'

Alice found that very plausible. He'd already put his foot in his mouth several times with her. He must have been way out of his depth with Fleur.

'What was it you said?'

James stood up, the shrill sound of his chair scraping on the flagstones slashing the silence, his eyes blackened with anger. 'It's none of your business. I've told the police about our conversation, but it's private.'

With that, he grabbed his jacket and strode towards the door. Alice was furious; of *course* it was her business. Her cousin was missing, probably because of what this man had said. 'James!'

But it was too late; he had gone, slamming the door behind him. The air in the kitchen had become thick with bitterness, Alice's emotions lurching out of control, and she had no idea how to cope with them. Confrontation was something she'd always struggled with; she'd tried all her life to avoid arguments, as she never knew what to say, finding it easier to keep her head down. She didn't want to argue with James; she barely knew him, after all. But he was infuriating, and he was the last person to see Fleur. He must know more than he was telling her. And perhaps more than he was telling the police?

CHAPTER TWENTY-ONE
FRIDAY 31 MAY

Picking up the little carved box, Alice opened it and looked at the earrings again. They were so pretty, but James's behaviour had put her in a sour mood. She closed the box and put it in a drawer. She might try them on later, when she was feeling calmer.

Fresh air was what she needed, and she remembered her plan to find some tools to help her look for Hettie's grave. After all, Octavia had mentioned in her diary that Hettie's burial mound was still to be seen, so Alice's gut feeling that she was buried close to her home was correct.

Braving the coal shed again, she found a rusty pair of shears and some thick gardening gloves that were brittle with age, strewn with greasy cobwebs. That would do; it was better than nothing. Donning her welly boots and stuffing her rain jacket and the gloves into her backpack, she left the cottage in a brighter frame of mind, swinging the shears as she walked. James might think she was being ridiculous, but what did his opinion matter? He'd said his argument with Fleur was none of her business; well, *this* was none of *his* business.

Following the path to Hettie's Hovel, Alice breathed in the

untainted air, delighting in the warmth of the afternoon, letting loose her worries. She had a purpose, and that made her feel better. As she approached the ruined bakehouse a soft breeze plucked at her hair, the leaves on the trees above rattled and shivered, and the dust on the path swirled in miniature whirlwinds. She put her backpack down, pulling out the rain jacket. She didn't think it would rain, but the jacket might save her arms from getting scratched.

The thicket of brambles looked dense and impenetrable, and Alice wasn't particularly strong, but she was determined to give it a go. Taking the shears and pulling them open and closed a few times to loosen the rust, she approached the edge of the patch. Thankfully, the blades still retained some sharpness, and they made easy work of cutting through the tough stems. Once she'd got into a rhythm, pulling the cut brambles from the clump and piling them well away from the path, Alice found the work quite pleasurable.

After half an hour or so, the patch was cleared, just the gnarly bits at the bottom left where she couldn't pull them from the compacted soil. Putting down the shears and stripping off the gloves, Alice sat on a rock to take a breather. The wind had died down, a strange stillness thickening the air. There was no birdsong, no rustle of leaves, and she barely dared to breathe for fear of disturbing the utter silence.

But clearing the brambles was just part of her task; she needed to find Hettie's grave, so her rest didn't last long. Using the closed shears, she poked about in the bramble stumps, jabbing into any exposed earth in the hope of finding something that would mark the site. A clang startled her as the shears hit stone, but closer inspection found nothing more than a few pebbles clustered together. Was there anything here, or had she been fooled by her own febrile imagination? She was about to give up, when a breeze whispered through her hair, and something black flashed across her field of vision. Another crow feather had dropped from nothingness; the hairs rose on the back of her neck.

Stooping to pick the feather up, Alice spotted something half buried in the soil. She instinctively felt it might be something important, so she put on the gloves and gently clawed at the earth. What emerged looked like tiny, shiny red eggs. Thinking it might be the spawn of some insect, Alice gingerly poked at them, then realised with a start that the "eggs" were strung together. In fact, they were not eggs at all, but beads on a necklace.

Taking off the glove so she could better feel what she was doing, she pulled the string of beads from the ground, and wiped away some of the dirt. They were oval, made of red glass, and linked together with gold-coloured wire, the two strands joined with a heart-shaped clasp. The necklace looked old, but that was probably just because of the dirt. Alice decided to take it home and give it a wash. It had probably been dropped by a tourist gawping at Hettie's Hovel, but still, it would be a shame to leave it lying there.

Octavia Denny-Hurst had mentioned a wooden cross marking Hettie's grave in her journal, but Alice knew that would be long gone all these years later. She shivered, and decided she'd seen enough. She had no spade to dig with, and in any case, she was not inclined to disturb Hettie's remains – if they were truly anywhere near there.

Picking up the shears and gloves, hoisting the backpack over her shoulder, and with the necklace safely in her pocket, she left the destroyed bramble patch, feeling a little guilty about the mess she'd made, and turned to begin her walk back to the cottage. But as she turned, something flashed, right at the edge of her vision. A light, or movement, she couldn't determine which. She snapped her head around, but there was nothing, just the blackness beyond the open door of the bakehouse, and the pile of brambles.

Feeling increasingly uneasy, her stomach fluttering, Alice walked quickly back to Crag Cottage. It must've been a bird she'd seen, flying into the ruins to its nest, or perhaps it was her imagination working overtime again. Still, even though the strange silence that had surrounded her whilst she'd worked had erupted back into the normal sounds of the countryside, she felt troubled by the scampering of unseen creatures in the undergrowth, and almost ran the last few hundred metres to the safety of home.

Alice started work on the necklace as soon as she got back to Crag Cottage. She was very careful, delicately scrubbing at the red glass and the gold wire with an old toothbrush she'd found in the bathroom cupboard. It now looked quite beautiful and, Alice suspected, very old and possibly valuable. Not tourist tat at all. It lay on a bed of paper towels on the kitchen table, the deep velvety red of its stones glistening under the light. Alice felt sure that the wire was real gold, and she wondered whether she should hand it in. Perhaps she'd ask Sergeant Cooper about it next time she saw him. For now, she enjoyed the triumph of having found something, even though she couldn't be sure it was to do with Hettie's grave.

A shower revived her, but she still felt tired and out of sorts, so she made herself comfortable at the table and spread the journals out in front of her. She settled on a lovely rose-coloured volume, written by Violet Denny-Hurst, and dated 1895. Checking the images on her phone, Alice realised Violet was the pretty blonde woman with a shy smile, in the salmon pink dress, who she'd liked the look of. But the first entry didn't bode well for an entertaining read; Violet sounded a bit miserable.

1st January 1895

It is a new year and, it seems, the year will bring naught but adversity. The passage I read as I dipped into my Bible was thus:

"When thou passest through the waters, I will be with thee; and through the rivers, they shall not overflow thee; when thou walkest through the fire, thou shalt not be burned; neither shall the flame kindle upon thee."

Oh Isaiah, would that I had chosen better. I shall attain forty-five years of age in a few weeks, and I fear my happiest days are far behind me.

Flipping on through the pages, it became clear to Alice that Violet was a bit tight-lipped and narrow-minded. By the time she'd got halfway through, she was convinced this woman was not someone she'd have got on with.

2nd June 1895

I am somewhat aghast. Countess Dalrymple has arrived from London, and is staying for a few nights, at Charles's invitation. She brought me a gift, a book, but I have no notion what to do with it. I certainly shall not read it. It is by that Irish man, the playwright Oscar Wilde. I cannot bring myself to speak his name; it is, indeed, hard enough to write. He is a base man, even now rotting in prison, and rightly so. Countess Dalrymple is, shall I say, overly flamboyant, and I suspect we will find little in common. I shall simply continue with my cross-stitch and feign ignorance, should she attempt conversation.

She was about to give up and look for someone more

entertaining, when she spotted some entries that hinted about another missing person.

> 8th June 1895
> Following her breakfast, which she took alone as I affected a headache, the Countess donned her cloak and riding boots, and determined to go for a bracing walk. I declined, as rain was threatening and I did not wish to risk my health, which has become a little delicate of late. It is now past luncheon, and she has not yet returned. Should I worry? I believe I shall wait a while longer, and then instruct the servants to find her and escort her home. Charles will be most annoyed with me if the Countess has encountered some small misfortune.

> 9th June 1895
> I cannot rise from my bed. Countess Dalrymple is missing, and no trace of her has been found. There is quite a commotion downstairs, with the police and half the village of Dennybridge continuing to search Pigswhistle Clump and Pedlar's Quag. The Earl himself has curtailed his business in Scotland, and is on his way to Nether Dennyfold. I have no notion what I will say to the man. His wife is missing. Is it all my fault? I believe I shall expire before he crosses our threshold.

Alice couldn't remember whether this Countess Dalrymple had been mentioned in the display in the museum, so she checked her phone. Sure enough, there it was:

A COUNTESS ADRIFT

In June 1895, a visitor to The Manor House in Nether Dennyfold, was reported as missing. Countess Bethesda Dalrymple was staying with Mr and Mrs Charles Denny-Hurst, when she failed to return from a walk. Her route towards Pedlar's Quag was witnessed by two locals, brothers Jimmy and Jed Ferris, who apparently watched as the Countess, dressed in "a posh cloak, mister, an' a big hat wiv fevvers" disappeared into a rising mist. A search was undertaken, but no trace of the Countess was ever found. Her husband the Earl of Huntesford travelled to the Moor from Scotland, where he joined the search and was heard to say, wearily, 'Perhaps at last I shall be free of that woman's unbridled passion.'

Alice giggled. The Countess sounded much more fun than the morose Violet. But something was niggling at her, again; something about these people who had gone missing. She couldn't quite put a finger on it. Grabbing her notepad and a pencil, she leafed through the journals she'd read, and jotted down all the names of the missing people she'd come across so far.

- *Judge Jeremiah Nisbet, the judge at Hettie's trial, disappeared in 1786*
- *Jack Malaface, the young farrier, disappeared in 1821*
- *The Reverend Peter Bailey-Bew, disappeared in 1910*
- *Sgt Fred Middleton, disappeared in 1910, while looking for Rev Bailey-Bew*
- *General Sir Clifford Denny-Hurst, disappeared in 1870*
- *Countess Dalrymple, disappeared in 1895*

All of them had been written about in the journals except for the judge; she'd read about him in the museum. She made a note to search for a journal dated from 1786; she'd have to go and see Genevieve quickly, before Finbar returned. She'd do that first thing tomorrow morning; it was too late now.

CHAPTER TWENTY-TWO

NOVEMBER 1776

Whether 'tis truth or ne'er but a lie, who dies?
With her breast pierced with loss and her feathers all torn
Drops the crow.

The moment's here – my final moment. I'm so numb, I can't feel nothing but the rough cord 'round my neck, scratching and chafing. When I opens my eyes I see a jeering crowd, strangers mostly, though there's one or two what I recognise: Reverend Bacon from St Brigid's, looking as pompous as ever, and that young constable what was on the jury, the one what looked so scared. He looks even more afeared now, poor lad. I try to catch his eye, but he don't look at me. He *won't* look at me.

I look up and see the branches, and the rope what'll bring me my end. 'Tis the Hanging Tree in Monkstown, a place of horror to all kiddies what live on the Moor. I never did see it afore, as my da never took me further'n Dennybridge, but if me or my sis was naughty, all we'd hear was, *"Wait till you see the Hanging Tree!"* I think 'tis a beautiful tree, a great spreading oak what must be a hundred years old, 'tis so big. But I wonder how many souls are snared in its branches, and whether its acorns hold the dying thoughts of people like me.

I search for my ma or pa, but they're not to be seen. I don't blame 'em; who wants to see their child hung for murder? All I see is ugly faces, screaming mouths, hate and bile, so I shut my eyes and think my last thoughts.

I think 'bout my child, my golden boy with his blue, blue eyes and sunny smile. I try not to think 'bout how scared he must've been, alone in the cave, and how hungry, but I know, deep in my heart, that he'd not have survived long without his Ma, and who knows what damage the storm did muster? I squeeze my eyes tight and we're back in Crow Pond, and the sun is warming our backs and we're laughing and singing, and the world is safe.

But a shout wakes me from my dream, and I snap open my eyes to see a man who I take to be the hangman, looming in front of me, faced towards the crowd. Dressed all in black, he is, and looks the part. He turns to me then and starts to pull a hood over my head. I never did see eyes so full of contempt, and I pities him, for all his hatred of me. I wouldn't like to spend my days killing people, and that's a fact.

But just afore the hood blinds me, I spot a face I know. Right at the back, away from the jeering crowd; it's a face so black and so beautiful, I feel a surge of joy in my bosom. 'Tis my Rose, a look of horror and sadness mingling with her tears. She looks straight into my eyes, piercing my soul, and she blows me a kiss... and after that I'm ready for my end.

The rope 'round my neck tightens. Then, all of a sudden, my feet are off the ground, and my neck feels like it's broken in two, and I struggle to breathe. I can't hear no more, and I don't care 'bout the pain, or the warmth on my legs as I piss myself. I just think 'bout my boy, until my body stops struggling and the world goes black.

THE HANGING OF HETTIE GALE

I'm s'posed to let my soul descend to hell, but I can't. I don't rightly believe in no God, so p'raps there's no heaven or hell, but my soul should go somewhere, flying off, or laid to rest, or some such. But I can't let it go.

I hear my ma, what must've been hidden in the crowd after all, begging with the hangman to let her and Da take my body to be buried at home. 'Course, I can't be buried in no churchyard, and that suits me fine. I never been in St Brigid's and I don't want to start now. The hangman wants to sell me to doctors what'll cut me up into little pieces and study my innards, but my ma's pleading works, and I'm took away in a cart. 'Tis a strange feeling, to know what's happening all around, but to be stuck in a body what has no life. To see the blackening sky, but not feel the chill of the first snowflakes as they fall all around; to hear the crow as he sings his lament, but have no voice to sing back to him.

At the end, my body, in its rough wooden coffin, is placed, quite tenderly, into a hole what my da must've dug, right near my barn. 'Tis a homecoming of sorts. My ma and da, Greta and little Daniel, dear Rose, and even Miss Patience and young Charles from the big house, stand and say prayers, and Rose sings a sad song, and then they each throw a little earth, which clatters gently on the coffin lid. Then they all go, 'cept Da, who carries on with the shovelling until I'm covered up.

Then he pulls summat from his pocket; 'tis a little wooden cross, and twisted all around the cross is a necklace of red glass beads. I recognise 'em! They are my ma's, and I used to play with 'em when I was a tiddler, pretending I was a posh lady and all. 'Twas Miss Patience what gave Ma the necklace, but I never did know why. Ma told me my da mustn't know of the beads, but now he has 'em and I s'pose that must mean Ma don't need 'em, and that's a good thing.

He pushes the cross gently into the earth, right above where my head is. ('Tis so strange to see my own, dead head 'neath the earth; the feeling don't sit right.) And then he stands awhile, swaying from the drink, tears clouding his eyes, and he whispers, 'I'm so sorry, Hettie. So sorry.'

And that pleases me; I can at last forgive my da, as he knows what he done was wrong, and he's sorry for it.

But I can't forgive the others. The ones what hanged me for a murder I never committed. The soldiers what defiled me and then lied to save their selves. I can't forgive them. I can't rest 'til someone pays the price for my boy's life.

CHAPTER TWENTY-THREE

SATURDAY 1 JUNE

Alice had been at Crag Cottage for a week. She should be getting back to work on Monday, but she couldn't leave, not yet. There'd still been no trace of Fleur, but something was balling itself up inside her, knotting her stomach and muddling her thoughts. There was something she wasn't quite grasping, but despite trying her hardest to make sense of everything, she was no closer to understanding, and she knew she had to stay here. For a while longer, anyway.

She'd sent her boss John an email at eleven the previous night, hoping he'd be the type to check his inbox over the weekend. She was pretty sure he was, despite the distractions of the girl from comms, and she was right. There was a reply that he'd sent at six thirty this morning:

```
Hi Alice.
    Sorry to hear you haven't found your
cousin yet. Yes of course, take another
week if you need to. I'll let your team
know. I think Sharon is sorting out your
workload, so they'll all do a bit. Don't
```

worry about that; you focus on your cousin. Keep me updated.

All the best, John.

The thing with the girl from comms must be going well, Alice thought with a grin. John was never usually that easygoing. So she didn't have to worry about going back just yet. She had time to try and figure out whatever it was that was giving her the jitters, and what the link was to Fleur's disappearance.

Her plan for the day was to visit Genevieve to see if she could find any more journals, particularly one from 1786 that might give more details about the disappearance of Judge Nisbet. Perhaps it would be another of Patience's; hopefully she was still alive ten years after Hettie was hanged.

After that, Alice would walk to Dennybridge and get a bus to Monkstown. She badly needed some more clothes; there was no washing machine in the cottage, and she'd only brought enough for a few days. Her jeans were still stained with mud and starting to stink, and she really couldn't raid Fleur's wardrobe anymore. The clothes weren't right for this part of the world, and anyway, Fleur would need something clean to wear when she was found – *if* she was found.

It was quite early in the day, still before nine o'clock, but Alice thought Genevieve would probably be up and about, and she needed to put a stop to the negative thoughts that were plaguing her. As she closed the door behind her, she thought she spotted a car parked further down the lane, near the path that led to Hettie's Hovel. Probably tourists, so nothing to concern herself with. It was a public right of way, after all, though she couldn't help feeling as though it was her own private place. She walked quickly to the big house, wishing she'd worn something a bit warmer; there was an unexpected chill in the air.

A rap on the lionhead knocker brought a swift response; the look on Genevieve's face when she opened the door was one of pure panic, swiftly followed by intense relief.

'Oh my goodness. Alice. Thank heavens it's you. Come in.'

'Who did you think it was?'

Genevieve groaned. 'I thought it must be Finbar. I'm expecting him to arrive today; not until late afternoon, but he's been a bit weird in his messages to me this time, so nothing would surprise me.'

Alice followed Genevieve through to the kitchen, noticing that the dead plant on the hall table had been removed, and there was a sweet smell of polish wafting through the air, mixed with the sharp tang of coffee.

'Fancy a coffee, or would you prefer tea? I needed the strong stuff this morning.'

'A coffee would be good, actually, thanks.' Alice sat down at the table and watched admiringly as Genevieve bustled around, rinsing and refilling the cafetière. She certainly had a sense of style, her hair caught up in a scarf, multiple bangles adorning her freckled arms. She wasn't afraid to wear colours, and clashing colours, at that. Alice felt dull and insipid in comparison. She vowed not to buy grey or navy clothes ever again.

'Why are you so worried about Finbar coming back, Genevieve? Is he that much of a monster? And how has he been "weird"?'

Putting a chunky mug of coffee in front of Alice, and grabbing another for herself, Genevieve sat down and began to sip the hot liquid. 'You met Finbar when you were younger?'

'Well, yes, sort of. I never actually spoke to him, but Fleur... You know, my cousin, who's... She really fancied him, so she made me come up here to spy on him over the wall. She tried to flirt with him, but he was always too busy fiddling with his bike. It was only that one year, though.'

'Hmm. I didn't know him when he was younger, but I gather he had a wild streak as a teenager. He became one of those privileged, bad-mannered young men who think they're entitled to the world. So different from his brother.' Genevieve looked sad. 'I don't suppose you knew Jenson either?'

Alice shook her head. 'No, I didn't. How did you meet them?'

A big sigh escaped Genevieve's mouth, and Alice thought perhaps she shouldn't have asked, but then it all came flooding out. Genevieve told her how she'd met Jenson ten years ago, at an exhibition of her work. He'd come along with a friend and, despite the big difference in their ages, they'd hit it off immediately. He'd asked her out, and that had been it.

'I was thirteen years older than him, but Jenson always had an old head on a young body. I hadn't had much luck with men my own age, but there was something so sweet and... I don't know... *trusting* about him.' She looked deep into her mug. 'He was my one true love.'

'So you only had five years together.' Alice found this deeply upsetting. Genevieve was such a lovely, funny woman; to lose the man she'd loved must have been devastating.

'Yep. The best five years of my life. The cancer took him very quickly; three months from diagnosis to...' A tear trickled down her face.

'I'm so sorry, Genevieve. I didn't mean to upset you.'

'Well, I'm lucky, really. I've been able to channel my emotions into my painting. And Finbar felt sorry for me. I'd pretty much moved in here with Jenson, you see, then suddenly I had no reason to be here. That's why he lets me come and housesit when he's away.' She paused. 'Jenson's always here with me.'

Alice shivered, and thought it was probably time to change

the subject. 'D'you think I could borrow a couple more journals? There's one in particular I'd love to see.'

Genevieve frowned. 'What is it you find so fascinating? I can't imagine much happened around here that makes for exciting reading.'

Alice told Genevieve about the people who had gone missing, and how she felt an urge to find out more. 'And I don't know why, but I keep feeling that there's some sort of connection between the missing people, Hettie Gale, and Fleur. Does that sound daft?'

Genevieve chuckled. 'Not at all. Don't forget, I'm a mad woman who doesn't believe in guardian angels or ghosts, but also thinks her dead lover is still hanging around.'

Alice laughed too, the tension broken, the sadness gone.

'By all means. But take them now, and let's hope Finbar doesn't notice they're missing. I'm guessing he's forgotten all about them; I can't imagine him being interested in long-dead women's ramblings.'

While they finished their coffee, Alice gazed around the kitchen, wondering if Patience had ever sat in here, chatting to the cook and the maids. She thought probably not, and anyway, perhaps this hadn't been the original kitchen. But for all Patience's correctness, she was beginning to feel a strong connection to the woman, and felt that reading her journals might provide the answers to some of her questions.

In the library, when Genevieve had unlocked the smutty cupboard door, the pair sat cross-legged on the floor and carefully took all the journals out. It seemed that some, pushed to the back, had suffered badly over the years. Bindings had rotted, and several of them had become unreadable, the mould extensive.

'What a shame.' Alice felt a real pang of loss; old books should be treated with respect, especially when they were part of a family history. 'I can't even read the names on some of these. All those memories, gone to waste.'

She piled all the unreadable journals to one side, and concentrated on the ones that could be of interest. She found some more that were written by Florence, Iris and Octavia, then there were others: Elizabeth, Emilia and Verity. Some names she recognised, others she didn't. She made a pile of journals that she thought might be of use, but was beginning to think she'd never find the one she'd really come for. There were a few more tucked away at the edge, and as she picked up the first of these, a shiver ran from her shoulders to the tips of her fingers. She looked at the name and date: *Patience Denny-Hurst, 1786*.

She ignored the shiver and smiled broadly as she added it to the top of her pile, then carefully put the others back in the cupboard, the mouldy ones well to the rear.

'I wish I could tell Finbar to take more care of these, but I guess he wouldn't take too kindly to being told what to do?'

The women stood up, and Genevieve produced a carrier bag for the journals. 'No, I don't think he would.' She locked the cupboard and put the key back in its drawer. It reminded Alice of what had happened last time she was in this room. She pointed to the desk.

'Have you ever seen that inkpot fall over for no apparent reason?'

Genevieve gave her a strange look. 'No, but then I don't ever come in here. Why do you ask?'

'Oh, nothing.' Alice felt silly, but couldn't shake off the feeling that someone was watching them. 'It happened last time I was here. I think this house needs new windows; there must be quite a draught coming in.'

Genevieve accompanied Alice to the front door, frowning as though in deep thought. 'Take care of those, won't you?'

'Of course I will. Thank you so much. And good luck when Finbar arrives. Will you go back home straight away?'

Genevieve sighed. 'Yes, I guess so. I've packed all my painting stuff away. I'll leave the canvases here, though. I'll be back as soon as he's buggered off back to London.'

Alice thought she detected a faint whiff of bitterness in Genevieve's voice.

'Well, I'll miss you. It's been lovely meeting you. I shall have to go back to London soon. If they don't find Fleur...'

Genevieve gave Alice a big hug. 'She must be somewhere. Don't ever give up hope.' She let go and delved into her jeans pocket. 'Here, my card. That's a bit pretentious, isn't it?' She burst into gales of laughter, as she thrust the brightly coloured business card into Alice's hand. 'It's got my email and phone number. Keep in touch and let me know when you find her.'

'I will, thank you. And let me know if you have any more exhibitions. I'd love to come and see your finished work.'

Genevieve winked. 'I will. I have a feeling you won't be staying away for long, anyway.'

Alice wandered back to Crag Cottage, carefully hugging the carrier bag that held the journals, wondering what Genevieve had meant. She knew she'd have to go home to London and back to her boring job sooner rather than later, but she really didn't want to think about it right now. That must be how Genevieve felt, having to go back to the city. This place had put a spell on them both, and it would be hard to say goodbye.

Monkstown was busy. Alice hated crowds; being jostled by enthusiastic tourists, having her toes trodden on by oblivious children, and getting hemmed in by slow-moving pensioners was not her idea of fun. But she needed new clothes, and

Monkstown had more choice of clothes shops than anywhere else, bar the city, and she didn't fancy going there. She was just leaving a clothes shop, bags in hand, when she heard a half-familiar voice behind her.

'Hey, Alice!'

It was Joe from the museum, his long white beard unmistakable, a big grin on his face.

'Hello, Joe. How are you?'

'Crow knows I'm as good as I could be, not as bad as I should be!' He chuckled, and winked, then his expression became serious. 'Any news yet? About your cousin?'

Alice shook her head. 'Not yet. But like someone said earlier, I mustn't give up hope.'

'Wise words. There's always hope in this seemingly hopeless world. You just sometimes have to look a bit harder.'

He scratched at the beard. A younger Alice would have expected bits of food to fall out, like that character in the children's book by Roald Dahl. She smiled at the very idea.

'So, how's the museum? Have you been busy?'

'Busy enough, I'd say. Ah, sorry!' He jumped out of the way of a woman with a pushchair. 'But I'm glad I've bumped into you. I went to the... *Sorry!*' Another near miss, this time with a wheelchair. 'Look, I've got a few minutes, and there's something I need to tell you. We're in the way here. D'you fancy a coffee?'

Alice happily accepted the invitation, and they made their way to Bean, the coffee shop she'd visited a few days ago. It was busy, but there was an empty table in the corner.

'Gamfer! What are you doing, skiving off work?' Maddie appeared from behind the counter, a huge smile on her face. She did a double take. 'Hello. Alice, isn't it? You met my granddad then?'

'I did, thank you, Maddie. He's been a real help.'

'And I reckon I'm going to be even more of a help when I've told Alice something I found out yesterday.'

Alice was intrigued, but tried to be patient while they ordered their coffee.

Maddie went to make the drinks, and Alice waited for Joe to tell her what he'd wanted to tell her, but he just chatted about nothing in particular until the coffees and his toast arrived. He wolfed it down, licking his buttery fingers when he'd eaten the lot, then he started on the coffee.

'Well, then,' he began, between sips. 'I went to the council offices yesterday, to research some new stuff for the dungeon. They've been clearing out their paper archives, getting everything onto digital, or whatever it is. I'm not very up on that sort of stuff.'

Alice smiled. 'I know what you mean.'

'Well, there's some old court papers that've been missing from our exhibition, and my contact reckoned they'd found them, stuffed away under the floorboards in an unused room.' He shook his head. 'The council's always moaning about lack of money, but they've got rooms in those buildings that haven't seen the light of day since the crow knows when. Shocking.'

Nodding her agreement, Alice silently urged Joe to get to the point.

'I found some excellent records that will add meat to the bones of the exhibits, if you get my drift. One of them was a transcript of the original court record of the trial of Hettie Gale.'

Alice's heart rate quickened at the mention of Hettie. 'Go on.'

'That old record's been missing for as long as I've been around, I'd say. So it was quite a surprise to see it, though it doesn't tell anything that we don't already know.' He paused, for effect it seemed. 'But there was another paper there, too. Something very unexpected. Something you'll find extremely interesting.'

'Why? What is it?'

'I had them give me a copy, and I asked my colleague Molly Webb to decipher it; the writing's very hard to read. She typed me out a copy. If you come to the museum, I can show you.'

'Yes, please. That would be wonderful.'

'Can I ask you something, Alice? Why are you so interested in Hettie Gale?' Joe gave her a quizzical look. 'Seems a bit odd, when you're here to look for your cousin.'

Alice felt her face reddening; Joe was right, she should be searching for Fleur, not faffing around looking for information about Hettie.

'I... This sounds silly, I know... but I've been becoming increasingly convinced that there's some sort of connection between Hettie, and Fleur's disappearance.' She kept her eyes down, unable to face Joe's mirth as he roared with laughter.

'I didn't have you down as a ghost hunter.' He stopped laughing and his expression became serious. 'What makes you think there's a link?'

'I don't know, really. A few things have happened that make me think Hettie's trying to tell me something. Silly things, which probably don't mean anything of the sort.' She could feel her face burning with embarrassment, and her voice trailed off to a whisper. 'I just don't think she was guilty. I think she was hanged for a crime she didn't commit.'

Joe gazed at Alice with an unreadable expression. 'Hmm, that's interesting. You definitely need to see what I found. Come on, drink up and I'll show you.'

Alice was truly intrigued now, so she gulped down the last of her coffee, and the pair walked out of the café, Joe shouting a cheery goodbye to Maddie as they left. They began to walk towards the museum, when a police car drove past, then stopped and reversed.

Briony leaned out of the window. 'Hi, Alice. I was just on my way to Nether Dennyfold. Can I have a word?'

'Hello, Briony. Erm, yes, of course.' She looked at Joe. 'Could I come and see your documents later? Or tomorrow, maybe. I expect this is important.'

Joe smiled and told Alice to go to the museum and ask for him whenever she had the time. 'I think you'll find it very interesting.'

Silently cursing Briony for delaying her visit to the museum, Alice chided herself for being so selfish. There might be news about Fleur, after all.

'Jump in the car and I'll drive somewhere a bit quieter.'

Briony drove out of town, stopping in the small car park near Greyfriars Priory.

'How are you, Alice?'

'Fine, thanks. What's this all about? Have you found Fleur?' Alice couldn't stop a note of excited anticipation from entering her voice.

'No, not yet. But we have found something.'

Alice's heartbeat raced. 'What?'

'Well, it may not be Fleur's, but we've found a shoe.'

'A shoe? Where?'

Briony took a deep breath. 'Pedlar's Quag. Sergeant Cooper sent me and PC Robbins to have one last search of the area earlier this morning.'

Alice nodded; that would explain the car parked by the path to Hettie's Hovel. Not a tourist at all, but the police.

'We got quite excited, because we found a pile of brambles that had been hacked away by the hovel, but there was nothing there.'

Alice blushed deeply. 'That was me. I'm sorry, I was searching for...' She felt too embarrassed to tell the truth, even to the police. 'I lost my phone. I thought I might have dropped it there.'

'Did you find it?'

'No, it was in my bag all the time.'

Briony frowned, clearly unconvinced. 'Anyway, we searched the Quag quite extensively and after a couple of hours, we'd got to Crow Pond and still found nothing, so we were just about to leave. Then Barry... PC Robbins... said he thought he'd seen something in one of the pools near the pond. We both fished about with sticks, and then he pulled it up. A woman's shoe, size seven, red sole. You know, one of those designer types: high heel, shiny. Expensive looking, even when caked in mud and weeds.'

Alice was stunned. That sounded exactly like the sort of shoe Fleur would have been wearing. 'Have you spoken to James... Mr Turnkey?'

Briony gave a sly smile. 'You can call him James. We don't need to be formal.'

'He'd be able to tell you if it was Fleur's, surely?'

'We did ask him, yes, but he couldn't be one hundred per cent sure. Apparently, he doesn't notice details like the shoes a woman is wearing.' A lift of the eyebrows was all that was needed to tell Alice what Briony thought about that.

'But it could be Fleur's. She's a size seven, and she loved – loves designer stuff.' Alice felt her spirits lift, then plummet as the consequences of finding a solitary shoe sunk in.

'It could well be. Sergeant Cooper has ordered another full search of the area. We missed this first time around, perhaps we've missed something else.'

'Can I help, Briony? I feel so useless.'

'Thanks, but probably best to leave it to the experts. The Quag is a dangerous place if you don't know what you're doing. That's why we haven't asked the locals to help; we don't want anyone else to go missing. Can I give you a lift home?'

Alice had lost interest in clothes shopping, and didn't have the heart to visit the museum, so she said yes. Briony chatted about this and that, keeping a deliberately cheerful tone. As she carefully made her way up the lane to Nether Dennyfold, she asked Alice about Joe, and what it was he'd had to show her. For some reason, Alice didn't feel like going into details, so she just muttered something about a piece she'd seen in the museum that had interested her, and Joe had promised to tell her more about it.

Thanking Briony for the lift, Alice watched as she did a three-point turn in the lane, and disappeared back towards Dennybridge. As she turned to unlock the door, she noticed a tall figure marching along the lane from the direction of the big house. She recognised the handsome face; it was Finbar Denny-Hurst, and he didn't look happy.

CHAPTER TWENTY-FOUR

SATURDAY 1 JUNE

Alice desperately tried to open the door, but the key refused to turn. She was half hoping that Finbar wasn't looking for her, and that he'd just walk on past. Finally, the door opened, and she scuttled through, but there he was behind her, hands on hips, glaring at her.

'You're Alice?'

'Yes. Finbar, isn't it?'

'Can I come in?'

Reluctantly, Alice stepped aside, gesturing for Finbar to enter. She felt very vulnerable, and horribly guilty, as he stepped into the kitchen and walked straight to the table where the journals were laid out. His family's journals.

'Genevieve said you had them.'

'I'm sorry. Please don't blame Genevieve. I pretty much bullied her into letting me read them. It's my fault.' She felt her face reddening as she waffled on. 'I've treated them with great care.'

Finbar's fingers lightly travelled over each of the journals, tracing the names and dates with an unexpected tenderness. 'I haven't seen these for years. Not since I was a boy, and Ma showed me.' His voice was calm, resonant, his words slightly clipped. The result of a private education, Alice assumed. But the angry expression had disappeared from his face.

'They're amazing. I've never seen anything like them,' Alice said, hoping a bit of flattery would sweeten him further. 'You're lucky to have your family's history written down.'

Finbar gave her an appraising look. 'Genevieve said you used to come here when you were a child. And you're here now to search for your cousin?'

'That's right. Fleur's been missing for two weeks now. I'm really worried.'

'Were you the two irritating girls who used to come and spy on me and Jenson over the wall? About... must be... twenty years ago?'

Alice felt the blush on her face deepen. 'Sorry. Yes, that was us. Fleur had a real thing for you...' Biting her lip, she wished she hadn't blurted that out, but Finbar laughed a deep, throaty chuckle, which brought a shy smile to her lips.

'Can I make you a cup of tea?'

'Thank you, no, I must get back. I only came to check which of the journals you had. There's a particular one I need, so I can show...' He tailed off, and poked about in the carrier bag that held the journals Alice had collected earlier. 'Ah, here it is.' Finbar pulled out a much newer-looking diary, bound in deep red leather, and held it reverently in his hands.

'Whose is that?'

He placed the journal down on the table so Alice could read the gold-tooled name and date: *Lady Emilia Denny-Hurst, 2003.* Alice remembered the portrait at the top of the stairs of Lady Emilia, her long blonde hair threaded through with daisies, a dreamy expression on her beautiful face.

'Your mother.'

Finbar sat down heavily, and picked the book up, handling it as though it were the most precious thing he'd ever seen. 'The last of the Denny Diaries, as we call them. She died in September of 2003; at least she made it to the twenty-first century. I was only twenty. She loved everything too much: my father, me and Jenson, vodka, cocaine...'

Alice was sure there was a tear in Finbar's eye. This was not what she'd expected, and she wasn't sure how to react. 'Did she write her diary right up until the end?'

Finbar gently opened the book, flipping through until he reached a blank page. The last written entry was dated August 2003, and from where Alice stood, the writing looked illegible. He flipped back a few pages, until he found one that looked readable; he read the entry slowly, mouthing the words, shaking his head sadly.

'This is what she became: a beautiful, damaged angel with the thoughts of a demon.' He pushed the journal across to her, so that Alice could read the entry too.

15th August 2003

My dearest, sweetest Diary, the skylarks sing above my head. Are they trapped in this hell with me? I think I must have displeased the Great Goddess herself, for my limbs ache and my thoughts run wild, and it is as though my life force is falling through an egg timer, and my time is running out. A wraith visited me this morning, as I lay in my bath. A shadowy witch with fingers as cold as ice, shivering my skin and my very soul. She wants me dead! They all want me dead! I screamed at the spirit, I denied her my life, but Rufus came before I could cast her out. He told me it was nothing, just a drug-induced hallucination, but I know. I know it was the spirit of Death, sent by the Great Goddess. They cannot have me yet! As long as the skylarks sing, I shall have life.

'That's so sad, but so lovely at the same time.' Alice had no idea whether that was the right thing to say, but she'd felt a connection at the bit about being visited by a wraith. And then the thought hit her. 'That was around the time I stayed here last. August 2003. I had no idea she was so ill.'

'Ill. Damaged. Hopeless. Call it what you will.' Finbar sighed. 'Perhaps it's not the best diary to show Grace.' He seemed to be lost in his thoughts. 'Have you finished with any of these?'

'Yes, most of them.' Alice sorted through, picking out three by Patience including the 1786 journal, and one by Susan Denny-Hurst that she hadn't yet seen. 'May I keep these for a day or two longer? I'll bring them back as soon as I've found what I'm looking for.'

Finbar gave Alice a strange look. 'What you're looking for?'

She wished she'd said it differently; how was she going to explain to this well-educated, highly successful man that she felt there was a connection between the females of his ancient family, Hettie Gale, and her own cousin?

'Oh, nothing, really. I visited the museum in the week and found the stuff about all the people missing on the Moor really interesting. Some of them are mentioned in these journals. That's all.'

'And your own cousin is missing. You think there may be some sort of link?'

Alice's eyebrows shot up; Finbar was very perceptive. 'Maybe.'

He lolled back in his chair, tracing a pattern on the table with a long, elegant finger.

'There are stories in my family. Old rumours, which are probably a load of nonsense. Nothing written down, but hints of hauntings at The Manor House. Apparitions. A young girl usually, sometimes a small child. I've never personally seen anything, but Ma swore she did, though that was probably just the drugs. Anyway, all old manor houses are supposed to have a ghost, aren't they? It's *de rigueur.*'

Alice felt a sizzle of excitement at the mention of a ghost, especially a girl and a child. Could it be? She felt bold enough to offer her thoughts. 'Hettie Gale, perhaps?'

Finbar looked surprised. 'You know about Hettie? I suppose you would, seeing as Hettie's Hovel is so close by. Could be, though why she'd haunt The Manor House and not her own little hovel, I don't know. Living in death how she couldn't live in life, I guess.'

He knitted his eyebrows together, and again appraised Alice. She felt uncomfortable being under so much scrutiny. 'There's supposed to be a letter, written by one of my ancestors, which had something to do with Hettie Gale. Some sort of deathbed confession. But then again, there are so many ridiculous stories about my forebears, I doubt there's any truth in it. At least, it's never been found.'

Alice perked up at this snippet of information. Perhaps her hunch that the Denny-Hursts were connected with Hettie in some way was correct. She was just about to ask Finbar more about the letter, when there was a knock on the door.

'Good morning. I brought you these. As an apology for my childish behaviour yesterday.' It was James, holding a huge box of chocolates, which he thrust towards her. 'I'm sorry. I've been a bit tetchy recently.'

Alice gazed at the chocolates, wondering how on earth he expected her to eat such an enormous boxful. 'Thank you, that's... not necessary. Really.'

James stood, expectantly, and Alice knew she should invite

him in; it was awkward, with Finbar sitting in the kitchen, but she couldn't just send James away.

'Come in, then.'

An endearing expression of gratefulness mixed with pleasure crossed his face, which rapidly turned to one of bafflement as he walked into the kitchen and spied another man.

'Oh, you have company.' He threw the box of chocolates onto the table, glared at Finbar, and began to retreat towards the door.

'James, please...'

'I'm Finbar Denny-Hurst, from The Manor House. I'm here to collect some of my family diaries that Alice has been reading. You're James Turnkey, I believe? From the bookshop? I imagine you'd find these very interesting.'

Finbar had leapt up and moved to stand in front of James, commanding the situation, his hand held out. His expression was unreadable, but Alice detected a slight hostility. James turned and looked from Finbar to Alice, clearly not sure what to say, but tentatively shook the other man's hand.

'I do hope you weren't planning on trying to sell these antiquities to Mr Turnkey, Alice? Is that why he's here?'

Alice was shocked; such a thing would never even have crossed her mind. 'Of course not! I told you; I'm just reading them to find out more about the missing people.' She tried to make her voice sound less whiny. 'Anyway, James hates books.'

Finbar laughed. 'Seriously? A bookseller who hates books! No wonder your shop looks so dreary.'

James's face reddened, but with anger rather than embarrassment. He squared up to Finbar, who was a little taller, but somehow less substantial. 'Your manners haven't improved with age, have they?'

Alice started to panic; she had no idea what to say to defuse the situation. She was saved by another knock on the door. She rushed to open it, thankful for the interruption. A woman stood there, probably about her own age, stunningly beautiful with cropped black hair that framed a face blessed with high cheekbones and full lips. She had eyes the colour of treacle, which sparkled with warmth and friendliness. The yellow dress she wore was short, complementing her flawless dark skin and long, elegant legs.

'Hi! I'm Grace. Is Finbar here?'

Alice managed to mutter that yes, he was here, and Grace should please come in.

'Darling! Did you miss me already?' Finbar spun away from James, a happy expression restored to his face, and grabbed Grace by the hand. He turned to Alice.

'This gorgeous creature is Grace Picton. I call her my *saving grace*, the *yang* to my *yin*. She's tamed my wilder excesses and made me realise that there's more to life than parties and profit-making.' Finbar curled his arm around Grace's waist and hugged her close. She giggled and tried to squirm away.

'Isn't it just beautiful here?' She grabbed Alice's hand. 'Looks like we'll be neighbours!'

'Oh,' Alice spluttered, 'I don't live here; I'm just staying for a few days. This is my cousin's house.'

Grace's hand flew to her mouth. 'I'm so sorry. Finbar told me about the missing woman. She's your cousin? How awful for you. If there's anything we can do to help?'

Alice smiled and sighed. 'Thank you, but there's nothing anyone can do, really.' She looked towards James, who was attempting to disappear into the background.

'This is James Turnkey, my... friend.'

'James, lovely to meet you.' Grace's warmth was infectious as they shook hands, and a smile spread across his face.

'Likewise.'

Alice frowned. 'Did you say neighbours? Are you going to be staying here for a while?'

Grace looked at Finbar, who gave the tiniest nod of approval.

'We're going to be staying here forever! Finbar has asked me to marry him.'

'That's wonderful! Congratulations to you both. Have you set a date?'

'Oh, not for a while yet. Next year, perhaps. But I can't wait to make this my home; I'm sick of London, the noise and dirt, and... phoniness, you know?'

Alice knew very well, and couldn't help a stab of envy, knowing that she'd be returning to the noise and dirt and phoniness very soon. Finbar scooped the journals Alice had finished with into the carrier bag, and held them towards Grace.

'This is why I need these. I want to show my soon-to-be-wife what's expected of her when she becomes Mrs Denny-Hurst.' He looked suddenly very ordinary, Alice thought, not the lord of the manor that he was.

'I thought the Denny Diaries were over, that Ma's were the last ones. But now...' he looked adoringly at Grace, 'now we can keep the tradition going.'

He led Grace towards the door. 'It was lovely to meet you, Alice. And to see you again, James.' He nodded towards them both. 'I didn't mean what I said about you selling the journals, Alice. I was just teasing. Keep those as long as you need them.' He indicated the four journals that still lay on the table. 'But, mate, you do need to do something about that shop.'

James began to bristle, but Grace laughed as she pulled her man through the door. 'You always need to have the last word, Finbar.'

He smiled. 'True. But at least I've got you to stop me, now.' He looked back as they began to make their way up the lane. 'I told you she was my saving grace!'

Alice closed the door, her head spinning. James was leaning against the kitchen counter, hands thrust into the pockets of his jeans.

'Well, that was unexpected.' Alice walked to the counter and busied herself with filling the kettle and drying two mugs that had been standing on the drainer. 'Grace is beautiful, isn't she? Perhaps she can change Finbar for the better.'

James scowled. 'I never did like that man. Not that I know him very well, but he was always lording it over us mere mortals.'

'Were you at school together? You must be around the same age?'

A snort was James's first response. 'No. He went to some private boarding school, not the local comprehensive. But he flashed his cash around the shops and pubs, and made it clear he expected the rest of us to bow and scrape.' Bitterness entered his voice. 'All the girls adored him, of course. Until he dumped them.'

Alice put two mugs of tea on the table and gestured for James to sit. 'But he's grown up now, and people can change. Maybe Grace is going to be the one to keep his feet on the ground.'

James didn't look convinced, so Alice changed the subject. 'I need to go to the museum. Would you drive me to Monkstown? Only if you've got time.'

'That's not a problem; I'm visiting Dad later anyway. Why do you want to go to the museum again?'

Alice opened the box of chocolates and studied them for a moment, before picking one out and shoving the box towards James. 'I went shopping earlier,' she indicated the bags which were still sitting on a chair unopened, 'and I bumped into Joe. He's got some records he thinks I'll find interesting.'

'Don't tell me: Hettie Gale?'

'Yes.' Alice couldn't read James's expression, but she caught a whiff of exasperation in his voice. 'I know it sounds daft, James, but I'm sure there's a connection between Hettie, the missing people and Fleur.'

'You're right.' James sipped his tea. 'It does sound daft.'

Not to be put off, Alice continued. 'I went to Hettie's Hovel yesterday, to look for her grave.'

James laughed. 'Why on earth would you do that?'

She shrugged. 'I just needed to see if I could find it, that's all. Don't you ever do things just because?'

'Not really. Did you find it?'

Alice got up and walked to the counter, where the red bead necklace still lay on its pad of kitchen paper. 'I don't know. I found this.'

James ran the necklace through his fingers, very gently. 'It's lovely. Very old. You should get it looked at by someone who knows about these things.'

Alice felt inexplicably protective of the necklace and took it out of James's hands, putting it back on its paper and shoving it into a drawer. 'Perhaps.'

She looked closely at James. 'Thanks for the chocolates. You'll have to help me eat them.'

He blushed, but helped himself to another. 'That's not a problem; I've got a bit of a sweet tooth.'

'So, they found one of Fleur's shoes.'

James froze, the chocolate poised in front of his open mouth. He put it on the table, and studied his hands. 'Yes, Briony asked me about it. PC Berry.' He glanced around the room, as though searching for an escape route.

'Do you think it was one of Fleur's?'

His face was stiff with misery as he looked anywhere but at Alice, unable to meet her gaze. 'I don't know. I think so. Like I told Briony, I don't really notice those sorts of things.'

Alice sighed. 'Oh well, if you didn't notice, you didn't notice. It does sound like it could be Fleur's, though. They're doing another search of Pedlar's Quag, so maybe they'll find the other one... or something else.'

Silence settled around Alice and James, a palpable barrier between them. Neither wanted to be the first to speak, but eventually it was James who broke the spell. 'Shall we get a move on? I'll drive you to the museum.'

CHAPTER TWENTY-FIVE
ALL TIME AND NO TIME

Whether 'tis truth or ne'er but a lie, who hates?
With a lust for revenge and his head full of spite
Loathes the crow.

'Tis a funny business, not having no body but still being able to see things, hear things, think things. Time passes but don't have no meaning, seasons change... but nothing changes for me. My heart hardens when I think of what I've become. 'Cept I don't have no heart, and that's a fact.

But my greatest joy is being back with my boy. He perished, he did, in our cave, 'neath the tree what fell when it got struck by the lightning and blocked his way out. He needed his Ma, but I was took away and so he shivered and shook, and the life drained out of him. He must've been so afraid, the poor little mite, and so hungry, and so desp'rate for his Ma that his soul couldn't rest, just like mine. He treads his own path, and cries tears what never stop, but when our lonely footsteps meet, even though I can't hug him, nor kiss his golden head, there's a deeper bond atween us that I just can't explain.

I will not rest till I've had my vengeance. 'Tis not for me, but for my boy. He'd barely begun his life afore it was took from him, and 'twasn't my fault, but the sin of those what dragged me from him. I know that now, though the guilt still lies heavy with me.

Mostly, we roam the Quag. I don't have to worry 'bout my boy falling into the pools, seeing as he don't have no solid body, and we fair skip along. Sometimes we go into my old home, but it in't our home no more, and 'tis falling out of repair. The reeds have long since blown from the roof and the walls are crumbling, and though someone puts on a tin roof to cover the emptiness, it's not home no more.

My ma sometimes comes to my grave to put flowers: bright, sunny daffodils in the spring, daisies in summer and darkest red-and-yellow pansies in autumn. She don't weep, but her hands fold in prayer. I don't rightly know why she does such a thing, as her foot never did step into any church, and that's a fact. Perhaps it's a comfort of sorts. My sis comes, and Daniel. How they've grown! Poor little Jack was a real innocent, and his soul has gone where it should.

But I like it the most when dear Rose comes, though the years are beginning to fade her and thread her black hair with silver. She brings sprigs of elder or hawthorn, sometimes a handful of blackberries, as though she frets that we're hungry. But best of all is when she sings, her voice winging through the air to touch every corner of the world, the words sometimes sad, sometimes happy. I try to blow her a kiss, which makes a little breeze lift the brim of her hat or catch at the collar on her dress. She knows we're there; I'm sure of it.

Yet though these times fill me with pleasure, there is a rage that is growing inside me. In the empty hours I cuss and I swear, and my breath forms little gusts of wind. My golden boy cries tears that'd fill the whole Moor, tears of anguish that raise a mist of sadness. We cannot rest, and I know what I must do.

I like to visit the big house, and now there's no gate nor wall that'll stop me going right inside. I watch Rose as she tends to poor Charles, who grows weaker by the day. I watch Miss Patience as she writes in her book, her hand trembling, her skin getting slacker and her bones pointier through her clothes, but I leave her be. Time is changing them, but not me. Not my boy. We're trapped in this emptiness, and I must do something to untrap us.

I watch as a man comes to the big house. 'Tis a man I recognise – the hateful brute what sentenced me to hang. 'Tis Judge Nisbet, and I hate him as much now as I did when he watched me drop from the Hanging Tree.

I call my boy and we wait and wait, until the judge finishes his business and comes out of the house to scold his man and summon his carriage. But afore the man is scolded, or the carriage is brung, me and my boy, we enchant him, and put it into his head that he wants to take a walk to the Quag. Don't ask me how we can tempt him so, for 'tis a mystery to me. But here he comes, his great, fleshy thighs wobbling across the quagmire, his finely shod feet sinking deep into the marshy ground.

My boy cries his tears of anguish, and a mist rises all around the cocky judge, and he does wail and whimper, but he must go on. We make him go on. Right to Crow Pond, where my black-feathered friends do cackle and accuse as he sinks deep 'neath the water. He is gone, down to his own hell, and me and my boy shiver with triumph afore we go after his bones.

But 'tis not enough. I am innocent of what they hanged me for, and I need to make 'em listen. Nine men judged me. Now nine must pay the price.

CHAPTER TWENTY-SIX

SATURDAY 1 JUNE

James dropped Alice off at the museum. She asked him to go with her, but he wanted to visit his father.

'Come round later? I'll cook you something?' Alice realised that she was beginning to enjoy James's company, despite his constant apologising, and the thought of another lonely evening dismayed her.

'Okay, about seven suit you? I'll bring wine.'

Alice walked into the museum and asked the girl at the desk for Joe. He appeared quickly and guided her towards a door bearing a sign that stated, *Strictly No Admittance*.

Leading her down a corridor dotted with doors, he opened one labelled *Records*. They were in a large room panelled in dark wood, with three cumbersome, old-fashioned, mahogany desks at one end, the other taken up by rows of moveable shelving. Two of the desks were occupied, an elderly woman at the nearest, tapping away at a keyboard and gazing into a computer screen; a young man at the other, poring through an enormous ledger of some kind, occasionally adding yellow Post-it notes to the pages.

Joe introduced Alice to his colleagues, then led her to the

third desk, which was almost empty save for a couple of folders and some books. He pulled up a chair and invited her to sit down. 'Sorry I can't offer you a drink; it's not allowed in here, what with all this stuff.' He gestured towards the shelves. 'I know I'd be the first to spill me coffee over a valuable document.' His chuckle was infectious.

He opened one of the folders and took out two sheets of paper. 'So, Alice, this is what I thought you might find interesting. These aren't the original documents – I made copies – but they're quite hard to read, so Molly,' he waved towards the woman who was still tapping away, 'typed me up a transcription. Some of the words and phrases were a bit archaic, so she changed it to more modern English, so they're easier to understand.' He thrust one of the papers towards Alice.

She read the first few paragraphs. 'Did you say you found this in a council office? Why would it have been buried away for so long? The original must be very old.'

Joe smiled. 'It's amazing, isn't it? A builder found it, with a load of other ancient documents, hidden under some floorboards that were being replaced in the Children's Services offices.'

The document Alice was reading was a transcript of the court report of Hettie Gale's case. It listed the names of the judge and other court officials, and related in very cold terms the fact that the three witnesses, the un-named soldiers who had found her drowning her son, gave clear accounts of what had transpired, and that Hettie had not been able to give a good account of her actions. It concluded with the jury's judgement that Hettie was guilty, and with the sentence handed down that she should be hanged by the neck in Monkstown. It also listed the names of the jurors, which Alice read twice so they'd stick in her head.

- *The Earl of Scaithe, Landowner*
- *Sir Eustace Denny, Landowner*
- *The Reverend Nathanial Bacon, Clergyman*
- *Thomas Hallissy, Physician*
- *Gideon Flemby, Volunteer Constable*
- *Edward Cox, Blacksmith*
- *Benjamin Theobald, Playwright*
- *Samuel de Flory, Painter*

'That one's quite dull, really. Doesn't tell us anything we don't already know.' Joe handed Alice the second piece of paper. 'This is the one I really wanted you to see.'

Alice's eyes widened as she read. 'Was this found in the same place as the other one?'

'Indeed it was. The Children's Services offices are separate from the main council building, in an old place that was originally some grand house. The only thing I can think is that whoever lived there originally had some connection with Judge Nisbet, and had this testimony hidden away. Who knows why things are hidden, but I'd say this would have been very inflammatory in its day. Anyway, now we've got it, and the crow knows it's massively important. I'll have to plead for it to be gifted to the museum; it should be displayed as part of Hettie's story. What do you think?'

Alice read the whole document twice, her hands trembling as she took in its implications.

> *On this, the nineteenth day of October in the year of our Lord 1776, this testimony is given by Gideon Flemby, volunteer constable, and witnessed by Arthur Fink, Serjeant-At-Law (retired).*

"My name is Gideon Flemby, and I am a volunteer constable in the parish of Monkstown. On the thirteenth day of this month, I was summoned to be on the jury that was to decide the fate of one Hettie Gale, a young woman from the hamlet of Nether Dennyfold who had been arrested on the charge of murdering her own child, murder by drowning in Crow Pond on Pedlar's Quag. The witnesses were three soldiers returning from action overseas, and their captain.

Presiding over the jury was Judge Jeremiah Nisbet, a man of low moral reputation who was at certain risk of losing both his title and his wealth due to his wanton and criminal conduct. Judge Nisbet warned the jury that he required but one more conviction and hanging, and that this conviction must take place immediately. Gossip reached the jury's ears, gossip of a most felonious nature, whereby Judge Nisbet was in thrall to General Sir Joseph Bunrutty, who was himself at risk of censure from his superiors due to misdeeds of an undisclosed nature, and who brooked no scandal regarding his soldiers. It was also clear, from talk overheard by more than one of us, that the soldiers had lied to save their own souls.

The jury was given an amount of twenty shillings each, on pain of imprisonment should they disclose this information to a living soul, on condition that they convict the Gale woman. With three young children to feed, I could not refuse this handsome sum, and to my eternal shame, I accepted.

But my conscience will not allow me to rest until I have committed this sin to paper. It is clear to me the aforementioned Gideon Flemby that Hettie Gale is innocent of any crime, and that she will be wrongly and most cruelly, hanged, and that the three soldiers should be tried for the sin of lying, and indeed for the abuse they showed that poor girl. I watched that dear soul as she struggled to tell her side of this most desperate of tales, and the tears she shed, and the dignity and fortitude she displayed as her words were rebuked and her sentence pronounced... and I knew, as Judge Nisbet proclaimed his victory, that not only he and the other jurors, but that I had committed a most mortal sin, all in the name of self-preservation and greed. She will be hanged, and my part in that grotesque miscarriage of justice cannot be denied. God will judge me harshly for it, and I deserve no better."

Her gut feeling was right: Hettie hadn't been guilty; it had been a sham to try and save the judge's reputation.

'But the date of this, Joe. It's dated in October, when Hettie was sentenced. She wasn't hanged until November.'

Joe's expression was sombre as he slowly nodded.

'So... they hanged her knowing full well that she was innocent?'

'It seems so. Shocking, isn't it?'

A tear trickled down Alice's cheek, but she didn't care. This was awful. Poor Hettie. She'd been right to suspect something wasn't as it should be.

'Oh, Joe, I feel so desperately sad for her. Even though she died so long ago.' Her eyebrows bunched together as a thought occurred to her. 'I wonder what happened to the little boy. He must have starved to death, or drowned. I wonder why his body was never found?'

'There are lots of questions, Alice. I'll probably have to show this to the police, in case they want to search Crow Pond for the boy's bones, but I doubt they've got time for such things. Might be best to leave well alone. But I'll certainly want to change Hettie's exhibit, once this has been verified and I've got permission from them above.'

'Why did you show this to me, Joe? I mean, I'm glad you did, but I'm not anyone special and you've only just met me.'

Joe gave Alice a long, appraising look. His eyes were so blue, and full of warmth and humour, she was comfortable under his scrutiny. 'There's summat about you that gives me hope for this sorry world.'

Alice frowned, an embarrassed giggle escaping her throat.

'Is that too deep? Well, then, you're a breath of fresh air, and I reckon young Hettie's picked you to be her judge and jury. How's that? Do you believe in the afterworld?'

Alice shivered, a chill running up her spine. 'Ghosts, do you mean?'

Joe nodded, slowly. 'If you like. Ghosts, phantoms, apparitions, visions, call it what you like. It's a bit of an interest of mine. Maddie'll tell you about the ghost stories I used to read her when she was little. Probably gave her nightmares.' He roared with laughter, and Molly gave him a cutting look. 'The Moor is famed for its myths and legends, stories of haunted houses and headless women, legions of soldiers tramping through the forests and piteous crying heard in the dead of night. Folks think they're just made-up stories, but I think there's more than a touch of truth in 'em.' He winked at Alice. 'One day I'll tell you about the monk I saw at Greyfriars Priory, drifting right through the pillars.'

Alice felt increasingly uneasy at the direction this conversation was taking and needed to get out of the stuffy room. 'That'd be great, but I think I need to go home now.'

Joe looked embarrassed. 'I'm so sorry, Alice. I've frightened you. I get a bit excited about this sort of thing, and I don't know when to shut my mouth.' He looked genuinely upset.

'Joe, you haven't frightened me. Really. It's just... I've got a bit too entangled with Hettie; my emotions go all over the place when I think about her. Thank you so much for showing me this.'

He thrust the pieces of paper towards her. 'Take them! They're just copies; they're for you. But please don't show anyone else, at least not until I've got approval to display them.'

Alice said that of course she wouldn't show anyone, and Joe led her back through the corridor to the main entrance, where he took her hand, very gently for such a big man.

'You'll find what you're looking for, Alice. I know it.'

Joe's interest in helping her was clearly genuine, triggered by a shared awareness of something that wasn't quite tangible.

'We'll have that chat about ghostly monks one day. When I've got to grips with Hettie. Thanks, Joe, and see you soon.'

Alice stood outside the museum for a moment, breathing in the warm air. She decided to get a bus to Dennybridge and then walk back to Crag Cottage. She couldn't face calling a taxi, in case she heard bad news about Harry. There was a half-hour wait for the next bus, so she walked into the park, automatically heading towards the Hanging Tree. It was late afternoon, and the park was full of school kids larking about. Several were near the tree, squatting down on the grass, or lolling against the trunk. Alice felt a pang of irritation. How dare they treat such a tree with disrespect? She chided herself for being such a prig. Why should young kids, or anyone, for that matter, have the same sense of horror that she had about the tree's history?

Feeling unsettled, she walked back to the bus stop and sat on the bench. Her thoughts were whirring around so much, her eyes cast downwards, that she didn't hear the car horn the first time. It was only when an elderly lady sitting next to her jabbed her in the ribs that she took notice. 'Is he honking for you, love?'

James had pulled up at the bus stop right in front of her, and she hadn't even noticed. He honked again, and gestured for her to get in.

She leapt up and turned to the woman. 'Thank you so much; my head's in a bit of a spin.'

'Ah, don't worry, my love, the crow knows 'tis a world full of unfinished business.'

Alice climbed in beside James and strapped herself in, the woman's words rebounding around in her head, though she couldn't make sense of them.

'You were off with the fairies. Did Joe have something interesting to show you?'

'Yes. Yes, he did. I've got a copy in my bag, but I'm not supposed to show anyone.'

'Very intriguing. What is it?'

'Oh, just an old court record from when Hettie Gale was tried.'

James didn't respond. He seemed to be concentrating on his driving.

'It gives me some real proof that Hettie was innocent.'

Still no response, so Alice stopped talking. Then she remembered that she'd asked him over for dinner and had very little food in the cottage. 'Can you drop me in Dennybridge, near the supermarket? I need to get some stuff for tonight. Do you like lasagne?'

Lasagne was one of the few things Alice could cook with confidence, and without a recipe, so she was relieved when James said it was one of his favourites. It didn't take long to reach the village, and he pulled in opposite the supermarket.

'Shall I wait, so I can drop you home?'

'No, thank you. I'll walk. It's so warm and I need some exercise. I've done a lot of sitting today.'

Alice watched as James pulled away, slipping into the stream of late afternoon traffic. There'd been a touch of awkwardness between them, though she didn't know why that should be. Perhaps his visit with his father had been difficult.

Twenty minutes later, carrying a bag filled with the makings of lasagne and a bottle of red wine, Alice wished she'd asked

James to wait and drive her back to Crag Cottage. Never mind, the walk would do her good, though her arms were already aching from the weight of the food. This evening had better be worth the pain.

A mouth-watering aroma filled the kitchen. The rich meat and creamy béchamel sauces had been layered with sheets of lasagne, and the dish stood covered in the fridge, ready for Alice to top with grated cheese and put it in the oven for its final bake. There were enough bits and pieces to put together little side salads, and she was pleased with her efforts.

There was time for a relaxing cup of tea and a read before she took a shower and changed.

Pulling the remaining journals toward her, she chose the one labelled *Susan Denny-Hurst, 1960*. This was the lady wearing the black-and-white dress with the Peter Pan collar; Alice remembered her portrait well. She opened it at the first page.

> *1st January 1960*
>
> *Well, here we are: a new year, another 365 days to make some sort of meaning of my existence. More than the start of a new year, this day is the fifteenth anniversary of my husband's death. I still miss Matthew, every single day, and I still feel rage at the stupid war that killed him. I'm not sure the world has learnt anything from the deaths of so many innocents. And I'm not sure I've learnt anything, except that although I've taken many lovers, no one will ever replace my true love. I shall make silly, meaningless resolutions: to lose weight, to drink less and read more, to wear longer skirts, and to stop having sex with men that mean nothing to me. But I shall fail at them all.*

Alice sighed. She felt slightly intrusive reading people's thoughts, especially when they were sad, even though Susan must've died a long time ago – possibly even before Alice herself had been born. But it was refreshing to read something a bit more modern; she liked the openness of this Denny-Hurst, so she flipped through a few pages, and read some more.

> *21st June 1960*
>
> *Today is the summer solstice. I spent it at Crow Pond, as I have done every year since Matthew died. I relish the peace and solitude, and today it was even warm enough to swim. I looked again for the cave Matthew told me about when we were first wed, but the pond is full of weeds, and though he told me the opening is in rocks beneath the roots of the fallen tree, they have spread themselves wide. I was scared I'd be tangled up and drown so, once again, I was disappointed. How I wish that Matthew was still here, so he could show me the way. And in any case, I don't think the crows wanted me there; they were making such a noise, and the pond was full of their discarded feathers.*

A cave? Alice read the entry several times, to make sure she was getting it right. A cave under Crow Pond – that *had* to have some significance. Perhaps it was just a hole left when the tree was blown over in the storm? She'd ask someone local about it. Maybe Finbar would know something.

Flipping through a bit further, Alice stopped in amazement as she found a long entry mentioning yet another missing person.

> *6th August 1960*
>
> *My son Rufus is a Knight of the Realm, and yet he remains unwed, living alone with his mother. I do wonder sometimes if I have erred in my parenting somewhere along the line, or whether*

it has been the lack of a constant father figure in his life that has caused him pain. He has certainly enjoyed a succession of beautiful women, yet none have stirred him sufficiently to knuckle down and marry. But I was glad of his presence today, when a rather portly American gentleman knocked on our door. The man introduced himself as Dr Howard Boone, visiting the Moor as part of a "whistlestop tour of Yew-rup" with a group of retired medical types. They were visiting Hettie's Hovel, but he got distracted by the sight of a "typical English dook's pad", as he called it, and ordered me to give him a guided tour of the Manor. Rufus was able to turn the repulsive man away, when I may well have caved in. Rufus pointed him in the direction of Hettie's Hovel and urged him to find his companions.

Two hours later, there was another knock on the door. A group of Americans crowded around, all jabbering at once. Eventually, we were able to make out that Dr Boone had joined them at the hovel, but then he'd wandered off towards Pedlar's Quag. He'd seemed to be in some sort of trance, they said, and a mist blew up around him, so they lost sight of him quickly. They thought he'd taken some drugs. He'd not returned, and though some of his companions had cautiously ventured a little way onto the Quag, they'd seen no sign of him. It is fifty years since the last disappearance, according to my mother-in-law's diaries. I was concerned enough to call the police. They are searching the Quag this evening; despite my dislike of Dr Boone, I hope he is found safe and well.

Grabbing her phone, Alice scrolled through her photos, searching for the ones she'd taken in the museum. Sure enough, there was an article about Dr Boone. She read it quickly.

THE DISORIENTED DOCTOR – THE LAST PERSON TO GO MISSING

In August 1960, a visiting American tourist – one Dr Howard Boone – retired surgeon, of Pennsylvania, USA, was visiting the well-known tourist site of Hettie's Hovel in the hamlet of Nether Dennyfold, with a small group of fellow retired medics. As the group admired the hovel, Dr Boone had, according to one colleague, 'gone into, like, a trance, and wandered off through a gate which had a prominent sign saying keep out, danger, or something like that. It got real foggy, and we lost sight of him pretty quick.' Dr Boone never returned, and though the police conducted a thorough search of Pedlar's Quag, his remains were never found.

So, a doctor to add to her list. Something was niggling at Alice's memory, but she couldn't quite grasp it. There was a pattern or a link that she wasn't seeing; she was sure of that. Then a thought hit her: Dr Boone was no longer the last person to go missing; it was her own cousin, Fleur. Or even Harry, though there was something about his disappearance that didn't quite gel with the rest.

And then there was the letter that Finbar had mentioned: a deathbed confession. That was very intriguing, but if he had no idea where it was, she'd have no chance of finding it. She knew now for sure that Hettie had been wrongly judged and unfairly hanged. What was it Joe had said? *"I reckon young Hettie's picked you to be her judge and jury."* Was that what was niggling her? Judge and jury. The idea needling her brain was getting her more and more agitated, but frustratingly it wouldn't coalesce.

Feeling unsettled, Alice decided to stop reading and have a nice long bath to ease away these troubling thoughts. It was time to concentrate on her own well-being, in the here-and-now, and stop trying to rewrite history. And anyway, she still had to decide which of her new tops to wear.

After dinner, Alice made coffee and they sat by the fire she'd built in the sitting room grate, eating chocolates as a substitute for dessert.

The room had a slightly neglected air, a smell of disuse that she'd tried to banish with some scented candles she'd found upstairs; candles which Fleur must have bought, as they were the posh, expensive sort. But it was cosy with the fire blazing, even though it was June and the evening was still bathed in warm sunshine. The sofa was tattered and squishy, and she felt comfortable sitting close to this man James, who she tentatively liked one moment and despaired of the next.

She felt good in the green top she'd chosen, matched with the new jeans and green sandals, and she was wearing the silver feather earrings that James had given her. She'd retrieved the little wooden box from the drawer and placed it in a prominent position on the mantelpiece, and his undisguised delight at seeing it there had pleased her.

'They look so pretty on you. I knew they would.' He reached across to gently touch one of the earrings, then let his fingers run through her hair, and down to her arm. She shivered under his caress but couldn't tell whether it was from desire or something else.

'Thank you. Tell me about your family, James. I think you said you have a brother and a sister. Are you close?'

Alice needed to gather her feelings, so she only half-listened as James withdrew his hand, and told her about his sister Jenn, who was expecting her first child, and his brother Billy, who sounded like a bit of a nightmare, going off the rails and living somewhere in the city.

'My dad's in a care home, as you know.' He looked sad and started fidgeting with the tassels on a cushion. 'I visited him earlier; I'm not sure he knew who I was. He kept talking about Fred, but I don't have a clue who Fred is.'

Alice frowned. 'An old friend, perhaps? Or an old workmate? It must be someone important to him.'

'Maybe. It's very unsettling.'

'I'd love to meet him.'

Why did she say that? She barely knew James – would he want her to meet his father?

'Really?' James looked puzzled. 'Why?'

'I... don't know. It's just nice to meet people.'

James's smile melted her heart. 'You feeling a bit lonely, tucked away up here? I can soon put that right.' He stroked her hair again. 'You can come with me tomorrow, if you like.'

'That would be lovely–'

Alice was stopped in her tracks as James leaned forward and kissed her, very tenderly, on the mouth. He smelled of soap and a touch of spice – cinnamon, perhaps – and Alice allowed herself to be wrapped in his arms, and kissed deeper, more passionately. A fleeting image of James with Fleur, just like this, embracing in front of the fire, seeped into her thoughts, but she quickly banished it, and concentrated on herself. On herself, and, it had to be said, on the muscles beneath James's shirt as his arms pulled her close, of the tension in her own body, and the yearning that flooded every part of her as she stripped off her T-shirt, finally understanding that this was what she wanted, more than anything.

CHAPTER TWENTY-SEVEN

SUNDAY 2 JUNE

Stretching lazily beneath the rumpled bedclothes, Alice felt warm and comfortable and happy. She reached an arm out, hoping to touch warm skin, finding nothing but an empty space. She sat up, shaking her hair from her face, the sleepiness leaving her and disappointment taking its place. He wasn't there, after all. Had she dreamed it all? If so, it was the loveliest dream she'd ever had, and she wanted to go back to sleep and delve back in. Then she heard a stair creak, and footsteps tapping across the landing.

'Good morning. I thought you might like room service.'

James stood in the doorway, wearing just his underpants, holding a tray laden with mugs of tea, a plate of buttered toast and a pot of jam.

Alice was delighted it hadn't been a dream. Now, in the clear light of a beautiful morning, she could really admire his body: the toned limbs and muscular chest, a light covering of dark hair curling across, and down his stomach. Tearing her eyes away, she tried to concentrate on the tray he was carrying.

'Thank you. This is lovely. I can't remember the last time I had breakfast in bed. Actually, I don't think I ever have, except perhaps when I was little and sick.'

James placed the tray carefully on the bed and unloaded the mugs onto the bedside tables. Then he gave Alice a plate and a knife, and offered the toast and jam.

'You're not going to do it for me, then?' she teased.

His eyes gleamed. 'I know what I'd like to do for you again.'

Making love in a bed full of toast crumbs wasn't quite the romantic experience of last night, when they'd stretched out in front of the fire on the old-fashioned plush rug, limbs entwined, lost in their passion; and then again on the squishy sofa, Alice on top, hungry for something she thought she'd never needed. But this morning it was lovely, lazy sex, each of them happy to take time to explore the other's body.

'Shouldn't you be opening the shop?' It was nine thirty, and Alice suddenly remembered there was a real world out there.

'It doesn't matter. This is more important.' James was lying on his side, gently playing with strands of Alice's hair, and tracing the contours of her face. 'You're beautiful.'

She wasn't used to being complimented and didn't quite know how to respond. 'So are you.'

He roared with laughter. 'I've been called a lot of things, but never beautiful.'

'Well, I think you are. You have beautiful eyes.'

She propped herself up on the pillows, delighted to see it was another fine, sunny morning through the semi-drawn curtains; another day to spend as she pleased. The urge to read more of the journals was strong, but not while James was here. He hadn't seemed too impressed that Joe had given her some information about Hettie Gale's trial; perhaps he thought that she should be concentrating on finding Fleur. He was probably right. And yet...

'Can I really come and meet your dad?'

James frowned. 'Are you sure you want to? He might not even know me.'

'That's okay. It might be nice for him to meet someone new. I won't if...'

'No, it's fine. I just hate care homes, all those empty shells of people, just sitting and staring.'

'But they're not empty; they still have memories and dreams, it's just harder for us to find them.'

The look James gave Alice as he took her face gently between his hands was one of pure adoration. 'You're such a sweet person. So different from...' He bit his lip.

Well, that ruined this perfect moment. Why did he keep bringing Fleur into things? He obviously still fancied her. She drew back from his embrace, trying to keep the hurt from showing, trying to quell the anger.

'I'm going to have a shower.'

But before she'd taken a step, there was a knock at the door.

Alice froze; what should she do? James slithered out of bed and peeped out of the window. 'There's a police car.'

'Oh. I'd better go and answer, then.' She wrapped herself in Fleur's dressing gown. (Why hadn't she brought her own? Probably because she hadn't thought she'd be here long enough to need one. And now James would know it was Fleur's and it would smell of Fleur and he'd be thinking about Fleur, and...)

Another knock sent her rushing down the stairs.

'Good morning, Alice. Isn't it a lovely day?'

Sergeant Cooper stood in the doorway, a broad grin on his face. For a moment, Alice's heart leapt into her mouth. 'Have you found Fleur? Or Harry?'

His smile disappeared. 'Ah, no. Neither of them, I'm afraid.

We've organised another thorough search of the Quag tomorrow. Hopefully that'll give us some answers about your cousin.' He hesitated. 'Can I come in?'

Once inside, his smile returned. 'I just wanted to let you know that one of my colleagues, Briony – you met her, I think? – has managed to talk to someone in Fleur's phone contacts. She'd not had any luck with anyone else, no one had seen Fleur for weeks or even months, but this one man was interesting because he'd been exchanging messages with her almost every day. Several times a day. Briony finally spoke to him yesterday evening; he's been a hard person to get through to.'

Alice took a deep breath. 'Do you mean he's a suspect?'

Sergeant Cooper grimaced. 'No, not at all. He lives in New York, hasn't seen Fleur since she was over there a month or so ago. It seems they are engaged to be married.'

'Oh!' Alice shouldn't have been surprised that her beautiful, glamorous, wealthy cousin had a fiancé, but somehow she was. Fleur had never mentioned anyone special to her. Though there was no reason why she should have done; they weren't exactly close.

'The thing is, this chap said the last time they'd spoken, they'd had a row. That would have been the day before she disappeared. We've had both his and Fleur's messages and texts checked out, and it appears he's telling the truth.'

Alice let this sink in. Fleur had had a row with her fiancé, and the next day she'd had a row with James. And then she'd disappeared.

'So how does this affect things?'

'Not much, really. I just wanted to check whether you knew anything about this man – if there was anything Fleur had told you about him?'

'You mean, could she be so upset about the row with him that she'd... do something silly?'

He looked solemn. 'That is a possibility, yes. We hadn't really considered it before, but with Harry... you know, his note and everything... and with Fleur being so upset...' He left it hanging.

'Well, I didn't even know she was engaged, so there's nothing I can add. I'm sorry.'

He sighed. 'Oh well, thanks anyway. It was worth a try. I'd better be getting back to base. Hopefully something will come of the search tomorrow. There'll be quite a few vehicles parked up around here, so don't fret; if there's something to find, we'll find it.'

Alice opened the door. Sergeant Cooper began to walk away, then stopped and turned round. 'Is that Mr Turnkey's car?' He tapped the side of his nose. 'Don't worry, I won't tell.' And with a chuckle, he walked towards his own car.

Retreating to the kitchen, Alice slumped onto a chair.

'Is everything okay?' James cautiously came into the kitchen. He'd dressed, and his hair was still damp from the shower, sticking out in clumps where he'd rubbed it with a towel.

'Yes, it was Sergeant Cooper. He came to tell me they'd made contact with Fleur's fiancé. In New York.' She watched James closely, to see his reaction.

'Oh. I didn't know she had a fiancé.' His face tightened slightly, his brows knitting together in a frown.

'James, did you and Fleur have sex?' Alice couldn't believe she'd asked him that, but she'd been itching to, and now seemed as good a time as any.

His eyes darkened as he fixed her with an intense stare. 'Would it matter if we had?'

She shrank back, knowing that yes, it would matter very much, but not wanting to admit it.

'Well, we didn't. She flirted like mad and clearly wanted some attention. But she never let me near her in that way.'

'But you tried?'

'We kissed. That's as far as it went.'

James was getting angry, and Alice was trying not to cry. The thought of him kissing Fleur made her feel a bitter jealousy she'd never experienced before, and she didn't like the sensation. He said they hadn't made love, and she believed him. She needed to get her emotions sorted.

'I'm sorry. I had to ask. At least she didn't cheat on her fiancé; that makes me think he must be very special to her.' She couldn't hold back the tears. 'He must be frantic, knowing she's missing, and being so far away.'

Alice crumpled into James's arms, and he hugged her tightly, planting tender kisses on the top of her head. They stood like that for a while, neither wanting to let go. Alice moved first, extricating herself from James's clasp and wiping her eyes on her sleeve.

'I'm okay now. This is all getting too much; I need to be stronger, for Fleur's sake.'

James took her face in his hands. 'You're stronger than you think, you know.'

'Maybe. Thank you for being so understanding. It means a lot to me.'

'Good.' He frowned. 'I've got to go. I should open the shop for a bit, at least.'

He gently kissed her cheek. The smell of his skin, and the feeling of the drop of water that escaped his hair and trickled down her neck, was delicious. She wished he'd stay a bit longer, but she pulled herself away.

'It's been lovely, thank you. I wasn't expecting...'

He smiled. 'Me neither. I would've brought clean pants if I'd thought...'

They both laughed, and all the tension disappeared.

Once James had left, Alice showered and dressed. She wasn't quite sure how she felt; her head was full of such a mix of emotions. The physical pleasure she'd felt with James had taken her by surprise, but there was also a touch of guilt at having been so brazen – she'd only known him a week, after all. Now he'd enjoyed her in that way, would he stop wanting to see her? And he'd kissed Fleur. Did he wish he'd made love to her, too?

But she was being silly; he'd arranged to pick her up at five o'clock and take her to meet his dad. She doubted very much he'd have done that with Fleur.

There was to be a full-scale search of Pedlar's Quag; the thought of finding Fleur's body was nightmarish, but the need to know what had happened to her cousin was getting stronger each day, and even a bad outcome would at least bring the not-knowing to an end.

Alice knew a mug of tea and a read would help banish any negative thoughts, so she sat at the table and spread the remaining journals in front of her. Her fondness for Patience made her pick up the oldest journal, labelled *Mrs Patience Wickens, 1772*. The very first entry betrayed Patience's sweeter side:

> *1st January 1772*
> *It is the first day of a new year. Mr Wickens and I dined alone last evening, and I went to my bed resolving to be a better wife to him, and a more generous benefactor to those around me. The house has been scrubbed from bottom to top, the ashes swept from the fires. Rose has assembled a large heap of rags, and quantities of potatoes and carrots, turnips and mutton. She will help me carry the baskets later as I visit the villagers and bestow these small offerings upon them. Mr Wickens has favoured me with his permission to do this small thing.*

Alice got a sense that beneath Patience's stern exterior lay a kind-hearted woman; but women were treated as possessions back then, and it must've been hard to have to get a man's permission to do even the slightest thing. Flipping through the pages, she stopped at an entry that contained another name she recognised.

> *13th September 1772*
>
> *This morning I bade Rose dispose of some threadbare blankets for which I have no further use. It is my earnest hope that she will take them to the wretched Gale child, who has been thrown out of her family home, sent to live in the old bakehouse. I saw the girl just yesterday as she crept up the lane to watch her sister playing by Mr Gale's cottage. I was horrified to see that her figure has become bloated, and it is surely not from greed, as there is little food to be had in the best of times for those sorry folk. I believe that the girl is with child, and worse, that the father can only be... No, I cannot put my thoughts onto paper, for they distress me so. Any child born of such a union must surely be at risk of peculiarity, or indeed lack of the senses.*
>
> *My own sweet Charles, though born of the rightful union between man and wife, becomes ever more lacking in sense. He reaches ten years of age very soon, and yet he is no more developed than an infant, with the gait of one just learning to walk and the speech of a simpleton. I would not wish such fate upon any mother, and though it would be unseemly for me to offer help, and Mr Wickens would be most unamused should I do so, Rose is a treasure that I will happily share, when the girl's time comes.*

Rereading the entry several times made Alice feel sick. Patience's meaning was clear: the father of Hettie Gale's child must have been someone close, possibly her own father. Poor

Hettie, her story just got worse and worse. She wondered who Rose was; she'd seen the name repeated several times. Perhaps she'd helped Hettie when she gave birth; the thought of such a young girl, pregnant by her father, banished from her family home and left alone to give birth, was too much to bear. She shut the journal before her mood was soured further.

Looking around for something else to read, she spotted her Holiday Diary sitting on the counter. Some of the entries were very amusing, but they brought back memories she'd tucked away.

> *Monday 4th August 1999*
> *Fleur told me something today, but I can't tell you what she said, Diary. It's too secret, even for you. I'm a bit confused; I didn't really understand. To cheer her up we went for a walk up to the big house, and guess what? Jenson and Finbar were there! Fleur went all soppy, and tried to make Finbar look at her, but he was too busy doing something to his bicycle. I don't know why Fleur likes him so much. Boys are stupid.*

Alice remembered that day when Fleur had told her about her father's abuse. She really hadn't understood; she'd had no idea about sex. Her mother had been too embarrassed to give her *that talk* and had left it to the school, but even though Alice had studied the anatomical illustrations, it had been with a mix of horror and disbelief.

But she giggled at the memory of Fleur trying to make Finbar look at her. No wonder he'd referred to them as irritating girls. She flipped through some very tedious entries that listed everything she'd eaten, or every pebble and flower she'd found, then stopped when she spotted the name Crow Pond.

> *Tuesday 12th August 2003*

Dad took us to Crow Pond today. It's only the second time I've ever been. Luke was busy arguing with Dad, so I spent most of the time on my own. There were so many feathers!!! I picked the first one up by Hettie's Hovel, then more and more were on the path. I picked them all up until they were like a bunch of black flowers. There were feathers all the way to the pond; there must have been more than twenty. Perhaps some crows had been fighting?

When we got to the pond I put the feathers down on a rock so I could paddle, but it got windy and some of them blew into the water, and they drifted to the old broken tree where they got stuck in the roots and I couldn't get them.

It was lovely in the sunshine, but we didn't stay long, partly because of Luke being a bastard and partly because it began to get misty. I still had about ten feathers left, but when I showed Mum she said they were dirty and I had to throw them away. But I kept one – the biggest, shiniest one.

She remembered those feathers, and the disgust on her mother's face when she saw them. Alice had felt sad when she'd thrown them in the bin, but the one she'd kept was here in the diary, stuck in with a yellowing piece of sticky tape, no longer shiny. She'd cultivated a morbid fixation on crows and feathers for a while after that.

With a start, Alice remembered the journal entry she'd read yesterday – was it Susan who'd been to Crow Pond and found the water full of feathers? How strange. Something about Crow Pond was beginning to tug at Alice's thoughts. She was coming towards the end of the Holiday Diary; the entries for 2004 were very sparse, but one caught her eye.

Saturday 14th August 2004
I'm so fed up with Luke. He's been moping around and

making us all feel miserable, so I suggested we went for a walk to Dennybridge, and said I'd buy him some toffees. Luke loves his toffees, but Mum's forbidden him to have any, because he's not very good at cleaning his teeth. We were walking along the lane, near the spooky cottage with the twisted chimney, when he disappeared behind the hedge. When I got to the cottage's gate, there was a skull stuck on the gatepost. I nearly jumped out of my skin. The skull looked like it was human, and it had blood on it, and there was a piece of rope dangling down. It made me scream a little bit.

When Luke came out from the hedge I shouted at him that he was horrid to scare me, but he said he'd been for a wee, and he swore it wasn't anything to do with him. He said anyway, it was only an old sheep's skull. When I told Mum, because I was crying, she told Dad. He went and had a look, but he said it was a sheep's skull too, and there wasn't any rope, and it wasn't on the gate but stuck under the hedge. He gave Luke a massive lecture anyway and said how disappointed they were in him. Luke looked quite sad, and I wished I hadn't said anything, because I think what I saw wasn't what was there, if that makes sense. Anyway, he didn't get his toffees.

Alice sat and stared at the page, barely breathing, frozen to the spot. She'd completely forgotten about the skull incident. The memory brought back all the intense, adolescent emotions she'd felt at the time: horror at the sight of a bloodied human skull (and she was absolutely sure at the time that it had been a human skull, and there had definitely been some rope); anger at her brother for playing a mean trick (although now she thought he'd been telling the truth, even though that didn't make sense); a thrill of excitement that the cottage they'd always told each other was creepy, Pedlar's Cottage with the twisted chimney, had actually *been* creepy;

and the idea that someone had been trying to tell her something.

Hettie! The skull had had a rope attached, she was sure of that; Hettie had been hanged. Had Hettie really been trying to communicate with Alice from beyond the grave? Was she *still* trying? The idea was steadily gaining strength. But then she thought about the sadness she'd felt for Luke and the guilt that she'd made things worse for him back then. She read the next entry, which was also the very last one.

> *Wednesday 18th August 2004*
> *Luke did one of his disappearing acts again. Dad says this is the last time we'll come here. I cried. Turns out he walked to Dennybridge and then hitched a lift to Monkstown, because he was bored. I could strangle him for being so selfish.*
>
> *Why do I have to be me?*
> *Why could I not be her? Or him?*
> *An invisible nothing, a waste of people's time,*
> *That's what I am.*
> *If I was a boy I'd be seen and heard.*
> *But I'm me, and I'm nobody,*
> *And perhaps I'll never feel the wind,*
> *Or hear the crows, or see the trees,*
> *Ever again, but at least I saw them once.*
> *I may be a nothing,*
> *But I am something, deep inside*
> *Where no one will ever notice.*
> *But I will notice, one day.*

Luke had only got more wayward after that holiday, and sadly, it *had* been the last time the family had ever stayed at Crag Cottage, as her father had died the following year. She'd never know whether he'd have stuck to his threat or not. Her teenage angst was clear as a bell in that dreadful poem, but she'd meant every word of it at the time.

She shut the Holiday Diary and pushed it away from her. All these snippets of real life were raising more questions than they were giving answers.

A growing headache prompted Alice to leave the kitchen and curl up on the sofa in the sitting room, drawing the curtains to block out the sunlight, allowing her thoughts to return to James, and the passion and tenderness they'd shared in this very spot. He'd be back later to take her to visit his father; he must like her, just a little bit.

CHAPTER TWENTY-EIGHT

ALL TIME AND NO TIME

Whether 'tis truth or ne'er but a lie, who cries?
With her breast gnarled with pain, sorrow breaking her heart,
Weeps the crow.

He's dead. Drownded, just like Judge Nisbet. My golden child cried his tears and the Quag filled with mist, and the young man did follow his path. Our path. He was at the big house, shoeing the horses, and I thought, there's one what'll do, he's near enough a blacksmith.

They're long dead themselves, those men what judged me and caused my death. I watched 'em grow old and die and pass into their own personal hell. The judge was the only one what paid his due. Him, and William Wickens.

For I was right to think that young man what wanted to poke my boy at Crow Pond seemed familiar. 'Twas none other than Miss Patience's older boy. I did find a way to end that man's life afore it should've ended. I made a sickness enter his lungs and now he's paid for not speaking up for me. For he knew the truth.

'Tis hard, finding the right folk, and a little part of me feels wicked for doing what I'm doing, but what else should I do if I am to feel at peace? If my golden child is to have his vengeance? Nine men sent me to my death, and in doing that, sent my boy to his grave too. So nine more must hear the truth, and though time is muddled and means nothing to me, time will be my saviour.

There's ladies up at the big house what I wish could be my friends. I do try to make myself heard, but none of 'em want to listen, and that's a fact. One came walking to my grave, and I made her see me and my boy, but she ran away, hollering and screaming, and never did come back. Sometimes I blow a little breeze into their hair, or ruffle the pages that they're writing on, or tip their bonnets, but mostly they don't notice.

Miss Patience, she do know the truth. She read the letter what William wrote, and though 'tis too late to save me, she might have told the world that Hettie Gale is innocent. But she be too under the thrall of her man, and so she hides the letter where she thinks it not to be found. Her weakness angers me, and when she writes in her journal I make a nasty blot of ink to spoil the page. 'Tis a childish thing to do, but it makes me feel better.

And so I am patient and wait for the right ones to come. The ones what'll be a new jury, and listen to me, and tell me that I'm not a murderess, and allow my soul to find its peace. There's a Denny, an army man he is, what'll do for Sir Eustace who was in on the plot with Judge Nisbet. And a posh woman, a right stuck-up sort with a title, Countess or the like, what'll do for the Earl. 'Tis a woman, and the crow knows 'twas men what judged me, but are not men and women equal in the end? If they're not, they should be, for we're all capable of good and evil, and that's a fact.

I feel a bit guilty 'bout the poor vicar what was visiting the big house for his tea. He crammed his pockets with cake, he did, and he crammed his mouth more as I enticed him t'wards the Quag. I don't know how he didn't choke on the crumbs, but he wasn't no better than Reverend Bacon, at the end.

And I do regret the policeman, what was only doing his best to find the vicar. But a policeman was needed, and so it was his lot to be called. I don't regret the doctor, though. He was swollen up with eating too much, and spoke with a strange voice, and he was rude to the woman at the big house. Men should respect women, and I don't like those as treat us bad. My da treated my ma bad; he hit her and beat her, and then he was bad to me. But he was sorry in the end, and so I forgave him. But 'tis not right for men to do such things.

And now there's just two more, and my new jury'll be complete. The two what I thought was dressed so strange, in flowing coats and garish colours. Now I do know them to be a painter of pictures, name of Samuel Deflory, or some such flowery title, and a writer of words, whose name I can't recall.

I shall be patient, and one day there will come a painter, and a writer, and my golden child will cry his tears, and the mist'll rise, and they will come to us. And then we can begin, and I will tell my story anew, and they will see that I am innocent, that my child is innocent. And they will change their judgement, and we will be free at last.

CHAPTER TWENTY-NINE
SUNDAY 2 JUNE

The knock on the door came at five to twelve. Alice should have expected James's early arrival, but she was still dozing on the sofa. She leapt up, trying to shake the sleep from her eyes and the crumples from her clothes. Rushing to the kitchen sink, she splashed some cold water on her face, then dried it with the sleeve of her T-shirt.

'You look like you've just woken up!' James smiled fondly. The cold water clearly hadn't helped, and Alice could only smile coyly and admit that she'd been taking a nap. 'Come on then; let's get this over with.'

Alice was a little shocked. 'That's a strange thing to say, when we're going to see your father.'

James sighed as he held the car door open, and Alice scrambled in. 'I love my dad. It's just that, sometimes, visiting him is hard work.'

The drive to Monkstown was quick, traffic was light, and they chatted about nothing in particular. Alice reflected on how much easier she felt in James's company since they'd been intimate, and she was starting to feel a pang of regret, knowing that she'd be leaving the Moor in the next few days.

'Here we are.'

They'd pulled into the rather grand gated driveway of a large Edwardian house, which had a sign announcing that they'd reached *Friarswood Manor - Residential Care Home*. James found a space in the small car park and led Alice to the entrance. Another sign stated that *"All Visitors Must Sign In At Reception"*, which was where they headed.

The Reception was in what must have originally been a very opulent entrance hall in a private house. A majestic flight of stairs swept upwards, lined with paintings and photographs of people and landscapes. Behind the reception desk, which was manned by a rather sour-looking woman, was a board titled *"Patrons of Friarswood Manor"*, together with a group of portraits. Alice was surprised to see a photo of Sir Rufus Denny-Hurst, his name in gilt letters beneath.

'Oh! I didn't know Sir Rufus had been a patron of this place. Mind you, I didn't know this place even existed.'

The sour-faced woman perked up, a smile rendering her almost pretty. 'Sir Rufus was a darling. It was so sad when he died. That must've been... ooh, eleven years ago, now. Do you know the family?'

Alice hadn't meant for the woman to hear her, but as she had, it would be rude not to respond. 'No, not really. I'm staying in the hamlet where their house is, and I've met his sons once or twice. Sir Rufus was always very kind to me when I was little.'

The woman's face dropped. 'Oh goodness, you're not the cousin of the lady who's gone missing?'

Alice grimaced; was there anyone who didn't know who she was? 'Yes, that's right. I'm Alice, Fleur's cousin.'

'You don't look very alike. My name's Audrey, glad to meet you. Any news yet?' Audrey thrust out her hand and had a surprisingly limp handshake.

'No, no news. There's going to be another big search of

Pedlar's Quag tomorrow.' Alice frowned. 'Did you meet Fleur, then?'

'Oh, James brought her here one day, didn't you, James?'

James's face turned a deep crimson. 'Just the once, Audrey.'

Alice couldn't believe it; James had brought Fleur to meet his father, even though he'd always insisted that they'd just had a quick fling. She felt betrayed and had to fight the urge to run out of the door. James must have realised how she felt; he finished signing the book, then took her hand, gently, and led her up the stairs and away from the smirking Audrey.

'She's an awful woman. Her own life is so lonely, she has to make trouble in everyone else's.'

When they reached the top of the stairs, he led her to a corner of the landing which contained a small elegant sofa, and a table stacked with glossy brochures and magazines. He took both her hands in his. 'I did bring Fleur here, but it was a disaster. Dad took an instant dislike to her, and she flounced off in a huff. I reckon she only wanted to have a nosey at the building and check out its interior design; the reality of what goes on in a nursing home was a step too far for her.'

Alice felt vaguely affronted on Fleur's behalf, but on the other hand she couldn't imagine her cousin in a place like this. But it was the fact he'd brought Fleur here and not told her that was most upsetting.

'It's not a problem.'

Even she could hear that her attempt at a nonchalant tone was unconvincing, but James smiled. He led her down a corridor towards a set of doors, where he punched in a few numbers on a keypad. Once through the doors, the atmosphere changed from one of peaceful, gracious elegance to a far busier noise-filled environment, nurses bustling up and down, popping in and out of the various doors that lined the corridor. James walked confidently towards the far end, Alice following closely, slightly disturbed to hear laughter and chatter intermingled with moaning and weeping from inside the rooms.

'Here we are. Please don't be surprised if he doesn't say anything. Or he might get angry, or start crying...'

Alice took James gently by the arm. 'Don't worry so much. I cared for my mum through pretty bad times. I know how they can be.'

The room was bright and airy, with large windows overlooking the gardens at the rear of the building. It was simply furnished, with a hospital-standard bed and locker, but also a few pieces that must have come from Mr Turnkey's home. James's home. A small, antique side table set with a cut-glass decanter and a Chinese-style vase filled with slightly wilting chrysanthemums, a grandfather clock in one corner, and some framed paintings. The effect personalised and softened an otherwise clinical environment.

'Hello, Dad. How are you feeling today?'

James strode towards a chair set by one of the windows, into which was slumped a shrunken Mr Turnkey. Alice was shocked at the disparity with her childhood memory of an intimidating, bad-tempered brute. This Mr Turnkey was an old, old man, withered by age and immobility. The persistent cough was still there, though reduced to more of a sigh. His expression was one of bewilderment, as James bent down and tenderly took one wrinkled, sinewy hand in his. 'I've brought someone to see you.' He gestured for Alice to come close.

'Hello, Mr Turnkey. How are you?' Alice really didn't know what to say, but she needn't have worried. The old man's eyes lit up, and he shakily reached out his other hand to her. She took it gently, noticing how cold his fingers felt. Glancing at James she saw his face transform with pleasure, but then crumple as his father spoke.

'Kath! Kath, my darling! Where have you been?'

Alice flinched, but kept holding the old man's hand and whispered, 'Who's Kath?'

'Dad, this is Alice, my friend. It's not Mum.'

Mr Turnkey shook his head, disbelievingly. 'It's my Kath! I'd know her anywhere.' Fixing Alice with a gaze from eyes suddenly sparkling with life, he continued. 'You've come back for me. You've come back for your Jimmy.'

Then, with a sweet smile that reminded her so much of James, Jimmy Turnkey fell into a fitful sleep. James sighed and stood up, and Alice carefully released the old man's fingers from her own. 'Does he often muddle people up?'

'He often calls me by other names. Yesterday it was Fred. I think I told you that. But I've never known him think someone was my mum before. It's kind of sad.'

'But in his own mind he's happy, if he thinks your mum is around.' Alice took a deep breath, not wanting to spoil the tender moment, but needing to know. 'What did he say to Fleur that upset her?'

'He told her he didn't like her. Just like that.' James sounded a bit bitter. 'She walked out. Didn't even try to understand that he has dementia and doesn't always know what he's saying.'

Alice frowned. Fleur was self-obsessed, but she did have a heart. Perhaps she'd just been having a bad day.

They pulled up chairs and sat quietly, chatting while Jimmy slept. Alice gazed out of the window, admiring the treetops as they swayed in the gentle breeze, appreciating the golden warmth that flooded in through the glass, feeling content.

'This is my son. Isn't he handsome? He'd make someone a very good husband.' The old man had woken without them noticing and winked at Alice. 'And I think you'd make him a very good wife.'

James went bright red, whilst Alice sat, open-mouthed, before collapsing in a fit of giggles.

All in all, the visit with Jimmy Turnkey had gone surprisingly well. He'd been quite lucid for a few moments, and once Alice had got over the shock of what he'd said, she'd managed to have a lovely chat with him about the Moor, and the bookshop. But then he'd suddenly become confused, called out for Fred, and started weeping. A nurse had come in and said it was time for his medication, so they'd left.

On the way back to Nether Dennyfold, James asked Alice if he could take her out to dinner again that evening.

'That would be lovely. My treat this time, though. Or I could cook for you again.' She'd frowned, desperately trying to remember what food she had in the fridge.

'No, my treat. As a thank you.'

'What for?'

James's eyes had brimmed with unshed tears. 'I haven't seen Dad have a normal conversation for a long time. You were so sweet and patient with him. And he really liked you; I could tell.'

By the time they'd reached Crag Cottage, Alice had given in and agreed to go out, but only if they had a simple pub meal.

'Do you want to come in for a cuppa?'

'I've got some things I need to sort out at home. Paperwork and stuff. If I don't get it done today it'll cause me problems. See you at seven?'

Alice had waved him goodbye, made herself a cup of tea and a sandwich, and was now sitting at the kitchen table, Patience's journal from 1786 waiting to be opened and read. There were more secrets to be discovered. Alice was increasingly sure of it.

> *1st January 1786*
>
> *At the beginning of this new year, I can think only of death. It is eight years since my dear Mr Wickens passed away, three years since poor, dear Charles breathed his last – though, in truth, that was a blessing for us all – and now, I fear, William is declining. The physician still has no cure for the strange sickness that has bound William to his bed. But my darling Edward will reach his sixth birthday this year, and for that I am truly grateful. I confess when Mr Wickens passed I married my cousin Frederick so that I might remain in my family home, and keep the Denny name safe, but the arrival of Edward is the one ray of sunshine in my dreary life.*

Alice found it interesting, and awful, that Patience wouldn't have been entitled to stay in her own family home once her first husband had died, simply because she was a woman. But she'd found a way to overcome that ridiculous obstacle, even if it did mean marrying her own cousin… so, good for her! She flipped through tedious entries about housekeeping and visitors, and the cook's disastrous concoctions, until she came to a page where a small cross had been carefully drawn in one corner.

> *12th March 1786*
>
> *My poor William is fading. I fear he will not last this night. He coughs as though trying to expel some terrible demon, and the blood is copious. The physician has declared there is nothing more to be done, and the woman Mr Denny-Hurst has hired to care for my son has constantly to change the linens but can do no more than wash William's face. It is hard to witness, and so I sit at my table and occupy my fingers with my embroidery, though there is nothing to occupy my thoughts but a creeping dread.*

How awful. Poor Patience, watching her eldest son die. William must have been very young, in his late twenties, perhaps. She read on:

> *13th March 1786*
> *May the Lord God hear my anguish and grant me peace. William lost his grasp on life as the sun began to rise. I am desolate, but his passing is surely a relief, as I could not bear to see him suffer so. At the end, my son gained sufficient strength to rise from his pillow, and as he grasped my hand he said three words, each uttered with much strife. "Letter. Desk. Sorry." I thought little of it at the time, but his eyes were consumed with fire, and his insistence such that I told him I understood, and at the last, that I forgave him. Though I knew not to what he was referring, my forgiveness was all that poor soul desired, and his soul departed at that very moment. I do not know how I shall survive this day.*

How strange, those three words. Alice was intrigued, and eagerly read on to solve the mystery. But there was nothing interesting in the next day's entry, and the one after that caught her eye for a different reason.

> *15th March 1786*
> *William has been laid to rest. Poor Edward asks repeatedly where his brother is, and I have not the heart to tell the child that he will never see William again. We have been blessed with a constant stream of visitors wishing to pay their respects. Reverend Bacon has barely left our sides, irritating me with his pompous speeches about wayward souls finally bending to God's will. I am well aware that William was no angel, but the man's condescension is insufferable.*
> *Even Mrs Gale came to pay her respects. I noticed that her*

face bore a yellowing bruise, but she was adamant that she had fallen, and that it was of no consequence. I enquired as to whether she still had the ruby necklace I had given her so many years previously, the first time I had noticed an injury upon her person. I told her it was to be sold should she ever need to escape her husband's violence. But she insisted that the necklace was in a safe place, and would never be sold. I fear for the woman. Mr Denny-Hurst may be bad-tempered and short of affection, but he would never lay a finger upon me. I pray that Edward will grow to be a kindly man and a good husband, who treats his wife with respect.

Alice's eyebrows shot up as she reread the passage. She got up and opened a drawer, and gently lifted the red glass necklace from its bed of kitchen paper. Rubies? Surely not. Patience must've been referring to another necklace altogether. But Alice placed it on the table next to the journal as she read on, rapidly putting pieces of this infuriating jigsaw together in her head. The next page was spoilt with an ugly inkblot, the first Alice had seen in what were uniformly neat passages of writing. But the words ramped the mystery of the letter up a bit further.

20th March 1786

There is a blot of ink spoiling the page of my journal as I write, and to me it is a sign that my life is forever sullied. William's final words have been haunting me, but it was only today that I found sufficient strength to think about their meaning. I entered his chamber, the first time I have found the courage to do so. My heart broke at the sight of the bed, empty of its linens, and the air of bleakness that filled every corner of the room. I found a letter in his desk, a letter that he had written on the first day of this year. Its contents have broken my spirit and caused me much suffering. I will never reveal William's words to a living soul, but the letter must live on as his testimony. It is safe with God. Our Lord, in His wisdom, will give sanctuary to the thoughts that cannot be spoken aloud, and a choir of angels will silently sing a lament for my errant child.

What did Patience mean? *"It is safe with God."* Did she burn it, or bury it somewhere? But she said it *"must live on as his testimony."* Surely that meant she hadn't destroyed it? Alice got up and stretched the cramps from her limbs; she hadn't realised she'd been sitting so rigidly in her fascination with the diary.

What had Finbar said? There was a family story that one of his ancestors had written a deathbed confession, something to do with Hettie Gale. Could it have been William? Well, if the letter was hidden in The Manor House, she'd have no hope of finding it. She could hardly barge in there while Finbar was around; he'd think she'd gone loopy.

"It is safe with God." Patience must have meant *something* by that. Could it be...?

Grabbing her phone, suddenly sure she knew what Patience had meant, Alice walked determinedly out of Crag Cottage and made her way up the lane and past the big house. Towards God.

CHAPTER THIRTY

SUNDAY 2 JUNE

The interior of the church felt chilly after the warmth of the sunshine outside. Alice stood for a moment until her eyes adjusted to the gloom, then quietly closed the door behind her. Silence thickened the air, and a faint smell of damp stone lurked in every corner. The aisle was striped with muted colours from the stained-glass windows, the carved backs of the pews either side glossed by the sunlight, the seats black where the light didn't reach.

Alice walked slowly towards the altar, her eyes flicking here and there, her mind desperately trying to make sense of Patience's words. *"It is safe with God."* The letter had never been found, according to Finbar, so it couldn't have been hidden in The Manor House, where a succession of Denny-Hursts would surely have discovered it; it had to be here, somewhere. But where? Where would be a good place to hide a piece of paper so it was safe but would never be found? She didn't know where to start; although this was a tiny church, it could be just about anywhere.

A low archway with a wooden door in one corner caught her eye. The vestry, she assumed. She'd start there. The door opened with a loud creak that made her jump; she felt vaguely naughty, that she'd be caught any moment in a place she shouldn't be. But there was clearly no one here, and the need to find the letter spurred her on. The vestry was a small room, containing only a desk, a set of drawers and what looked like a cupboard. She opened that first, to find a rail on which were hung various items of ecclesiastical dress: a couple of white cassocks and some coloured silk stoles. She rummaged around, but there was so little in there, and no hidden corners where a letter could be concealed.

She moved to the desk. The large drawer beneath opened easily, but despite a thorough search she found nothing but random pamphlets and papers and a notebook filled with someone's ideas for sermons, the ink faded with age. She even checked for hidden panels, but the furniture was solid. There were few places that she thought might act as hidey-holes. She checked behind the pictures that hung slightly lopsidedly on the walls, and even in the pockets of the single, lonely coat that hung on a hook behind the door.

'For goodness' sake!'

The words she hadn't meant to speak out loud sounded deafening in the small space. She chided herself for being ridiculous. Patience had hidden the letter in 1786: it would hardly be in the pocket of a coat that was probably only a few years old. Would a woman in those days have had access to the vestry, in any case? Probably not; it seemed the world had been dominated by men back then. Leaving the vestry and walking back towards the middle of the church, Alice gazed around, and tried to imagine where a lady would have sat over 200 years ago.

She walked to a pew towards the front; Patience was a woman of some standing in this hamlet, so surely she would have had a front-row seat? She sat down and looked around. There was nothing there, just a row of old kneelers –were they called hassocks? – on the floor, dusty from disuse. The covers, lovingly embroidered, were threadbare and tattered. The pew held no secret cubbyholes where a letter could have been hidden.

She left the pew and wandered up towards the altar. It was highly unlikely Patience would have hidden anything there; surely that was the domain solely of the vicar? In front of the altar, to each side, was a row of pews facing towards each other, where the choir sat. Alice couldn't imagine there would ever be enough people in this tiny place to fill the choir stalls, but lots of churches had them. These were elaborately carved, with high backs, each seat separated from the next by a wooden divider pierced with cross-shaped patterns. Although beautiful, and much fancier than the stalls in the church Alice sometimes visited in London, they looked faintly absurd here, in such a small church in a rural hamlet.

She didn't know where to look next and was beginning to think her imagination had got the better of her. Patience hadn't meant the letter was hidden in the church at all. But then she remembered Patience's other words: *"a choir of angels will sing a lament,"* or something like that. Looking around again, Alice noticed that each end of the shelf that fronted the choir stalls was decorated with a metal sphere, etched with angels and topped with a cross.

Excitement balled up in Alice's chest. Could it be? She made her way to the nearest of these and ran her fingers over the metal; once gleaming brass, the metal was tarnished to a dull brown, pitted with age. She tugged at the orb, tried to twist it, but it was stuck firm. The idea wouldn't leave her head, though: *"a choir of angels"*. That must mean something.

She examined the orb at the other end of the stalls, but it was equally unmovable. Walking across to the other side, she tried the third one with no success, and was beginning to feel silly, when she tried the fourth. This one was a bit wobbly. She pulled and twisted, but years of dust and dirt had made it stick at one side.

Worried about causing more damage, and realising she was probably completely wrong about the letter being in the church, Alice admitted defeat. She was about to walk back down the aisle when the door opened. It must be the vicar, and she'd be caught in the act of committing vandalism! But there was no one there. A gust of wind must've blown it open, though she was pretty sure she'd closed the latch securely. Goosebumps rose on her arms and the back of her neck as a chill breeze blew towards her. The breeze intensified, almost as though it was becoming a sentient thing, and the orb she'd just been fiddling with rattled, caught in a tiny whirlwind.

Then everything became still and silent. Sunlight streamed through the doorway, flooding the church with a sense of sanctuary once again. Despite the warmth, Alice felt her limbs shaking; had something just happened, or had she imagined it? She glanced at the orb that had wobbled so furiously before; it looked no different to the others. Perhaps she was losing her mind. But she felt compelled to take another look.

This time, as she took the orb in her fingers, she was able to twist it free of its base. She turned it around, tracing the outline of the angel that was flying, wings spread, in eternal flight. With a thrill of excitement she saw that the orb was indeed hollow. Prodding her fingers into the hole, she felt something. Was it paper? It was, she was sure of it. Very carefully, making sure she didn't pull too hard so as not to rip anything, she managed to wiggle her forefinger and thumb into the space, and grab a corner, extracting it slowly from its hiding place.

The paper was yellowed and felt rough, yet it had a fragility that she was terrified of as she carefully opened it out. The writing was haphazard, in black ink that looked almost fresh, probably due to it having been hidden away from any light. And it was a letter. The first words she read were *"My Dearest Mama"*, and the date, *"1786."*

Alice's hands shook as she folded the paper again; she'd found it. She placed it gently on the pew while she screwed the orb back into place, then concealed the letter under her T-shirt as she walked quickly down the aisle and back outside. She intended to give it to Finbar, but she needed to read it first, and felt it would be better to do that in the safety of the cottage.

She was in such a hurry to get back to the cottage that she didn't notice the solitary black feather that fell onto the pew where she'd just been standing.

Back home in the kitchen, Alice carefully opened the letter, spread it on the table and began to read. The writing was clumsy, as though written in difficult circumstances, and it took her a while to decipher it all.

1st January 1786

My Dearest Mama,

I write this as my deathbed confession. I implore you not to show this letter to Father. I would wish that he meets his maker innocent of such knowledge. But I am impelled to tell someone, and dear Mama, you have always been wise and countenanced honesty above all else.

Ten years ago, I was approaching the end of the long and arduous journey from distant Nova Scotia. My comrades and I had been evacuated there from Boston after several wretched years of occupation, and we were lucky to be finally sent homewards, wounded but safe. This you already know.

We arrived in Plymouth and enjoyed a good quantity of ale before taking a carriage as far as Great Bercow. There we stopped for the night, filling our mouths with song and our guts with meat, and our throats with the finest Irish whisky. The following morning, we vowed to walk the last ten miles to the Moor, where my two comrades Billy Shelton and Godfrey Brown would reunite with their families in Monkstown.

I know not why, but I felt a desire to see the wildness of the Moor, and so I bade them journey with me across Pedlar's Quag. From there, they could find their way home by way of Cleator Forest.

As we reached Crow Pond, surely my favourite place of all, we spied a young woman and her child, warming their limbs in the sun. It was a pleasant scene, but Billy and Godfrey felt a stirring at the woman's nakedness, and before I could counsel otherwise, they raced to the pond.

The girl took fright, and we witnessed her take hold of the child and jump into the water, sinking beneath the surface. When she reappeared, the child was gone, nowhere to be seen.

It is a hard thing for me to confess, but I did not attempt to stop my friends as they attacked the girl. They each took a turn with her, then urged me to do likewise. But I am not as other men, Mama. This is also hard for me to confess, as I know it would be of great distress to Father, as it must be to you, but you are the stronger, so confess to you I must.

I prefer the company, and the bed, of men. And I find small boys enchanting. There, it is said. Please do not despise me.

Before my friends could do further harm to the girl, our captain appeared. He had not proposed to accompany us, and I know not why he was there, but I am glad that, in the end, he saved that wretched girl from further defilement.

To hide their shame, Billy and Godfrey told the Captain a lie; they told him that they were trying to stop the girl from drowning her child. The Captain ordered us to take her to Monkstown, where she would be tried for murder. He no more believed my friends than did I, but my shame is that I did not tell the truth.

I understood that she was not attempting to drown her child, but to hide him. There is a cave beneath the tree, which I had thought to be my own secret. She put the child in there, where it would surely have perished due to our wicked lies.

This is my confession Mama, as I lay awaiting the judgement of Our Lord, and I fear He will judge me harshly, as surely I deserve. Blood adorns my kerchief, and it is as though my very insides are deserting my body. But the pain I feel is as nothing to the pain that poor girl endured. I ask you not to hate your eldest child, but to accept my contrition, and to remember me as your caring son.

Yours with love,
William

Alice was shocked beyond anything she could put into words. This letter was the answer to everything she'd needed to know about Hettie Gale. Hettie had not only been innocent of the murder of her child, she'd been raped by two soldiers, and she must have known her child would starve to death or drown as she was marched away to face trial and be hanged.

The tears flowed freely, and a great knot settled in her stomach as she reread the letter, again and again. Finally, when there were no more tears to shed and her insides felt hollow, she carefully folded the paper and slid it inside Patience's journal where it would be safe.

A loud noise rattled the windowpane in its frame, waking Alice from a deep sleep. She leapt up, terrified, thinking someone was in the cottage. Then another rumble, this time a little softer. Thunder. Peeking between the curtains, she saw a huddle of dark clouds blotting out the sun, and a flash of brilliant white as lightning streaked across the sky. The weather was on the change and the tightness of the air, the pent-up energy in the sky, only added to her sense of impending disaster.

William's letter to Patience had really shaken her, and now she knew for certain what she had suspected all along: Hettie Gale was hanged for a murder she hadn't committed. But there was something else, something she couldn't quite grasp. And she was sure it was connected in some way to Fleur.

It was five thirty; she needed to shower and change ready for her evening with James. But first she had to try and work out what it was that was needling her. She sat down at the table and neatly laid out all the journals, her notebook with the ideas she'd been jotting down, and her phone. She started with the list of missing people she'd made a couple of days ago:

- *Judge Jeremiah Nisbet, the Judge at Hettie's trial, disappeared in 1786*
- *Jack Malaface, the young farrier, disappeared in 1821*
- *The Reverend Peter Bailey-Bew, disappeared in 1910*
- *Sgt Fred Middleton, disappeared in 1910, while looking for Rev Bailey-Bew*
- *General Sir Clifford Denny-Hurst, disappeared in 1870*
- *Countess Dalrymple, disappeared in 1895*

Now she could add *"Dr Boone, disappeared in 1960"*, to the list. And Fleur, and Harry. Nine people, missing with no trace over a period of nearly 240 years. And all, bar the judge, Fleur and Harry, were mentioned in the Denny Diaries. She pulled

Patience's 1786 journal towards her, and flipped through the entries that came after William's death. It seemed Patience had swiftly resumed her stony disposition – William wasn't mentioned again. But then Alice came across an entry that mentioned Judge Nisbet, who'd presided over Hettie Gale's trial.

> 15th October 1786
>
> The sky today has become dark, with a gathering of clouds that is almost sinister in its countenance. It heralded the arrival of Judge Jeremiah Nisbet, on the invitation of Mr Denny-Hurst, who wished to discuss business with that pompous and wine-soaked villain. I declined to take supper with them, feigning a headache. There is only one thing worse than watching an overweight and overbearing man become inebriated, and that is watching two such men. It was my fervent hope that Mr Denny-Hurst failed to secure the man's interest.
>
> It seems, however, that God was listening to my fears, for the man has disappeared. Mr Denny-Hurst rushed to my parlour, seeking advice, as Judge Nisbet had gone deathly pale in the face and had not uttered a single word since consuming a second helping of orange pudding and imbibing an abundance of port. I would have preferred to stay in my chamber, but I am a dutiful wife, and so I reluctantly followed Mr Denny-Hurst, only to find Judge Nisbet gone. On questioning the staff, one of the grooms declared that he had seen "a portly figure dancing along the lane." The groom had been amused, and so had followed this figure, but it had turned up the path that leads to Pedlar's Quag, and the groom declined to follow further, for fear of "the ghosts that do live up in those parts."
>
> Mr Denny-Hurst will call for help at first light on the morrow, and a search will be undertaken, but I suspect that wretched man will be back for his nightcap e'er long.

Something tugged at Alice's memory: *nine people missing*. She raced up the stairs to the attic, and pulled out the *Myths and Legends* book, hurrying back down to the kitchen. The fuzzy thoughts that had been rushing around in her head were finally gaining clarity, but she couldn't quite believe what she was thinking. The book automatically opened at the page with her favourite poem, "The Hanging of Hettie Gale", and she ran her finger over the relevant verses.

The clergyman, called for his nearness to God;
The constable for upholding the law;
The physician to vouch for the girl's state of mind;
The blacksmith to speak for the poor.

An artist, a soul with the vision of gods;
A man from the purest of castes;
A writer of words to make sense of the charge;
And an Earl of the Realm at the last.

The clergyman – well, that was the Reverend Peter Bailey-Bew. The constable was Sergeant Fred Middleton; the physician was Dr Boone; the blacksmith, young Jack Malaface. The rest were trickier. "The Earl of the Realm" could possibly be represented by Countess Dalrymple; they were both titled. And General Sir Clifford Denny-Hurst was from a long line of Dennys and Denny-Hursts – could he be "A man from the purest of castes"?

That left "An artist", and "A writer of words". Of course. Harry! Harry had told Alice he was trying to be a writer; it must be him. And Genevieve was an artist, though she wasn't missing, she'd gone back to the city. Then Alice's insides flipped: Fleur had trained as an interior designer – did that count as an artist? The thought was both shocking and sobering. The sudden surge of hope that she'd discovered something related to the missing people started to unravel. This was silly; she was clutching at straws.

Then a fresh wave of certainty hit her – the words she'd just thought: *"The Earl of the Realm could possibly be represented by Countess Dalrymple." Be represented by.* It was almost as though... Hettie was assembling a jury. A new jury. Then she remembered something Joe had said yesterday: *"She's picked you to be her judge and jury."*

'Oh, don't be ridiculous, Alice. You're tired and overwrought, and you've got to get ready for a night out with James.'

Speaking the words out loud to herself had the right effect. It was almost six thirty, and James had a habit of arriving early. She needed to shower and do something with her hair, and she had to stop all this silly daydreaming about Hettie.

The thought of being with James obliterated everything else, and she headed upstairs.

There was nothing quite like pub chips; Alice wondered how they were always so golden and crispy, and delicious. She dipped one into the gravy that smothered the steak-and-ale pie that accompanied the chips, and briefly shut her eyes as she savoured the taste.

'You look like you're enjoying that.'

James was grinning. She was enjoying his company, and no longer felt awkward in his presence. And he looked particularly handsome this evening. He'd trimmed his beard again. He was wearing black jeans and a dark green T-shirt under his heathery tweed jacket, and Alice felt an unexpected rush of desire.

'It's delicious. Nice and warming for this horrid weather.'

The weather had turned: the warm sunshine and blue skies smothered by a blanket of threatening cloud, although the thunder and lightning had stopped. Rain pattered gently on the window and Alice gazed out at the people rushing by, umbrellas raised, and car headlights creating an orange glow and reflections in the puddles forming along the gutters.

'You look lovely. That colour really suits you.'

Alice had dressed in her new jeans and the second top she'd bought yesterday, the berry-red one. It was a good job her feet were hidden, though; it was too wet to wear the new sandals, so she'd had to resort to her muddy trainers.

'What did you do this afternoon?'

James had finished his food, and poured Alice a second glass of red wine before she could stop him. It was a delicious Rioja. Alice found herself drinking more of it than she'd intended. The effect loosened her tongue, and she found herself telling James about finding William's letter in the church.

'Hettie Gale was innocent? That'd cause uproar if anyone ever found out.'

'What do you mean?' Alice felt slightly deflated by James's lack of enthusiasm about her discovery.

'Well, it's one of the more famous stories about Pedlar's Quag. They'd have to rewrite it all, at the museum and so on, and then all the books would be wrong.' He sounded faintly disapproving.

'But if she *was* innocent, and I think the letter proves that she was, surely everyone *should* be told? She should be vindicated, and if that means having to rewrite her story, so what?'

'She died over 200 years ago, Alice. It's too late to make any difference to her, so why bother? Leave well alone.'

Alice was saddened by James's lack of understanding. It *would* make a difference; Hettie would at last be able to find peace. The thought jolted her: Hettie had been trying to communicate with Alice ever since she'd first holidayed at Crag Cottage. The book that had always opened at the same page with the poem; the crow feathers; the little breezes that had blown out of nowhere; the skull on the gate. Everything was becoming clearer now, and Alice felt a surge of energy as she dismissed James's antipathy and launched into a spirited account of the list of missing people that she'd managed to match up with the jury members who'd originally condemned Hettie to death.

Alice was relieved that she'd finally told someone about her discoveries. But James sat there stony-faced, shaking his head. 'Seriously? Alice, I think you've got too involved in all of this. It doesn't make any sense. Not unless you believe in ghosts.'

His dismissive laugh touched a nerve, and Alice felt herself bristling. 'Well, I think I do believe in ghosts...' Her voice trailed off as she realised she was tipsy from the wine. She didn't want to argue with him, so she changed the subject. 'I'll have to go home on Tuesday, unless the police find anything when they do their search of the Quag tomorrow.'

James's eyes darkened for a moment, then he looked down at the table, fiddling with his glass. 'Oh.' He looked as though he might burst into tears.

'I don't really have any choice, James. I need to get back to work. I've already had more time off than I should have done.'

'What if they find something tomorrow?'

She hesitated, the thought of the police finding Fleur's body causing a shiver of dread to run up her spine. 'Well, if they do, at least I'll know. I'll face that if it happens.'

'Please don't go.' James stopped his nervous fiddling, and looked Alice straight in the eye, taking her hands in his. 'I really like you. I thought you liked me.'

'I do. I like you very much, but I don't live here. I don't belong here; my home is in London.'

James let go of her hands, his own trembling with emotion. 'Well, there's no point in all of this then, is there?'

He got up and trudged to the bar, his shoulders sagging, pulling his wallet from his pocket; he was clearly intending to pay the bill and end their evening out. Alice let him do it; she'd no energy to try and stop him. What was she supposed to do? Her home and her job were back in London. She liked James – she *really* liked him – but it wasn't enough to stop her from going home. After all, he'd had a fling with Fleur, too, and for a while she'd thought perhaps he knew more about her cousin's disappearance than he was telling. How was she supposed to know whether he was telling the truth? He probably got cross with Fleur when she said she had to leave, too; in fact, that was quite possibly why they'd argued.

Earlier, Alice had tidied the sitting room at the cottage, plumping the cushions and laying a fire ready to be lit. She'd remade the bed with fresh linens, and even found some old single-blend Scottish whisky in a cupboard so they could have a nightcap. But her excited preparations were all for nothing; James drove her home silently, the rain pattering loudly against the windscreen, her tears threatening to fall yet again.

CHAPTER THIRTY-ONE

ALL TIME AND NO TIME

Whether 'tis truth or ne'er but a lie, who hears?
With her courteous nature and patience to wait
Learns the crow.

A lady has come into my hovel, and I'm that glad to see her. 'Tis the same girl what used to read my story in the book in the cottage up the lane from Ma's, and sit on the rock in Pigswhistle Clump, and walk to Crow Pond, and I've not seen her for a goodly time. I try and touch her, but 'tis tricky with no solid hands, and that's a fact. Her name is Alice.

She has a rare thing, does my Alice: she has a heart that is open to those of us who live only in the shadows. I make her read my story, over and over, and I blow kisses to her, but she never does notice. When she visits Crow Pond, I leave her a trail of feathers so she's safe. The crows are my friends, and they know she's special, and they do lend me their black plumes. I try and touch her at the Hanging Tree, though I don't like to be at the place of my dying. I follow her to the museum, where she gazes at my image and at my little box of shells, and

THE HANGING OF HETTIE GALE

I try and tell her I'm a good girl, but she don't hear. Not quite. Not yet.

Alice sometimes visits the lady painter in the big house, and I'm pleased, 'cause that lady has a sweet soul. Sometimes I watch as she paints her pictures full of colour and life, and I help her think to make a little mark what is meant to be me, watching over her shoulder, though 'course she don't know it. I thought to bring her to Crow Pond and make her be on my jury, for she'd know the truth, but I don't have the heart to hurt one so agreeable.

But I want Alice to find the journals what Miss Patience and the other ladies wrote, and I knock over the inkpot so she'll find the keys. My plan works, and Alice has the journals. I watch over her shoulder as she reads the words, and I know one day she'll understand. I'll make her understand.

There's so many ladies at the big house; they arrive all happy, and winsome for their men folk, but they soon do change. 'Tis the men what push the ladies down, make 'em think they're only good for 'broidery and playing little songs on the piano. And for making babbies, of course. But I like the ladies, 'specially Florence, what makes me laugh, and Octavia, who has a fire in her soul. The last one, Emilia, has a sad heart, like she's lost all hope. I did try to be tender with her as she lay in her bath, the water all bubbly and smelling like flowers, but she didn't want no help. 'Tis a shame, for she was sweet once, but her head's full of demons now.

Alice might not be a *big house lady*, but she's a lady to me, and the best one there ever was. She has a loneliness 'bout her, same as I have, and her 'magination don't shut me out, unlike most folks. I got to make her see me, feel my presence. She must, 'cause there's no one else what cares 'bout me.

So I make her see things, at the graveyard, and in the church. I watch as she searches for William's letter, and she must find it, for 'tis all the proof she needs to tell the world that I am innocent. Old Patience, though, she did choose a good place to hide it, and I must help Alice a little. But she has it now, and she knows. And soon the world will know.

And here's Alice, cutting through the brambles what cover my resting place. She don't give up easy, and that's a fact. She digs a little and finds the pretty red beads what Ma let me play with when I was little, what made me feel like I was a *big house lady* too. Miss Patience gave the necklace to my ma, afore I was even born, and Ma told me they were just in case, though I never did know what she meant. Alice has 'em now; she washes 'em and makes 'em all sparkly again, and I want her to keep 'em, for they'll make her feel special. And she *is* special.

I hope she'll come, afore it's too late. I'll make her come, and my boy will cry his tears and the mist will draw her to them. She'll see the golden lady's shoe, and she'll know.

See, I wanted a new jury for to judge me right, but now I know my folly. For I took the judge, what was a bad 'un, and that was right, but I took six men and women what are innocent souls, and I did steal their lives from 'em, just as mine was stole from me. I am ashamed of my mistake, but p'raps I can put it right.

The golden lady, what was to take the place of the artist, she has been through what I been through. Her da... And she has a box of shells, like mine. We're kin, and I don't mean her no harm, and now I know I done wrong.

P'raps it is not too late, and I can save this last soul. And then my own soul can be free, and me and my boy can rest. P'raps.

CHAPTER THIRTY-TWO

MONDAY 3 JUNE

Alice had finally cried herself to sleep, after what seemed like hours of tossing and turning, thoughts about James, Hettie and Fleur all rushing round unchecked inside her head. But once sleep had finally claimed her, things got worse. Dreams took over – or rather, nightmares – in which she was either being chased, or chasing something or someone that may or may not have had evil intentions towards her, or someone else who was also trying to flee, or perhaps trying to catch her and do her harm, or stop her from running or asking for her help, then she was falling into a deep, deep pool unable to escape and someone tried to help, but really they were trying to push her under and there were crows, so many crows, black feathers raining down and gravestones and shadows and books with words that screamed at her, and...

A loud bang shattered the curdled air, waking her with a start. The thunderstorm had reappeared, or more likely this was a new one, and the bedroom was caught in a frozen second of spectral phosphorescence before the dark of night reclaimed its place. Rain was drumming an insistent beat on the windows, echoing the urgent beating of her own heart. A glance at her phone told her it was 5.40am; there was no way she'd get back to sleep with the storm making such a racket, so she pulled a jumper over her head, slipped her feet into Fleur's slippers, and made her way downstairs.

It was cold, the kitchen filled with a pungent dampness. Rain had seeped under the front door, soaking the mat and creating a growing puddle. The windows rattled with each clap of thunder, and eerie shadows played across the walls with every flash of lightning. Alice switched on the lights to banish the darkness, and decided the cottage needed some warmth; *she* needed some warmth. She raked the ashes in the wood burner, scrunched up some newspaper to make the base of the fire, then looked for some kindling. The basket was empty, no logs either; she remembered now that she'd meant to fill it up yesterday after she'd set the fire in the sitting-room grate, hoping for a second lovely evening when she and James would make love in front of the flickering flames.

Sighing deeply, Alice grabbed the log basket and made her way through the scullery to the coal shed. Picking up the torch, she found her way to the log pile, selected three good big ones, and a handful of smaller sticks. As she turned to make her way back, she nearly dropped the basket. By the door that led back into the scullery, a clutch of black feathers lay in a tangled heap on the floor. Her heart raced and fear began to knot itself in her stomach; she was sure the feathers hadn't been there when she'd come through just now. And how would birds – crows, she supposed – get in here in the first place?

Stepping gingerly over the feathers, forgetting to replace the torch in her alarm, and shutting the door quickly behind her, Alice made her way back to the kitchen, and busied herself with getting a good blaze going in the wood burner. She tried to keep last night's thoughts from getting a grip; perhaps James had been right when he'd dismissed her talk of ghosts, vengeance and new juries. Crow feathers and breezes out of nowhere and rising mist were all perfectly normal things in isolation; it was just her overwrought imagination that made them into something more.

Tea made, Alice pulled a chair in front of the wood burner and stretched her feet out to enjoy the warmth, cradling a steaming mug of tea in her shivering hands. She was beginning to relax and enjoy the sound of the rain drumming against the windows, and the occasional flash of light and gentle rumble of thunder, the storm moving further away now to wake somebody else from their sleep.

But she couldn't just sit there. She drained the mug and, feeling more herself, moved to the table, spreading all the journals, books and notes out. She kicked off the slippers, then began to pore over everything she'd already read: all the journal entries about missing people; all the notices and cuttings that she'd captured on her phone; her own Holiday Diary.

In her heart she was hoping that she was mistaken, that she'd made it all up in her head. But as she jotted down her thoughts in her notebook, her writing became more and more illegible, her haste fuelled by the idea that somehow Hettie had lured nine people across Pedlar's Quag, including Fleur and Harry, to form a new jury to judge her innocence. William's letter proved Hettie to be innocent, the testimony that Joe had given her did too... but she was hanged, and her child would have died wherever she'd left him.

Wherever she'd left him...

One of Fleur's slippers, lying on the floor where she'd kicked it off, did a sort of flip. The movement startled her. She put the slippers back on, feeling a chill snaking up her limbs and through her body.

Wherever she'd left him...

She knew. She knew where Fleur was, and the sudden understanding filled her mind with thoughts and images that thwarted any sense of caution. She raced upstairs to put on a pair of jeans and a T-shirt under the jumper, then back down to pull on her socks, welly boots and raincoat. She grabbed the torch from the table where she'd left it, and shoved it, together with the slippers into her pockets – Fleur would need them; she'd be so cold. Then, forgetting to turn off the lights, forgetting to pick up her phone, forgetting to close the front door behind her, Alice raced off down the lane, wind grabbing at her hair, rain nipping at her face, heading for the path that led to Pedlar's Quag.

James was pacing around the kitchen at Crag Cottage, anguish etched into every line on his face, when Sergeant Cooper cautiously pushed open the front door, shaking off the rain that had drenched him in the short distance from his car.

'Thank God you're here!'

'Came as fast as I could, Mr Turnkey. You sounded rather distressed on the phone. So where's Alice gone, do you think?'

'No time, we have to go now. Crow Pond.' James gestured frantically towards the books and papers spread out on the table. 'She thinks that's where Fleur is. I'm sure of it.'

Sergeant Cooper frowned. 'We've got a team of divers conducting another search today.' He looked at his watch. 'It's nearly nine o'clock; I should think they'll be here soon. Perhaps we should wait.'

'No!' James shouted in his panic. He took a deep breath to calm himself down. 'I'll explain on the way, Sergeant Cooper, but we need to go now. I didn't follow Fleur and look what happened – she vanished. I'm not making that mistake again.'

His face was stony. 'I'll go on my own if you won't come.' He made for the door, but Sergeant Cooper grabbed him firmly by the arm.

'Okay, okay, calm down. I'll come with you, of course. But we need to be sensible and take some stuff, just in case. Blankets, a torch, water – that sort of thing. I'll fetch my bag.'

While he returned to his car to get his stuff, James picked up Alice's notebook. Her writing became increasingly messy as the passage went on, but the note was just about readable:

Hettie is innocent; the Gideon Flemby testimony and William's letter both prove that. Her soul cannot rest until she clears her name. Nine missing people. Nine men on Hettie's jury. She's collecting a new jury. Including Fleur and Harry. There's a cave under the tree on Crow Pond. It's the only place...

The writing tailed off at that point. James had no idea who William was, or whether there really was a cave, but this was where Alice had gone, he was sure of it. And he had to find her. He *had* to.

'Here we are.' Sergeant Cooper came back in wearing a heavy rain jacket, a large backpack strapped to his back. 'There's a first aid kit, rain gear, everything we might need. Good job I was a boy scout – always prepared.'

His attempt at lightening the atmosphere failed, and the smile quickly disappeared from his face as James thrust the notebook towards him.

'This! This shows she's gone to Crow Pond.'

Sergeant Cooper read the words, shaking his head. 'But I was going to tell her when I saw her later. We've *found* Harry. He was at a writer's retreat on the other side of the Moor.'

James frowned. So there weren't even nine missing, only

eight. He knew Alice had an overactive imagination... which was why she was such a good writer...

'Oh, shit.'

The list Alice had written showed that each of the missing people had a type of connection with the original jury. It seemed Harry was a writer, and he was missing, that's why she'd thought...

'We have to go. Now!'

Alice was soaked to the skin, but she barely noticed as she raced along the path towards Hettie's Hovel. As she passed the ruin, a little gust of wind blew out of nowhere and was gone as quickly. She smiled, sensing that she had company, and that she'd be safe, but the smile disappeared as she made her way through the gate and onto the Quag itself.

Even though it was almost seven thirty, and the sun should have been well on its journey to illuminate the day, it was still half-dark, black clouds smothering any light that tried to sneak through. Alice took no care of where she was going; her boots sloshed through the waterlogged ground, her heart hammering an urgent beat that urged her onwards.

She could no longer see her feet under the thick mist that rose and swirled, as high as her knees now... but some force was guiding her, and though she had no idea where the path was, where the black pools lay that waited to trip her up and swallow her, she knew where she was going, with an absolute certainty.

The story of the little boy abandoned by his parents, who cried so many tears that a mist rose to smother the Moor, crowded into her head. The boy was Hettie's son, it could be no other. Not abandoned by his mother, but by the actions of a group of soldiers. It was no wonder Hettie and her son couldn't find the peace they deserved; they'd been treated so appallingly badly.

Tears flowed down Alice's face, mingling with the rain that still fell, needling her skin and chilling her to the bone. Her feet carried her onwards with little effort from herself, and she allowed her mind to wander back to her childhood, to her sunshine days here on the Moor, comparing them to the gloomy days in suburban London. She'd been so lucky; her parents had loved her, even though they hadn't always demonstrated it physically. She'd been allowed to be a child. But she hadn't totally appreciated that, in some ways, she was more blessed than Fleur.

As she raced on, the mist rising to hip level, Alice tried to concentrate on the here and now. On her reason for making this journey. On her desperation to find her cousin. Fleur was in the cave. That was the only thought she allowed herself, now. Fleur was in the cave, and it was up to Alice to find her. The air was clotted with menace, and her breaths were coming in increasingly painful gasps. Shadows snaked around her, shadows of things that couldn't possibly be there on this open, desolate, tree-less stretch of ground. She ignored them and concentrated on her goal.

Suddenly the mist was all around: above, below, swirling and thickening the air into a shroud that blinded her. Alice felt as though she'd been walking forever, and time had lost any meaning. She was suspended in a nightmare, losing any sense of reality, almost forgetting what she was doing, who she was. Soundless voices called to her, gossamer fingers prodded at her, the shadows became rarefied to her unseeing eyes. She was in the presence of dark angels hiding mute threats within their ethereal wings.

A splash brought her back to herself; the mist had cleared, abruptly, totally, and a glance downwards showed that the toes of her boots were underwater. Another step forwards and she'd have found herself falling into the pond. Crow Pond. She was here.

A single crow sat atop the fallen tree, silently watching her, it's eyes beady and knowing.

Craw!

It called and another joined it, appearing as if from nowhere.

Craw!

Another bird glided to the tree – then another, and another – until a whole line of them sat, soundless, watching her, judging her. Nine of them.

Alice woke from the nightmare of angels and found herself in the nightmare of reality. She was alone at Crow Pond. The mist had gone, but had been replaced by driving rain, and she was cold. So cold. And afraid of what she must do next. She stood for a moment, shivering, indecisive, scared of what she might find. She might have stood there for a good while longer, had a glint in the water not caught her eye. Where the branches of the fallen tree drooped into the water, and the roots spread out in search of nourishment, an object had become caught in the tangle. It was shiny, and there was a flash of red.

It was a shoe – black patent with a distinctive red sole. It could only be Fleur's. The pair of the one Bryony had found. Shocking Alice into action, she checked her pockets, finding the torch still there, but realising with a blow that she'd left her phone at home. She should be calling someone: Sergeant Cooper, an ambulance, James... She wished she could call him, explain properly why this meant so much to her, why she had to find her glamorous, damaged cousin. Talk to him, one last time, just in case this went wrong.

Shaking the fear away, Alice slipped off her welly boots, then slowly unbuttoned her coat, and peeled the wet fabric from her shivering body as though shedding a layer of doubt. She could do this. She took the torch and the slippers from the pockets, then folded the coat and set it down on a rock at the edge of the pond. A part of her wondered whether she should take the coat with her, in case Fleur was still alive and needed the warmth, but it was soaked and wouldn't provide much protection. And anyway...

No, she wouldn't give herself a chance to consider what she might find. She waded into the pond, gasping as the chilly water hit the skin beneath her jeans, grasping the torch as though it was her protector. The crows sat silently, watching, waiting, wings restless as though nudging each other. She walked on until her feet no longer touched the ground. Everything felt heavy, but she kept going, frantically paddling her arms, until she reached the shoe caught in the roots. Size seven. It was Fleur's. Madly treading water, and hanging on to a root for dear life, she freed the shoe from its watery grave and flung it as far as she could onto the grass edging the pond.

What had Susan written in her journal? *"...the opening is beneath the roots of the fallen tree..."* There was nothing for it but to dive under and look. Alice could swim, but she'd always been a little scared of water, especially going beneath the surface. Her schoolmates had mocked her for being the only one to refuse to put her face under, teasing her for wanting to keep her hair dry. They hadn't understood that she'd been terrified. Since she'd left school she'd avoided swimming pools like the plague, but now she had no choice. She'd have to go under the surface if she was to have any chance of finding the cave. Of finding Fleur.

It was just light enough for James to see the solid bits of ground as the path snaked between pools of blackness. Sergeant Cooper had insisted on going first and was making good pace for an older man, but it still wasn't quick enough for James. The knot of panic that had settled in his stomach was only getting bigger and tighter, and he felt as though he might fall apart at any moment.

A bank of fog was ahead of them, but strangely they never quite reached it; it was as though a gentle wind was pushing it forwards, keeping the way clear for them. James was alert for any clue that Alice might have been this way, but there was nothing, just an eerie silence punctuated by the rasping breaths of the two men, the slosh of their boots on the waterlogged ground as they hurried onwards.

Sergeant Cooper had called a colleague as they'd walked, and requested that the search team, or at least a couple of divers and a medic, be dispatched as a matter of extreme urgency. Hopefully they'd be on their way already, and not too far behind the two men; James knew they'd need help, if they found what they were hoping to find. And Alice might be in danger.

After what seemed like forever, the crescent of low hills that protected Crow Pond loomed up ahead, and they knew they'd reached their goal. The mist had finally disappeared, a watery light casting soft rays across the gently lapping water. The silence was heavy with tension, the air thick with threat. Nine crows sat on a branch of the fallen tree, silent, bearing witness.

'Here!'

Sergeant Cooper had walked to the edge of the water, and now James saw what he was looking at: a blue raincoat, soaking wet, neatly folded on a rock next to a pair of grey welly boots. They were Alice's. And then, nearby, a single shoe: shiny black, spike heel, red sole. It was Fleur's, he was certain, the match for the one the police had already found.

'What do we do now?' James frantically scoured the pond for any sign of movement, the smallest sign of life, but there was nothing, just the gentle lapping. Except... what was that near the roots that plunged down beneath the surface? Feathers. A tangle of black feathers, clinging together in a mass, floating just above a black shadow that seemed to go down to the very depths of hell.

The cold slap of water on Alice's face shocked her. Taking a deep breath, she sank beneath the surface, tentatively opening her eyes, but seeing nothing but shadows and roots, and tangled weed. She panicked and returned to the surface, gulping in great lungfuls of air. She couldn't do it. But the nine crows still sat on the tree, watching her, cawing gently as though in encouragement. She went under again.

This time she grabbed one of the roots and tugged it apart from its neighbour, using the torch as a sort of club. There was nothing but water, murky from the mud that had been dislodged. Rising to the surface, she took another gulp of air and went back down, finding two roots that looked as though they had already been torn apart. There was a gap.

She needed another lungful of air before returning to the parted roots, and this time, though fearful of becoming entangled, terrified of being trapped, she forced her body through. Her grasping fingers found a rocky ledge, above which there was a void. She grabbed the ledge and pulled herself through and upwards, suddenly finding her head above the surface of the water.

Heaving her numbed body onto the rock, Alice found herself in chilled air rather than cold water, and a thrill of delight ran through her as she realised she'd found the cave. But the thrill was short-lived; it was dark in here. So very dark. She fumbled for the switch to turn the torch on, shivering so badly she almost dropped it. The light was muted, the batteries almost spent. Her immediate surroundings were dimly illuminated, but shadows, untouched by any light, stretched away into utter blackness, so it was hard to tell how big this space was.

She froze, her heart hammering wildly in her chest, as she allowed her senses to adjust. There were muffled sounds – slithery, scuttling noises – that terrified her. The smell was of something metallic, something nauseatingly organic that wormed its way into her consciousness and made her heave.

Wriggling her body so that she was kneeling, looking inwards, Alice directed the beam of light across the rocky floor of the cave. She gasped. There was something lying there. Someone. A body. Her heart began racing so fast she thought she'd pass out, but she crawled towards the body, her head telling her to expect the worst, her heart screaming that it couldn't, wouldn't be bad.

First, as her fingers groped into the shadows, she felt something hard. A box. A small wooden box. Just beyond it was a woman, lying on her side with her knees brought up to her chest, foetus-style. Long blonde hair was plastered across the woman's face, obscuring it, but Alice knew. It was Fleur. She gingerly pulled at the hair, which was caked with dirt and stuck to the pale skin beneath. 'Fleur! Fleur, it's me, Alice. I've found you.'

There was no response, and Fleur's skin was cold, so cold. She was too late; Alice had failed, and now her cousin was dead. She tried once more, grabbing at Fleur's arm, squeezing as though trying to force life back in, hot tears scalding her own, chilled face. 'Fleur!'

Was that a movement, or was it just her imagination? Turning the beam of light towards Fleur's face caused the tiniest twitch of an eyelid. Alice placed her fingers on Fleur's neck, and she felt a pulse. Faint, barely discernible, but a pulse.

'Help! She's alive! Someone help us!' Alice yelled into the

blackness, not really expecting anyone to hear her. How could anyone be out there, when no one knew she was in here? Then the batteries in the torch gave out, and the cave was plunged into total darkness.

But not before Alice saw the bones. So many bones.

CHAPTER THIRTY-THREE

MONDAY 3 JUNE

Warmth crept slowly through Alice's limbs, but the dull throbbing in her head wouldn't go away. She was wrapped in an aluminium blanket, one of those things she'd seen on medical dramas on the telly, never expecting to be shivering underneath one herself.

What had happened after the torch failed was a bit of a blur, but James had filled her in, sitting with his arm protectively around her, his face a mess of anguish and relief.

'I knew where you'd be, because of your note, and I knew you'd gone to find Fleur. Sergeant Cooper was with me, but we didn't know how to get to the cave. A team of divers was just behind us, so we waited for them.' His tears were tears of remorse. 'I'm sorry. I should have jumped in, looked for you myself.'

Alice placed her hand on his arm. 'No, you did the right thing. What if you'd got stuck in the roots or something? I can't bear the thought...'

He'd told her how the divers had arrived quickly, with a team of experts who'd swiftly set up spotlights, organised stretchers and medical equipment, and the area had become a swirl of noise and activity. James had felt helpless, praying that Alice would be brought out safely. He'd not even considered that Fleur might be in there too, yet alone still be alive.

Fleur *was* alive, but only just. The divers had brought her out first; goodness knew how they'd done it. She'd immediately been worked on by the medical team: drips set up, special pads to warm her, and a team to race her back across the Quag to an ambulance waiting in the lane, as there'd been nowhere nearby an air ambulance could land safely. She was already in Monkstown General Hospital, where they were doing everything they could to save her.

Alice had been brought out soon afterwards, and James had almost broken down as he'd not been allowed anywhere near, not until she'd been checked over. She'd refused the offer of a stretcher to take her back to the lane and, after the medics had done their work, dressed her in warm, dry clothing and wrapped her in the aluminium blanket, James had folded his arm tightly around her waist and guided her tenderly back to Crag Cottage, Sergeant Cooper leading the way.

The three of them were now sitting in the kitchen. Sergeant Cooper set the fire in the wood burner and made mugs of tea, which they used to warm their hands. The little carved box was sitting on the table, too. Alice had grabbed it before she was rescued, refusing to leave it in the cave. The wood was dark and discoloured from being in water, but the delicately carved shells were still clearly visible.

'She took it with her, James. She didn't just dump it; it must have meant something to her.'

James half-smiled; the shock of the morning's events still had him in its grip.

'How did you know I'd be going to Crow Pond so early in the morning?'

James sighed, embarrassment in his eyes. 'I couldn't sleep

after we'd argued...' He glanced at Sergeant Cooper, who was studying the shell box. 'I kept thinking about what you'd said, about Hettie Gale and the missing people, and all of that. You'd been so... passionate about it, and even though I don't believe in ghosts, especially not ghosts who make people disappear, when you talked about Fleur and Harry making up the eighth and ninth places on the jury, something clicked in my head. I knew you wouldn't let it go, and when the thunderstorm started I just wanted to come here, make sure you were safe, and tell you how sorry I was not to have taken you seriously.'

Alice stared at James, her eyes sparking with fear. 'But Harry *wasn't* there. I was wrong.'

Sergeant Cooper decided this was the right time to stop fiddling with the box. 'Ah, Mr Deegin. Harry. We were wrong about him. Remember the note I showed you that he'd left on his table?'

Alice did remember: *"I can't go on like this anymore. My mind has turned against me. I have to find solace in that other place. There is no comfort for me on this earth."* At the time, she'd thought it a bit odd; Harry seemed so down-to-earth; he didn't normally speak in such a dramatic way, but then, when a person is desperate they might say anything.

Sergeant Cooper chuckled. 'You won't believe this. There'd been a mix-up at the taxi rank; Harry had requested a few days' leave, but somehow the coordinator hadn't entered it in the system. Turns out, after his morning shift he went away to some writer's retreat over at that hippy place, you know, Silent Hill.'

Alice had never heard of Silent Hill, but she did vaguely remember Harry mentioning something about a writer's retreat. 'So why did he leave that note?'

'Well, that's the thing. It wasn't what we thought...'

'A suicide note?' Alice whispered.

'Not one of those, no. It was a piece of creative writing he'd done for the retreat. It'd fallen out of the folder the rest of his writing was in.'

'You're joking?' Alice laughed; she was so relieved to know that Harry was fine. Then she frowned. 'So my theory doesn't hold up. Fleur's a designer; she could have been the artist Hettie wanted for her jury, but she needed a writer, too. I thought that was Harry. I think my imagination has got a bit out of control.' She shook her head, sadly.

'No, I think you're right, Alice.' James's eyes were brilliant with a fevered energy. 'Don't you see? *You're* the writer Hettie wanted.'

'But I'm not a writer...'

James looked sheepish. 'When I got here earlier, I found the door open and all the lights on. I rushed in, yelling for you, and ran up the stairs, but you weren't here. Your phone was on the table, but your coat and boots were gone. I was frantic, so I called Sergeant Cooper. While I was waiting for him to arrive, I checked all the stuff on the table: the journals, all the notes you'd made in your book. And I read the poems. I'm sorry.'

Alice's eyebrows shot up. 'My poems? The ones in the back of the notebook?'

James nodded, his face reddening.

'Oh.' Alice didn't know whether to be angry or flattered. 'They're private, you know. No one's ever read them before.'

He took her hands in his. 'But they're so good. So full of... emotion... passion... like they're the real you, on the page.' He went even redder. 'You're a writer, and a very good one.'

Alice blushed too, and the tender moment forced an embarrassed Sergeant Cooper to rise from his seat and pace purposefully around the kitchen, anxious to diffuse whatever it was that was overtaking his companions.

'Nobody knew there was a cave under the tree, you know. It's come as quite a shock to some of the so-called experts who claim to know everything about the Moor.' He chuckled, then coughed, his face taking on a more serious expression. 'It's only thanks to you they were found. The bones are being removed and sent for forensic examination. I think you might well be correct, Alice; from the first reports I've been given there are at least six, maybe seven sets of remains, all in varying states of decay.'

Alice was brought back to reality with a jolt. The *bones*.

As the torch had finally flickered out, she'd glimpsed bones everywhere: long, chunky leg bones, spiky ribcages, and skulls with small creatures slithering in and out of gaping black eye sockets. That was when she'd screamed.

Once Sergeant Cooper had left, promising Alice that he'd report back on the findings as soon as he could, James insisted that Alice rest up for a while before he drove her to the hospital to visit Fleur. 'You need to regain your strength, warm up properly, so you're in a fit state to see her.'

She stripped off the bulky clothes she'd been dressed in at the pond, had a lovely hot bath, and put on her comfortable old jeans and a warm jumper. James tenderly towel-dried her hair. He heated up a tin of soup and made some toast, and they sat quietly together, sipping and munching, until Alice felt restored to some semblance of normality.

'So, it's all over now. You can feel so proud of what you've done.' James took her hands across the table. 'I'm prouder than you'll ever know.'

Alice frowned. 'I *am* proud, and I just hope we got to Fleur in time. But...'

'But?'

'Well, Fleur's hopefully safe, Harry's safe, and I'm safe. But what about the others? The bones. They all died. She found her jury, but what now? I know that she was wrongly hanged, but nobody else does. How can I make that right? So she can rest?'

James gazed into Alice's eyes, no longer trying to hide his admiration. 'Well, if anyone can do something to right the wrong, I'm pretty sure it's you.'

Alice lit up. She frowned again, thinking hard. 'If I get all the evidence together,' she ran her fingers over the journals that lay in a neat pile, 'and ask Joe at the museum to help me, perhaps there's something we could do.' She grabbed James's arm. 'I just want her soul to rest; I want her to be happy.'

'And I want *you* to be happy.' James smiled, but the smile quickly vanished as a thought struck him. 'Will you go back to London tomorrow, like you said?'

'I... I don't know. I don't really want to.'

The thought of leaving this place – the Moor, Pedlar's Quag, Crag Cottage – was horrible, but the thought of leaving James was even more devastating. She might have only known him for a couple of weeks, but he was everything she'd ever dreamed of in a man: a friend, a companion, not a shred of vanity, someone she could laugh and dream and explore with, someone who would treat her as an equal. Okay, she didn't know that for sure, but there was something about him that told her he was as good a risk as she'd ever take.

'What would I have to do to persuade you to stay?'

She laughed. 'Not much, really. It's just all the practical stuff. Where would I live? Would I be able to find work?'

James leapt up from his chair and sank to one knee. 'Marry me?'

She giggled. 'No, I will not marry you!'

James's face couldn't have dropped any lower.

She put her arms around his neck and planted a kiss on his mouth. 'Ask me again in six months, then we'll see.'

Even attached to wires and tubes, her blonde hair filthy and matted, and her face pale and thin, Fleur managed to look delicately beautiful. She was asleep when they arrived, so a nurse took them into a side room, where the doctor treating Fleur could talk to them in private.

'Your cousin has had a very lucky escape. And I believe it was you who found her? You should be very proud of yourself, Alice. Another day and the outcome might not have been so good.'

'But she is okay? She'll make a full recovery?'

'Yes, we think so. She's lost a lot of body heat, of course, verging on hypothermia. It's lucky the weather has been so warm lately, and she was in a dry, sheltered place. She's also lost a lot of body weight, although there is evidence she managed to find berries to eat, though they weren't very ripe, which has caused some gastrointestinal problems... and fresh water must've been close at hand. Otherwise...'

The doctor left the words hanging. Alice couldn't bear to think of what might have happened had she not found Fleur when she did. She'd have ended up like the others.

'How long will she be in here?'

'Well, that depends how quickly we can get her temperature back to normal, and we'll need to get her eating patterns re-established. Just water and glucose to start, but we should be able to get her to take in some bland food soon, some protein. Luckily, she doesn't seem to have suffered any organ damage.' She looked closely at Alice. 'It sounds like you've been through some trauma, too. You must make sure you look after yourself, and don't worry about Fleur. She'll be fine.'

So now Alice and James were sitting, one either side of

Fleur's bed. Alice held one of her cousin's hands, talking gentle, soothing nonsense to her cousin.

'Doesn't she look lovely, James? Even in a hospital bed. No wonder you were smitten.' There was no malice in Alice's words; she felt no jealousy, and totally believed James when he said he and Fleur had just had a meaningless fling.

They chatted about this and that, Fleur sleeping away her dreadful experience between them. Apparently, her fiancé was on his way over from America. She chatted to Fleur about that, too. 'I'm looking forward to meeting your man. I didn't know you'd got engaged. I don't even know his name.'

She directed her words at Fleur, but looked lovingly at James. 'It must be so nice for you to have a special someone at last, someone to share your life with.'

He smiled and went pink, and blew her a kiss across the bed.

'Looks like both of us might be...'

'She brought me berries.'

Alice stopped dead. 'Who did? Who brought you berries, Fleur?'

Her cousin had opened her eyes, beautiful green eyes glazed with exhaustion and shock. Her voice was tiny, the words spoken in a hoarse whisper. 'The girl. And the little boy cried me tears to drink.'

Alice looked sharply at James. There was clearly more to be done, and Alice was the only one who could do it.

CHAPTER THIRTY-FOUR

THREE MONTHS LATER

Paperwork was not Alice's thing; it reminded her too much of work. And there was so much of it. First, stuff to do with the sale of Crag Cottage. Well, not the sale, exactly.

Fleur had made an amazingly speedy recovery. She was out of hospital within a week, thinner, perhaps less confident, humbler, but displaying an enormous amount of courage, considering the ordeal she'd been through. When her fiancé Adam had appeared in her hospital room unannounced, she'd gone to pieces, but then all she'd wanted was to get out of there and fly back to New York with him.

Alice liked Adam. He was undeniably handsome. He had that brashness that some New Yorkers have, but when she'd witnessed how he'd been with Fleur – so gentle and tender, treating her like the most precious, delicate jewel – she knew Fleur's future was assured, and that she'd be safe with this man.

They'd come back to Crag Cottage for a few days before flying home, and Alice had found herself in the role of mother, sister and friend. She'd enjoyed keeping the cottage warm and cosy, and she'd remade Fleur's bed as beautifully as she could with what was available. Fleur had laughed when she'd seen the cushions and throws heaped up.

'You're so sweet, Alice, thank you. But I've finally realised that there are far more important things to worry about than how beautiful something is.' Her expression had become thoughtful, sad. 'If there's one thing I've learnt since being in that place... it's that people are more precious than anything. I might have stylish homes and gorgeous handbags and expensive shoes, but when it comes down to it, it's only the people we love,' she'd gazed at Adam, gripping his hand tightly, 'that matter.'

Fleur hadn't said another word about her time in the cave, or how she'd got there, other than talking briefly about the inexplicable urge she'd felt to walk to Crow Pond, the mist that had risen around her and gently pushed her onwards, and a strange comment about "the *little boy whose tears nourished me*" and "*the pale, sweet girl who brought me berries*". She'd spoken briefly to James, alone, apologised for walking out on him and having neglected to mention her fiancé. Then she'd talked to the police, and emerged from that grey and drawn, so Alice hadn't asked her anything, or told her anything.

Alice hadn't pressed her because she knew exactly what Fleur was talking about and who she was talking about, and it didn't matter anymore anyway. Things were in place, and soon it would all be over. But Fleur had talked about Crag Cottage. She'd watched Alice as she bustled around, prodding the logs in the wood burner, scuttling out to the coal shed to replenish the log basket, serving up simple, delicious meals of home-made soups, salads, roasted chicken-and-vegetable platters, lasagne. She'd watched as James helped her, bumbling a bit, mostly getting in the way, but the love and affection between the pair was obvious.

The two men had hit it off, and the day before Fleur and Adam were due to leave, James took Adam to Crow Pond, so he could see for himself where his fiancée had been. Fleur had taken the opportunity to make Alice stop what she was doing and sit down.

'When are you going back to London?'

Alice had sighed, her face crumpling a little. 'Soon, I suppose. I don't know, my boss said I could have another few days, but...'

'But you don't want to go back at all, do you?'

Alice had pretty much collapsed, all her energy and bravura from the past few days gone. She'd confessed to Fleur how much she hated her job and London; how she felt like a shadow in suburbia, and of course, how she felt about James.

Fleur had sat quietly, holding Alice's hand, nodding. She took a breath once Alice had finished speaking. 'This cottage. I don't like it, never have. I think you know that. I've put it on the market. But I don't need the money; I've got a fabulous apartment in New York, another in Paris, and the sale of the London house will make me plenty. And Adam isn't exactly a pauper.'

She'd stopped, watching as Alice frowned, her expression betraying a suspicion of where the conversation was leading.

'I'd like to gift the cottage to you, Alice. It's not enough payment for what you did for me. I mean, you literally saved my life. But you look so comfortable here – so right, like you belong – like you've always been here, and always will. You looked after your mum for years – I wish I'd had the chance to do that for mine – but now it's your turn to live life how you want to.'

Alice had cried, and they'd exchanged memories of their dreadful shared holiday, collapsing in fits of giggles. Alice told Fleur that Finbar was back in the big house, and he was actually quite nice now, and very happy with Grace.

'See, you're making friends already. You belong here, Alice.'

And so, Crag Cottage was now nearly Alice's; just some more

dreaded paperwork to read and sign, and it was all hers. Fleur had insisted that the place be updated and made more comfortable; perhaps new windows, and the roof looked a bit dodgy, and maybe an extension at the back with huge windows overlooking the garden. She'd transferred an enormous amount of money into Alice's bank account for this purpose. Alice had thought she might get some new curtains, maybe some rugs and cushions, and possibly she'd have the front door fixed so it kept out the rain... but otherwise, she loved the place the way it was.

She'd given her notice in at work straight away; John had sent an email in response that had been very terse. That had made her giggle; he'd probably been dumped by the girl from comms. Alice did have to briefly return to London though, to sort some things out with her parents' house. She didn't want to sell it; besides, it was half Luke's, and until he bothered to answer her emails and texts there was little she could do. James had driven her up; he'd wanted to see where she'd lived her previous life, but he'd been very unimpressed by the rows and rows of anonymous houses, by the lack of greenery and the smell of exhaust fumes.

Some of the paperwork she was tackling now was to do with the London house – utility bills, and that sort of thing. But the most exciting thing she had to sign was a contract, sent from the museum in Monkstown. It was an agreement for Alice to undertake research on their behalf, and write her findings in what could eventually become a book. Research into Hettie Gale and all the evidence Alice had uncovered about the girl's innocence and wrongful hanging.

She'd spoken to Finbar and asked for permission to use extracts from the Denny Diaries, which he'd gladly given. He'd been stunned when she'd shown him William's letter admitting Hettie's innocence, and even though it showed that particular Denny-Hurst in a bad light, Finbar was determined to help in any way he could. His only stipulation was that the Denny Diaries be properly conserved; the ones that had begun to go mouldy were probably beyond saving, but James had agreed to help with the others, as well as with the contents of Finbar's library. Alice was delighted; she'd probably have more of a hand in sorting through those amazing old books, given that James had all the knowledge but none of the interest.

She spread the contract in front of her, a mug of tea in hand to keep her going as she went through all the small print. Just a few short months ago she'd been working in a tedious job with nothing to look forward to; a hopeless nobody who'd thought eating a donut on Freebie Friday was reckless. Now she was living in the place of her childhood dreams, with the prospect of working with the two things she loved the most: books and writing.

A glint caught her eye, and a grin spread across her face as she gazed at her left hand, and the diamond that adorned her ring finger. The *three* things she loved the most. She'd told James to wait for six months before proposing to her again; well, he couldn't wait that long, as it turned out. He'd taken her for a walk to Pigswhistle Clump, sat her on the Whistling Rock, and got down on one knee. The ring had been his grandmother's; a single, lovely diamond surrounded by tiny sapphires, set in gold. Of course, she'd accepted.

As they'd left the woods, arm in arm, each secretly happier than they'd ever expected to be, a single black feather floated down from the sky, marking the place which would forever be their special, private sanctuary.

'There were eight in total.'

'Eight? Oh, I thought there would only be seven.'

Sergeant Cooper coughed, his expression solemn, a typed report lying on the table between him and Alice.

'No, eight full skeletons. It's taken a while for forensics to piece a couple of them back together, being as they were pretty old, but there were definitely eight.'

'Have they been able to identify them?' Alice was desperate to know who the bones belonged to; she *had* to know, so that she could write her book.

'The oldest was dated to around 1786, male, a big man. Likely to be the remains of Jeremiah Nisbet.'

'The judge.' Alice nodded to herself. That made sense.

'The next oldest dates from the 1820s, a younger man, slight of build.'

Jack Malaface, the farrier.

'One set was identifiable from its DNA, which has been matched with the Denny-Hurst family. Finbar kindly agreed to have a DNA sample taken. That would have been...' He scrabbled through his notes.

Alice completed his sentence. 'General Sir Clifford Denny. Went missing from the big house in 1870.' Alice knew every one of the missing by heart.

Sergeant Cooper chuckled and carried on. 'Then we have a female, middle-aged; first tests show the bones to be from around the end of the 1800s, and likely the remains of the wife of the Earl of Huntesford.'

'Countess Bethesda Dalrymple. That's quite a name.'

'That's her. Then it gets easier, 'cause we're into the 1900s. The Reverend Peter Bailey-Bew went missing in 1910. Church records tallied with our findings.' His face dropped. 'Then it's one of our own: Sergeant Fred Middleton, who was searching for the Reverend. He was only thirty-four, had two young kids. His great-grandson Peter Middleton is a copper, too. He's my boss, as it happens.'

Alice interjected. 'Let me guess: the last skeleton was an American doctor?'

'Dr Howard Boone, retired surgeon from Pennsylvania, USA. That's right. He went missing whilst visiting Hettie's Hovel. Just wandered off and never returned, so the reports go.' He hesitated, not quite sure what to say next. 'But that wasn't the last skeleton. There was an eighth.'

Sergeant Cooper shook his head, sadness clouding his usually jovial face. 'It was one of the oldest. And by far the smallest.'

Alice breathed in sharply. 'Of course, Hettie's son.' A tear escaped her eye. 'How could I have forgotten the little boy?' The thought of a small child, sitting alone in the cave in total darkness, calling for his mother who never came, through no fault of her own – was too much to bear. Alice found herself sobbing. He would have been so hungry, and cold, and frightened. It was dreadful.

Sergeant Cooper hugged her, a bit awkwardly. 'There, there. It's all over now, Alice. At least Fleur survived, thanks to you.' He let her go. 'What we can't work out is how all those people got into the cave in the first place. The little boy was put in there by his mother, but the rest are a mystery.'

'Hettie put her son in there, to keep him safe... at least, that was what she thought she was doing. She put the others there, too.'

Sergeant Cooper looked at Alice with an expression that was half-amused, half-scornful. 'And how would she have done that, being dead an' all?'

'I don't know. I don't suppose we'll ever know, but that's what she did. She was assembling a new jury, based on the original one, so that she could be re-tried, and her innocence discovered.'

He shook his head, clearly flummoxed by Alice's theory.

'Well, you're right about one thing – I dare say we'll never find out the truth.'

'What happens now? What will they do with the remains?'

'Well, we've got to sort that out, but I expect there'll be a special burial in St George's Church graveyard in Monkstown. Seems the best place, really.'

'But not the boy. Not Hettie's son. He should be with her.' Alice was surprised at the ferocity in her voice. 'He must be buried with his mother, so that they're together. I won't let him be buried anywhere else.'

'But, Alice... no one's entirely sure where Hettie Gale was interred.'

'I know exactly where she is, and that's where his little bones will be buried. With Hettie.'

A small crowd was gathered at Hettie's Hovel; not nearly as many as the crowd that had gathered for the burial of The Missing, as they'd started to be called, in the graveyard at St George's in Monkstown yesterday. There'd been various dignitaries there: the Mayor of Monkstown, the local MP, high-ranking officials from the council, the health service and the police force, Colonel Andrew Jackson representing the army... and the Bishop of Winchester, no less, had presided over the service.

The press had attended in large numbers, such was the local, national, and even international interest in the story of the remains found in the cave. And last, but certainly not least, had been the descendants of the missing: local men and women, mostly, but also the present Earl and Countess of Scaithe, and of course Finbar representing the Denny-Hurst family. Even a group of descendants of Dr Boone had travelled from

Pennsylvania, an excitable bunch who were only too delighted to be part of this *"English Murder Mystery"*.

Alice had stood quietly at the back of the crowd with James, to keep clear of the press; although she'd given a couple of interviews for the local news channels, attention wasn't something she particularly wanted. It had been a nice service; the seven coffins had all been sombrely lowered into the ground in a row, tucked into a corner at the back of the graveyard. New headstones had been carved, already in place; flowers were laid, hymns sung, people had cried, and then it had been over.

Today was a much more intimate affair. For a start, there wasn't much room for a huge crowd to congregate on the little path that ran beside the ruin, and even though some of the ground had been cleared of brambles to exhume Hettie's remains and dig a new grave, it was still tight for space.

Alice had had quite a struggle to get the authorities to agree to bury the child's remains in unconsecrated ground, but they'd agreed in the end, bowed by her newly discovered, dogged determination to get things done properly. There was no way she'd let the little boy be separated from his mother any longer than was necessary; 243 years was quite long enough.

Even though the burial was taking place outside of church grounds, the current incumbent at St Brigid's, a newly ordained, nervous young vicar called Anita, had agreed to lead the proceedings. She gave a hesitant, but very beautiful address about the nature of love, and loss, and how good will always overcome evil.

Joe was there, with a couple of colleagues from the museum, including Molly who'd typed up the lost testimony, and his granddaughter Maddie. He'd hugged Alice tightly, his beard tickling her chin.

'Don't forget, I've still got to tell you about the ghostly monk at Greyfriars.'

Alice had laughed. 'I haven't forgotten, Joe; we'll have that chat very soon.'

Sergeant Cooper and Briony looked smart in their uniforms, representing the police. There were people Alice didn't recognise; officials from the council, she supposed. Several people were introduced to her as local historians and experts on Moorland legends. They seemed thrilled to meet her and clamoured for information on how she'd found the remains. She exchanged phone numbers with a few of them; she'd be happy to tell her story to people who really understood, and they'd no doubt be invaluable sources of knowledge for her research.

Finbar was there with Grace, and even Genevieve had made the journey. She'd knocked on the door the previous evening, much to Alice's delight, and presented her with a large object wrapped in an old, paint-splattered sheet. When Alice had opened it, she was astonished to find the painting of the Whistling Rock, the one that Genevieve had been struggling to get right. It was gorgeous.

'Have you changed something? It looks different, somehow. More complete.'

Genevieve had smiled. 'That's down to you. All the paintings I did in the big house seemed to have a pale stroke somewhere, remember?' She pointed to the top right-hand corner of the canvas. 'See? It makes all the difference.'

Alice had gazed at the painting in wonder. 'Your guardian angel.' She'd known then it was no angel, but a spirit of a different kind, which had watched over Genevieve as she'd painted.

But best of all, Harry had turned up, embarrassment written all over his face. 'I hear I got folks in a spin. I'm so sorry, Alice, if I scared you.'

She'd laughed, and given him a hug, which made him even

more embarrassed. 'It's not important, Harry. You're okay, and that's the only thing that matters. I'm so pleased to see you again! Did you enjoy the retreat?'

'Well now, I wouldn't exactly say enjoy, but it was interesting. I need to up my game if I want to be serious about my writing, the crow knows. But one lady did say my words "flowed like milk", so I'm not quite a hopeless case.' He chuckled. 'So, you found your cousin. You're quite the hero in town, you know. How is she?'

'She's fine, thank you, recovering quickly. She went home to New York with her fiancé; she couldn't face coming back for all of this.'

Alice paused, thinking about Fleur, wishing she was here but understanding why she wasn't. James had driven them to Bristol airport, Fleur looking too thin but radiant, as though she'd just had a few days at a spa, not been stuck in a cave half-dead for two weeks. James and Adam had shaken hands, but she and Fleur had hugged – warmly, affectionately, genuinely hugged – and Alice knew they'd always have a special bond. Fleur had left the shell box James had given her, requesting that it be buried with Hettie. James had been a little miffed to start with, but when Fleur had explained that it was ruined now anyway, from being in the cave for so long, and she thought Hettie would like to have it, he'd ended up being quite touched by the gesture.

Now the little crowd, complete with two journalists and a photographer specially chosen for the task, stood silently as the willow coffin containing both mother and son, was lowered into the ground. Alice had asked if the red necklace could be buried with Hettie's remains, but apparently the risk of theft had been too great; though who in their right mind would dig up a coffin to steal a glass necklace, she couldn't think. She was wearing it today, just the once, and then she'd donate it to the museum to go with the new Hettie Gale exhibit that was being planned.

Alice was asked to throw the first clod of earth, and wept openly as she did, dropping in a small posy of daisies too. She thought Hettie would have appreciated the simpler things in life. A few more people did the same, photographs were taken, and then everyone began to disperse.

Afterwards, as everyone drifted away, she and James stayed back with Grace and Finbar, and Sergeant Cooper. They stood and watched as the grave was filled, and flowers placed reverently on top of the fresh earth.

Alice read the words on the single gravestone. It was a graceful slab of natural rock, its face smoothed, the words carved in simple font:

Here lies Hettie Gale
1758 - 1776
And her son

Underneath was the boy's name, his dates tragically short: 1773 - 1776.

Together forever
To sleep the long, tender sleep

Alice took James's proffered hand and waited as the others started making their way back along the path. 'Can I catch you up?'

He nodded, reluctantly letting go and leaving her there, understanding that she needed this moment alone with the girl she'd freed from her sadness.

Finally on her own, Alice crouched down at the foot of the grave, staring as though she was trying to look beneath the floral tributes, beneath the crumbly earth, and into the willow coffin; as though she was trying to see Hettie – not her bones, but the flesh-and-blood girl who'd become such a big part of her life.

Shutting her eyes, she felt a breeze blow up around her, prickling her skin, raising the hairs on the nape of her neck. But this time it didn't scare her. Hettie was there, right there with her, and she held out her arms to welcome the precious contact, relishing the feeling of togetherness. When she opened her eyes, a gentle mist had grown up around her, and she knew the little boy was there too. Hettie and her son, together again. Now they could let go of this world, and sleep the eternal sleep, hand in hand.

Reluctantly, knowing that her search for the truth was at an end, Alice stood up and blew a kiss towards the grave. As she turned to make her way back to the cottage, a pair of crows, their feathers glossy and black, alighted on the gravestone, touched their beaks lightly together, and cawed gently into the wind.

CHAPTER THIRTY-FIVE
ALL TIME AND NO TIME

Whether 'tis truth or ne'er but a lie, who knows?
With the wisdom of age, and the gift of the truth,
Knoweth the crow.

She's here! My Alice has come to Crow Pond, as I knew she would. My boy cried his tears to guide her, and she found the shoe what I made to be in the pool, and she knows. She's in the water now, 'termined to get to the golden lady, and I help her, the crows help her, and suddenly she's here, in my cave.

She's so tender with the golden lady, and I'm pleased the lady didn't die. Not like the others. I could have saved them, I s'pose, but 'tis too late now, and perhaps they wasn't worth saving anyway. Their bones lie scattered all about, company for my boy's bones, though poor company they are.

I did watch each one as they lay, afeared and hungry and helpless. I watched 'em as they cried out, and I watched as they drew their last breath. Does that make me a bad person? For I was watched as I played with my boy, I was watched as the soldiers defiled me, and I was watched as Judge Nisbet spoke my sentence. I was watched as I stood, shivering at the Hanging Tree, and I was watched as the cord tightened 'round my neck, and I was watched as my life was took.

It was only Alice what understood. All the others – the ladies at the big house, Miss Patience, and Octavia and Florence, and dear Rose – they knew I was there, some of 'em; they felt my breath, I'm sure of it, but they didn't understand. Not like Alice. I shall be sad to say goodbye, but I must... for my golden boy is tired, and I'm tired, and 'tis time to leave.

'Tis done.

A little crowd gathers round my old home, and words are spoke. Alice is there, wearing the red beads, and she looks so pretty, though her dear face is stained with tears. When she's all alone, I reach out to her and try to give her the biggest hug, my boy at my side. She knows we're with her, she knows we're safe. Don't cry for us, Alice, for you have done what nobody else could do. Our bones are snug, and my reputation is mended, and that's all a simple girl can ask. 'Tis nearly time to close our eyes and sleep the long, tender sleep.

But I have just one last thing to do. I must leave my sweet Alice a kiss, so she knows how much we love her, and how much we owe her. We wait by Crag Cottage 'til she's awake, and I blow my hardest at the door, and raise a little cloud of dirt what spatters 'gainst the wood. My boy cries a cloud of tears, though this time 'tis tears of happiness. My friends the crows do help me leave my kiss. I try and make her see us, but we've almost faded to nothing and I'm afeared she won't know 'tis us. But she sees the kiss, and she knows 'twas me as blew it, and all's well.

And now 'tis time to leave the world, me and my golden child, comforted by knowing that Alice will be happy with her man, and her own sweet boy what's growing in her belly. For 'tis a boy, I know.

And that's a fact.

New version of original, nineteenth century poem, by Alice Turnkey. Taken from "The Hanging of Hettie Gale", an in-depth, beautifully written history of Hettie Gale, her wrongful conviction, and the mystery of the bones in the cave at Crow Pond. Published by Moorland Books.

THE HANGING OF HETTIE GALE

*'Twas a bright, sunny day, and the girl and her child
Were happy, and laughing, and free
As they played at Crow Pond, in the cool of the shade
Of the elegant alder tree.*

*She thought they were safe in their own secret glade,
And their joy was so loving and true,
But unknown to them both, on the hill that stood
    guard
Three men appeared, out of the blue.*

*The soldiers were full of bravado and ale,
And the girl feared for her innocent child.
She bade him retreat to the depths of the cave
As the weather turned cruel and wild.*

*She covered herself as they raced down the hill,
And pleaded for mercy, but none
Was shown to the girl as the men had their way,
And accused she had drowned her own son.*

THE HANGING OF HETTIE GALE

The Captain, a man who desired only fame,
Charged the men to take Hettie to gaol,
Where a plot was devised by the devious judge
To condemn her to death without fail.

Nine souls there were, nine men to judge
The girl who had been so defiled.
Hettie Gale was her name, a sweet, simple soul
Who cared only for her abandoned child.

The clergyman, called for his nearness to God;
The constable for upholding the law;
The physician to vouch for the girl's state of mind;
The blacksmith to speak for the poor.

An artist, a soul with the vision of gods;
A man from the purest of castes;
A writer of words to make sense of the charge;
And an Earl of the Realm at the last.

The soldiers told lies to the jury of men,
Who'd been bribed to believe what they heard.
Poor Hettie tried hard to tell her side of the tale,
But her fate was pronounced with one word.

Crowds jostled and jeered as they gathered that morn,
For the spectacle they had travelled to see.
Hettie Gale was strung up and met her sad end
At Monkstown's Hanging Tree.

Her soul could not rest for her unlawful death,
And the fate of her child 'neath the tree.
She searched for new souls to discover the truth,
But there were none who could hear her pleas.

Then came a young woman, a girl who believed
That Hettie had been unjustly shamed.
She searched for the truth, and fought for the right
For Hettie's name to be forever acclaimed.

ACKNOWLEDGEMENTS

Hettie and Alice's story was conceived and written in the mountains of County Kerry, Ireland, but the inspiration for the setting came from the beautiful wilderness that is Dartmoor, England. I wanted to write a story that showcased women's strength in the face of adversity through the centuries.

My own strong women include my beautiful daughters, Lucy, Sarah and Caitlin. You've bolstered me on my writing journey and provided much needed encouragement. Jo, Beth, Caroline and Aly, you've been equally supportive. My biggest advocate, my dear friend Polly: you are one of the most positive forces in my life, thank you.

I must also mention my writing group friends. Gail, Anna and Jess – thank you for sharing your wisdom, and for your considered and extremely helpful critiques.

This journey wouldn't have started if I hadn't entered the self-published version of *The Hanging of Hettie Gale* in the Dorchester Literary Festival's local writers' competition in 2022, which to my amazement, I won. The boost to my confidence that gave me was immeasurable and prompted me to enter the Cheshire Novel Prize competition in 2023. I wasn't longlisted, but the incredible feedback I was given found me rewriting large parts of the book.

And so to Bloodhound Books. I was beyond thrilled when I received an email offering me a contract. Thank you to the team, to Betsy and Tara for your belief in me, to my editor Rachel (you were right about the ending!), my proofreader, cover designer and marketing team. You've all done an amazing job.

Finally, I'd like to thank my husband Steve. You've never once doubted me, and the sacrifice you make by staying in bed a little longer every morning, so I have quiet time to write, is invaluable.

Dreams can come true, whatever your age – never stop believing.

ABOUT THE AUTHOR

Tess has loved words and storytelling since she was very small, but only started writing seriously in her late fifties. The Hanging of Hettie Gale is her debut novel, though she has written four more in varying stages of completion and various genres.

After a few years living in Ireland, Tess has now moved back to her adopted county of Dorset, where she lives with her husband and works as a medical secretary in the NHS.

You can find Tess at the following:
www.tessburnett.co.uk
Twitter/X: @tessburnett56
Instagram: tessburnett_author
Facebook: tessburnettauthor

If you'd like to contact Tess you can do so by emailing tessburnettauthor@gmail.com

A NOTE FROM THE PUBLISHER

Thank you for reading this book. If you enjoyed it please do consider leaving a review on Amazon to help others find it too.

We hate typos. All of our books have been rigorously edited and proofread, but sometimes mistakes do slip through. If you have spotted a typo, please do let us know and we can get it amended within hours.

info@bloodhoundbooks.com

Printed in Great Britain
by Amazon